Christine Paice is the author of the novel *The Word Ghost*, the children's book *The Great Rock Whale* and two poetry collections, *Staring at the Aral Sea* and *Mad Oaks*. Her work has been published in *The Best Australian Poems*, *Australian Love Poems*, *Prayers of a Secular World*, *Recent Work Press*, and *Not Very Quiet*, and has been performed on BBC Radio 3, *Jazz Alive* on Vox FM, and *Poetica* on Radio National, and published in the UK, the USA, and Ireland. She won the prestigious Josephine Ulrick Poetry Prize in 2009 and she has been shortlisted for the Blake Poetry Prize, the UK Bridport Prize, the Australian Catholic University Prize for Poetry, the University of Canberra Vice-Chancellor's International Poetry Prize, and the Alan Marshall Short Story Award. She works as a manuscript assessor and a creative writing mentor, and is an acclaimed observer of shadows, fields, and driveways.

THE
OXENBRIDGE
KING

CHRISTINE PAICE

FOURTH ESTATE

Fourth Estate
An imprint of HarperCollins*Publishers*

HarperCollins*Publishers*
Australia • Brazil • Canada • France • Germany • Holland • India
Italy • Japan • Mexico • New Zealand • Poland • Spain • Sweden
Switzerland • United Kingdom • United States of America

HarperCollins acknowledges the Traditional Custodians
of the lands upon which we live and work, and pays respect
to Elders past and present.

First published on Gadigal Country in Australia in 2024
This edition published in 2025
by HarperCollins*Publishers* Australia Pty Limited
ABN 36 009 913 517
harpercollins.com.au

HarperCollins*Publishers*
Macken House, 39/40 Mayor Street Upper
Dublin 1, D01 C9W8, Ireland

A catalogue record for this book is available from the National Library of Australia

ISBN 978 1 4607 6749 8 (paperback)
ISBN 978 1 4607 1637 3 (ebook)
ISBN 978 1 4607 3172 7 (audiobook)

Cover design by Emily O'Neill
Cover images: Feather detail by Vicki Jauron, Babylon and Beyond Photography
Feather on pages 58, 187 and 226 by Adobe Stock
Author photograph by Freya Beth Jansens
Typeset in Bembo Std by Kirby Jones

Printed and bound by CPI Group (UK) Ltd, Croydon, CR0 4YY

For Mary Paice, mother, grandmother, great-grandmother and head gardener in the garden of love, laughter, faith and stubborn resilience you planted in us all. I finally finished the book, Ma, and this one's for you.

Memory is a fact of the soul.
Plotinus, *The Enneads*

He shall cover you with His feathers,
And under His wings you shall take refuge.
Psalm 91:4

1

Truth is a lonely thing

under a grey defeated sky. The soul of King Richard is still on the battlefield at Bosworth where God has left him. History has changed on this day, 22 August 1485, and the battle has been won, but not by him. He is cold and confused. Unable to absorb the enormity of death. So many dead are leaving the living in cool grey light, and Richard is one of them, but he doesn't know that yet. His head pounds with uncertainty. A great heaviness invades his senses. Somewhere in this deserted place he has lost his horse. The weight of his body is still in the saddle, like a dream he is trying to remember. All around him fields stretch to horizons. Under his feet the earth is churned and muddy. Men have fought here, and men have died, but where are they now?

Human voices echo in his head, but when he turns, no one is there. A shiver runs through him. He can barely feel his fingers or his toes. He has no armour, no helmet, no clothes, and cannot see where they have fallen. *What has happened here?* A desolate wind sweeps the acres and thunder rolls in the heavens. There comes a time in every person's life when they seek answers from their creator and now is that time for the king. He searches the sky, praying for God to show Himself, but all he sees is a raven flying over the empty land. What use is a bird to a king?

Memories rise and fall. At dawn he was in his tent, calling for his priests, but none could be found and this unnerved him, so where were they? There was a thumping in his heart, a breeze picking up, his enemy waiting. He remembers a sick feeling in his stomach before the sun appeared.

He whispers to the Lord, 'Save me,' but the Lord does not reply, only the raven calls.

'Walk,' says the raven. 'You've a long way to go. *Walk. Walk.*'

'Where am I going?'

'Well,' says the bird, 'you're always going somewhere.'

'I am waiting for the Lord,' says the king, 'and you mean nothing to me.' God is testing him. Sending him dark matter, a trick to lead him from what he knows.

'This is going well,' cries Raven, flying over his head in great dizzying loops. 'Out of all these souls, you are the one who is interesting to me.'

The bird looks at what's left of the king. He knows too well the brutality of battle, the piercing screams. He has heard triumph and defeat in equal measure. Vanquished or surrendered, it makes no difference to Raven. The bird does not care about the glint of the crown. He is only interested in the quality of the soul, and, whether the king likes it or not, and he probably doesn't, Raven will show him how far he has fallen. When the king is desperate for the Lord, the Lord sends His favourite bird, His treasured guide for lost and stumbling souls. He will help the soul of Richard be clothed anew. He will guide him through shadows so one day he can find the light.

The king, in his time, has seen plenty of ravens, but this one, so uninterested in the bodies of men, is now walking over the muddy field. Stopping every now and then to scratch his chest with his beak. The king cannot bear it; he closes his eyes, muttering to himself, 'God is Goodness Incarnate, God is Wise.'

'Splendid,' says the bird, drawing closer. 'Glad to hear it.'

There's nowhere to hide and at first the king thinks whatever is falling from the sky might be another bird, but it's a cloak of shiny feathers. Covering him with its light feathery warmth.

The bird inspects him with an inquisitive eye. 'You'll need that where you're going.'

'Where am I going? Tell me, *I am the king.*' Richard adjusts the cloak on his lop-sided shoulders.

'You were, you was, and you has been,' says Raven, 'but you ain't anymore.'

Truth comes rushing through the clouds like a roar of fiery wind and knocks the king to the ground. He stumbles and falls, desperate for God to answer him as He has always done before. 'Most Merciful Lord, show me Your Gracious Mercy.'

'A little late for that, don't you think?' says Raven, offering him an outstretched wing. 'Come on, up you get.'

The bird is the voice. That is all there is. There is no sign of the Lord. Richard is alone in this world. No one is coming. He struggles to his feet, touching Raven's wing. It's a relief to be told what to do when you are broken.

2

Months before Bosworth,

on a small hill above the village of Oxenbridge, spring sunshine warms the stones of the Abbey of Stern. Apple blossom drifts through the air and the devout press on with their rigorous application to prayer and duty, which fulfils their daily purpose. In the fields and farms surrounding the abbey, animals welcome the spring with their usual cacophony and chickens lay eggs in lengthening light. A monk, Dedalus, crosses the small courtyard tucked away at the northern end of the abbey between the stables and the cloister, on his way to the kitchen to see Sister Alice and surreptitiously find something to eat. Wickedness waits for him round every corner, but he's getting good at trying to avoid it, working his way through the pitchers of sin that slosh about inside him with increasing regularity. He wonders, scuffing the stones with his toes, why God makes it so hard to be good, or if this is peculiar to him and others have an easier time doing righteous things. Surely he would know by now, after so much diligent prayer and devotion to God, the answer to this question that bothers him every day, like an irritating companion, but he does not, and he considers this to be his singular failing.

Blue sky, wispy clouds, warm air, a day bathed in God's glory. He stops for a rare moment to breathe in this goodness, before the ever-watchful geese shatter the peace and sound the alarm. Their contemptuous racket is soon drowned by the thundering of hooves in the courtyard. Clouds of dust billow over Dedalus as a steaming mass of beasts and men surround him on the cobbled stones. All thoughts of food have fled. The abbey does receive travellers, but they usually walk, like good pilgrims, their holy sandals in pursuit of holy things, and never in such numbers. Banners of the white boar and the white rose of York flutter in the breeze and thrill his long thin bones. He's about to fetch the others, but they have heard the arrival and fetched themselves. Father Jessop comes running with his robes flapping, his gingery head bowing so low he's almost scraping the ground. The Holy Mother and Sister Alice appear like two small ghosts on the other side of the courtyard, eyes averted, not looking at anyone or anything. Copying Father Jessop, Dedalus bows to the horses, and when he looks up again, King Richard the Third of England is standing before him.

He can see the face of the king. He lets out a feathery little sigh without knowing what he's doing and in that instant the king extends his hand, fingers covered in rings, and, like Father Jessop, Dedalus kisses those fingers.

'This country is ours,' says the king. 'Your prayers will help me keep it.'

He means all those at the Abbey of Stern. He means Father Jessop and the Holy Mother, and Dedalus, lurking and watching everything with his big round eyes. He means all of them on their knees, penitent and humble, beseeching the Lord to save England for their lawful, rightful king.

'I remember you.' The king tilts his head at Dedalus. Two years ago, the newly crowned king and his triumphant glittering procession bestowed their grace on the Abbey of Stern, and

Dedalus is easy to remember. Thin like a stick, the monk in charge of the horses. What's left of his hair curling round the circle of his head. Large grey eyes astonished at the world. Plain robes in keeping with his estate, a belt to bind them, a small wooden cross attached to that belt, and leather sandals with a strap to keep them on his feet. A plain and simple monk fascinated by the king.

Now the king's voice floats through the air like birdsong. When he's not talking, he's chewing his bottom lip and, for a moment, being so close, Dedalus almost believes he and the king are the only people alive in the world. Excitement surges through his chest. Dedalus can see the king's teeth, shining and perfect, no gaps or breaks, each tooth appointed by God to be in his head and remain there. Although he is slightly shorter than Dedalus thinks a king should be. Kings are chosen by God to be rulers of men; therefore they have to be taller, stronger, and wiser, but despite his coat and hat and trimmings, the king looks much the same as any other man. This is how Dedalus remembers him, a slight figure dipped in sunshine, running his hands over the tips of the lavender.

Accompanied by a retinue of men, the king walks beside the Holy Mother and Sister Alice, glancing at them as if he's searching for holiness.

Dedalus wonders what Silas is doing. Amongst all the commotion he is nowhere to be seen. *Latrines*, thinks Dedalus, *that's where he'll be.*

In the small solid church, the king kneels and crosses himself as Father Jessop intones the Prayers for Righteousness and Victory and the Holy Mother blesses him with all the grace she can summon, which is a reasonable amount seeing as it is almost midday and she has been awake since three am for the first Service of Redemption. Dedalus eagerly watches the king, remembering how the inhabitants of the abbey were always astonished and delighted by his presence. They had never met the previous king, his brother, Edward. He had never journeyed to the abbey for a blessing, and neither had his young son, the boy who was meant to be king after the death of his father. No one knows what happened to him. His uncle, Richard, is the one kneeling in the church with Dedalus.

After the blessing, the king returns to his throng of men and the Holy Mother takes Dedalus aside. She has agreed that the physical presence of Father Jessop and Dedalus will be required in attendance on His Grace, as and when the king commands. The Holy Mother is half the size of Dedalus and three times holier. She is fierce and wise, always seeking redemption for all people in all things, and she can see the look on his face. 'You will go where the Lord needs you, where his faithful servant, the king, needs you to be.'

Humility at all times is needed in the service of the Lord and in the service of the king. Dedalus wonders about the enemy, so full of sin, as he overhears snippets of talk. According to a red-faced duke, the Tudor is the man who believes he has some kind of claim to the English throne, and what is he doing? Sheltering like a sheep with his uncle in France, picking at the fluff in his navel while planning his invasion of England. The idea of him is distant, unrelated to daily life, and daily life is what Dedalus requires. He does not know who the Tudor is or why he would be anywhere at all. One king is enough for him. Blessings bestowed and agreements made, the king is back in the saddle and leaves as quickly as he came. Sunshine disappears into dust as Dedalus watches him ride away.

3

Since he was a boy

Dedalus has learnt that what he wants simply does not matter. From the day his aunt brought him to the abbey door, Dedalus yearned to return to his family and his unfinished life in the small smoky house no longer visible to him. No one told a lonely boy how the needs and wants of daily life would linger under his skin, tucked between his itchy robes and bony chest. Every day, duty balanced against desire and duty always won for the boy growing into a disciplined man. With his vows taken before God, he attempts to lead a life of abstinence and hard work leading to salvation, but now this faithful servant of the Lord finds himself in turmoil. The Holy Mother would never refuse a request from the king, but she isn't the one going, and the desire to stay within the abbey walls, and close to Sister Alice, rises in him like sap in the spring.

Dedalus prays for the king, but for his prayers to work as best they might, he needs the sanctity of Stern. He needs to see Sister Alice every day. Just a glimpse, and then he can go on. Whenever he brushes against Sister Alice in the kitchen, hanging bunches of dried herbs, or preparing chamomile daisies for the tea, he seems to grow taller, his bones filling up with a purpose that might lead him to God's grace.

He prays fervently that the Tudor will be struck with sickness. Felled by plague. Halted by tempest and a sour-faced malevolent wind that refuses to blow any ship carrying his skinny pustular form to the coast of England. And if fortune turns his way, then let the waves drown him and the fish chew his bones. God will make sure His Divine Providence works for the Righteous King. *That will surely do*, thinks Dedalus. *Everyone can be happy with that.*

Weeks later,

the geese make their usual fuss as a messenger arrives, dirt-spattered from the road. He wipes the dust from his eyebrows and begs whoever he can find for water, wine, ale, anything, so he can recover and give the message from the king. Dedalus, Jessop, and Silas all look much the same to him and Dedalus does not want to welcome him but cannot deny a thirsty man his drink.

'The Tudor has sailed to England. The forces of darkness are gathering. Now is the time to fulfil your duty of prayer.'

He reads the rest of the king's letter but Dedalus has stopped listening. Despite the advent of the Tudor, all Dedalus has heard is that Dedalus and Father Jessop must join the king at Nottingham. A place he's never been to. What is Nottingham? Somewhere that barely exists. Who would be there? Dedalus imagines a great hall piled high with the king and his men, with bows and arrows, axes and armour and swords. The idea of such a place, humming with the pent-up energy of fighting men, fills Dedalus with dread. He understands they must make haste, but both Jessop the Fiery Believer and Dedalus the Reluctant take their time packing and repacking their meagre stores: rolled cloth for sleeping, the relic box as Jessop has requested, and bread and cheese for the saddle bags. Dedalus finds four green apples and fills the travelling pouches with water. When they are finally ready and have said their goodbyes to Silas, Sister Alice, and the Holy Mother, the horses make their way over the courtyard. Past the entrance, which looks like a pile of stones but marks the beginning and end of Holy. Past the geese, who recognise horses and riders and for once in their lives say little. Then along the overgrown path that follows the river to the outskirts of the village. One fierce thought about Sister Alice stirs inside Dedalus before he kicks his horse in the right direction.

The longer they ride, the looser Father Jessop's tongue becomes. 'That stream of unworthy, that pile of piddle, that *Tudor*, thinks he can take the Crown, and we're all going to what? Lie down and kiss his feet? If they fight, the king will win. Anyone who doubts *him* will be mistaken.'

They have just reached the outskirts of Oxenbridge. Miles and miles to go. Dedalus watches the line of the river snaking back through the village, to the abbey, to the familiar. It's all he can do not to tug the reins of Squirrel, his sturdy mount, and turn her in the direction of home. Instead, he pats her thick little neck. Clouds of dust rise and hang in the air. If he turns back now and does not do his duty, what does he then become? He has no answer. Jessop is waiting, duty is his calling, so Dedalus follows him. They tack across country. It's safer this way, there being only two of them, and neither much suited to self-defence, but if it came to that, Jessop would probably fare better than the long piece of straw riding alongside him.

After the flat fields of Thame and Oxford, they arrive at Little Squyrewell, to a placid reception from the brothers of the Sacred Cloth. The brothers from Stern are greeted, and food and bedding given with calm acceptance. The further north they travel, the fresher the air becomes. Dedalus has never been so far from Oxenbridge in his life. Their journey takes them to the soggy-strawed inn at Fylche. Tired from riding, they welcome frothy ale into their stomachs with gusto and wake in the morning belching and farting, but only with each other to mind. They spend two nights in Lesser Dytchewicke to fully recover, and longer than they intended with the whey-faced monks at Shroude, where Dedalus develops severe stomach cramps, blaming the unrelenting pottage. Some foul thing found its way into the bubbling mass of beans and cabbage, the turn of a brother's finger most likely, and he is unable to ride until his cramps have eased. God is telling him, king or no king, he should have stayed at Stern.

From Shroude, they set off again, Dedalus still weak and wobbly, Squirrel staunch and standing no nonsense, just a simple horse giving a simple ride, thank you. Then on to Streede and Pincham.

Roads and paths churn with hoofprints. They haven't reached Nottingham but find themselves following crowds of people through the gate of the great square, the Newarke, in the city of Leicester. The wind is blowing from the west on a late afternoon. It's 22 August 1485, and the battle between the king and the Tudor has already taken place without them.

4

By the time

Dedalus and Father Jessop make their way through the crowd gathering in the Newarke, Dedalus is tingling with nerves. He ties the horses at the trough. The water is dirty grey, insects wriggle on the surface. It's past noon. The sun pounds his head, a bead of sweat rolls down his face, his heart beats an anxious tattoo at the procession of soldiers coming into the square. He can't see the banner of the white boar. The crowd murmurs and people start pushing and shoving one another to get a better view. Dedalus squirms forward, then wishes he hadn't. Something doesn't look right with the horse at the front. It's restless, twitchy, tossing its big head up and down. Closer and closer it comes. A lot more murmuring, some gasping. Dedalus cannot tear his eyes away. There's a naked man hanging over the horse, his buttocks and legs streaked with blood. His hands are tied and pointing to the ground. *Is he dead?* He looks dead. The fighting men seem to think he's dead.

The man's body moves with the rhythm of the horse. A mass of bloody hair flops about, his arms flop, his head flops, so for a moment it looks as if he's come alive again. Dedalus has never seen anything like this in all his twenty-five years. The dead need respect, so 'Cover him,' he can hear himself shouting, 'Cover him. Where is the king?'

A soldier bellows in his ear, 'King Richard is deeeeaaaad, Long Live the King.' The smell of blood makes him queasy, and the nakedness upsets him, and as he tries to back away from everything he bumps into the unyielding form of Father Jessop.

'They've killed the king,' says Jessop, nodding at the dead man on the horse.

The longer Dedalus stands there, the more the world shrinks to those words. *How can that be the king?* Not long ago, Dedalus had kissed those hands, now look at them. He covers his mouth to try and stop an overwhelming urge to puke. The body on the horse bears no resemblance to the king in the courtyard. *His king.*

Father Jessop speaks in a low voice, 'We didn't pray hard enough, did we?' In his sinking heart, Dedalus knows that to be true.

The dead are dead

and the air is warm and sticky. God did not send the malevolent wind. The Tudor marched through Wales and marched to Bosworth and met the king, and now look what has happened. As the day progresses, people come and go from the Newarke, trooping under the great archway and out again when they've seen enough. The Tudor and the Plantagenet fought, and the Tudor won. Dedalus wants to protect the body of the king and take him back to Stern, although riding through England with the dead man and his battered head would be difficult. He checks with Jessop. 'We're taking him back?'

Jessop frowns at Dedalus and shakes his head. 'How can we? They won't let him go.'

A couple of dirt-splattered soldiers take the body down from the horse and place it on a stone ledge near the entrance to the church, the hands still bound. *Release him*, thinks Dedalus, *untie him, he cannot draw his sword.* A pool of bodily fluid seeps out from under the king. His mouth is half open, jaw at an odd angle, dried blood covers his face. A scrappy piece of cloth covers his privates.

'Look what they've done,' cries a woman, edging closer, weeping. The mood grows sombre.

'Where are his clothes?' Father Jessop asks.

'Father, the question is, where is his crown?' says one of the soldiers.

Dedalus stops himself from shouting out, *On his head, that's where his crown should be.* He can barely bring himself to look at the king's head. *I remember you.* Only a few months ago the king was alive; now he's a blood-streaked body at the mercy of his enemies, which is exactly what the Tudor's men wanted.

'Look upon this man,' the soldier commands. 'Tell your friends, your neighbours, your families, the Plantagenet king is dead.'

Dedalus can hardly bear it. Exhaustion swims through him, his legs shake, he rubs his eyes. All he wants to do is cry and cry and cry. Desperate to leave the terrible sight behind, he lurches into the church away from the heat and clamour and lets his eyes slowly adjust to the gloomy interior. This is the biggest building he has entered in his life. It's at least three times the size of the abbey church and he can almost feel God pulling him up to Heaven, but he is definitely still on earth. As if from nowhere, half a dozen men make their way past him, breaking the quietness, and taking no notice of the monk lurking in the corner. One man is taller than the others, those around him showing a determined deference, so he must be more important than the rest of them. Is that the Tudor? Their accents are peculiar, he can't understand anything they're saying. Should he creep out? *Who is that man?* Dedalus tries to get a better look.

The man has a long narrow face with watchful eyes. He's tall and thin, extruded from air like Dedalus. There's nothing wide or generous about him. If he is the Tudor, perhaps he is unable to believe that England is now his, just as Dedalus is finding it hard to believe that King Richard is dead. But that's how it goes. Jessop said Wales was where the Tudor had the most support. Dedalus has never met a Welshman before but might not be able to avoid it now.

'Two days,' says the tall one. 'Let everyone see.'

'He'll stink.'

'Then we'll put him in the ground.'

The men leave the church and Dedalus follows, wondering what to do. If the monk from Stern attacked the Tudor, he would soon be sliced with swords, stuck with daggers, close-shaved with halberds. Then where would he be? Lying next to the king, who would know nothing of this. He takes one last look. Death has whitened the king's skin, and it almost looks like he's sleeping, but death is death, no matter how many times he looks.

As Dedalus emerges into the harshness of daylight, Father Jessop reappears with the relic box under his arm, accompanied by a monk from the Grey Friars monastery, who is surveying them with his watery eyes. Dedalus can see he's not impressed. The Grey Friars monk has probably never met a brother from Stern before, and certainly not Dedalus or Jessop. One looks like a scoundrel and the other like a stick of willow. *We're all wrong to him*, thinks Dedalus. That's what you get with a mixed order, no matter the piety of the Holy Mother, or the blessing of the Pope.

'I've seen the Tudor,' he says, to lighten the mood.

Jessop shrugs. The Franciscan coughs.

'He's tall.'

'Closer to God,' says the monk.

'We will pray for the king now, where he lies,' Jessop says, as if he's in charge.

'There's only one king,' says the monk, sniffing. He'll still offer rooms for the monks from Stern because he's a Franciscan.

'We'll not be staying,' Father Jessop replies, rescuing him.

'As you wish,' says the monk. 'I pray for your safe return. I pray for your strength against all temptation.'

With a renewed bout of coughing, the monk disappears, gliding into shadows. It has been a long day. Dedalus's bones ache with tiredness. People are leaving the Newarke, going back to their lives and families, whatever they were doing before the battle. Life goes on, king or no king. Father Jessop has a word with the soldiers. 'If you allow me time to pray for the dead, you will be one step closer to Heaven.' The men cannot resist the grace their actions will bestow on them. They need every last drop.

Jessop spends his last few moments in prayer with the king, the relic box still tucked under his arm. The soldiers are tired and yawning and pay him little attention. Horses need water, the dead need prayers to continue their journey. When Jessop is done, he ties the box to his horse with quick, deft movements and covers it with his saddlecloth. 'Time to go.' He nods at Dedalus.

The horses are ready. Jessop has the saddle, Dedalus has his bony buttocks and not much in between. The sky is full of light and Jessop is fixed on what lies ahead. Shadows swim under his eyes. In the distance, a dog barks while the rest of the world sleeps. The dead are dead. No one follows them from the square. No one asks where they are going, or what their business might be. They ride in quiet prayerfulness through the ancient town.

5

Raven is in far better spirits

than the king, being observant and light of frame. He is considering the king's personality as he digs his great beak in his shiny black chest, searching for the source of irritation. 'He was magnificent in battle', says Raven to the wind and the darkness. 'You should have seen him.

'I did,' continues Raven. 'I saw him and claimed him, and now look at him. Who would have thunk that the king would be so squirmy, so miserly miserable, being unavailed of his purpose. Still, once you've been king it's all downhill from there and it's always harder going down than up, let's give him that. And perhaps he is wondering if he has been kidnapped by his enemies, so let's give him that too.'

The king flaps his arms and his cloak billows out. 'What is this?' he asks Raven. 'And where are we going?'

The air is thin, as if they are in the mountains, but the path winds inexorably downhill.

Maybe it's my magnificence, thinks Raven. *He just ain't used to the dazzle.*

*

Richard will not be fooled

and he wouldn't put it past his enemies to conjure up a talking bird. They all want to harm him, and it could be the French. The battlefield has disappeared far behind him, and his legs ache and he can't see straight. His knees threaten to give way. If this is eternity, he's not impressed. There are no servants to tend to him, no counsellors to proffer wisdom, no one to ask what His Grace desires. His family have not gathered at the foot of his bed. There is no bed. There are no outstretched hands, no sobbing of women. And if he's right about things, there should be angels, at least one, to guide him up to Heaven, because he will not ascend to the Almighty accompanied by a bird. He's a king, and a king will have an angel. He demands one, he deserves one, he'll tell Raven to fetch him one. No, he won't tell him, he'll *command* him. Threaten him with his sword.

He has no sword. No town, no welcoming door, no houses, no fires. He has crossed fields and rivers, boulders and stones, listening for voices, dogs, horses, and the breath of the Lord, who surely knows him to be his most devoted servant. Time wears on. No one comforts him.

'First things first,' says Raven. 'Seeing as I am Raven, what shall I call *you*? My Kingly King? Richard? Rich? Dicky? Dick? Ricardo?'

'Am I not still myself?'

'You're you, but you're not you, if you get what I'm saying.'

Richard's thoughts unwind like a skein of wool.

'Ricardo it is then,' says Raven, 'and I'm going to tell it to you straight, old mate: when you're with me, life's a bit upsy downsy.'

You and not you. Stones loosen under his feet. He once was Richard, now he is *Ricardo*, until he is no longer.

'I would like some proper clothes, and a goblet of wine.' He rubs the back of his head; there is an imprint, a memory of pain. 'Here' – he keeps rubbing – 'it hurts.'

'No surprises there, Ricardo,' says Raven, 'that's where they did you in.'

Raven shakes the ragged ring of feathers round his neck. He has to tell it straight sometimes, but straight is hard for a soul to hear.

Ricardo takes a good look around. Twisted trees grow from the hillsides. A steep-sided valley spreads before them, with a tower looming upon them. If the tower belongs to a church, Ricardo can take sanctuary. That word tastes sweet in his mind. He will be saved. There will finally be an end to this.

'Are we still in England?' he asks Raven, just to make sure.

'Once in England, always in England,' says Raven, but this England is a strange country. Ricardo has never seen a place like this. The tower quickens out of the mist with a door that takes up half the sky as the cold mist thickens round them. Raven hops onto one of the great trees and sits there bobbing by the door, which seems to have no end.

Ricardo points to the sky. 'Is that Heaven?' he asks, heart pounding with relief.

The wind shakes the trees and Raven makes a thumping sound deep in his throat. 'Could be,' he says. 'God might be waiting with a pot of Lady Grey tea and a nicely turned out millefeuille just for you. Why don't you knock and find out?'

The king stays where he is. He does not understand half the things the bird says to him. Everything here is the devil's work.

Raven tries again. 'What are you waiting for, O Kingly King? Your brother made you Duke of Gloucester at nine years old, Admiral of England at ten, and Constable of England at seventeen, and you were married to the good Lady Anne by the time you were twenty. King of bloody England before you were thirty-one, so what's stopping you now? If you think that's Heaven, knock! *Knooock!*'

A bird cannot know about his life, yet the bird is all he has.

'All these years, Ricardo, I have seen you with my beady eyes,' says Raven, flapping his wings and nearly falling off the branch. 'And now here you are.'

'What is this place?'

'It's been called many things over the infinite years. Some say it's Purgles, Monseigneur, or the Hairafter, or the Great Yawn of Nothing, but we in the business of souls call it Threadbare. It's what's left of you, my Kingly King. The thread of you, the bare of you, the who you really are of you, and it's all yours.'

'Threadbare,' says the king, tasting the word for the first time. Rolling it in his mouth like a stone. Through the fog there are walls now towering above him. Turns out Threadbare is a keep of solid stone and the longer he looks at it from the outside, the more he knows if he does nothing, nothing will do him. If he opens the door, the rest of his eternal life might begin. Whatever that life turns out to be. In all the places he has been, in all the countries he has visited – France, Bruges, Scotland – none has ever been like this.

The cold is ferocious. This is not what he envisaged in his quiet moments. On his knees, with his Book of Hours, with his God, with his cross, with his deep belief. He's never heard of Threadbare, England. Never ridden through its winding streets, never slept at the inn, never walked its cobbled stones. His *Book of Ghostly Grace* does not detail the prayers or meditations necessary for Threadbare. His mother has the same book and she's never mentioned it once, and if anyone would know about Threadbare, she would. God hasn't said to him, *Wait for me in Threadbare.* Priests and bishops have not once uttered the word from their penitent Christian mouths. No one at the Abbey of Stern offered prayers for his safe passage through Threadbare to the Glories of Heaven.

The earth creaks and shudders beneath him. The bird is right. He was made Duke of Gloucester when he was nine years old, so he knows one thing: he has never let fear stop him, and he won't start now.

A blast of icy air engulfs him. The walls close round him as if the place is breathing by itself. Steps rise from the ground, leading in every direction. *Think, Ricardo, think. Which way do I go?*

The stairs down might lead only to dungeons and despair. His enemies hiding, waiting to pounce. He knows how it's done. The steps closest to his feet keep bumping against him.

'You'll soon get the hang of it,' says Raven. He thought this was going to be a quick trip to Threadbare, up or down the stairs (their choice), to the Rooms of Remembering, where new arrivals are given every opportunity to remember their deeds. One final sorry before Redemption, then Angel, Soul, Heavenly Light (possibly, if all goes well, and sometimes that's a big if). 'It's early days. Go on then.' Raven nods. 'Time to find out.'

Ricardo's not having *any* days and the bird is starting to upend what's left of his reason. He's halfway to nowhere, chewing his bottom lip.

'Ricardo, for a bright fellow, you're exceedingly slow. Nothing stays the same, not even you. I'm a bird and you're a soul and here is where you are.'

'Here is where you are, also,' says the king.

Raven inclines his wary head. 'True, but you prayed for everlasting life, and this is it. My advice? Tap yourself a tune, otherwise the darkness comes upon you.'

'Are you coming too?'

'Do I look like I need Redemption?' says the bird.

Ricardo listens for something more, but all he hears is Raven making scratchy little noises with his tripod feet.

6

Red kites whistle above them

on their journey back to Stern. *One day*, thinks Dedalus, *I will be like those birds, body and mind joined in one effortless journey.* But he doesn't know how, and he doesn't know when. Jessop rides beside him, a little taller in the saddle, bum against the relic box. Dedalus would like to know what's in it, but his head is full of king and for once he's happy to smell the summery stink of the river telling them they're home. His stomach rumbles, desirous of filling. He wonders why he is always hungry, why there is a hole inside him that can never be filled no matter how hard he prays. He longs to see Sister Alice. He longs for a mouthful of that fine white cheese that stinks of goat and skips along his tongue. Squirrel pricks up her ears, she knows she's home, but Dedalus is suddenly filled with pangs of guilt and wants to keep riding. It's his fault the king is dead. He could have saved the king if he had arrived in time and asked God to save his soul. Perhaps as penance he should leave the abbey, bed down at the inn, drink a flagon of ale, and vomit on the rushes with a mangy dog chewing at his ear. His beloved sandals will be stolen in the night, and he'll shout in his dreams for his mother, but she won't hear him. She's buried in the long grass. He chastises himself: *God sees you always wanting to be somewhere you are not.*

By the time they clatter into the courtyard, the Holy Mother
has appeared to greet them. A slender reed of righteousness, her
robes flapping in the breeze. She looks searchingly at the Royal
Pilgrims, their faces telling her everything she needs to know.
The king is dead, and they were not there to save him. Jessop
carries the relic box to the church and Sister Alice joins them,
treading lightly with each step, her eyes fixed on the ground.
Summer has not brought many travellers to the abbey, but the
kitchen can still accommodate as many mouths as there are
to feed. Having fed and watered the horses, Dedalus does not
want to eat dried lavender or sage. He soon finds what he's
looking for. White and heavenly in a bowl covered with cloth,
freshly made. He cannot resist. *You glutton.* He's licking it off his
fingers when Silas walks into the kitchen. He's the last person
Dedalus wants to see. He wants to tell Sister Alice about the
king himself, instead of leaving it to Jessop – *He's deeaad, he's
deeaad* – and he wants to tell her about the king before he speaks
to Silas. But it's too late.

Silas is the youngest inhabitant of Stern, and therefore the
most annoying and the most forgivable, but not for Dedalus.
Silas is wed to his beloved broom, drags it everywhere, cleaning
and comforting, like his own personal indulgence. Dedalus has
christened him Rat Face, on account of his large front teeth.
His head balances like a moon on his skinny body in his skinny
robes. Silas reminds him of himself, whiny bones groaning for
the light, all elbows and knees, as most boys are. But Silas is
really not like him in any other way. He claimed not to know
his family, or where he might be from when Father Jessop took
him in. The broom is his family.

'Dedalus?'

He burps. The boy watches him.

'Silas,' says Dedalus.

The boy takes his time, running his tongue over his teeth. 'Father Jessop said the king was …' Rat Face grips the wooden handle.

Dedalus stares at him. 'We pray for all the souls on God's earth and most especially we pray for the soul of the king. We act in all ways in accordance with the divine instruction of Stern.'

Silas nods. 'Exactly so,' he says. 'Did you see him?'

Dedalus grimaces, he has no wish to describe what he saw. 'The king is resting with Our Lord, and we, Silas, are but His weak and feeble messengers.'

'Only I've seen Father Jessop with the relic box.'

'The relic box is blessed. Not for the likes of you.'

'What's in it then?' He wants to know, just like Dedalus does, but Silas hasn't finished yet. 'Travellers came while you were away,' he says, his face burning with knowledge that cannot be forgotten. 'The soul of the king will be in the eternal flames of Hell because he was wicked and killed his nephews. That's what they said.' Silas gives his teeth a final suck and his words land in a pile at Dedalus's feet.

Dedalus sighs, and the air sticks to his bony ribs. This is what happens when he leaves the abbey. The natural order of belief is provoked and disturbed. The abbey supports the king, the king pays for that support, the king is a good man because he is the king. *Was* the king. The cheese rises in his throat, his face is covered in a sheen of sweat. *Killed his nephews.*

'Brother,' he says to Silas, very calmly, very quietly, 'do not speak of things you do not know, or I will break your broom.'

Then he rushes past him to be sick.

A wave of exhaustion

washes over Dedalus. He walks to the church, cutting behind it to the brambles growing over the path. Juicy fat blackberries cleanse his palate. Sunlight falls in slivers to the ground. Oxenbridge spreads below him, green and tranquil, cottages and farms dotted amongst the fields and sheep. He pictures the woods where he and his brother, Will, went hunting. He hasn't thought of his brother for a very long time. Rat Face's words bounce around in his head. It is true that the young prince did not become king. Rumours abounded that summer when the king was crowned and visited the abbey, but in the excitement of those days, who really knew what happened? People said all kinds of things, and he never took notice of them. The king was the king, so why, now, does Silas bother him so much? *Killed his nephews.* Dedalus liked the king. The king called him by his name, touched him on the shoulder. *I remember you.*

When Dedalus lies on his mattress, belly grumbling and moaning, tiny devilish creatures burrow into his skin. Sleep won't come. Every time he shuts his eyes, there's the body of the king, holding out his bloody hands so he can haul himself to his feet.

7

The question is

will Ricardo ever be bright, confident Richard again? Will he ever leave Threadbare and see sky above him, earth beneath him, men beside him, horse under him? Be ready for the swell of power. The authority of command. Will his words matter? Will his footsteps be heard? Here, there are too many stairs to count. Just when he's ready for some light in his darkened eyes, another set of stairs appears and the walls threaten to squeeze him like a bunch of grapes.

'Raven.' He calls for the bird. 'Tell me how I get out of here.'

'Climb, Ricardo, climb.'

Every set of stairs leads to a passageway at the top. He must be brave, inching along in the dark, still believing this to be a trap because he knows about those. An ambush to fetch a little boy from sanctuary takes fifty armed men hiding in shadows. And while they wait, the boy's mother, the queen, is told by someone that she respects, let's say the Archbishop of Canterbury, that if she refuses to hand him over, then Richard and those men will fetch him themselves. Even though she has taken refuge with her family. *And that is how you take your nine-year-old nephew to his brother waiting in the Tower of London to be crowned, is it not?*

27

A dull ache spreads across his chest. A child's trusting hand in his. A mop of tousled hair. A small high voice. At the end of the passageway there is a door half open to a room where someone is sleeping. He can hear little raspy breaths in the chilly Threadbare air. He creeps closer. A sense of familiarity washes over him. He and George, his older brother, once slept in a bed like this, covered in furs and blankets, snowflakes breezing past the cold, thick walls. It's been such a long time since he thought of him. He remembers how they shivered in that long dark night when they knew something outside their own happiness was happening, as children do. He and George both alert to the meaning beneath the voices that adults think children cannot hear. Two young boys with their mother, while his father and his brother Edmund fought the enemy. He can feel, in what's left of his emotional self, a sadness rising, a lump of regret, a memory, a darkness. He remembers the sound of their mother's footsteps coming to the chamber to wake her sleeping children. The torch held by the servant hovering behind her. The way she shook him and he sat up, pretending to have just woken, but neither he nor George had slept at all, as if they both knew she would come and had been waiting for her all night long.

Your father and your brother. They are gone. Gone.

He remembers how he and George clutched each other. How their breath hung in front of their faces in their nice warm bed. How for the first time in his life the evil of the world crept along the stones and frightened him. He sees himself in the cloudy distance, a fatherless boy learning to reorientate himself in the world. One brother dead, one brother fighting, one brother alongside him. His mind tumbles into chaos. He grew up in the company of men who taught him how to be, how to fight, how to take what's his.

He does not enter the room. He walks quickly back along the passageway, down the endless stairs, intent on finding the door, flinging it open, breathing in the icy air, walking back through the valley, back to the battle, finding his horse, killing the Tudor, wearing the crown – anything not to be here, anything to reclaim his breath, his bones, the undisputed power of life. But Threadbare doesn't work like that. Every time his feet touch the ground, the stairs reappear. The hope that he will ever find God at the top, surrounded by divine light, begins to fade. Where are the gates to Heaven? Where is the choir of angels? They are not here.

8

Autumn swirls through the Abbey of Stern

with rain and blustering wind, a prelude to the white-tipped joys of winter. The hens won't lay – too cold, not enough light, come back in spring. The miller brings up sacks of barley and rye on his rickety cart to the kitchen door. The abbey still has a bake oven in the wall, left over from the days when it was the largest double abbey in England. Now it's the smallest. Days are filled with ordinary things.

In their strictly limited discourse, Dedalus always finds it hard not to offer a blessing or a greeting when he works alongside Sister Alice. If their arms accidentally brush against each other in the busyness of God's earth amongst the cabbages, they give each other small sideways glances and move away. Where once he yearned for his family, for the life he was taken from so abruptly, it is the warmth of another that he now seeks. He is glad of the limitations placed upon him by his vows, for how else would he know how to live, or how to walk the path of righteousness, where God is to be found. There is always living to be done, and life is work and duty. The accounts don't write themselves. The abbey's household ledger must be maintained, the ins and outs of daily life, the visitors, the expenses, the donations. God bless the king and God save the king because Dedalus and Jessop didn't.

When Dedalus sits in the small solarium sharpening his quill, cold draughts winnow round his ankles. He runs his tongue over his lips as he concentrates, gripping his favourite knife. As he works, his mind wanders back to the king. He thinks of Jessop and the relic box, how easily he slid in and out of the church, how carefully he placed the box on his horse. He wonders what would happen if he looked inside it, just once, to see what might be there. He thinks of the king's matted hair, and his knife slips and cuts his finger. Drops of blood squeeze through a flap of skin. Now there's blood on the feather. He sucks his finger, and it stings. The blood tastes unpleasant. He sits for a while with his bloody finger wrapped in his robe.

He doesn't know how long he sits there. When it stops bleeding he starts again. Scraping the knife down to the end of the shaft, where it sat in the poor old goose. He finishes sharpening the shaft to a fine point and tests it on his finger. No blood. Letters can be clearly drawn. He balances the feather between his thumb and forefinger. How can something so light be so useful? *Better tools, easier tasks*, as Jessop has told him many times.

Writing eases his mind. Solitude becomes less burdensome when he's doing the accounts. Grain and tallow, linen and leather – things they cannot make themselves – cost money. Sometimes Silas floats into his mind, a thin lad at the end of his thinner broom. He has an idea to beat him once, like his father did to him, to try to make him better.

He hasn't spoken more than a few words to Sister Alice since he returned. Whether working, writing, or praying, he might glance at her, but makes certain not to speak, although he wants to. He worries his tongue might have a life of its own and say things he might regret. *O Lord, help me be good.* In the kitchen garden he takes great interest in turnips pulled from the earth with clods of dirt dangling from their roots. Weeks have passed. Sometimes he sees the king standing there, accusing him: *You did not come. I asked you, but you did not.* If his tongue loosens, it will open the portcullis of his teeth, and words will rush from his mouth, falling over themselves in their haste to be heard. *The king is here*, he wants to tell her. *We failed and look what happened.*

Dedalus beseeches the Lord for the soul of the king to go straight to Heaven. He prays desperately for that soul and shudders at the thought of Hell, replete with demons breathing fire on his softly spoken king. And then on him. The wind howls and the river trembles in the rain.

God's punishment

for dithering under a cold November moon is a chilly wind. Dedalus is passing the women's quarters, on the western side of the abbey, the small stone block with two doors side by side. Those doors are part of the landscape of his life, landmarks, like the church and the stables, deeply familiar, like candles and straw and sinful thoughts. His eyes water, his nose runs, and, above the wind, faint but audible, the sound of crying rises in the air. He has no business near the women — no man ever does — but tonight he stops and listens. It's been a long time since he heard a woman cry and he's sure it's a woman. A strange soft sound, like water running through his hands. As a child, crying came naturally, but he has learnt emotions are subjugated before God, like all things.

He remembers his aunt with her red face and dripping nose. When she cried, he always cried too, although he had no idea what she was crying about. It didn't seem to matter. If his aunt was sad, then he was sad too. If one of the women is crying, then God will comfort her, he tells himself, although God hasn't been comforting him, so maybe there'll be none for her, either. *Walk on, Dedalus, walk on.* The moon hurries behind clouds; no sign of Jessop or Silas, not yet dawn, not yet time for Devotions. There's a long pause, an owl shrieks in the night, and the sobbing starts again, and through the tears he knows it's Sister Alice. His body moves before he realises what he's doing, there's some part of himself he cannot deny — *It is her* — and he soon finds himself outside the familiar door. He imagines the king treading on the cobbles and stopping behind him and placing a hand on his shoulder. He can feel the weight of it, but when he turns, no one is there. He clears his throat and coughs, the crying stops.

He coughs again. 'It's me,' says Dedalus, and the door opens a fraction, just enough for an eye to peer through, and before he can stop himself — *She'll bless me and that'll be it* — he's stepping into the small cell of Sister Alice, who pulls him inside and closes the door. His heart yammers in his chest, he should not be here. Turmoil jumps across his face. In smoky light he sees her eyes are wet; she dabs at them with her sleeve. On her upper lip, reflected in flickering candlelight, a row of fine hairs he's never noticed before. Behind her is a narrow bed, a blanket, her rosary, a small wooden cross in the niche by the door. Two candles, one unlit, one smoking with its tall black wick and saucer full of tallow. Not much else apart from Sister Alice and her big sad eyes. Barely a hand's width between them. A tear makes its way down her cheek.

'Dear Sister,' he says, and then stops because he doesn't know what else to say.

Her eyes brimming. The screech owl cries its terrible cry.

'Listen,' she says, kneeling on the floor, ear tilted to the ground. His arm tries hard not to touch her.

'There, there they are!'

He wriggles down as best he can; the sound of his breathing fills the tiny room. Blood rushes to his head, unbidden images pour into his mind. Logs spitting in the fire, a kiss on the top of his head at night as a child, hearing things that are not his business, shallow breaths, groans, the rustling of linen. Shadows cross her face, her eyes shine in the dark. He holds his breath and listens to the muffled noises coming from the ground. Thumps and scratchings, cat or fox, stoat or badger. A moan, or a cry, not the bark of a fox, nor the growl of a badger. He listens again, harder: it's a cat, ratting in the dark, catching a nice juicy rat. Then a softer but still insistent repeated request, rising between them: 'Save me, save me, save me.'

She turns to him. 'Dedalus, the Lord is telling us there are poor souls asking to be saved.' A strand of dark hair has escaped from her veil.

'Foxes,' he says, looking at her hair, his voice stuck in his throat, 'or cats.'

She grips his arm and her eyes widen as if she's been struck by a terrible thought.

'Can you not see, Dedalus,' she says softly in her passion, 'these are the unredeemed souls? And the king is amongst them, is he not? And God has allowed us to hear them' – she clutches at her chest – 'and our solemn purpose must be to save them, Dedalus.' Her eyes fill with tears again.

'Hush now, hush,' he says, laying a hand on her arm. She flinches but lets it rest there; her voice grows a little higher. 'We must bring them back to the Lord. We must pray for the soul of the king. That is why we are here.' She dabs her eyes and gazes up to Heaven where the Lord is waiting. Dedalus struggles to his feet. *Leave now and do not return.* This is the closest he has been to a woman since he was a boy, and his feet try to keep their obedient distance.

'Help me,' he whispers. He doesn't want to let anything into this moment and certainly not the king. Beneath the ground there is nothing but beasts and worms, but what if she understands salvation better than he does, and the king is one of those lost souls unable to rest in peace. *Look what they did to me, Dedalus, and you weren't there to save me.*

'I see him,' he says to Sister Alice. And all the words come tumbling out, weeks of the unspoken, falling onto the humble dirt floor and into her arms. It's his fault that the king is dead, he didn't pray hard enough, or long enough. He wanted to stay with her. 'With you,' he says, choking with the effort of saying too much, of just wanting to save himself.

She strokes the back of his hand with her fingers. He shuts his eyes, and the lost boy rises, desperate for a warm loving touch and all the things imprinted on his skin he once had but now can barely remember. A pressure builds inside him, he can't stop it, can't control his usually well-controlled body. He touches the top of her lip. *So soft.* That same sinful finger touches her cheek. Her skin sinks into him. He sighs, his legs shake. The chambers of Hell will now devour him, but surely for once the world can stay out of this. Sister Alice brushes his mouth with her fingers, his chin, his cheeks. His heart jumps, his body trembles with pleasure. He thinks he might be dying.

'Dedalus,' she whispers, 'God is showing you the king.'

A low little moan escapes from his lips.

'And the king is in the bowels of Purgatory asking you to save his soul. You are a messenger of God, Dedalus. You must save him.' She gazes upwards as if she can see the path to glory before her, the path of righteousness for a sinner such as he.

Save yourself, Dedalus, but he's not sure what that means and when he opens his eyes he's still in the room with Sister Alice, which is the only place he wants to be. He can't stop himself shaking, so she holds him, and he leans into the comfort of her arms, her soft warm body. He can feel her breasts beneath her robes, he dares not touch them, but he wants to. Neither has any idea what they are doing. He's becoming someone else, not the name she keeps calling him – Dedalus doesn't behave like this. He's sinking further and further into himself, all his knowledge draining back into the earth, like a dribble of water. Brain full of stars, body expanding into the heart of love, into her arms, and before he knows what's happening, it's too late. He's shuddering and moaning, there's a wet patch on his robes, and, very soon after that, beneath the ecstasy, his cock softens like a fat little worm.

Dazed, he's not sure what to say, so says nothing. She closes her eyes, pushes her hair back under her veil, into virtue. They sit beside each other on the hard little bed, wrapped in the comfort their normal life denies. He takes her hand, but everything is different now.

'Sin has tempted us,' she says, 'but we will pray for forgiveness.'

When he walks back to his small cell, the moon has gone into hiding and flames flicker at his feet. The ground hasn't swallowed him yet, but soon it will. Father Jessop will appear like a demon shrieking in his dreams, *I see you, Sinner! I see you!* He will be beaten and put in a cage where he will die a terrible lingering death. His body will blacken. His eyes will be eaten by crows and there he will dangle, through frost and snow, rain and wind, as a warning to the village, so that every day his beloved family can watch his bones twisting in the wicked air. All of them suffering shame, and no salvation for the young man who chose sinfulness instead.

He wakes and his throat is dry. His eyes swim in his head. The goats bleat insistently, ready for milking. He pictures her amongst their hard little bodies as they butt against her skin, her soft warm hands fastened round the soft warm teats. He listens to his thumping heart, so full of wickedness ready to burst on the cobbled stones. He runs his hands up and down his body, feeling for the weak spots where the Devil may enter. In his mind, there she is, smiling at him, eyes as wide as a summer's day. *It's too late, Dedalus*, she says, *I'm already in.*

9

The Tudor has become

the new king, seventh Henry, with the burden of the crown of England on his long thin head, weighing down his long thin face. Everything that King Richard put into place, King Henry must undo. He says, 'This is a new country now,' but England has never been and never will be new, no matter what the Tudor wills it to be. Old families keep old allegiances, and grudges and dislikes grow like moss over stones. The Tudor sits on his throne wondering who is for him and who is against him and who will betray him at the drop of a crumpled boot.

First things first. King Richard's claim to the throne is to be repealed. The *Titulus Regius*, the Act of Parliament that passed in January 1484 and stated that Richard was the lawful king, is declared wrong. All copies of the Act are to be destroyed. Abolished. Richard was, but never should have been, king. It was a tale of fancy in a scroll of words. Richard had no right to the throne. He took the crown from the head of a boy, his brother's beloved son, the nephew he had sworn to protect. Richard had him declared illegitimate along with his brothers and sisters and this was endorsed by Parliament. Richard was the only one left. The crown could only be offered to him, the legitimate, last surviving kin, brother of the Poor Dead King.

The Tudor is to marry the uncrowned prince's sister, and the Tudor's bride cannot be, and never has been, illegitimate, and that includes her brothers. All the future heirs the Princess Elizabeth will bear the Tudor will forever be lawful claimants to the crown of England. No one is to mention Richard, and if you do, you'll get your tongue cut out and fed to the dogs. The reign of Richard the Usurper is over. He was defeated. His bones are in the ground.

10

Raven sits on the tower of Threadbare,
letting the wind ruffle his feathers. Far below him, fog keeps
swirling and souls keep stumbling along. Raven remembers the
unkindness he once belonged to. Him and all the other ravens
circling and wheeling over the Tower of London. At least he's
not a crow, as then it would have been a murder of crows and,
being Raven, he's never killed anything in his life that he didn't
want to eat. Raven has seen this king from beginning to end; he
knows more about this king than the king knows about himself.
Sometimes Raven has looked away. Humans will do what they
choose to do and Raven cannot stop them. Sometimes he has
had to return to the Gathering of Birds and Angels just to regain
his equilibrium. Mostly he remembers where that is. He digs his
beak into his feathery chest. There is always some wormy itch
that drives him mad and one day it will stop like all things must.

Raven admires himself for his unsentimental approach to
the soul, but by now the angel should have arrived and the
unrepentant king should be down on one knee, confessing and
kissing the angel's hand before the great shaft of light bears him
away. Raven is looking forward to that, for that is the reason for
it all. Raven fluffs his windblown feathers. He really is a most
magnificent bird, and also a most patient bird. If he had nothing

else to do with his time, he would carve the greatest medal in the world for himself out of stone.

Every soul he accompanies on this demanding journey through the afterlife must admit the truth of their actions before they can seek forgiveness. What if accepting the truth for this kingly king is harder than it looks? And if Ricardo can't admit the truth to himself before his final confession, then he will have nothing to confess and they are going to be here for a very long time.

'Still,' says Raven, squawking to himself, 'them's the breaks, the stops, the get-out clauses, and what's a humble bird to do other than keep himself ubiquitous and hold the world in the centre of his all-seeing eye?'

Ricardo likes to think of the good

parts of the summer when he became king. His glorious coronation in Westminster Abbey. Days were long and light and he was the one with the crown fixed on his head. He was the one rejoicing with his family. At his coronation feast he was the one eating peacock and swan, eel and carp, custard and jelly, cake and spiced fruits. He was the one riding through England, with his wife, the queen, and his son, the prince, and his splendid crown and his splendid cross, so his subjects could kneel before him and see his grace and benevolence. Sometimes the thought comes to him that when he took himself on his kingly procession, his nephews stayed behind in the Tower of London. How could they possibly have joined him? The support they might have gathered would have detracted from his glory, and the glory of being king was his.

If his nephews had been seen waving from their handsome mounts, people might have wondered why he, Uncle Richard, was crowned instead of the older boy, but he shoos that thought away. Banishes it from his kingdom of soul so his soul does not whisper in his ear, *You were the one who left them there.* Raven didn't see them. The servants in the tower didn't see them. Dukes and earls and lords and commoners did not see them. Their horses didn't feel their light bones on their backs. The grass didn't bear their tread, the walls did not hear the echo of their laughter. All of that was two years before he met the Tudor at the battle of Bosworth.

Raven nudges him; he can see his face, hear his thoughts swinging in the wind. 'Everything here is you, O Kingly King. This is the life you have lived. There is no other.'

Raven is right. Ricardo cannot remember any other life than the one he has lived.

'Call me old-fashioned,' says Raven, 'for it is true I am a most ancient bird, and you, Ricardo, may call me what you like, but if you take the hand of a child and lead them to a tower and they never come out again, you are then responsible for that child. Goodly old Uncle Richard, sworn Protector of All Lads. Then weeks later you're bobbing about with your nephew's crown on your noggin. Am I right, Ricardo?'

Ricardo pretends he cannot hear the bird. He is not ready to hear the bird. Talking nonsense as usual. Another staircase finds his feet. Every time Ricardo reaches the top, the passageway leads to the dark of a muffled room. Every time he goes into that room he finds a bed with two sleeping boys curled next to each other. Nether boy stirs. The memory of summer billows through him. He doesn't want them to wake. He doesn't want to look at them now or ever, standing there in his bare feet, in his odd cloak. He does not want to smell that warm summer scent of strawberries and milk. He will not give in. He will not admit anything to himself about the boys.

Raven briefly wonders

what it's like to be human, then gives up and considers playing a game of solitaire. Is the truth so hard to tell? That weight in the heart that can only be dropped like a stone in a pond when the soul demands. And Raven has dropped plenty of stones everywhere, so he should know, and here's the thing: Raven can see Ricardo is a soul who still believes he is a good man.

Ricardo tucks his hair behind his ears. Before he met him, Raven had heard rumours that he had no ears, but he's looking at them now.

Ricardo says to the walls, 'Bring my enemies here so they may see the truth of me,' but the walls of Threadbare have not yet heard the deep truth of his life and they close round him, hard against his soul.

He cannot get away.

'What do I do?' he asks Raven, his voice trembling. 'Who will remember me?' He wants to cry but the tears won't come. 'Who will mourn for me, who will kneel at my grave and pray for me? I'm not going up again,' he shouts. 'I refuse. Do what you will with me.'

Raven is inches from his face. This is much more interesting than solitaire; what was he thinking?

'Question for you, my Kingly King,' says Raven. 'What's the point of being good if you're not happy when you're dead? You should be rejoicing, Ricardo, that this world is not laid out before you like a Feast of Easy. Everything here has already fallen through time. That's what eternity is, old mate. When you are dead, you are dead, and you, Ricardo, in your current state, are nothing more than a teeny meeny fraction of light.'

The king looks at his cloak. He cannot stop whatever is happening to him.

'Will an angel take me straight to Heaven?'

Raven stretches his wings and yawns. 'In case you haven't noticed, Ricardo, and you haven't, angels aren't the most reliable creatures. When you need them, they're nowhere to be found. So, here's my tuppence worth. If you don't want to be here, and I'm wisely surmising that's the case, old bean, you need to spit it out, open up, tell the truth, lay it all out.'

That's how it's always worked before. He's done kings, a couple of queens, he's done citizens of the world, good and bad, simple, complicated, preternaturally sad, happy, mostly young, sometimes old, mostly England, mostly south of the north, but this one, left reeling on the battlefield, doesn't want to give anything away.

Raven's seen him in all the castles he's lived in since he was a boy. Him and his good lady mother, his siblings and his brother the king. Him and his nephews. Ricardo is a soul with a lot of life to transport. He hasn't sat still for the last thirty-two years. He's grown and learnt and ridden and fought and loved and married and become a father and ridden and fought again and fought bravely and fought right to the end when he could fight no more. Along the way he's lost his wife and son and the kingdom of England and two little boys. He definitely needs an angel.

'I'll say it plain, Ricardo: you are here to face the things you have done. Whether you go up or whether you go down – Heaven is never where you think it is. And when you've had a good look, try asking for forgiveness. Cough up the old sins. Do it for you and me, Team Raven. You might find a chair to sit on – there's usually one around here. And when you are upon that chair of lonely, my Royal Royalness, your head may become heavy and your heart fill with sorrow, and that, my friend, is the pointy point of what you are doing here. Bring it all up, then take it down deep and throw it out wide and hope the angel's light catches you. Then, Ricardo, we can get out of here. Forever and forever, mine is the glory, kind of thing. And as I am your conduit between Heaven and earth, and seeing as I am free for the weekend, I am heading earth-bound to find the angel. And one last thing, if you need me, you can't reach me. Where I'm going is a different dimension, so goodnight.'

Ricardo's head droops onto his chest and he stands very still, considering Raven's words. 'Don't go,' he says, 'don't leave me in this place alone.'

'Well, if I don't go, you can't go, and all time is malleable here. Don't wait up. I'll be back soon, my Kingly King.'

And Raven leaves him standing there. A small silhouette in a cloak of lonely.

Without Raven, waiting is all

Ricardo can do. He wants the years to stop, but they never can, and never will. His life has been lived, determined, taken. All his decisions, all his actions, all his thoughts, everything he did or did not do, day after day, year after year. The truth is still alive, even if the king is dead. What he really wants to do is leave, slip out the door, over the boulders, find home, have a sleep, a good lie-down, a break from the endless stairs. No one will miss him here.

11

Omnipresent Rat Face

with a beady eye. Frosty grass, clouds of breath, slow mornings, fingertips blue with cold. Rat Face lurking beside him. If he's grinding gallnuts for the ink, Rat Face fetches the jars and water, taking his tedious time. When he breaks the ice from the pail of water, Rat Face is looking on. When he gathers moulted feathers from the geese, the geese don't make a fuss over Rat Face. They seem to welcome his presence.

In the quiet of the toilet, Dedalus sits on the round wooden hole, not minding the general stink, his feet on the straw, his mind contemplating the walls. There's nothing much to see. Rat Face sidles onto the latrine furthest away from Dedalus, thank the Lord for His blessed mercies. Business done and grateful for the little shitty cloths, otherwise it would be a handful of straw, Dedalus takes a moment to gather himself. Father Jessop once told him how some monks, in lands so far away that Dedalus cannot even begin to conceive of their existence, use a stick to scrape the shit away. *A stick*. Rounded, not pointed – too sharp and you'll get into all kinds of trouble.

Rat Face sits on his small wooden throne, gazing at the handle of his broom. 'Brother,' says the never-ending voice, 'I have seen you at night being where you should not be.'

His words sink into the pit of Dedalus's stomach. Silas saw him. A shiver runs through him. Fear seeps into his hands, he curls his fingers as his stomach revolts and farts his fear into the waiting air.

The following night, after Midnight Redemption, Dedalus sits on his bed all tense and jangly, his stomach in knots. As far as he knows, Silas is the only one who saw him. He waits, listening for any sounds of activity, but all is quiet, as usual. He takes a few deep breaths to settle himself, then creeps to Silas's cell. He can hear Jessop snoring from here. The door is not locked, and Silas is not asleep. He is sitting on his mattress, arms behind his head, as if he has been waiting for him all night.

'What brings you here, Brother?'

Dedalus keeps his voice low; last thing he wants is Jessop poking his nose round the door.

'You saw nothing, Silas.'

'I saw something, and it was you.' Silas yawns. Can't help himself, it's late. 'I've seen you with our Beloved Sister,' he says, in a way that makes Dedalus want to tap a stick of willow against his head.

Silas moves first. In one fluid movement he grabs his broom and shoves Dedalus as hard as he can against the wall. 'And you're so very righteous, Dedalus.' Wielding his broom, Silas hits Dedalus in the face with the handle.

Dedalus yelps in pain, but Silas doesn't budge and keeps him pinned there, squirming. He says in a quiet angry voice, 'I've seen you, and I'm going to tell Father Jessop, O Most Holy Brother of Mine.'

Grunting with effort, Dedalus pushes Silas and his bloody broom away, determined not to be thwarted by Rat Face. His face hurts where the broom whacked him.

Silas is working up a head of steam, snorting like a bullock in the small cell. With his broom in hand, he's coming for another go. 'If I tell Jessop, you'll hang for it and the crows will eat your eyeballs,' he hisses.

'Silas, listen to me, just listen.'

But Silas isn't listening, he's brandishing his broom. 'You Sinner, Dedalus. I'll shove this up your arse and break your teeth when it comes out.'

Before Silas can do anything else, Dedalus is fumbling for the door and running past the stertorous sounds of Jessop. *Leave the boy alone*, he thinks, his face throbbing, but the boy doesn't want to let Dedalus go. He's coming after Dedalus and he's fast, but Dedalus, in his sandals, is just a bit faster. Silas almost catches up with him but can't quite get him, and halfway over the courtyard Silas hurls the broom and it flies into Dedalus, sending him sprawling onto the cobbles, smacking the sore side of his face. Pain shoots through him. *Leave it*, he tells himself, *go to bed, make peace with the Lord*. He sits up and tries to break the broom handle over his legs, but the wood won't split.

Silas, breathing heavily, grabs the broom from his fallen brother and heads towards the church.

'Shit,' says Dedalus under his breath.

Squirrel hears the huffing and puffing and pokes her head outside the stable door. She snorts hello to her lad, Dedalus – he always gives her a nice little treat, an apple core, or a handful of oats, and pats her neck just the way she likes it. But not tonight. Dedalus bends his face to her forelock, his nose throbbing and his eye half closed. He strokes her soft muzzle. She flicks her ears backwards and forwards. Maybe he should take Squirrel and leave, it would be so easy – *So do it, Dedalus, do it* – but what would happen to Sister Alice if he rode away like a sinner?

Silas saw a shadow on the earth, and that shadow was comforting a sister in distress, and that was all. A shadow on the night of the moon. *Save me.* A nun and a monk with their vows before God, but when someone is distressed, do we turn away? Does the abbey not take in travellers who need comfort? Can we not help each other as well? He must make Silas understand, then everything will be all right.

The usual scent of musky incense fills the church when he reaches its quiet insides. A layer of straw cushions the floor, scattered throughout with rosemary sprigs, and Dedalus knows that is her scent, and he stops for a moment in the stillness. On the altar, a slab of Oxenbridge stone. Nestled between candles, the relic box. *Open it, and see what Jessop took from the king.* An enormous lassitude comes over him as he thinks of the church in the Newarke, the roof soaring to Heaven. He has half a mind to lie down and sleep – *Forgive me, dear Lord* – but before he knows what he's doing the relic box jumps into his arms. *What are you doing, Dedalus? Put it back.* He thinks of those eyes, and those fingers. *Save me.* Pain reverberates through his body. The night is breathing softly. *Put the box back, Dedalus*, but he doesn't. Silas will tell Jessop. So let him. His face hurts so much. *Let the worst things happen.* Opposite him is the door to the crypt. He opens it, half thinking Silas is hiding there, but there's only a gloomy set of stairs leading down to darkness. 'Silas?'

Thinking about the crypt makes him shudder. Jessop took him down there once to show him the tombs, long since occupied by past inhabitants of Stern, those bony instruments of God. He'll go there when he's dead, and not a moment before if he can help it, and only then will he be one step closer to the Lord.

'Is that you?'

Dedalus turns round to find Rat Face behind him.

'Look,' he says, holding up the box. Sensing a trap, Rat Face stays where he is.

Dedalus doesn't move, the entrance to the crypt yawns behind him.

'Come, let us examine this together.'

'If I do …' says Silas.

'If I let you see in here, you don't say a word to Jessop.'

Silas thinks. 'All right,' he says, edging closer to Dedalus and the door.

Whatever the box contains is not theirs to know. What is required is steadfast faithful prayer and a life without sin. Neither of them is managing much of that. Opening the relic box without benediction or blessing adds to the list of sins, but now they are both complicit. A blast of wind rattles the church door, making Silas jump, and yet there is the box, finally, in front of his nose. It is dark in the church but there's just enough light to see, and he wants to see.

'I was comforting a sister in distress,' says Dedalus, closing his fingers round the small brass lock.

Silas slides his tongue over his teeth. 'Was the comfort of prayer not enough?'

A trap, and one Dedalus will not enter. The Lord is always enough. The lock will not budge. It is a small brass circlet: turn it one way, the lid is released; turn it the other, it holds fast.

'Let me,' says Silas, 'I have smaller fingers.'

It still won't open. Dedalus has another turn, picking and poking at the lock.

'She hears the souls beneath us, those who need saving,' says Dedalus, his fingers hurting as he twists the lock. 'They are beseeching us for help. She says we must go to them.'

Silas considers this for a moment. 'We pray always for the salvation of souls,' he says, trying to wrestle the box from Dedalus, but Dedalus hangs on to it and, with a burst of greater force, the lock begins to move.

'Does she think she can pluck them from the flames?' asks Silas.

Before Dedalus can answer, the lock undoes itself and the lid opens. A quick look at each other before they both peer inside. Silas tries to nudge Dedalus out of the way to see what is in the box, and he picks up something in his hands and holds it up.

Dedalus gasps.

'And you thought …'

'As did you.'

'Well, at least it's not his finger,' and Silas laughs, which is altogether not a pleasant sound.

Flop, flop, flop. Dedalus feels sick at the lock of matted hair poking from a cloth. 'Put it back,' he says.

Silas replaces it slowly in the box.

An impulse lasts a few seconds, the results stay forever, but you never know what you're going to do before you do it. Silas's brain is on fire thinking of Dedalus the Wicked, touching the woman who must not be touched, threatening the stability of Stern. The reason they're holy is because they don't do what Dedalus has done. Comfort for the soul is the work of the Lord. Comfort for anything else becomes part of the wickedness, the sinfulness.

'All those souls you're so worried about,' says Silas, with a sneer on his face, 'you go to them,' and he shoves Dedalus with all the strength of a frustrated boy. 'Get out of my way, I've had enough of you.'

Just before he falls completely off balance, Dedalus grabs the relic box from Silas's hands and tumbles down the first few steps leading to the crypt. He leans against the wall, trying to regain his footing. 'Silas, help me.'

But Silas doesn't want to hear what Dedalus has to say. No good talking about devoting their lives fully to God when the actions don't match the words. Without thinking what he's doing, Silas shoves the struggling man down a few more steps. There will be no more sinning from the monk who never liked him. Let him suffer. 'You stay there,' he says to Dedalus, closing the door.

The stairs are slippery and Dedalus is trying to stay upright, but his feet catch in his robes so he cannot keep his balance. At the top of the stairs he can hear Silas locking the door with his quick little hands.

'When you no longer have the devil inside you, Dedalus' — Silas leans against the door — 'I'll let you out.'

Silas is halfway over the courtyard, cradling his beloved broom, before Dedalus makes his way back to the top of the stairs and calls through the door.

By Dawn Devotions, Dedalus has given up, his voice reduced to a painful croak. He's slumped on the top step, resting against the door.

Meanwhile, Silas has returned to the abbey and answered questions from the Holy Mother and Jessop about Dedalus. 'He never misses Mass, never misses Devotions. Is he sick? If he has a fever, then Sister Alice should attend him.'

Sister Alice also asks of him, 'Where is our brother? Have you seen him?'

Silas shakes his head, no, he has not seen Dedalus.

Dedalus has heard them at Devotions, but they haven't heard him. The latch sticks and the handle won't turn. In a great panic of fear, he yells and bangs until he has exhausted himself. The door shakes as he pounds it. No one hears him. No one comes. The staircase is so narrow he almost falls again before he finds his footing.

He pictures Silas talking to the Holy Mother, and Father Jessop and the Tudor and anyone else who will listen. *He was skulking like a cur, with this woman. They're all sinners at Stern.* Sister Alice is condemned, and the Holy Mother and Jessop do nothing to help her in their fierce piety. She knew the rules, she had taken vows before God, and if you break the rules, well. *And he has the relic, Your Grace. Taken from He Who Was Never Rightfully King.*

They will both bear the punishment of their sin. Each step makes his nose throb, one eye is closed and swollen so he must concentrate hard. He cannot think what they might do to her. He will not leave her. It's daylight now, he's worn out, hungry, thirsty, needs a piss, needs to find another way out.

When Jessop took him to the crypt, he had paid scant attention. *Dedalus, ingrate, are you listening? I'll tell you anyway. If you take this path, the one that winds through the tombs, there, can you see it?*

What path?

That one.

In a few hours, they will be back in the church for Morning Redemption, and the only thing he can do now is try to find the way back to the kitchen. As he walks, the only sound he hears is his own wheezy breathing. The steps are crooked, uneven, wide, then narrow, built like this to stop the thieves and sinners. Only the righteous will not be defeated. Further down he goes, legs shaking, muscles protesting, and just when he thinks he can't go on, there's the last step and the ground levels out. He rubs his aching thighs, his tight painful face, he must surely be near the kitchen with its fires blazing. He follows the path round the tombs — *I'm not ready for these yet* — imagines the look on Silas's face when he walks in for supper. *Not expecting me, Rat Face?*

A bowl of broth swims before his eyes. He's light-headed from the pain, not sure he can eat even if food presents itself, which it doesn't. *Dear Lord, please grant me the gift of a candle.*

Dedalus, you are such a disappointment to me. You know that don't you?

Yes, Lord. Forgive me, for I have tried to be good. Isn't that what you wanted?

It is too late now.

Last time, Jessop had candles to light the way between the narrow tombs. *Saints are in there, go this way*, said Jessop, pointing to an arch barely visible in the wall, one dark space in another. But now he can't find it. Ahead lies damp and stink. He might be under the stables or the courtyard. The last thirty seconds of the life he knows so well will be quickly over, but he remains oblivious to the future. This is still his present life. He holds his breath, listening hard for voices, but all he gets is a couple of fat rats scurrying along. *God has sent us to remind you of Rat Face and now he is punishing you.* Jessop told him to follow the path, but there is barely any path, so he does the only thing he can do. He follows what little he can see; he is still the most faithful servant of the Lord. Sometimes he thinks he hears footsteps, but when he turns to look behind him, no one is there. Every so often he stops and listens, but soon he's on his way again, going deeper and deeper into the silence.

12

Sister Alice rebuilds the fires,

seasons the water, blesses the turnips, grinds the rosemary. Days drag by without Dedalus. Weeks pass. Nights come and go. The moon shines bright, then withdraws to a shining silver slice above the world. Sometimes she thinks he'll burst through the door, hungry as usual, brow furrowed, a blessing on his lips, and a smile when he sees her, but he never does and this is how the months pass as time creeps over the cobbled stones.

The Holy Mother prays on her knees for Dedalus, one half of her with the Lord, the other listening for the sound of Jessop, the rough scent of his skin and his unwavering strength as he cups her face in his hands when no one can see. In the early days, Jessop was almost tempted to go after Dedalus himself and he did search everywhere for him, but now he knows he must be dead. Curled in some dark corner like a beast and the Lord will take his unworthy form to Heaven and that's all right with Jessop. Everyone has extra work, and life goes on without him. Still, Dedalus hovers in their thoughts, especially Silas's, as he tries not to think of him at all, though Dedalus ends up in his head most days anyway. Perhaps he'll turn up next spring, his body feasted on by worms, his soul on the narrow path to glory.

Sister Alice lies alone and prostrate in her cell every night, beseeching the Holy Father to find Dedalus. Every day she thinks of him, hoping he'll reappear, and trying to explain his absence as some Divine gift: *God took him to the edge of the world and showed him the souls amongst the dead, and yet when he returns he will be with me, and we will hear them calling and we will save more souls together.* Her heart believes, but Dedalus stays stubbornly invisible. The man who never was. His meagre possessions collected and reused: a string of rosary beads, two candles, felt booties for winter that he hardly ever wore. In his absence what has he become? The outline of a man, the man himself missing.

Now her knees ache when it rains and grumble when she prays. Her hands stiffen in winter. She is stricken by the idea that he is close, that she just might touch him through layers of earth and soil. 'I am here, Dedalus,' she whispers, clutching her cross, trying to press the truth of it into the floor. 'The Lord will save you,' she cries, but in her darkest moments she is angry with the Lord for allowing His faithful servant to be lost like this.

'Dear Lord, let me see him one last time.'

What use is prayer if no one answers? Prayer is all she has in her pain; prayer is what she knows. A poultice of onion and herbs has not soothed her. The headaches have increased. Prayer does not bring sleep. Tightness spreads across her chest. Flesh falls from her bones. Her joy in life is diminished. In the sacred offering of Mass, her lips move, but the love and gratitude she always felt for the Lord has withered into the straw, into Father Jessop's eyebrows, into the rain and wind, into a leaf, a flower, a cloud across the sky.

Nothing she can do will atone for the sin she committed with Dedalus. Her thoughts fall like soil through her fingers. She is a sister of God, and everything that happens to Sister

Alice is by Him, through Him, and because of Him, but no one notices the gradual deterioration of a woman. For what do women do other than obey the Lord, or their husbands, and weep for the men they have lost. She begins to see that the more powerful the prayers, the more God will listen. Will He not listen to a hundred priests, a hundred men, more than one nun on her bony knees? God will tell her, *Yes, I have heard you, but I hear them louder and I hear them better than you.*

God doesn't help her when the pain spreads across her chest and makes her gasp in the rain-spattered night. God doesn't bring Dedalus back, although she has listened for him every night alone on a cold floor. That's how the Holy Mother finds her in the morning, clutching her cross, her head uncovered, her eyes open, her body stiff and cold. The tombs are already taken. She is buried in the abbey churchyard. Her soul gone straight to Heaven. Her body given to the earth that gave her so much joy.

13

Happiness for a little girl,
in the modern world of 1993, is her father telling her a bedtime story. Marcus Stern rearranges the pillows behind him and squeezes onto his daughter's little bed in her cosy bedroom in Oxenbridge House.

'Budge up then, Molly Polly.'

'All of it, Daddy, from the beginning.'

She's so tired and in two minutes she'll be sound asleep, but that doesn't stop her asking because there's nothing she likes better than this.

'So, we were eating dinner that night and the whole house was very busy.'

'So *busy*,' she says.

'We had lobster soup,' he says, miming a huge pair of snapping claws, and she does the same with her tiny fingers.

'Then we had …'

'Roast beef,' she says, because they always had the same meal.

'And Uncle Frank was handing round …'

'Potatoes.'

'When suddenly, *bang*,' and he claps his hands, and she laughs when he does that, 'the dining room doors are flung *wide open* …'

'Go on, Daddy, *go on*,' she squeals, as this is the best bit.

'It's Him,' he says. 'It's the Angel. Coming into the house for the very first time.'

She nods, seeing it all before her.

'There's crashing and banging, and all the plates smash on the floor, and the spoons fly into the air and Uncle Frank tries to catch him, but he can't catch him, and Aunty Peggy tries but she can't catch him, and Mummy tries too but she can't catch him, and then he runs away, *quick, quick, quick*, and no one ever sees him again.'

Molly tugs her father's chin. 'Why can't Mummy catch him?'

He taps the end of her nose with his finger. 'He was too quick.'

Molly is wide awake now, shaking her head. 'No one could catch him,' she says with a sigh. 'You should have made him a nice cup of tea, shouldn't you, Daddy?'

'Yes,' says her father, 'I think he would have liked that.'

'And no one ever saw him again,' she whispers.

'Except …' He holds up one finger.

'*Once*,' she says, holding up her pointer just like Daddy.

'I was going to fetch some wine from the cellar, and Max was with me, trotting along …'

Her hand waves in the air, becoming Max's tail. 'Miaow, miaow.'

'Down we go and there's a shadow in the corner and Maxie, he's so brave, he hisses and *hisses*.'

'*Hiss, hiss*,' she says, her fingers becoming claws.

'And there he is. The Angel.' Daddy's voice goes a little lower and a little wobbly and he makes a big sad face with big sad eyes, and his daughter clutches her hands tightly together.

'He's very polite. He says, "Thank you for letting me stay here, but now it's time to go," so I open the door and before he flies away, he says …'

'He will always watch over us.'

'That's right. He will always watch over us.'

He kisses her on the head and tucks her in tight. 'Night-night, Molly Polly.'

'I miss Mummy,' she says, because that's what she always says.

'So do I, sweetheart, so do I.'

'Night-night, Daddy.'

He waits a few minutes for the soft rise and fall of her breath before going downstairs to the kitchen, where he stands in darkness gathering his thoughts. One day, when she's older, he'll tell her what happened. He stares at the cellar door at the far end of the kitchen, but the door says nothing, and the years fly past, and the story stays the same until it's almost forgotten.

14

Molly has taken

hardly any notice of the abysmal winter weather of 2013. As far as she's concerned the apocalypse has come and gone and left a few sad people wandering the streets of Oxenbridge, one of whom turns out to be her. Nearly done with being twenty-five years old Molly M. Stern. Smoky diesel from the London train lingers in the air. She's fraying round the edges. Life without her father has unhinged her, and life without Stefan, her man, has tipped her into the never-ending rain and blustering wind. This year has not turned out the way Molly thought it would. Her heart has fallen from her body and rolled into the dirt and every day she leaves it there, flopping about in front of her like some mad injured thing.

Get up, O My Heart. Account for yourself.

But Heart says, *I don't think I will.*

What you long for does not happen. What you desire doesn't matter. Trees shake their branches at her, the world wags a finger. *Weren't you listening, Molly, can you not see? He does not love you like you love him.* She goes over and over it in her head. The moment when he told her it was over. She'd been looking at him adoringly, like she always did, and they were holding hands, like they always did. They'd just been to see the latest film version of *Romeo and Juliet.* Her choice.

'I loved that,' she said, 'but why do all great love stories have sad endings?'

'Maybe that's just the way it is, Molly, that's all you get.' Stefan sniffed and lifted his hand to scratch his nose.

Her hand followed his, the other hand cold in her pocket. No gloves. She squeezed his hand. He loved her. They were always going to have a happy ending, weren't they?

She thinks of that conversation now and look how it turned out. Friday afternoons were always more exciting than any other, because they had two wonderful days to spend together. They each usually ended up working, but the feeling that time lay ahead of them was a good one.

Once back in the flat, he poured the wine, she opened the crisps, some cheese, crackers, half a beetroot dip, her favourite, but not anymore. Stefan with his glass of red, she with her glass of white. His serious face, mouth tight, eyes tense. Frowning. 'Mol, Mol, I need you to listen.'

So she listened. She twisted the ring round and round on her finger. The ring of commitment, the ring of their future. Her lovely ring, chosen together, now slipping the wrong way. As he talked, she knew that all this was her fault, her grief about her father eating into everything, her doubts, her fears, but Stefan didn't have any doubts about this. The biggest decision of his life, he must be true to himself, so he said, and part of that – 'Molly, Mol, please listen' – was he didn't want to be with her anymore. The rest of their lives were not going to be spent together.

'You've met someone else.' She shouted those shaky disbelieving words.

'No,' he said, 'there's no one else,' but all her friends told her there must be. That a man doesn't end a five-year relationship without having met someone else first who makes him feel good.

Men are like that. They do things they want to, just because they can. They betray you, no matter what they say.

'Mol, it's not like it used to be,' he said.

'It is,' she said. 'It is always like it used to be.'

She finished her wine and poured herself another, but apparently he was still talking. His mouth moving through all the clichés she never once thought would be directed at her. No longer Stefan the Viking, Stefan the Gorgeous Guy, Stefan the Aren't You Lucky to Have Him. Now he was Stefan the Betrayer. He'd made up his mind without talking about any of it with her. Is that what people do? You do everything together then they decide, and you're relegated. Fourth division, officially Unimportant in the Next Life of Stefan the New. As he left the room, the pepper grinder flew towards his back. He'd bought it for her as she'd always wanted one of those ridiculously tall grinders, and *Here it comes, Stefan, it's all yours.* Missing him, it hit the wall instead and black pepper floated through the air. Sneezing and covered in snot, she sobbed on the bed in her small warm flat for half the night.

This is how the year has turned out for Molly. She tries not to think about Stefan, but all she can do is think about Stefan. And her father, and the fact that she's back in bloody Oxenbridge again. Which is where she always and never longs to be. She tells herself grief is just a little down patch, and everyone has them, but she's not fun anymore. Every winter tree and field asks her the same question. *How does something once so solid and good change so quickly?* Everything makes her cry. She's like a flower with a droopy head since the death of her father, nine months ago, and now this. Stefan had come down for the funeral, but mostly he stayed away. He knew how close she was to her father.

He said, 'I'll just get in the way.'

He said, 'I'm taking up yoga, Molly, to make myself more flexible. It'll be easier, you won't get distracted by me.'

He really meant that in her absence he could put himself first. His glorious self, first and first and first, and follow his desires and be free. He could walk into his future, while she returned to sort the past. All the self-help books in the world have told her nothing about where to put her sadness. Do you keep it in a box in your bedroom, and try to close the lid? Do you mail it to a town that doesn't exist, or bury it under a stone so it becomes an unavoidable lump in the ground that trips you up every time you pass? Do you boil it up and dissolve it, or shred it into a thousand pieces and throw them into the sky?

Molly's come back for Christmas to escape her loneliness and because Aunty Peggy said she had to.

'You are not eating KitKats out of an old sock and pretending to be happy.'

'I'm not pretending anything, am I?'

Last month, walking down Baker Street, after selling nothing in the gallery all day, she'd marched into a hairdresser and demanded that the boy lounging by the door cut off all her long thick hair. She'd looked the same for years, but now it was time to be different. *Start with the hair, Molly.*

'Do it now, please, before I change my mind.'

She doesn't care what anyone thinks anymore. She tugs her beanie over her ears. Her father bought it for her years ago. *Must stay warm in Oxenbridge, Antarctica, Mol.* Legs made of wire, heart made of stone, rain on her face. The town lit up for Christmas. She turns her collar up, tucks in her scarf, *I'm alive*, she says, *yippee*. Her fingers turn purple with cold and the weight of her bag. She's nearly reached Off the Peg, Peggy's shop, practically an institution in Oxenbridge. It stands on the corner of Crown

Street, a beacon of light for lovers of wool and linen. It's the last
shop in town before the road takes you past Oxenbridge House,
then further south to nowhere.

Oh Peggy, tartan trousers, what are you thinking? The models
in the window wearing the season's finery wave at her with
moulded plastic hands. She'll invite them round for drinks and
try to be sociable.

The shop bell jingles as Peggy's assistant, Edward Farraday,
scoots in with the coffees and finds Peggy hugging a beanpole
at the counter.

'Hello, Edward,' says Molly.

Edward stares blankly at her.

'It's Molly, Edward,' says Peggy.

'Yes,' he says, 'of course it is,' and he ducks into the back
of the shop to recover from his embarrassment. Molly sighs to
herself. She's known Edward since childhood and she's always
found him annoying, with that silly hair of his and his general
oddness, like he's leaning against a crumbling wall. Her aunt
sips her coffee and appraises her niece. Last time she saw her, she
had shoulder-length hair, two matching earrings, and looked
healthy.

'Thought I'd pop in and say hello.'

'Well, you'd be in big trouble if you didn't. Had brekkie?'

'I'm not eating carbs, Peggy.'

'Goodness, why ever not?'

'Not good for you.'

Peggy snorts, *Here we go.* 'Does that mean rice as well?' She's
straight on to food logistics. At the Tremble household, Saturday
nights are curry nights.

'Any problems?' she calls out to Edward, tapping at her
phone, thinking that the biggest problem is two inches away

from her, turning her nose ring round and round. Peggy's not at all sure what she's going to do about that. Ten minutes later, they manage to nab their favourite seats in the window at Flour Power, the café closest to them.

'Edward's always asking about you,' Peggy says. '"How's Molly getting on?"'

'Sold out, commissions flooding in, why is he interested in me anyway? He didn't even recognise me.'

'Molly, he's known you half his life, so I tell him.'

Molly stirs her sugar-free coffee. 'Well, don't.'

Peggy grimaces, two coffees in one morning, she'll be insane by eleven o'clock. Oh well, all for love. She squeezes Molly's cold fingers. 'Come over tonight and see what Frank has been getting up to.'

'Can hardly wait,' says Molly.

Molly's destination

is hidden behind a six-foot wall on the old London Road. Iron gates mark the entrance to Oxenbridge House, and they clang shut behind her as she walks up the driveway. Patches of green appear through the sodden grass and the pair of lions at the front door are doing what they always do, yawning. Her father loved teasing her about them — *They're roaring, Molly, that's why I bought them* — but she knows better. They're tired of everything, like her. She draws a deep breath and opens the front door, glimpsing, for a split second, her father standing in the hallway. She blinks and the shadow disappears. The first time she returned after his death, she buried her face in his favourite tweed jacket still hanging on the coat pegs. The shape of the man caught in the fabric, in the creases round the leather patches on the elbows.

She doesn't have the heart to remove it, despite Peggy's wisdom. With Molly's blessing, Peggy's already taken bags of her father's clothes to Oxfam, but the ones that are left are precious. She knows his favourites and the ones he didn't like but wore out of duty. There's a tender vulnerability about that, and Molly doesn't want to get rid of them yet. Maybe not ever.

Someone could be keeping warm with that jacket, Molly, which is what your father would have wanted.

Molly doesn't care what her father would have wanted. He's not here. He's left her, so if you can be angry with the dead, then she is. Grief is personal, it belongs entirely to her. She doesn't want to hear any more advice from anyone. *Keep busy. Let it all go. Move on, move forward. What's the point of hanging on to things, Molly, he's gone, he doesn't need them.* Her father's presence is confirmed by his absence. He is inevitably part of the house, just as he is deeply part of her, and Molly Stern will do things in her own way, in her own time, whenever and whatever that turns out to be.

Her ancestors stare at her from gilt picture frames. Her paternal grandparents, Jacob Stern in a prim and proper suit, and the lovely Elizabeth seated in front of him, hair all done up, a smile frozen on her face. Her father's second cousin Eleanor, with that glinty stare that never changes. *Go away. Leave me alone, stop judging me.* Sometimes she wants to tear them from the walls, burn them.

'I'm going to sell you one day,' she says, brightly to them all, 'especially you,' pointing to her grandfather, who died before she was born but whose stern patrician features remind her of her father when she argued with him. The painting she loves the most hangs at the top of the stairs in an ornate frame, making it look twice as big as it really is. The artist has depicted the old abbey church and the surrounding fields, with two tiny figures in the foreground walking forever into an unchanging world. It's a comforting sight that always reassures her.

She calls out to her father just because she can, 'Dad! Dad! I'm back.' And here he comes, giving her that welcome-home bear hug, his head almost brushing the ceiling.

Kettle on. Earl Grey will be with us soon.

The house is cold. There's a spoonful left of the Earl Grey in the tin marked *Jasmine Tea.* 'Just enough for me, Dad.' She stirs in a teaspoon of honey because that's how she likes it.

Phillis Stine, putting sugar in your tea.

'It's honey.'

Same difference. How's Stefan?

'Fuck me, Dad, it's over.'

She's forgotten to buy milk, but there's always a litre or two of long life in the cupboard. Not the same as fresh but who cares? The radiators creak into life.

Still. There we are.

There you are. Still.

Half a bottle of white wine, a half-empty tub of butter, and nothing else in the fridge. Why would there be? It's been weeks since she was last here. If she leans as far as she can over the kitchen sink she can see where he's buried, south of the abbey walls. The old joke: if you're not Stern, you can't get in. Another story her father told her: if you're not here then you're in the Land of Gone. She's lived with these crumbling walls all her life. They're the never-changing landmarks of her childhood, and they're all that's left of the Abbey of Stern, although now it's called Stern Abbey on the website. The Ruins. The north-facing wall of the abbey church still exists, but that's at the top of the hill, not visible from the house. She's never understood the endless fascination people have for walls and the remnants of a latrine block, which was once the drainage ditch. Why would anyone want to spend the day here, when they could be in the Tate, or the National Portrait Gallery, or the Weissman Gallery, looking at all those clever pictures, including some of hers.

A wall is a wall. A picture has infinite possibilities. Maybe now her father's there, she'll become entranced with the past. Maybe she won't. Maybe she'll make pancakes just the way he liked them.

Molly, you've outdone yourself this time.

'Sure have, Dad.'

She sleeps half the day, and when she wakes, her father is still in the Land of Gone, and Uncle Frank is on the phone.

'All right, Molly Chops, it's massaman curry with chicken tonight because Peggy won't eat red meat. You're coming, aren't you? Peggy said you were.'

'I'm busy.'

'Come on, Mol, you can do the poppadums in the microwave the way you like them. How can you resist?'

'If I must.'

'If you massaman,' says Frank.

Peggy has temporarily banned him from the shop. He makes a different curry every weekend. 'I had to let him go, his hands are always yellow, it's the turmeric. Can't have that on the clothes, can I?'

By the time she walks the fifteen minutes to 10 Castle Road, the semi-detached she's spent half her life in, Peggy and Frank are tumbling with joy to see their niece again. Their familiar routine and warm loving faces comfort Molly in a way little else can. They avoid all talk of rainfall totals and relationships. Frank Tremble, Man of History, will steer them all to safer waters with his current favourite subject, the bones of King Richard the Third.

'It's exciting Molly, now they know for sure it's him.'

She yawns. 'Nothing's as exciting as Bradley Wiggins.'

Frank shakes his head. 'It won't work, Molly Chops. I shall not be deterred. Richard Plantagenet was the last English king killed in battle.'

Molly rolls her eyes. 'Why am I so massively unimpressed?'

A blob of curry sauce drops onto Frank's cardigan. 'Oh bugger,' he says, 'but I'll just say this before I launder myself into oblivion' – he makes a face at Peggy – 'it's bloody amazing that he was found at all, after so long buried under the centuries. No one knew what happened to him and now they do. It was quite awful, actually.'

'What difference does it make to anyone?' says Molly. Frank gets up and kisses the top of Molly's head. She squeezes his hand: *I'm still in here somewhere.* He squeezes it back: *I know, I know.*

'He still has family, descendants.'

'Bet they're thrilled Uncle Richard's back again.'

'When did you turn into this wise compassionate being, Molly Stern?' asks Frank, on his way to the kitchen. 'Peggy where's the stain remover?'

'It's under the sink. More wine?' asks Peggy. 'Such a fuss over a pile of old bones.'

'If it keeps him happy,' says Molly.

That's the thing Molly relies on. Her aunt and uncle's warmth and happiness. They have each been grieving the loss of Marcus in their own ways; they all miss him greatly and no one more than Molly. Her aunt and uncle have become the fixed points in the emotional landscape of Molly Stern, and she needs them more than ever.

Frank reappears with a wet patch on his cardigan, completely unperturbed, like an amiable genie, with a round face and grey beard and eyes twinkling with mystery.

'Molly, no one knew what happened to him after Bosworth, and finally there's an answer. He didn't stand a chance, he was sliced—'

Peggy pats Frank's hand. 'Thank you, Francis Tremble, but we're just not as interested as you.'

Frank will not be dissuaded. 'And his curved spine, poor bugger. His bones are telling us all kinds of things: what he ate, all his injuries. We actually get to see a real-life medieval king close up.'

'Frank, it was all a long time ago and it's over and done with,' says Peggy, finishing her wine.

'History's never done though, Peggy, is it?' Frank has never sounded so keen. *Must be the sauvignon blanc,* thinks Molly, studying their faces. She would like to talk about Marcus with them, but something is different tonight. If grief makes you a bit edgy, then Peggy is definitely that. There's a thread running between her favourite people that pulls a little tight. A half-glimpsed moment when the truth wants to be revealed, but remains hidden beneath the surface in an unspoken pact, if life is to carry on as normal. They're tired, she thinks, everyone's tired. Too much wine, too much king. Yawning loudly, she gets up from the table.

'Time to go home.'

'You're staying. The bed's made up.'

Peggy knows Molly better than she knows herself. Clean sheets, drawers tidied; she always has her room ready. Frank looks like he's about to burst out of his cardigan; he was just warming the room up with history and there are so many things to say, but he kisses Molly goodnight because he adores her.

'Night-night, Molly Chops, sleep well.'

Peggy pushes her up the stairs, rolls her into bed, and turns out the light. She watches her for a few minutes until her breathing settles. She looks so vulnerable lying there, her face half buried in the pillow, arm over the blanket just the way her mother used to sleep. Peggy's heart skips a beat. Part of her wants to stroke Molly's head like she always did and tell her everything that has sat in her chest for so long. But the little girl has grown into a woman and, more than anything else, Peggy wants to protect her from all the sadness in the world and keep her safe forever.

15

When the bones of the king

are discovered during the previous year, Edward Farraday is busy dealing with his own discovery, which is that bustling about in the kitchen keeps the sadness at bay. Whisking the eggs with salt, pepper, and a sprinkle of chilli flakes. No parsley, nothing fresh or green – *sorry, Mum.* She used to do this for him, even when she was exhausted after a night shift. She believed in God, but God doesn't show up in the kitchen. God doesn't vacuum, or dust, or empty the compost bin. He doesn't adjust the timer in the linen cupboard for the boiler, and he certainly doesn't put Edward's dirty laundry in the washing machine and remember the short wash. Three eggs today. Hungry. Half a saucepan of last night's pasta congealing on the stove. Microwave scrambles, she called them, her speciality. Now he's doing it, he's nearly eighteen, and at least he can cook.

Promise me, Edward, always make sure you have a good breakfast.

'I promise.'

Scrambled eggs are a devil to clean, so that's something for later. He scrapes the pasta into his lunch box, leaves the eggy saucepan with the others in the sink.

Hurry up, Peggy will kill you.

'I'm going, I'm going.'

Backpack on — *Don't forget the keys* — door closing behind him. He's meant to be in the shop at nine, he'll never make it; he scurries along, sucking in the cool summer morning. He's just passing the medical centre and the last set of lights before the high street when he remembers he's left his lunch on the kitchen bench. Bugger. Not going back for it now.

You'd forget your head if it wasn't screwed on.

He texts Peggy and she texts him back with her coffee order. He can relax, take his time, he's getting the lattes, plus a cheese and spinach muffin, which is better than day-old pasta. Flour Power is busy today, but he waits patiently in line. They make the best coffee in town, and Peggy will see all the extra trouble he's gone to, which is none, to make up for being late. A soy latte for Peggy, a cappuccino for him. He waves to Mr Khan in the newsagency over the road. *Hello. I am Edward.*

Mr Khan gives him a little wave back. *Yes. I know who you are.*

He was meant to be

in the shop fifteen minutes ago, and Peggy spreads the paper on the front counter and tries to swallow her irritation. He's never been late before, and she understands why, but she'll still have a talk with him later. Right now there are more interesting things to look at. The photos in front of her, for starters. An archaeological excavation, in the remains of an old friary in Leicester. Well, stands to reason, if you're digging things up, everything's going to be old, isn't it. *Stay calm, Peggy, everything's going to be fine today.* Anyway, there's a pit, with measurements and signs and mounds of dirt, and lying in the earth is a skeleton with a twisted spine and no feet. Hands on one side, skull with its mouth open, still with most of its teeth.

When Edward finally turns up with her latte, he's wearing the new polo shirt Peggy gave him. *Pink, Peggy? It suits you, and colour belongs to everyone, Edward, I want you to remember that.* Edward with his jeans, leather belt and mop of wild hair.

'Sorry, Peggy, bit of a queue. It's going to be hot today. Mid-twenties, almost tropical.'

She can't stay cross with him for long.

'Look at this,' she says, slapping the paper.

'Bones,' he says, peering at the page, unimpressed.

'They think it's Richard the Bloody Third.'

'Evil Uncle Richard,' says Edward, sipping his coffee. 'We did him at school, Shakespeare, it's engraved in my brain.' He drops into a low voice, '"Deformed, unfinished, sent before my time into this breathing world, scarce half made up." What's all the fuss, anyway? They're always digging someone up.'

Her latte isn't strong enough, she should send it back.

'They're not sure it is him, though,' Edward continues. 'They found him under a council car park. It's not a very grand place for a king, is it?'

'That's bloody parking in this country, Edward. You die before you can find a spot and then they dig you up years later.'

Her mind races ahead. Frank is going to love this, something new to get his teeth into before turmeric and ginger take over his life. A few tourists are already bobbing past the shop, heading to the old abbey walls with their cardigans and walking boots. *If that were me*, thinks Peggy, *I'd be down at the seaside.* She has her finest range of pure cotton T-shirts on display, with some linen shirts and shorts, and funky drink bottles in matching colours for extra enticement. The buzz of the Olympics is already fading, even though it's still September.

'Frank will be happy,' says Edward. 'He'll be able to get his plaque done now, won't he?'

'His beloved plaque. We'll get loads more tourists.'

Peggy sighs as if that's a bad thing. *King Richard woz here.* Ever since Frank retired from Oxenbridge Council, the plaque has been his pet project to promote the town. A plaque would be proof of the king's visit, as Frank calls it, and it would be based on words written on the precious parchment found in an abbey ledger when the foundations for Oxenbridge House were dug four hundred years ago. The writing is barely legible now, but it is still possible to make out the amount paid by 'Rex Ricardus III' to the Abbey of Stern for prayers for his soul. Ten pounds per annum for Father Jessop, enough to pay a craftsman his wages for a year in those days. The rest of the entries are illegible due to a water stain or tears or a nosebleed or spilled ink, all preserved for eternity in a thick plexiglass case standing in the foyer of the council's main building.

'Peggy, it's already listed on the website: "King Richard the Third visited the Abbey of Stern in the Spring of 1485, months before his defeat at the battle of Bosworth." The plaque makes it real and people will love it.'

'More people will mean less parking, Edward. Wait until you start driving.'

She likes the influx of tourists for the business that it brings but hates the struggle to find a place for her beloved Mini. The lack of parking in Oxenbridge makes her boil with frustration, especially when people park in front of her house. She knows it's a public street but surely one little spot could just belong to Peggy Tremble. At least since Frank built the shed she doesn't have to drive down that awful pot-holed road to the garage anymore, which used to fill her with despair. *Calm down, Peggy*

Tremble, everything's going to be all right, but somewhere inside her she doesn't really believe that.

'He was found under a space with *R* on it, Peggy.'

'That means Reserved, not Richard. What's a king doing down there anyway? Typical, isn't it, for a man to have his own parking place for five hundred years.'

'He doesn't have any feet.'

'I should think that's the least of his problems,' says Peggy.

16

Raven has left Ricardo

and is following the map in his head through the skies that uphold him. Centuries exhaust him. As he flies from one dimension to another, his body leaves little bumps and gaps along the way. He's never had to find an angel before. The angel has always shown up, done their duty, sorted it, taken the soul for a day trip to Margate before the final reveal.

What is a bird compared to an angel but a feathery provocation? A ruffle. A tender merciless thing. A flap of the bones and the wings. For sure, an angel has the heft of the Lord. An angel can juggle three turbulent souls all night and still be home for breakfast, and Heaven is at least sixteen miles further north than anyone ever thinks it might be, but Raven is nothing if not magnificent.

Dude of all Dudes, am I not?

He's never had the soul of Richard the Third to deal with before, and the town has changed over the years, but it's still much the same – rivers and trees, tunnels and caves, gardens and gravestones – that's the landscape Raven knows. Now there are shops and cars and trains and people. A massive lightning-struck oak is what Raven is looking for. *Aha, there it is.* On the side of a path leading to a field, at the back of a pub called the King's

Head. Half the tree has gone, leaving a hollowed-out version of itself, with branches sprouting from its sides. Visible and hidden at the same time. It's right where he's sitting; of course it is, the map in his head is never wrong. The hollow tree marks the entrance to a cave, but that's for later, thinks Raven, and he's not going there without his Kingly King.

A house martin zooms past, giving Raven the eye, cautious of a large bird being in such proximity.

'Oi, Martin, you're up early, have you seen an angel anywhere round here?'

The house martin shakes its little head and a red kite shrieks in the sky. Raven loves birds. Poor humans, no wings. The thought's unbearable. A jackdaw sits on a wall watching him warily.

'Hello, Grey Head,' Raven says. The jackdaw cocks his head to one side.

'Yeah, welcome. Long journey?'

'Tell me about it,' says Raven. 'Five hundred and twenty-eight years, if you must know. It's hard work being a conduit between Heaven and earth.' The jackdaw nods without understanding. A few minutes ago, he was sitting on a road sign minding his own business before a truck startled him.

The red kite circles above them. 'Now that's what I call a bird,' says Raven.

'We're all birds, aren't we?' says Jackdaw, inclining his head. Jackdaw sticks to what he knows, which is everyday, ordinary kinds of things.

'So, Monsieur Daw, if I may call you that,' asks Raven, 'I am searching for an angel, and wondered if you might have seen one?'

Jackdaw turns his head, blinks, sees nothing extraordinary. Blinks again.

'If you must know Mr Daw, I have flown from Threadbare, that's the afterlife to you, and the current soul I am escorting is having a bit of trouble with acceptance.'

'Don't we all?' replies Jackdaw.

'Hey, Daw, how come I really wanna call you Dave?'

Screw loose, thinks Jackdaw.

'Anyways, just so you know, *Daw*,' says Raven, 'Ricardo, the soul, used to be a king, and now he's not too happy. He prayed so hard for salvation but doesn't seem to want it when it's happening to him. Which brings us back to the angel.'

The red kite lets out another shriek.

'Do we have a name?' he asks Jackdaw, who thinks for a minute.

'I have heard something, but I cannot now remember what it is.' Jackdaw flies into the endless sky. The wind under his wings jogs his memory. 'Tremblings,' he calls through the clouds, 'the name's Tremblings.'

Raven watches Jackdaw getting smaller and smaller as he flies towards a house in a long street with a shed at the bottom of the garden.

17

It's a cold clear night

and the New Year of 2014 has departed and Molly doesn't give a
fig about it. So long as it's better than the last one. She and Peggy
are heading to the shed for a light supper with Frank.

'I'm worried about him; he's not been himself recently.'

Frank grunts from the kitchen, 'Don't touch anything in
there, will you, there's a method to my madness.'

Since the renovations, the shed at the bottom of the garden
is now officially a studio, but Molly still calls it the shed. It has
replaced the garage, and the compost patch.

'Apparently we don't need a compost anymore,' explains
Peggy. 'It's a miracle: the council wants our leftovers.'

They slip into coats and hats and boots, and Peggy twists
what's left of a tissue round her thumb. Molly puts her arm
round her aunt's shoulder. As they wander over the lawn to the
shed, a large black bird flies onto the garden fence.

'Mr Crow,' says Molly, 'always watching.'

'Always messing down the fence, more like it,' says Peggy.

'Harsh words, Madame, harsh, harsh words,' mutters Raven,
for once letting the insult of *crow* pass him by. He is growing
more curious by the minute. These must be the Tremblings.

Peggy flaps her arms at Raven, but the bird does not move.

'Madame, are we dancing?' Raven gives her a sideways stare, but Peggy doesn't hear him.

How strange, thinks Peggy, *it's not at all scared*. 'Molly, you'll never believe this. Uncle Frank is going off the curry. It's the bones. He's obsessed with them. Spends all his hours in the shed.'

'So now we'll see what he's getting up to, won't we?'

Frank follows them down the garden, wearing his best winter hat and carrying bowls of food on a tray. 'Uncle Frank can still hear you,' he says, 'and he happens to think this is an exciting discovery, thank you very much. Come on, hurry up, don't want this to get cold.'

He doesn't see Raven watching and listening in the darkness.

'Don't worry about me,' says Raven, 'I'll just eat a miserable lump of earth for my tea.' Apparently that is his fortune tonight, as no one takes any notice of him, and he is left with the sky, and the stars, and the fence. 'A spoon for me earth and custard,' he says to the moon as it slides out from a scuttering cloud.

Peggy has a head full

of worry about Frank. He has gone from one thing to another. First it was Charles the First, then Oliver Cromwell, then he skipped a bit and went straight to the Regency period. He even started writing Regency romances but found it hard to think of the next part of the story after he'd made the coachman stop outside the large house with an unexpected gentleman caller. After that, he fell in love with the Brontës but could not persuade Peggy to join him on a pilgrimage to the parsonage at Haworth.

'Too cold,' she said, 'too sad. All those lovely girls.'

He returned with a small book of Anne and Emily Brontë's poetry, which had appealed to him during the visit but has since stayed unopened on his bedside table. After that, he decided there was no place on earth quite like Tudor England, and after months at the court of Henry the Eighth, he tired of that king and found Henry's daughter, Elizabeth the First, much more compelling. After his long-awaited, much-threatened retirement from Oxenbridge Council, he joined the Oxenbridge Cookery Club and found new meaning in life with his first ever green curry.

He became spellbound by the fact that he, Frank Tremble, formerly Deputy Mayor of Oxenbridge Council, devoted husband of Margaret Tremble, astute businesswoman and owner of Off the Peg boutique in Oxenbridge, England, the World, could cook. He graduated from mid-week cheese and mushroom omelettes to the beauty of freshly ground cardamom, and turmeric, cumin seeds and fenugreek, and bright red chillies. Peggy liked this version of Frank. He was a better man when he cooked, more aware, more switched on, as opposed to the man now spending hours in the shed reading biographies of kings and books about Richard the Third and his bones.

Peggy loves facty fiction, World War II stories, Bletchley Park and spies and women in their Land Army breeches. Now they're what she calls fundamentally proper attire.

'Stories are so much more engrossing,' she says, 'than bones.'

'The stories you like are based on facts, Peggy; so are mine. History is who we used to be.'

Peggy likes a beginning, a middle and an end. History is full of speculation and too many dates and unanswered questions and she knows those kinds of questions always raise more problems than they solve.

'Some of us, Francis Tremble, are working too hard to care about the affairs of kings.'

That's unfair of her, she knows it. She is busy running the shop, and she likes being busy. The mortgage has been paid, thanks to some help from Marcus, and she works because she enjoys it, not because she has to. Losing Marcus has pulled a pin out of her neat orderliness. One grief reminds her of another, and she does not know what to do with the emotional havoc that threatens to overtake her. Wild unpredictable feelings were never any good for anyone.

All Peggy wants is for Frank to spend time with her, at home, when the day is done, like he did when he was cooking. Each new obsession takes his mind elsewhere and a little further from her. Perhaps she could join him in the garden shed occasionally. It's nice to sit at the bottom of the garden and look back at the house; it gives you a different perspective. A bit chilly in winter, granted, but so what; they are fit and healthy for their ages. Frank is sixty-one, Peggy is five years older. That has never bothered Peggy before, younger or older, what does it matter, but now doubts have started creeping through the doorway of her heart and she finds herself wondering if she has become too old for him. As if the years have caught her off balance and she is unable to be the Peggy that Frank once adored.

Bright beautiful Peggy is now uptight anxious Peggy, without any sign of the calm wisdom she hoped might be heading her way. Perhaps Frank is becoming interested in almost everything except her. Is her hair too short, her face too old? She has never once questioned the reality of Peggy and Frank, but now she isn't sure what that might be. She can't bear to think what he might be doing in the shed. In the early days they had longed for a child of their own, but it was Sally, the wild and gorgeous Smallgood sister, not Peggy, who married Marcus and had Molly, though Molly became theirs and they loved her. Peggy needs to talk to Frank about Molly, but once they start she knows where that will lead, and she isn't ready for what that will bring. Not yet.

The shed consists of a small bathroom with shower and toilet, a neat little corner kitchen with a bar fridge, microwave, toaster and kettle, and a sleeping space with a futon on a fold-up base. A radio perches on the shelf in the corner by the door. There's a nice rug on the floor and the rickety trestle table groans with newspapers and magazines, *History Today*, and *Discover This!*, and *KINGS of Britain*, suggesting the whole country was populated by men, and women only arrived with the first potatoes, conveniently in time to thicken the stew.

'Out of the way, my hands are full.' Frank plonks the tray on the table, over his newspaper mosaic of graves and bones and crowns. Molly takes the only comfy chair while Peggy and Frank sit at the table. The shed is warm and full of food and family, and Frank swells with pride.

'Cosy, isn't it, Molly?'

She nods. Supper is wine and a kind of Frank version of tapas, which is anything left in the fridge. Olives, yesterday's quiche, houmous, cheese, and some pitta bread that he toasts so the smell drifts languidly through the air.

'Everyone warm enough?'

Without waiting for an answer, he rubs his hands together. 'Right,' he says, 'let us begin.'

Peggy rolls her eyes.

'The thing is, Richard the Third wasn't a hunchback. Shaky Bill, that's William Shakespeare in case you didn't know, had that wrong, but Richard's spine *was* twisted, because he had scoliosis, poor lad, which meant that one shoulder was a bit higher than the other.'

Molly takes a huge gulp of wine.

Frank fossicks about and finds a newspaper article under the bowl of olives. 'The right one, that's it.' He raises his shoulder in sympathy.

'You sound as if he's an old friend of yours,' says Molly.

Frank looks at her. 'You know, Molly, I almost feel as if I know him. I walked past the ledger with his name in it every day at Council, so maybe the vibe's rubbed off on me. You do know that a woman's intuition found him?'

'Didn't she have anything better to do with her life?' asks Peggy.

'Perseverance and dedication, Peggy,' says Frank. 'She knew where he would be. It's not every day that happens, is it? Just goes to show when you look hard enough for something you can find it. Cheers!' He sips his wine.

'To women's intuition!' says Molly.

'To women,' says Peggy. 'He'll talk about this all night if I don't stop him.'

'This, Peggy, is far more interesting than coriander and coconut milk. They've found the most wicked king that ever lived – what's not to like about that?'

Molly looks from Peggy to Frank and there it is again, a strange knot of tension dancing between them. They've always shared a lightness of existence with their old jokes and new laughter. Peggy crisp and smart and tut-tutting at Frank's many and varied misdemeanours, and Frank making sure she never stays cross with him for long.

Molly has never seen her beloved Uncle Frank quite so engrossed in anything before. She has learnt from many arguments with her father that some things are not open for discussion. That deep difficult things take their own time to surface, but if Frank and Peggy aren't okay, then the world isn't right for Molly. If Frank doesn't stop this madness with the king, she will have to take him to Tate Modern for a fresh perspective on life that will soon sort him out.

Frank has no idea what's coming his way. He sips his wine, his eyes glittering with facts.

All this time

Raven has been peering into the shed with one eye pressed against the window, not a favourite pastime for a bird with an amazing beak. These people have been talking about the king as if they know him. That's what humans do, they gather information as Raven gathers souls, and they are the Tremblings, as Jackdaw showed him, in their bony little shed. For Raven, so used to the limitless skies, humans always surprise him with their happiness inside such little boxes.

He talks to the Tremblings, but they cannot hear him. 'Mayhap and mayhem, do tiny spaces make you feel safe in your perilous lives?'

Raven tries again. 'Come Tremblings, tell me of angels, and I will tell you of kings, for I must not stay long.'

Raven has his work cut out keeping his glimmering eye on both the living and dead. The line between them is so easily drawn. One step and you're over, but he doesn't say that to the Tremblings in their small snug shed. Now he knows where to find them, he flies again into the cold night air.

18

Once back in Oxenbridge House,

Molly checks the cellar door in the kitchen is locked. It has a large cat flap at the bottom, which Marcus made. Marcus never did small. Max had once been trapped in the cellar and Marcus hadn't realised and wanted to make sure that didn't happen again. He wanted to make life easier for Max, but the flap makes Molly uneasy. Anything could get through. She leaves a small offering to the God of Ordinary beside it, a bowl of I Love Tuna biscuits to entice Max home. She calls him again: 'Maaax, Maaax. Puss, puss, puss.' Her plaintive voice rattles round the room and no one answers her, not even the cat.

The next day, dreary and grey, clever old Max slips through the cat flap into the kitchen, waving his tail and turning his nose up at his fish-shaped biscuits. He gets better offerings than this when Peggy and Frank feed him, but that's what you get with Molly Stern, Maxie. Still. She's happy to see him and have some company even if his breath is stinky. Molly makes a big fuss of him. 'Did you come to say hello, Maxie? Uncle Frank is mad about the king, yes he is, and Peggy doesn't like it.'

He stares into the distance only cats can see. She sips her tea, Max jumps onto her lap purring loudly, and she strokes him absent-mindedly, so she doesn't notice anything different about the cat at first because she's not thinking about anything except calling Stefan just so she can hear his voice again. *Molly, don't.* She flicks through photos on her phone: Stefan and Molly at the seaside, on the pebbly beach, Stefan squinting at Molly, the decision in his face already forming. *There it is, see that, Molly Stern? That's him saying goodbye and you didn't even realise.*

Max digs his claws into her. She loves his soft white fur and blows into the face of her beautiful green-eyed cat, but then stops and double checks. One of his green eyes has turned blue.

Max?

There's no large rat still attached to his whiskers. She runs a hand over the rest of him, nothing obvious, no lumps or bumps or scratches, no blood anywhere. All legs are working. He's not wobbly or shaking his head from side to side. Tail's not been chewed, both ears okay, including the tips. No bald patches, no fur missing anywhere. Her brief examination reveals nothing amiss and it's too late for the vet. She'll take him in the morning. She scoops him up and carries him to his bed, but he won't settle like he usually does and sits miaowing on the carpet. It's too late to call Peggy. She looks at Max. He definitely has one blue and one green eye. Right in the middle of his new blue eye she thinks she sees a thin black shape move, but a second later his pupil lengthens, then goes back to normal and the shadow disappears.

The next day Max is a prisoner

protesting from his cat basket. The vet, sensible down-to-earth Laura Briggs, is well known and liked in Oxenbridge. She'd briefly dated Marcus Stern when Molly was a surly teenager, and Molly still feels awkward about that. Should she apologise? Laura examines Max with wise knowing hands. He quietens down, Laura strokes his ears. No, she will not apologise, she was sixteen, protective of her father.

Laura gives her a quizzical look. 'I can't find any obvious injuries.' She checks him again. Max has calmed down and now looks as if he doesn't have a care in the world. 'So, what I think has happened, to give it it's fancy name, is acquired heterochromia.'

Molly groans. 'It's not a hideous disease, is it?'

'No, it just means he's had a spontaneous colour change in one eye. White cats are more susceptible to it, that's all. He'll live, Molly, his sight seems unaffected.'

'Only, yesterday I thought his pupil changed shape …' She trails off. Saying it out loud sounds strange.

'If you're at all worried, just bring him back, but I think he'll be fine.'

'Thank you.'

I'm worried about me, thinks Molly, wondering what things would have been like if Laura, kind sensible Laura, had become part of their lives. No silly shadows, that's for sure.

Max agrees. *Take me home*, he says. *Set me free. Feed me biscuits shaped like a fish*. Molly imagines Max flying through the sky, happy and wild, furry little wings quivering in the clouds, oceans spilling from his one blue eye, as he circles the earth. Cloud or cat? No one's sure. *Fly, Max, fly*. He races out of his basket when they're home. If Max could speak from his little catty mouth he would tell Molly how, in the cellar, he has seen the shadow of a man. A sliver of energy turning his eye cells blue. *A little bit of him has crossed into a little bit of me, and if you're not careful he'll do the same to you*. But Max does not speak. He just keeps washing his ears and licking his paws.

She pours herself a glass of wine. *No, Molly, no, it's two in the afternoon.*

'Dad, I've had a shock, I need something and does time really matter?'

Never drink before five, Mol.

'It's almost five, Dad.'

What is wrong with me? wonders Molly. Ever since she was small, she's felt misplaced in the world. Odd. A jigsaw puzzle with a piece missing. She didn't fit in the way others did. Her mother left when she was little and her father told her she was in the Land of Gone. Marcus made the Land of Gone into a place with dragons and mountains and exciting adventures and Molly could only travel there in her favourite red spotted pyjamas. This was how she always imagined herself, sailing the seas and fighting monsters that came her way, her father by her side to comfort her with his carrot sticks and certainty.

Deep in her child's heart, Molly knew her mother must love being in the Land of Gone more than she loved Molly because she never came home. Her father loved her. Peggy loved her. Frank loved her. But her mother had left her, and whenever Molly wanted to talk about her mother, Marcus always wanted to talk about other things. Molly could never bear to upset him and as she grew older she learnt the way for everyone to stay okay was by saying nothing at all about Mummy.

When she was young and missing her mother, she remembered the story her father had told her and would search the house for the angel who said he would watch over them. She never found him, but just in case the angel turned up and needed more feathers for his wings, she spent hours in the garden collecting them. Shiny black ones were her favourite and there always seemed to be a lot of those. Sometimes she imagined a bird that could talk; she called him Mr Crow and had many splendid conversations with him.

She kept the feathers on her chest of drawers, and Uncle Frank helped her make a big scrapbook of feathers and twigs and bottle tops and leaves. She drew endless angels with long hair and pointy wings. Every cat they ever had was always called Max, and when one died Marcus acquired a replacement. So Molly drew Max and the angel. Molly and the angel. Mummy and the angel. Peggy and Frank having tea with the angel. Those huge wings took up most of the page and took hours of colouring in. The angel saved Max from the pond, and from barking dogs that looked like they would eat him. She wanted an angel she could believe in, who could keep her safe from every scary thing. She thought in her heart perhaps her mother was an angel, keeping watch over her when she slept. Invisible Mummy in the Land of Gone.

Peggy preferred reality. She wanted Molly grounded in the world outside the window. 'Take her to the zoo, Frank, show her zebras and giraffes. Talk about real things, for goodness sake.'

'Zebras don't have wings, Peggy.'

19

Molly knows she is lucky

in many ways and working at the Weissman Gallery is one of them. Lenny Weissman was a close friend of her father and stuck by his promise to look out for Molly if anything happened to Marcus. Lenny's daughter, Suzi, is the same age as Molly, and Lenny's paternal instincts work well enough for him to rent the flat above the gallery to Molly for a reasonable amount. Suzi often stays at weekends and it's an arrangement that works well for everyone. Lenny always kept his undeclared love for Sally Smallgood a secret, and Molly's photographs have a quality that reminds him of her, a dream-like mystery in the everyday world, which intrigues him. Several collectors are interested in her work and customers love her. Suzi loves clothes more than she loves art, but Lenny considers himself blessed with both of them in his life.

Returning to Oxenbridge is Molly's great escape, but when she's back she misses the bustle of London and when she's in London she yearns for the peace and quiet of Oxenbridge. On the weekends she's home, she tells herself it's the last time, she'll sell the house and say goodbye to Peggy and Frank, but number 10 and her big draughty home always draw her back. It's been just over a year since her father's death and months since Stefan left her, and she's still at a loss and wide awake in the middle of the night, and it's Saturday night again. She briefly wonders what Suzi is up to – a party or dinner with her boyfriend? What's the point? Nothing works out anyway. Her eyes roam around the room. Window, wardrobe, chest of drawers.

When Molly was little she thought furniture moved around when no one was looking and, just before anyone entered the room, it skedaddled back into place and spent the rest of the day recovering from its exertions. The coffee table trembled, the chairs suppressed laughter, the walls shook with secret knowledge.

Now her bones ache, her throat itches, she wants a bucket of wine to drink and another one after that. She wants to stop the darkness gathering behind her eyes. She hasn't mastered the part about being a grownup yet, the art of self-control, of being less impulsive. *Mol, just say I will consider your request for sex and then say no.* She has to stop sleeping with men to fill the void before she faces the world again. Her filter between thought and action is missing. Misplaced under the bed along with last year's *Vogue* magazines and half a packet of chewing gum.

The nuns at the abbey that once stood here didn't have any of this doubt and self-loathing. Surely life was simpler when you said yes to God and no to everything else. Easy. *I'll become a nun then, won't I? Maybe I am a nun, just not practising.* She'll tell Gabe, the guy she's sleeping with just because she can, because he has a wife already and came into the gallery and didn't leave for hours and didn't buy a print or a card or one of her photos. But bought her a drink instead of going home. 'My wife is seeing someone else,' he said. She imagines telling him she's thinking of taking a vow of celibacy, and as she thinks about Gabe she sees how much she likes being loved, even by someone who may not really love her at all. She should have said, *No Gabe. Not a good idea. You are married, and it will end in tears, mostly for me*, and with that thought, her father, the moral arbiter of all things, pops into her head.

Molly, how many times do I have to tell you, don't give your problems to other people and expect them to solve them for you — 'I was so fucked up, Your Honour, so I fucked up everyone else too.' Think before you act. Ask yourself what it is you want and say no if it's not right for you.

'Yeah, Dad, I'll try,' although she knows she won't try very hard.

She plays with her nose ring; it's tender, she can't sleep. The loneliness inside her threatens to explode. Going downstairs she treads on the creaky stair, the one to be avoided when she was a teenager creeping to her room much later than the time she had agreed, but that hardly matters now. Her father is never going to wake up, though he is still with her, scolding and teasing.

In the chilly hallway her grandfather shakes his dusty head.

Don't you judge me, Jacob Stern, or I'll—

What? What will you do?

For goodness sake go back to bed, Molly Polly and lie down and close your eyes.

Can't. Won't. Leave me alone.

For as long as she can remember, the house has yawned and stretched and moaned and groaned. The wood remembers the trees, the stone remembers the quarry, the foundations remember the mud and the sand and the water. Last year, when the house was busy with comings and goings and funeral arrangements and visitors, the noises receded so she barely noticed them, but now she's on her own the usual thumps and bumps are amplified. The old story whispers in her ear. Radiators gurgling, it's the angel. Toilet won't stop flushing, it's the angel.

She takes a good look around. The house never used to look like this. The kitchen's a mess and smells of old socks, and there's no sign of the cat. She asked her father once, if the angel can make bad things happen, why can't he fix them? It's two am and she can't sleep, anxiety's gnawing her bones. What if someone breaks in? What if the roof blows off in a freak storm, or the power lines break over the house while she sleeps and the whole of Oxenbridge explodes in a cloud of dust and atoms?

Above her frantic thoughts she hears a tap, tap, tapping sound.

She listens hard, she's only a few metres away from the kitchen, in the hallway of fears and dreams, but there it is again. She tiptoes back towards the kitchen, stops at the door, her feet freezing on the cold floor. The noise ceases, and the house is quiet again.

Going mad, Molly Chops.

It was a bird scratching at the window, a branch falling on the roof, a lump of solid air asking to come in. *Back to bed, Molly, put your headphones on, close your eyes.*

She does what she has told herself to do. She snuggles under the duvet with her phone and listens to the waves rolling on the shore. She walks down the steps to the beach. Explores the sand with her toes. She observes the pod of dolphins on the horizon. They are jumping out of the water with joy, with joy, *with joy.* She trawls her hand in the warm welcoming sea. She tries to completely relax her body. She takes a big breath in, a big breath out. *Breathe, breathe, breathe.* She's drifting in the tranquil sea.

She does not see Max careering through the cat flap in the kitchen. She does not see the long thin arm snaking out behind the cat before pulling itself back into the darkness. Molly Stern is safe in bed listening to the sounds of the ocean.

20

It was such a shock

blasting through their world when a year ago Frank walked round
Oxenbridge House calling for Marcus, then Max, then Marcus
all over again before treading softly down the cellar stairs. Frank
was the one who found him. Frank with his torch and his calm
sensible manner. Frank had often spent time with Marcus in
the cellar, in his world away from the world, sitting in the old
armchair, sharing a bottle of plonk, while Marcus reclined on
the camp bed, his long body hanging over the end as if he was
relishing the discomfort. Marcus kept his wine bottles in the
cellar, so it was only natural, in this man cave, that they would
let them breathe, then drink them, *Right, Frank?* They talked
about nothing or something. Soccer or food, or how Molly was
getting on, and sometimes Marcus opened up about Sally, and
what he should do, if anything, although Frank thought that had
been sorted out years ago.

At first it looked like Marcus was sleeping. He had one hand
on his chest, the other hanging by his side. Frank leaned over
him, the tassels on the lampshade moving gently with his breath.

'Marcus?'

His brother-in-law's eyes were closed, his feet hung over the
edge of the bed as usual, his body half covered by the sleeping

bag, a glass of unfinished wine on the table. With an unstoppable wave of panic rising in his chest, Frank shook him again. 'Wake up, Marcus, *wake up*.' He barely knew what he was doing, his mind desperately trying to catch up with his thoughts. Some part of him still waiting for Marcus to speak.

'Marcus. Come on. Open your eyes, Molly needs you. We need you.'

Frank touched Marcus's face, and his skin felt cold. He didn't know what to do. He fumbled for his pulse but knew he would find nothing. A deep peaceful calm circled Marcus, and Frank sat down beside him, trying to digest the fact of his death in this space they had so often shared together. Someone he had known more than half his life was now no longer with him, with them, with Molly. He had no idea how long he spent there. Time floated round him in a sea of nothingness before the chaos of emotions kicked in. Marcus looked completely himself, yet different. Perhaps his jaw was just a little slack, his hair a bit messy, but surely any moment now he would reach up and pat it back into place as he had done so many times after his post-prandial doze. The hand on his chest was resting on a black notebook, and when Frank's heart had calmed down from that wild tattoo, he pulled it out gently in case it was something important he needed to know. He recognised it straightaway, Sally's old sketching book. He could not bring himself to open it, not then, not there.

'It's all right,' he said in a quavering voice, 'I'll look after everything, it's okay.'

Frank had never shared a time like this with anyone before. Marcus had been his friend, not just his brother-in-law, and he would miss him. He thanked him for his life, for everything they had gone through together. 'I will always, always, look after her.

After them.' Then he couldn't say anymore. He was not used to praying, but the occasion required it, so he clasped his hands together and asked God, if there was one, and if he was listening to Frank Tremble, to take the soul of Marcus M. Stern and let it rest peacefully in Heaven. 'Let him be a watchful, helpful presence for Molly, for us all. As he was in life, let him also be in death. So, thank you, God, and one last thing, if you could just help me, Mr Francis Tremble, with my shaking hands.'

That was all he could do. He went back up to the kitchen, trying to quell the tears and stop the dread washing over him as he reached for his phone.

21

Back on the great turrets of Threadbare,

Raven taps his claws and nods wisely to himself as if he knows already the things he has forgotten. From what he has seen in the shed, at least one of the Tremblings is interested in Richard, and somewhere on the earth Raven can feel the energy of an angel. Maybe the two are connected, although none of the shed dwellers are of the Heavenly Realm. 'No siree, not yet, no way.' He knows an angel when he sees one.

'More than that I cannot say, or can I?' Raven opens his beak and the sky rushes in. Time catches in his throat, curling his feathers as he hops about chatting to himself and searching for Ricardo.

'Once a king, always a king. *Mais oui, bien sur.* When in doubt, speak French, it refreshes the mind. Most unlike me to become sentimental, but where is the recalcitrant soul of this strategic opportunistic king? If you gives me a body on a battlefield,' says Raven, 'I knows what to do, but down here the soul is a much harder thing. A soul like Ricardo will always be getting up to sumpthing, won't he, oh yes he will, because that's how he became king.'

Raven knows that in his keep of lonely, Ricardo is still Richard with that kingly life pulsing through him. He lived his life in a brutal time when you faced your enemy and fought until one of you was dead, but Raven also knows Threadbare is not that world. Threadbare is the chance for redemption.

'And what, my dear Soul of Feather and Rain, could be better than that?'

Raven searches for a ghostly trail, a set of steaming footprints. Ricardo must be here, as there's nowhere else to be.

One eternal hour

is much the same as another in Threadbare, as Ricardo is now discovering. Raven was right about the chair, a plain hard little chair, so unlike his majestic throne, but there he sits, swinging his legs at the walls. Wondering how to go down. At first he always wanted to go up to Heaven and light and glory, but after so long he is getting tired of nowhere. He believes the trick now is not to be overcome by the multitude of staircases, but just to pick one. He tries step after step after step until with an unexpected lurch he finds, to his unbridled joy, that the staircase finally goes down.

So much quicker, seems to take half the time, even though Raven says time is all he has. His cloak blows in the downy breeze. When he reaches the bottom there is another corridor with a distant flickering light. This must be the one. There are no other doors, no other rooms, and only one way to go. Although he's loath to admit it, he misses the company of Raven. At least he could talk to the bird. It's darker and gloomier here and even though he wanted to go down, now he's here he doesn't like it, and the stairs have disappeared. The air is warm and stuffy, and everywhere is the same, which is what Raven said Threadbare was all about. His life.

With each ongoing step, the truth begins to bite. He can feel it seeping through him. What else did Raven say? Time is malleable here. He wonders where his dear young son might be, and his wife, Anne, crowned queen when he was king. Memories slide through him. So many people loved him. So many questioned him. He remembers carrying a cross for the Lord. He remembers being cheered in the streets in a life that has drifted away and in that life there was another Edward. A few years older than his son. A boy who trusted him. Now look at him, he has no lungs, he cannot breathe. All he can do is walk closer to an open door and he knows what he will see. What if he goes back? It's the same. What if he runs away? It's the same. What if he stays where he is? It's the same. Every staircase leads through every door and in each room the boys will always be waiting. Their faces swim before him. The trust they placed in him. They wait and they wait and they wait, and if no one can see him here, how is it someone always knows what he does? Time alone here is interminable and he welcomes the sound he hears joining him in the darkness. For here comes the scratching of claws.

'Did you miss me?' asks Raven, his shadow lit by the light of the room. He inclines his head, ushering Ricardo in with his great bird wings. 'There you go, my Kingly King.' He is a most irreverent reverent bird. He understands seeking forgiveness is the hardest thing of all.

There is nothing else for Ricardo to do but walk into the room and let time swallow him. Take him in one huge mouthful of dust. He stands so still and so calm by the side of the bed, watching the sleeping boys. *Edward*. That name floats towards him in a current of cold air and sits on his shoulders. For a moment the boys stir, and he hears them say, *Uncle, what did you do to us?* But when he looks again, their eyes are closed. Beyond this, there is nothing and nowhere to go. He is beginning to understand there is no escape from the things he has done. He sinks to his knees and everything he knows about himself falls away.

'Forgive me,' he says. To the midnight air. To the walls. To the bird. 'Forgive me,' he says in a low soft voice to the boys.

22

'**Everybody dies in April,**'

says Frank. 'And I'm talking about great leaders, Peggy. I'm talking about Edward the Fourth, Henry the Seventh, and our very own Iron Lady, who died last year, I know, but it was also in April.'

Peggy wonders what's coming next. 'I always liked Maggie,' she says. 'She was a woman of conviction, even if I didn't agree with half the things she said. I can't imagine what it would have been like for her with all those *men*. She had to be strong, didn't she, to be heard. And I like that.'

Peggy tilts her chin at Frank as if to say sometimes it's just hard being a woman and she wants Frank to say something nice about how he always loves and respects her, but he doesn't.

'Yes, but Peggy, don't you think it's odd that she died at the same time as King Edward the Fourth?'

Sometimes Peggy wonders what the point is of being alive. 'You only think it's odd because only *you*, Francis Tremble, think like that. You've got to go some time.'

'Edward died in April, Henry died in April, and Margaret Thatcher died in April, so, technically, it's the same.'

Peggy sighs. 'Technically, there's the inescapable fact that they're five hundred years apart, and two of them were medieval kings and one was the first female prime minister of Britain.

You knew where you stood with Maggie, which is more than you can say for the lot we have now. Most of them are hopeless.'

The rest of the day

arrives in a flurry of rain and Peggy weighs up the possibility of the delivery truck mounting the corner of Crown Street and driving straight into the shop. Part of her likes the idea of some large destructive force sweeping everything away, lights flashing, driver edging closer to the kerb. The streetlights make the entrance to Abbey Lane and the toilet block look much more interesting than they are. *Light it all up*, thinks Peggy. The toilet is mentioned in the guidebook, the nearest public convenience to the abbey ruins. *Maybe we should get a plaque for that as well* — King Richard the Third sat here — *which would be undeniably fascinating.*

The key for the toilet is kept in Off the Peg, and Peggy has grown used to people asking for it, so they can relieve themselves before traipsing to the station or the abbey, depending on how weak their bladder is at either end of the day. The toilet sits at the start of Abbey Lane, before the path winds through nettles and brambles up to the abbey ruins.

The driver hauls two boxes up the steps — at least the delivery's arrived on time. Edward can unpack it all when he arrives, but he's late. Peggy doesn't know what's going on with Edward these days. He spends far too long staring out of windows, but Peggy tells herself it's okay, he's still grieving for his mum, and Peggy's not been the same since Marcus.

Molly says she will never come to Oxenbridge again if Peggy doesn't take the tartan trousers out of the shop window, but Molly says a lot of things, not all of them reliable. Peggy can't wait to tell her she sold three pairs last week to a hiker with a flushed face who thought she'd found God in the abbey ruins. Peggy had to admit they suited her, and she gave her a discount for being brave enough to buy them in the first place. That's what spring does for you, makes you wild and reckless.

She offers the delivery driver a cup of tea, but he doesn't have time, and Edward appears, umbrella dripping on the floor.

'Hello, Peggy,' he says, brushing raindrops from his jumper.

'Late again,' she says. 'The shirts have arrived.'

His punishment is cleaning the toilets. A requirement of the assistant's position because Peggy's not paying someone and doing it herself.

By midday, Edward Farraday has been gone almost two hours. She puts the *Back in Five Minutes* sign on the door and goes to find him. Now she's a detective; there are the cleaning sponges and the Sink-O-Cleen, and the sinks are shining, so at least he's done something. Everything looks clean. She pouts in the mirror — *Don't be silly, Peggy* — and checks the Peggy signature bob. Very sleek, well maintained, she's the regional Anna Wintour, always wearing the same chic look, just with no one to appreciate it. Edward has refilled the toilet paper and the towels, but there's no sign of him anywhere.

'Edward?' she calls. No answer. He wouldn't be hiding in the toilet, would he?

She promised his mother she'd look out for him and that means keeping him in this job. Peggy pats her hair again and decides on giving him ten more minutes to make his entrance. When he does finally reappear, his cheeks are pink and there's a bit of dirt smudged on his face.

'Where have you been?'

'Lunch,' he says.

'It's nearly two o'clock. Only I thought you might have fallen down the toilet.' A late frost appears on Peggy's eyebrows. 'Look, I know things aren't easy, but just tell me if you don't want to work here anymore. It will be easier for both of us.'

'No, Peggy, I mean I do, I'm sorry. It won't happen again.'

He puts the key in his pocket, checks himself in the small wall mirror, wipes the dirt off his face, and by the end of the day Peggy's forgiven him. She drops him home with a couple of meat pies, a large pepperoni pizza that should last ten minutes, a litre of milk, a packet of digestives, and a jar of instant coffee. She's doing it because he's young, and because she can, and because she told Edward's mum, Nancy, that she'd look out for him because it's the right thing to do.

She'd like to give him a hug, and whisper in his ear, *If there's anything you need, just tell me.* She decides against it, as she's still a little bit annoyed with him from this morning and he'll be twenty later in the year and knows where to find her. She turns the engine off and sits in the car, remembering Nancy's gaunt exhausted face the last time she saw her. How her own body felt light and unreal, as if by some thread of empathy with Nancy, she, Peggy Tremble, was also floating with the inevitability of life and death, and there was nothing she could do to stop it. Except buy biscuits for a boy. She still has that feeling, as if she is hovering over her own life, and sometimes nothing really matters anymore. How has time passed so quickly? It seems like only yesterday when England was buzzing with the Olympics and Bradley Wiggins won the Tour de France and Mo Farah won both the five and ten thousand metres and everyone was feeling good about themselves. Now Edward's getting used to life without his mother, and Molly is missing her father and Frank has gone all fifteenth century.

Things change, and Peggy hardly knows what to do about that anymore. Peggy misses Marcus, but she's tried to tuck her grief away. She and Marcus always had Sally dancing between them, but not anymore, and not for a long time. Now Peggy sees the years stretching in front of her, a panorama of missing Molly all the way to the shed, and if the unthinkable is happening she might have to include Frank in that. Maybe she should join Frank at the court of the Plantagenet king before it's too late, make sure history is the only thing he's burying his head in.

Perhaps it's time to give Molly the notebook. Peggy has kept it hidden away since the day Frank found Marcus in the cellar. When Frank brought it home, Peggy opened it and looked at her sister's private world, before closing it with a sigh. She could feel the old sadness inside her flowing through her and meeting up with her new sadness over Marcus. Is this what has been driving Frank away? She wants to ask him, *Do you still love me, Francis Tremble?* She wants to know the truth but doesn't want to ask because once you know it, you can never not know it. Molly hasn't been the same since her father's death and her breakup with that bloody man, and Peggy doesn't want to add to her stress, but she knows life is nothing without the real things, and the real things are the hardest things of all. Molly's not eating, has shadows under her eyes, and that ridiculous nose ring.

Frank calls to her as she walks in, 'Need any help with the shopping?'

She dumps the bags in the kitchen, her heart beating loudly. 'I think it's time for Molly to know, Frank,' she says, too quietly for him to hear.

23

Edward Farraday rolls up his sleeves,

ready for the baking. His mother's baking trays are so old-fashioned. None of them will do. His new bendy pink silicon tray makes a dozen mini muffins at a time and the tray itself looks so good he wants to eat that too. He assembles all the dry then the wet ingredients. Chocolate chip tonight.

Don't make a mess this late in the kitchen, please, Edward.

'I'll clear it all up, Ma.'

The kitchen is the place where he feels most connected to his mum. Cooking helped her unwind after a stressful week at work and she found baking as calming as he does. He pictures her at the stove, stirring the gravy, before she became too tired and sick to enjoy the taste of food. Her lovely dark hair framing her face. Her face is so familiar that he almost *can't* remember it, and he wonders how that happens to someone he spent every day of his life with. She always listened to Radio Four, so he does too. It keeps him company and he talks to the presenters even though they can't hear him.

'Just because you're not here doesn't mean you're not somewhere.'

A nice light touch when you're mixing.

Handfuls of chocolate melts make their way into his mouth.
He spoons the mixture into each muffin case, slides the tray into
the oven, licks the bowl, always the best bit. Dinner is spaghetti
with chilli sauce from a bottle, and cheese, mostly the same every
night unless Peggy's bought him a pizza, which she did, but he's
already eaten it. Afterwards, slurping a cup of tea in the living
room, he lights a pink scented candle, tea rose, his favourite.

You were always scared of the dark, Edward.

'Not anymore, Mum, not with this.'

He's bought a head torch and straps it to his head and nods up
and down with it. She laughs. The sky grows darker. He settles
down for a nap in front of the telly, he needs the company, and,
like the radio, it soothes him. When he wakes with a start he
jumps up, blows out the candle and closes the curtains, before
limbering up for his nightly travels. The muffins have cooled.
He scoops a handful into his old school lunch box, stuffs it into
his backpack, puts on his puffer jacket, beanie, and head torch
over his beanie. Soft clunk of the front door, no one around,
everyone asleep. Walking quickly, it takes fifteen minutes to
reach the high street. Nearly midnight. Streets are deserted.
There goes Edward Farraday, all in black, no one will notice
him, but if anyone does, they might ask what he's doing out at
this time dressed like that. Grief has turned his head just a little,
so we'll give the boy some leeway.

You're not doing anything silly, are you, Edward?

Down the high street, past the quiet shops, his shadow turns
into Abbey Lane, the sign for the abbey lit up by his head torch.
This way, one and a half miles, mostly flat.

Like me, he thinks.

He fumbles for the toilet key he's kept in his pocket. No
one's doing a shit in the public toilet at this hour and it's a relief

once he's inside and out of the cold. The pungent smell of the toilet cleaner hits him. *Ocean Breeze, that's a laugh.* Oxenbridge is at least seventy miles from the sea. Why are the cubicle doors so short? Less door, less money on materials, he supposes. His head torch flashes past the sinks and the mirror, to the wall. Running down the length of the wall is a solid wooden beam with a sign beside it.

This beam dates from the 15th century
and is all that remains
of a public house on this site.
Please treat with respect.

His mind ticks over as the fear kicks in. He'd like to tell Peggy about his discovery, almost did, but doesn't know how she'd react.

It was an accident, Peggy, when I was cleaning the toilets. I leant against the beam and almost fell through. Peggy, the world is full of things that need undoing and discovering, and here's one of them.

He loves seeing how things work and finding the secrets. His mother had an old typewriter that he dismantled, much to her dismay because he could never put it back together again. Once he'd finished with it, he left it like a dismembered animal waiting for her on the carpet after her eight-hour shift.

'Edward!' she yelled. 'Come here now.'

After that he hid his screwdriver in his school bag. His mother thought he was doing it for attention, missing his father, but as he never knew him, he doesn't think it's that. Now he keeps his trusty Phillips screwdriver in his backpack for emergencies. He runs his hand over the tiles. *Please treat with respect. I will.* He lays his hand on top of the beam. The wood is stiff and does not want to move, but after an extra hard shove with his palm, it moves, just the same as before, and his eyes widen as the hole in the wall is revealed.

He didn't get very far earlier today, but now he has more time he's excited. He throws his backpack through first, then the rest of him follows, leaving the wooden beam ajar in case he has to get back in a hurry, like he did today. Opening it from the other side is hard and he didn't want Peggy to see anything out of the ordinary if she came into the toilets. The wood is heavy and doesn't swing back into place by itself. He's brought a little packet of glow-in-the-dark stars and planets, and once he's on the other side he sticks them on the beam and some on the wall just in case the others fall off. Now there's a haphazard map of the heavens to guide him back. The beam is a hard grainy wood, full of splinters, and he wonders what kind of tree it came from. Perhaps one of those lovely Oxenbridge oaks scattered over the fields.

Peggy almost caught him this morning. He'll have to be more careful. The first time he discovered the beam could move was after giving it an almighty slap when he'd finished cleaning the toilets. Just because he could, just because it was there, and he was thinking of all the people who would have sat drinking ale with their friends in the tavern as it once was then. That's when the beam shifted and revealed its secret. He almost fell through with surprise.

Now he's walking into the space that lies ahead, gingerly feeling his way along and wondering where he's going. He thinks he's following the direction of Abbey Lane, and that will take him to Oxenbridge House. If he ends up there, then he might bump into Molly Stern. Molly never takes any notice of him, but he likes her. Especially the nose ring. If he keeps walking, he thinks he'll end up under the abbey ruins as well, and who knows what he might find there? The air is musty and damp, and after twenty minutes he stops for a swig of water, seeing nothing ahead but more walls and a low roof, all of which he's finding a little claustrophobic. *Keep going, Edward, don't give up.* He's a bit tired now and not really enjoying it, but on he goes.

There's no mobile reception down here, but he double checks his phone is still in his pocket. His head torch shines on the walls. If Molly could see him now, would she be impressed? *Hey, Molly, how goes you? My grand accomplishment in life so far is walking under your house, if that is where I am, so what's yours?*

That's wonderful, Edward, come and have a drink with me.

Edward, you should be at home in bed and asleep.

'Thanks, Mum.'

Since he was little he's visited the abbey ruins countless times, with his mother and his friends. He's smoked dope there, laughed, cried, and fallen off the walls. He's wandered round looking at graves and chunks of crumbling stone. His mother is buried in the graveyard of St Stephen's church and, as much as he misses her, he doesn't like going there to see her.

The further he walks, the colder the air, the narrower the walls. People must have been small to build passages like this. Perhaps this wasn't such a good idea. All he really wants is a girlfriend to watch soccer with him, and a car of his own. *Go home, Edward Farraday, join the gym, go to the pub, learn to drive, find the way forward.*

He's about to turn around when he hears something scratching in the dark. His spine tingles. He says to himself, *I am not, and never have been, frightened of rats.* Maybe it's his mum, tapping on the window, telling him to come home for tea. *Edward do not panic, no one knows where you are.* His torch light flashes up and down, there's just wall and nothing but wall surrounded by the solemn dark, as if the darkness has a weight, a heaviness to it. He wonders if this is where people were brought to be killed and now their souls are here, crying out for revenge. Quite when this happened or who did it he doesn't know, but it might have happened, and now he can't unthink it and a gulpy panic rises in his chest. Maybe the tunnel stretches for miles, but here is the end of his adventure. He sniffs. He should be tucked up in his nice warm bed. He should not be wandering about Oxenbridge with his dead mother telling him he's somewhere he really shouldn't be. He knows that. His watch says he's been here for an hour already.

In the world above his head life goes on. Frank tidies up the shed before turning in for the night. Molly moisturises her dry scaly skin and checks her phone multiple times for all the messages that aren't there. Peggy cleans her teeth and checks the light in the shed is out before she gets into bed and reads a few pages of her latest self-help book, *Change, Courage and Letting Go*. She's tired and not concentrating, so she has to read the last few pages again as she waits for the unmistakable sound of Frank huffing and puffing up the stairs to bed.

In the world below Oxenbridge, Edward rests against the wall. As far as he can see it's a dead end. His lunch box is digging into his back. He turns off his head torch just for a second, to see what it's like, but the dark is ferocious and he switches it back on. The red light first, then white, then the brightest version. Red, white, bright, he flicks them on and off, and that's when something walks past him, brushing against his leg, and a bolt of terror shoots through him. His heart leaps into the wall and thuds so loudly that whoever or whatever it was is bound to hear. He tries not to fart in terror. He's too afraid to move. *You shouldn't have come here in the first place, should you?*

He inches back the way he thinks he came, head torch on red, too afraid to change it. The light bobs up and down as he searches for the way out, but all he sees are walls. He has no idea where he is, and the more he walks, the smaller the space grows round him, until he finds himself stooping under a low vaulted ceiling, where an odd yeasty smell floats through the air. He edges forward. The darkness is thick, as if the shadows are breathing. 'Whoever lives here is a very short person,' he says to himself and just as he says that the room widens out and he breathes a sigh of relief and straightens up. Head torch on white now so he can see properly; there's a rack of wine bottles running along the wall, and alongside them a small table with a lamp and a fringed lampshade, which reminds him of his nan, as she always told him off whenever he played with the tassels.

Next to the table are a camp bed with a sleeping bag on the top and a pillow, and an old armchair. *What is this place and who on earth sleeps in a wine cellar?* Though maybe a glass of vino would quell his shaking legs.

'Hello?' he says in his thin reedy voice, regretting it as soon as he's spoken. What if someone answers him? In the darkness he thinks he can hear the unmistakable sound of someone breathing, and, before he can stop it, a fart he has been holding in releases itself with a loud raspberry. He almost laughs, but then he looks down and breaks into a gabble of relief. 'Shit,' he says. 'Shitting shit, shit, it's a bloody cat.'

The bloody cat winds itself around his ankles, purring loudly.

'Oh you silly, silly thing.'

His legs tremble. Cats usually make him sneeze, but with gratitude and relief he makes a huge fuss of this very solid cat, with its gleaming white coat shining in the darkness, and plonks himself down in the old armchair. The springs poke into his bottom, and the cat jumps onto his lap, but he doesn't care, not now. He welcomes the cat and rubs his itchy nose and sneezes five times in a row, deciding in the light of his newfound happiness that it's time for a muffin and a drink. He breaks off a bit of muffin and offers it to the cat. After a few minutes he relaxes, absorbing the quietness, and his brain calms down, and he's fairly sure this is Molly's cat, Max, the great white ratter. Peggy has told him many tales about him, and if this is indeed Max, then he, Edward Farraday, is sitting in the cellar of Oxenbridge House, and Molly Stern, the woman he thinks he loves, might be upstairs asleep, or watching a film or reading a novel, or writing a novel or snogging her boyfriend, or running the world or doing anything else that girls might do. He has no idea. If Molly came into the cellar he would say, *Don't mind me, Molly, I'm just having a tiny little adventure and I will support you in any of your life choices, anything at all.*

Another muffin. The cat starts miaowing as he fossicks in his lunch box and that's when Dedalus steps from the darkness and the cat flies off his lap and Edward sneezes and sprays half his muffin over the floor in astonishment.

He jumps to his feet. 'Who the fuck are you?' He gets ready to swing his backpack in front of him like a weapon if he needs to.

Dedalus shuffles forward

with absolutely no idea of what he looks like or how that might affect another human being. He has no idea of anything; he's emerging from stasis, a deep dreaming sleep during which his cells were rearranging themselves. Old Dedalus from the Abbey of Stern has quietly turned into new Dedalus, awakening with the same face and the same heart and the same mind but now also different. He has dreamt all these years of what he will become, yet still he does not know, but the world is waking him. He takes a deep breath and his lungs shudder, unused to such exertions. His robes hang round his knees, his sandals curl with age. His hands and feet are filthy. He has not washed for five hundred years. Bedraggled hair, hollow eyes, cheekbones jutting out. An ancient living being caught in the light from another time.

A man stands between him and the light, and the chair, and the sleeping bag. Dedalus rubs his eyes with a sense of familiarity. Years earlier, another man stood in the cellar, filling the air with scents and odours that washed over Dedalus, just as it's happening now. The world creeps up his nose and into the myriad folds in his brain, overcoming his senses. What to do? *Take me back Lord, where everything is known and understood.*

The man in front of him

looks impossibly weedy, and Edward thinks he might be one of those thin wiry men who resemble a pencil but can tear a book in two, if pushed, and Edward doesn't want to take any chances. Pencil Man sways as if he's about to keel over, but you never know. Edward slowly backs out of the cellar, edging past the chair, past the table, past the wine rack – *Slowly, slowly, there we go* – all the while his eyes fixed on the stringy man. At the point where the ceiling lowers and the tunnel begins, Edward ducks and runs as fast as he can, back the way he came, backpack over one shoulder, lunch box half open, spewing out what's left of his muffins, like huge Hansel and Gretel crumbs. *Look who was here, look where he went.* If he was Mo Farah he'd be super fit and could run like this all day, although Mo Farah wouldn't find himself in this situation, would he? Neither would Lewis Hamilton, but Edward is not Lewis Hamilton and he's not cool and he can't even drive. He's out of breath and slowing down and desperately searching for the stars that he stuck on the beam.

Edward Farraday, son of Nancy, begotten with love, grown with vegetables and routine, discipline, tidiness, and love, fills with gratitude as he sees the Constellation of Rescue ahead on the walls. The glow-in-the-dark rings of Saturn and the full moon are his guide, both half an inch high but doing the job for now as his head torch slips on his sweaty brow. *Quick, come on, through the hole in the wall.* He scrapes his face against the wood as he clambers back into the toilets. It's much harder pulling the beam back into place than pushing it out – *Move, you bastard, move* – and when it finally does slot back into place with a slow *thunk*, he tests it to make sure it will not budge, then dabs his cheek with toilet paper when he's feeling brave enough to move.

He is never doing this again. *Ever.*

He locks the toilet door behind him and double checks it, hands shaking. He's more marshmallow than man: nose dripping, blood on his face, can't help the tears, looking over his shoulder every once in a while to make sure he's not being followed. Back home, he kicks off his trainers, closes the curtains, locks the doors, checks the street, the back garden, front garden, no one there, swabs his cheek with antiseptic, *Ouch, that bloody hurts.* Gets into bed, pulls the covers over his ears. He desperately misses that safe quiet feeling in the house when his mum was there. He punches the tears from his face.

The next day he walks into town, twitchy as anything, still picturing that man's face in front of him. By the time he's reached the shops and encountered no one unusual except his own reflection in the windows, he feels able to continue and buy a dozen multicoloured muffin cases. He takes a great interest in all the items on the baking shelves. Baking powder, flour, calming and soothing. From Mr Khan, the newsagent, he buys the next instalment of *Universe Monthly*, with another set of glow-in-the-dark stars, yellow moons, and planets. There's a girl at the counter who serves him, he's never seen her before; he hands over his change, she smiles at him, he gives her a nervous little wave in return. 'Thank you,' he says. He keeps an eye on everyone. It must have been a Hare Krishna, a hermit, a rough sleeper, living off the grid, living under the world. *Who is he? Does Molly know he's there?* What should he do? If he tells Peggy, she'll ask him what the hell he was doing in the toilets in the first place.

24

Dedalus now finds himself

as a spirit from another time living in a thinner, taller form, and is having difficulty coming to grips with this. It's not made any easier by a five-hundred-year gap without food, which was bound to upset him. He follows the trail of sweat and sugar left by his visitor and gathers up some muffins as he goes. He sniffs and takes a bite and what's in his mouth almost tastes good, but as he chews his tongue sticks to the roof of his mouth and he gags and spits it back out. *Who is giving me this?* The muffin cannot sustain such inquiry and crumbles like dust in his fingers. There have been intrusions and disturbances, but none has brought him food. He walks back to the cellar followed by the stealthy white cat, which goes in and out of the cellar door through another little door. He perches on the edge of the camp bed in the darkness that he knows so well and rubs his hands together to warm them up. He yawns. Warmth comes and warmth goes. The boy disappeared through the wall, just like the cat through the door. He has woken from his spirit sleep, but his feet are still cold.

It seems like no time at all to him since the last time he woke. He could hear voices, a baby crying. He listened to that sound as if it were telling him everything he needed to know. *I am young, I am new in this world, I need your help to stay alive, I am hungry, I am scared, love me, love me, love me.* He listened, he waited, and then the cellar door opened, and a man walked down the stairs and turned on the light. Dedalus could see him, but the man could not see Dedalus. The man was dressed in odd clothes and strange shoes, and this was the first time Dedalus began to understand something had changed in him. *Who am I?*

His heart muscle pounded with life. Blood skipped along his veins. His hair was still growing, his mind still working. *How have I come to be like this?* Unknown to himself, unknown to the world, finding his way back to God, wherever that may be. With these strange vibrations, was the man showing him the way?

The man was singing something to himself and Dedalus had never heard a sound like that travelling through the air. The aromatic scent of food laden with spices drifted round the cellar. And the man brought light. The yellow bulb almost touched the top of his head when he walked down the cellar steps. As light flooded the gloomy shadows, it was accompanied by an intense smell of moss and lavender and geranium all wriggling into Dedalus's brain at once and threatening to overpower his senses. He lay on the floor wondering if he had really woken in the afterlife and, if he had, why did it smell like that? The man selected two bottles of wine, blew dust from them, then climbed back up the steps and turned out the light, leaving Dedalus in darkness once more.

The man forgot to close the cellar door behind him. Dedalus could still see the light through the gap in the door and stood, sniffing the air. His senses started springing into life as if the Lord was showing him the way. This was God's reply to his eternal questions: *Follow the light, Dedalus, and there you will find me.*

How will I know when to ascend?

Ask and the door will open.

Up he went.

Making his way past shapes of things he'd never seen before. His breath caught in his throat. What would happen next in the afterlife to help him draw nearer to Heaven? It seemed so unreachable, so full of all the temptations. He was alive and hungry now and the smell of food drove him on. God was watching him, as He always had done before. There were so many scents and odours he did not recognise, voices he did not know. His thin little legs creaked like twigs as he walked. He wondered how many seasons had passed since he had stepped on the earth, and he wasn't there yet, he was walking through a house.

Be in this world now, my faithful servant.

One hand against the wall, he lurched unsteadily along, until the doors to Heaven opened with his unsteady hands and there he found the feast that God had prepared for him.

It was impossible for Dedalus to know

it was not God in Heaven who had cooked, but Francis Tremble, helped by his fiancée, Peggy Smallgood. They were having dinner with Marcus and his wife, Sally, Peggy's sister, and their baby daughter, Molly, who was meant to be asleep upstairs. It was not a feast for him.

A thousand things happened at once. There were the shocked faces, the open mouths, the surprised cries, the hands of people touching him, pulling him. Being exhausted and hungry in equal measure, he sprawled on the dining room table, his robes barely covering him, his hands grabbing whatever he could find. A tablecloth, a plate, the arm of a woman, he was in the middle of such a noisy multitude that he was overcome and closed his eyes to keep everything out, because if this was eternal damnation, then he was firmly in it. Voices echoed round him.

'Frank, for God's sake, who the hell is he? Where did he come from? Help me get him out of here. Bloody well put that down. What on earth do you think you are doing? What's wrong with him? Don't think he can hear me.'

'Sal, Sally, look Molly's here,' said Marcus. 'Hey little one, how did you get out of your cot? It's all right, Sal, Sally, calm down. Peggy, take Molly back upstairs would you? It's all right, Sal. Sal, it's *okay*, we've nearly got him.'

Peggy scooped Molly up in her arms. 'It's okay, darling, there, there, sh, you're safe, sweetheart, come on, let's get you back to bed.'

Then Dedalus finally understood.

This was how the fiery circles of Hell began. They were here now and he was with the demons who were burning his skin. There was so much terrible noise. A knife cut his fingers, a spoon hit him on the head, wine spilt from the table, something hot and sticky landed in his hands. It smelt good, and he didn't care, he crammed it in his mouth.

A woman was watching him, her eyes wide with disbelief. She was saying something to him, but he didn't understand, so he reached out to touch her. To reassure her. And for a few seconds the madness stopped, and the noise fell away, and she looked at him, amazed.

This febrile man, with his long hair and thin arms and shaking legs.

He did not know what he'd become, and neither did they.

More words he did not understand.

'Hold him, Frank, he's covered in gravy, slippery as a bloody fish. Frank, hang on, he's bloody strong, keep hold, don't let go, bloody hell.'

A man tried to cover him with his coat.

Peggy was anxious

to take the loudly sobbing Molly away from all the noise and commotion as quickly as she could. Sally was telling everyone, 'It's the angel, it's the angel,' but no one was listening. Dinner was completely ruined, and Sally was left sitting on the stairs, the colour drained from her face in shock, as they dragged Dedalus away. Amongst all the noise and fear, they bundled Dedalus into the cellar, which was the only place they could think of to put him, through the door that had finally opened for him.

They tied him up – *Not too tight, Marcus* – and left him in the darkness and closed the door behind them until they could work out what to do and calm everybody down. The sound of poor Molly crying still echoed through the house.

'Keep him here for now.'

'No, call the police.'

'What are *they* going to do?'

'Leave him alone, he needs help.'

'We have no idea who he is or what he's doing here or how he found his way into the house.'

'What if he's injured?'

'He's not injured, Sally. He's all right.'

'No, you can't see if he's all right, he might be dangerous.'

'Sally, it's all right, calm down.'

'Did you see him?'

'We all saw him.'

'Isn't he beautiful?'

'I would not use that word to describe him.'

Sally said she had seen him before in her dreams and she knew who he was. 'He has come for me.'

Marcus said, 'He hasn't come for anybody, sweetheart, he's just a tramp who found his way into the cellar.'

They locked the cellar door and bolted it from the outside and took it in turns guarding the kitchen in case he tried to get back into the house again.

'Where did he come from? How did he get in?'

After that, they all searched everywhere. They checked and double checked every corner of every room and then the cellar, and he wasn't there. He had gone.

'He has gone, he has gone, he has gone, you drove him away,' said Sally, busy drawing in her notebook.

Even when Molly was crying. Sally kept drawing with such intensity that Peggy became worried for her.

Over the next few days, they searched again and again, and did admittedly drink a bottle of wine down there just to help calm their nerves, but there was no sign of him, and in the end, in a unanimous decision, they decided not to call the police, as no one was there.

25

The man who was no one

crawls on his belly in the dirt out of the cellar, his ribs playing
a tune on the ground. All he really wants to do is go home,
but he can barely remember where that is or was, as the world
above him has changed. Another twenty-odd years in the blink
of an eye.

'All my life,' he cries, 'I have tried to be good.' He addresses
God but has given up waiting for an answer. He thumps his bony
chest. 'And when I tried to get into the world they beat me.'

The rats stop scurrying and stare at Dedalus, covered in dust,
resting against the wall. 'Tell me,' he says, 'who I am, that I am
meant to be like this?'

The rats blink and sniff the air. Perhaps they are a little scared
of him, although they are creatures of darkness. Perhaps they can
hear the pounding of his heart. So what is he? They have never
seen anyone like him before. He is not like the others, coated
with their smells and flesh. They appear to have no answers as
they rock backwards and forwards on their little ratty feet.

Like these rats, Dedalus has spent a large portion of his life
curled in dark corners, but unlike them, he has been deprived
of company and sustenance. He is shaky on his feet and just a
little bit shitty. He's edgy, jangled, his senses worn by too much

stimulation. Most of the years he has slept, much like Jessop thought he would, curled like a worm round the relic box.

Look at all the years I have given you.

I did not ask for them. I asked to go home.

Seek, Dedalus, and you will find God.

Will I, though?

He leans against the wall. A man with a cake came to see him. Is this God pushing him to begin his life anew? He drums his fingers on the wall and breathes deeply, as that is all he can do. He is so alone. Incubating in the dark. Sparks fly from the ends of his fingers. Light pulses through his long thin body.

26

Ricardo is still

with the boys, who remain curled round each other like fox cubs
in their sleep. The air turns chilly. The older boy's ashen face
turns towards him. Ricardo shuffles forward, wants to touch
him, but it is so cold now he can hardly move and his eyelashes
stick to his cheeks. The boy's hand lies on the bed beside him, the
rest of him covered in death. The boy's cold face is the endless
reckoning of Threadbare. He steels himself and reaches out to
touch that small cold hand. A shiver runs through him. He stays
like that for a bittersweet moment between nephew and uncle.
Family to family.

He kneels by the bed and clears his throat. 'When your father
died,' he begins, 'I swore to protect you.'

He stops. He remembers his horse thundering beneath him
as he rode through half of England to meet this boy. How
welcoming he was. How like his father he looked.

'When I brought you to London, I did not know how it was
going to be. I was confused. There was so much going on, but
I should have told you, then and there, *You will never be king*.
Everyone was with me, the Lords, Spiritual and Temporal, and
the Commons, all of them begged me to accept the crown.
Richard, last legitimate York standing. You were out of the

line of succession. Can you not see? Your father's first secret marriage made his second marriage to your mother invalid and you could not rule. They beseeched and petitioned me. I told them, yes, if I had to, I would accept, yes, I said, I would take this burden of duty and take the throne to safeguard the kingdom. I did you both a favour, do you see? I saved you from that.' This boy trusted him, he put his hand in his and let him lead him to his fate.

Now look at the man who was king. Strands of frosty hair stick to his face, his feet are slipping on a frozen lake, sliding towards the truth. Icicles form on his fingers. Thick white flakes of snow fall on his cheeks. His feeble hands pull at his cloak for warmth and comfort, but there is none. His breath freezes in front of him. Snow creeps through his hair and into his mouth. He is gulping it down and he's colder than he ever knew he could be.

Ancient breath heaves from his ancient body. The years have caught him, his actions have caught him; this is what it means, laying bare his soul.

'Being king is power,' he says to the cold little boy. 'You saw that in your father, and you felt that from me. Once you are king, you do everything to stay king.

'Being king is death to those who do not want you to be king, but you cannot fear death when you are king. No one wants a king who cannot kill his enemies. This is what you felt from me.'

He staggers to his feet. Tries to flex his icy fingers. The ice cracks with the weight of his soul. It feels like ice is cracking his brain. His heart is frozen. He imagines his teeth dropping out of his mouth one by one. He watches himself like a bird above his body, gathering teeth in his bare cold hands, threading them round his neck like an amulet. He remembers his own son and he says his name because that's what's left, the memory of love. If he could not save his own son from death, how could he have saved these small and tender boys? Water pools at his feet. His teeth are still in his mouth.

He sways at the side of the boys' bed and shuts his eyes. 'In my heart, I am sorry. I am. I should not have left you. I should not have sought my own glory so easily. There were many things I could have done or should not have done.' Words catch in his throat. His chest heaves with shame. He leaves the sleeping boys and stumbles from the room. A shadow of something raggedy looms towards him on the wall.

'Raven, is that you?'

'Who else would it be?' replies Raven. 'Although I hate to tell you, *mon ami*, this is not the end. Come with me.'

He follows the bird to the edge of the parapet on the battlements of Threadbare. A fierce wind shrieks through him. If he looks very hard into the distance, he can see a town and houses and a church spire, all beckoning.

'A little bit of self-acknowledgement does wonders for the soul. In my next life, I will have that on a T-shirt. What you're looking at, Ricardo, is the town of Oxenbridge. I do believe you've been there before.'

Ricardo sighs. What did he do there that he must atone for now? In the small dark holy of his soul, there is a void, hollowing into bone. Ricardo just wants to sleep.

'You can either walk from Threadbare to the rest of the world, and most souls do, or you can ascend through the skies in the arms of an angel.'

'I'm sick of walking.'

'If the angel won't come to Ricardo, Ricardo must go to the angel. You will soon find that Truth is effortless, my Monseigneur of Gloom. It won't take long,' says Raven, launching himself into the air and spreading his beautiful wings. A moment ago, the bird was before him but now it is behind him, squawking in his ear. 'One last walk, Ricardo. Trust me and remember: all life is illusion. Here one minute, gone the next.'

Raven doesn't tell him he once saw a man go up in flames, completely spontaneously when he realised what he had done. He had just said, 'I am really sorry for everything,' then flames hit the ceiling and he was gone. Some things need telling, some don't.

They walk in companionable silence, like an old married couple, weighted with what has gone before, finding solace in each other's company. From time to time they stop and Raven offers Ricardo his wing, which Ricardo accepts with a cold hand, desperate for a sliver of comfort. Then they continue on. His feet hardly touch the ground. His cloak holds him together and he walks for as long as he can remember, and then he walks some more.

Halfway between here and there,

no royal trumpeters appear to welcome him to the next part of his eternal existence, but Ricardo's not bothered by that now. He's getting used to not having things, and he's tired. Always tired. Once it would have been nice, but lots of things are nice and he doesn't need them. Jewels and brooches are nice. He used to like wearing them as king, to show a bit of oomph and awe — otherwise what's the point of being king? He shrugs. Doesn't know the point of anything now. What he has done, he has done. Threadbare has shown him there is never an escape from that.

After what feels like an interminable amount of time, there is still dirt beneath his feet, but he is somewhere else entirely. He takes a good look around and as far as he can see there are no stairs, no rooms, and no sleeping boys, and he thanks the Lord for that, wherever the Lord may be. Stray feathers drift in the air. He is standing in a massive chamber with huge sparkling walls. Ricardo doesn't mind sparkly. 'Are we …?'

'Not yet,' says Raven. 'Remember the Thread of Acknowledgement. Forgiveness. The New You, Ricardo.'

All Ricardo wants is simple.

'I cannot be anything other than myself.' Ricardo's toes curl into dirt.

Raven stretches his left wing and his right leg, which is a bit stiff and crinkly after all that walking. It was a long journey without the air under his wings, and still no angel, but easier than flying through the hollowed-out tree. Raven has always liked this cave. The space and grandeur are a fitting tribute to immortality, so what is it with Ricardo? These humans can be so … what's the word? *Silly* springs to mind. All this inner stuff fighting the outer stuff for recognition. But that's the human condition, *is it not, my Magnificence?*

It is.

It is.

I love you.

Yeah, I love you too.

Now he can continue. Raven clears his throat. 'You were a man of your time, old mate, you did what any king would do, but it's the same for everyone here. Judgement is a skewer through the heart, my Kingly King.'

At least now Ricardo feels lighter, less troubled. His soul may redeem itself. If he must confess in public, then he'll confess in public, but he's exhausted and can't think about the next bit. He did once, years ago, and look what happened. After that, a man invaded England and killed him.

27

Molly stays in London,

absorbing herself in her work. She is learning that changing the angle of light can reveal details of a leaf, the bark of a tree, a petal, an expression in someone's eyes that she never saw before. She even helps Suzi with the launch of an exhibition, which makes both of them happy, although Molly slightly less so. Suzi's excited. Lenny's excited and Molly's buying soya milk lattes, or three-bean salads and five bags of Percy Pigs at Marks & Spencer. When she's not working, she's walking in Regent's Park, taking close-ups of raindrops on leaves. She wonders if Suzi's mother encourages her or buys her clothes and says things like *Well done, Suze, I knew you could do it*, no matter what she's doing. Molly has an anger simmering inside her that makes her feel she can never get close enough to anything, no matter what she does.

She wants to dive into every tree and become the tree. *My arms are the branches. Hold me.* She wants to swallow the world, crunch on the bones. She wants to be wanted. She wants to be loved. She wants to drink buckets of rain. Dress in pink like a carnation, or red like a poppy, or white like a daisy. She is a bride of the oaks, a sister of every blade of grass. She talks to unfriendly dogs: 'I know how you feel.' She falls in love with the ducks in the pond. Gives them dried-out madeira cake and sets a table for tea in the park and invites the moorhens and gulls to join her. Her hands itch to capture every ounce of light refracted in the world. On every bus ride she lopes up to the top deck so she can see all of everywhere. At Westminster she waves to the statue of Boudicca: *Fuck those Romans, Boudicca, fuck them all*. Bach and Beethoven swirl through her headphones. Sometimes she plays Midnight Oil when her energy threatens to turn her inside out. When she crashes, it's Max Richter, or any other slow beautiful music to take herself down. She sings loudly in the shower and when she undresses she throws her clothes in a heap on the floor and tells every single item to fuck off – 'Go on, socks, jumper, jeans, off you fuck.' She eats a banana and a spoonful of yoghurt for breakfast, listening to the passing traffic in her small chilly flat. Mostly she's lonelier than she's ever been.

She reaches for the phone. *Call Gabe*, she tells herself, *come on Molly Polly, tell him you want to see him when* you *want to, not just when it suits him*. She decides against doing anything with Gabe, but then does it anyway. He's a friend, it's just a chat. *I'm lonely.*

They meet in her favourite Vietnamese restaurant, Pho, on George Street, close to his work in Hertford House. This is the first time she's seen him for a while and his eyes sparkle and his hair flops about in that usual beguiling manner. He looks good kitted out in jeans and a leather jacket. Classic. Her heart does a little hop and a skip. She orders her usual, a bowl of beef pho, and he has the tofu, and they slurp and eat, and their fingers touch as they rest their spoons on the table. It's a cold clear night as he walks Molly back to her flat.

'Val and I, we're not together anymore,' he says, brushing the hair out of his face.

'Oh, I didn't know, I mean you didn't say.'

'It's okay.' He shrugs.

Run, Molly, run. She imagines she is speaking. She says, *Thank you, but no. I've asked myself what I want and it's not you, Gabe. Even though I called you. Because I have a very full life, Gabe, so we'll leave it there, thank you,* but her mouth doesn't appear to be moving.

He sleeps with one arm over her like a fallen branch, too heavy to move. There's an awkwardness in him that wasn't there before. A new hurt coming from an old love. A history not made with her. A familiarity and yearning that belong to someone else. He's so warm and handsome but if it's comfort she wants she can get that from the cat.

Molly, you said you weren't going to be like this.

Did I? I don't remember. Besides, look at him, how can I say no?

In the morning she kisses the sleeping man, scrawls a quick note: *Going now, may never see you again, love M.* Not long to wait for coffee, she orders two more, then three, then five, energy pulses through her, setting her hands on fire, her brain whirling like a dynamo. The more she thinks, the worse everything gets. *Make it extra strong, stand the bloody spoon in it, please, there's a good barista.* At ten o'clock she unlocks the gallery door. She has a good mind to take all the paintings down and show the empty walls. Someone would buy them and talk about the intrinsic beauty of space and how priceless that is. Seeing Gabe again has stirred her up, especially now he's free to be with her. *Ask yourself what it is you want, Molly Polly.* For a second she's tempted to spray paint the walls. Black out the moons, the pond, the pictures, the beautiful rippling water. Triple the prices, bless the enigma, the absence, the void inside. Watch Molly Stern as everything she's ever done slides off the walls. When she gets like this, which is more and more often these days, she asks Suzi to cover for her, and leaves London and heads back to Oxenbridge. She could ask Peggy about her mother, but then her father wouldn't like that, and she doesn't want to upset him, even though he's dead. She's sure Peggy will know what to do with her, as she doesn't know what to do with herself.

28

Shed business

happens when Frank tucks himself away and animal-shaped clouds scud across the sky, when days of wild winds and stormy weather scatter branches and sticks across roads and pavements. In the manual Frank is writing in his head, it's important to tell the world what really happens when you age; the first thing he will declare is how your teeth shift and change as your bones wither on the vine. Food gets stuck where no bits of food have ever been before. Frank recommends taking dental floss everywhere you go. This was something he never thought of in the days of long ago when he was young. Every time he eats, he runs his tongue over his teeth to make sure he hasn't got a piece of spinach stuck anywhere. He spends hours researching in the shed, nibbling at things, checking his teeth, wondering if there's any way he might be an ancestor of Richard the Third or anyone else related to kings. When she was doing the hoovering, his mum always used to say, 'Don't know what happened to the castle, Frank.'

'It's here, Mum, this is it.'

*

The Trembles' shed

takes up the whole back end of the garden and makes the Farraday shed seem small, and dilapidated, which it is. From his bathroom window, Edward watches old Frank Tremble trundling up and down the garden path in his anorak.

When are you going to learn to drive, Edward?

'Soon, Mum, soon.'

Edward sniffs down the phone to Peggy that he has a bad cold. He can't make it to the shop. He hasn't been out of the house for days.

I love you, you are my son, even though you do not yet know how to be in this world.

Most nights Edward eats and sleeps in front of the gas fire in the living room. The warm gassy flames send him into a coma in less than ten minutes. Grey skies hang over everything like a blanket. In the end he has to talk to somebody and grabs his coat. *Mum*, he says to the drumming rain, *tell me who I'm going to be.*

Frank is thrilled to have a visitor.

'You hungry?' Because boys always are. 'What happened to your face?'

Edward shrugs. 'Didn't see the wall.'

'Next time then.'

'Next time what?'

'You'll see the wall. Cup of tea?'

It's just past five in the afternoon, which is usually wine o'clock, but Frank thinks better of it. Can't ply the lad with alcohol in the shed. Frank gives him an awkward smile and Edward hopes desperately that Frank isn't going to start talking about all the important things in life. Frank's never done that before, so why start now? He just wants to sit in the shed with another human being. Despite the renovation, the shed still somehow smells like a shed. Books and magazines and newspaper articles are scattered over the table.

'You like all this historical stuff?'

'Love it,' says Frank, peering over the top of his glasses.

'Frank, do you ever think you're related to someone famous?'

'My mum always said her side of the family was descended from nobility.' He pulls a face. 'Maybe it's true, but apart from that, not really.'

'Don't you want to find out? You might be a lord or something?'

'Maybe,' he says. 'What about you?'

'I wouldn't mind being related to Lewis Hamilton,' says Edward.

'He's great, isn't he?' replies Frank.

'Yeah,' says Edward, wondering how exciting it would be if Lewis Hamilton taught him to drive on the Silverstone track.

'Do you think people would still like you if you were related to Richard the Third?'

'They would love me even more,' says Frank, tapping away at his phone. 'Hold on, I'll show you something.'

A face swims into view on Frank's phone. The reconstructed face of Richard the Third. Kind eyes, bit of a chin, brown hair in a long bob. Edward thinks he looks a bit girly, with his hair and hat and sticky-out chin. Nothing special apart from the fact that you know it's Richard the Third.

'Doesn't look much like a child killer, does he?' says Edward.

'He looks kind,' says Frank, overcome with love. He sighs. 'This forensics professor, she made this from the measurements of his skull. It's so life-like, isn't it, looks as if he's about to speak.'

'Yeah, the boys were a pair of little shits, and he was glad to see the back of them.'

'Very funny,' says Frank, who for some reason appears to be taking flight, his arms spread out like wings and his cardigan flapping as he zooms round the shed. Edward rubs his eyes. Frank Tremble is still talking.

'Imagine being king at twelve years old. Although he wasn't, was he? The boy.'

I'd love it, thinks Edward, *being king. No one to tell you what to do.*

'No, poor boy, he was never crowned, but if he had been, then Uncle Richard was going to be regent until the prince was old enough to rule in his own right.'

'The woman who found Richard, she might find the princes.'

'She might at that,' says Frank.

'They'll be in a car park with the letter *P.*'

'They've all got those,' says Frank.

Frank offers him a biscuit, slice of toast, bit of Marmite and cheese, topped off with the tea. Edward briefly considers telling Frank about his escapade in the tunnel but decides against it. A lad must have his secrets, after all.

'Where's Peggy this evening?'

'Up at the house with Molly, sorting things out. Lots to do,' he says. 'Not much fun on your own.'

Edward sips his tea.

'Sorry,' says Frank, blundering around with his size ten feet, 'I know you're on your own too, Edward. You're always welcome here. Pop round any time.'

'Any chance of some more toast, please?'

'There's pizza if you'd rather.'

Five minutes later the microwave pings and a warm fug of food floats through the shed. Now he's feeling more relaxed, Edward changes his mind.

'Frank, this might sound like an odd question …' *Don't ask; once it's said, it's said.* 'But do you know anything about any tunnels in Oxenbridge? Being with the council and all?'

Frank has been chewing a bit of mozzarella cheese that has gone all stringy and resistant like the last piece of cheese in the world, but now he swallows it and wishes he hadn't. His glasses slide to the end of his nose. 'You mean a hidey-hole for a priest, like a secret passageway?'

'Yeah, something like that. Some places have them, don't they, where people hid in the war, stuff like that?'

The mozzarella has left a squeaky rubbery feeling in Frank's mouth. 'Not as far as I know,' he says, 'although Oxenbridge House does have quite a big cellar, and who knows what's hiding in there.'

Edward thinks of the man in the darkness.

'Why do you ask?'

'Just wondered. How old is Oxenbridge House?'

'I should know this. I think the original house was built over four hundred years ago, so Queen Elizabeth the First was still on the throne. Maybe she came to Oxenbridge too. Her grandfather was Henry the Seventh – he's the one who defeated Richard at Bosworth. He didn't kill Richard himself, his men did it for him, but I'd better not go on about that.'

'Oh, I don't mind,' says Edward. Hearing Frank talk makes him all warm and cosy, like his mum reading a bedtime story to him. He yawns. *Forget about the tunnels, then.* Rain throws itself at the window. Edward flicks through one of Frank's favourite books, *The Way We Used to Be*, with illustrations of the town from the sixteenth century through to the present day. One of them is a map of Oxenbridge with the Abbey of Stern on the hill behind Oxenbridge House, before the house existed.

'Can you imagine how it would have been then?'

'Not really,' says Frank, his feet slipping on the rug under the table, revealing a small brass handle inlaid in one of the floorboards.

'That looks interesting,' says Edward.

Frank keeps looking at the ground. 'That was there when we redid the place, it's just a silly thing really,' he says, sliding the rug back into place then yawning conspicuously loudly.

Edward checks his watch; it's ridiculously early but Frank is ridiculously old and anyway he can take a hint. 'Thanks for the tea.'

Funny lad, thinks Frank, when they've said their goodbyes. Why on earth would Edward Farraday ask him about tunnels? He packs things away, rinses plates and mugs, locks the shed door from the inside, checks his phone in his pocket, then pushes the table back against the wall and rolls back the rug. *It never gets any easier.* He's grunting and groaning – *very undignified for even a deputy mayor, but I'm not that anymore now, am I? Manual for old age: once you're down, stay down. Getting back up can cause delays.* He pulls the brass ring towards him with practised dexterity and the floorboards rise, revealing a square trapdoor with a folding aluminium ladder beneath it. He zips up his jacket, squeezes through the hole and carefully climbs down the wobbly rungs.

'It's storage,' he says determinedly to himself, 'somewhere for the boxes. There are no tunnels in Oxenbridge.'

Frank is wearing his comfy trainers

for the grip they give him on the sandy slippery ground. Once his feet are firmly on the floor, he double checks the ladder – *Yes, it's still there, waiting patiently for the return of Mr Tremble.* He praises the wisdom of his thrifty self. The tunnel he is now walking along is covered in a string of fairy lights. He bought them in the garden centre sale after Christmas; there was nothing in the bargain bin that stretched further, so after a hundred yards the lights end, but they're better than nothing. He's Blu Tacked a little battery-operated switch on the wall for them, and it gives him great pleasure turning it on. The place is so quiet he can almost hear the thoughts pop out of his head like bread from a toaster.

Edward Farraday can't possibly know anything about this tunnel, can he? The shed is clearly visible from Edward's house, same as all the back gardens in Castle Road. Frank has an odd tizz in his stomach. Why did Edward ask him about tunnels and why hasn't he, Francis Reliable Tremble, told his wife what he's been getting up to? He's worried about Peggy, doesn't seem quite herself these days. He doesn't like keeping secrets from her. His irrational self has always believed something terrible will happen without Peggy knowing. Their lives will explode, the house will burn to the ground. Molly will stop loving them, the garden will slide into the depths of the earth and nothing and no one will stop it.

His rational self says, *Stop it, nothing will happen, you're just a bloke investigating the darkness*, and even though he's quietly outraged by his own behaviour, he's reluctant to let anyone else in on Frank's Great Secret. The longest darkest tunnel he has ever known. Time stretches in a discombobulating way without familiar landmarks. He's in a catacomb of possibility, and later when he's thinking straight about everything he'll admit that, yes, it was odd how the tunnel appeared under the shed one day, before the renovations, after he put his boot through the rotting floorboards and nearly fell into it, but life is nothing if not odd.

After he says goodbye to the fairy lights he uses the light from his phone to guide him. There's a place where the tunnel roof threatens to drop on his head. He always stops here, never brave enough to go further, but if he's never going any further what's the point of coming down at all? A voice in his head whispers, *Go on, Francis Tremble, what do you have to lose? Take another step. It's so much easier than you think, doing something you've never done before. Who knows what you'll find, Frank.* He takes a deep breath, ducks, and keeps to the left like a good citizen of England.

There's something comforting about being so far away from all the noise and bustle of everyday life. In his head he measures the distance and can soon straighten up – professional potholer he is not – as the roof gets higher. The plan of the tunnel so far is mostly a reasonably straight line of twenty minutes' walking, before the gradual incline. The boy in him grows excited as the air grows fuggy and warm. Before long, the excitement gives way to panic, and a hot tight feeling grows in his chest. *I'm not a boy, just a silly old man who might be having a heart attack. Not now, for God's sake, not here.* He leans against the walls. *What am I doing?*

In the light of his phone the walls twinkle. *Steady, Frank, steady, you'll be okay.* 'Calcite,' he says to himself. Made from water dripping through the good old limey Buckinghamshire rocks. *Peggy, we've lived on top of this for years without knowing anything about it.*

He's soon to discover the walls are just the warm-up act. He takes a couple of big deep breaths, easing the tension in his chest. Another few steps and the tunnel leads into the mouth of a cave, widening out into a vast chamber with a thousand glittering stars.

Oh my goodness, get a cracking load of this.

He gazes silently around him, taking it all in. Crystals cover the roof, his torch light flashes up and down, back and forth, from the walls to the cave ceiling, one glittering shining thing after another.

Peggy, you will not believe this place.

This, Francis Tremble, is your reward for being brave, for pushing on. The size of it takes his breath away and the anxiety he was feeling soon disappears at such a magnificent sight. The walls are so shiny they look wet, but they are dry and rough beneath his fingers. He hardly dares breathe his germ-ridden breath upon them. Behold the tiny human in this amazing place. It demands a certain reverence, like a museum filled with ancient artefacts.

Mouth open, neck craning everywhere. If he's not careful, he'll get a pinched nerve in his shoulder. The cave roof must easily be fifty or sixty feet high. Layers of stony ridges run horizontally along the walls, and it looks a bit like an amphitheatre, but who could possibly come here? He marvels at the way nature has carved out such stony abundance.

Along one side of the cave wall is a series of little hollow grooves that look like steps, no doubt made by the ice-cream seller at the interval with tubs of vanilla ice cream and wooden spoons. It's dangerous on his own, but Frank cannot resist a little climb. He could edge his way from one side of the cave to the other along the stony ridges. Most are wide enough to sit on. He checks his footing as he goes and finds the gap between the steps varies hugely, so sometimes it's easy and other times he's not sure he can scrabble up to the next one. He stops for a bit and sits down. He didn't realise how far he had climbed.

A few lost feathers float through the air. The top of the cave can't be too far away. He checks his phone in his pocket. There must be a hole somewhere that allows the birds in. Much as he'd like to stay in the peace and quiet of this underground chamber, it's getting late and it's dark and he's left the lights on in the shed, and Peggy will wonder what he's doing. He gazes upwards, his heart full of churned-up anxiety about Molly and Peggy and Marcus and everything that's happened, and how he has to be there to catch Molly when she's falling, and she's falling now, and he knows it. He always tries to be there for her, and one day he knows he and Peggy will talk about her mother, but in the quiet of the cave he wonders if it is the right time for that now, or whether they should just wait a little longer.

Frank edges his way back along to the steps, and starts clambering down, which is much harder than going up, and his heart thumps loudly in his chest, protesting. *Come on, Frank.* His legs shake as he goes. *You're far too sedentary, Tremble, need to use the old pins a bit more.* The closer he gets to the cave floor the more his sense of urgency rises: he doesn't want to trip or fall or break an ankle. He misses the last step and slides most ungraciously the rest of the way to the ground. *Thank God*, he says, picking himself up and dusting himself down. The more he shines his torch light on the walls, the more they sparkle, until it looks like the whole cave is full of tiny stars, all twinkling at him.

'Wow,' he says, wishing Peggy was beside him to see this. A wave of warmth washes over him, he's sweating from his exertions, and for a split second he thinks he sees his mum sitting at the old dining room table with the lace tablecloth, drinking a cup of tea. He blinks hard and then she's gone. His mum always knew when he was up to something, but his mum isn't here. He shines the torch around just to make sure. His mum is tucked up in his heart, forever sipping tea. It's being alone in the dark that's made him like this. It's keeping secrets from Peggy that's made him guilty.

He reorientates himself, heads for the stone archway, which is where he came in. The air thickens and he goes as fast as he can. He really wants to be home with Peggy now, back in the warmth of what he knows. The safety and comfort of his dear little house in a dear little street, and the more he thinks about that the greater the panic in his chest. His heart thumps, it's nighttime, and a drop of sweat rolls down his face. *Hurry up*, he tells himself, with nothing but the swish of his trousers to accompany him as he races along, determined not to look behind him until the fairy lights come into view. *If there's a choice between freedom and knowledge*, thinks Frank, *I'll take freedom. Knowledge can wait.*

Frank's lungs

haven't worked so hard in years. He's as slow as an old tortoise lurching against the walls. The back of his throat itches and he sneezes, so feathers and dust must be here somewhere. *But I'm not in the cave. It's birds, bloody birds everywhere you go*, he says to himself, *this is madness, madness*, and just when he thinks all is lost and he's never getting home again, the fairy lights twinkle on the wall. Thank the Living Lord for that, what a relief, it's all okay. Now he can be happy that he was brave, and first thing tomorrow he'll tell Peggy about his discovery, because he can't stand that guilt, the red-hot shame of keeping a secret from someone he loves, the closest person in the world to him. *Silly old Frank*. He stops for a moment and takes a deep breath of gladness and then nearly jumps out of his skin because right in front of him is a large scary-looking bird, its round blinking eyes lit up by the torch.

He clasps his chest in relief. What a shock, it's only a bird, but still his legs go extra wobbly. At the same time, he spies the ladder right where he left it.

'Oh my goodness,' says Frank, 'oh my deary me, what are you doing here? How did you get here?' And as he's talking to the bird he's hauling himself back up the ladder without even thinking about what he's doing. He can hear the bird hopping beneath him. *Scritch scratch.*

Don't break now, ladder, he thinks, scrambling up the last steps. *Oh bugger, my knees. Come on, Tremble, you elephant.* With a massive effort he hauls himself into the shed. *Thank bloody goodness for that.* He turns to close the trapdoor and there's the bird, frightening the living daylights out of him, peering into the shed with its terrible beak and swivelling eyes.

In a wild panic, Frank shoos the bird away and hurriedly lowers the trapdoor into place. He can hear a big squawking fuss and sits quietly trying to gather himself, afraid that the bird is injured or will somehow come bursting through the floor, but how can it?

He double checks the hatch is firmly shut. Then he rolls a stone on top of it, then a boulder, and a mountain, then parks a truck on top of the mountain, and moves the shed down the road, leaves the country, moves to a farm in France, in the Loire Valley, where he lives with Peggy for the next twenty years, making goat's cheese from a herd of yellow-eyed goats, and he never ever mentions the night of the cave. He dreamt it, he was overtired, it didn't happen, and Molly spends every summer on the Farm of Great Happiness, and they all live happily for centuries like the free endless spirits that they are.

He listens for birdlike sounds, but what he hears is a voice coming through the floorboards. 'Oi, Mr Trembly, what did you do that for? Let me in, Tiger.'

Tiger? He snorts. *No one's ever called me that before.* His heart hasn't beaten like this for twenty years. He needs a whisky. The whisky is in the house. He turns off the lights. The rug is over the trapdoor. *Tap, tap, tap,* the bird is still there.

'I've come a long way to find you, Monsieur Tremblay. Well, not that far if you count to ten and whistle sixpence.'

Frank doesn't understand what the bird is saying.

Raven scratches his beak on the rung of the ladder, 'Come on, Tiger, there's things to say, like I love you, and have you seen an angel and perhaps we could have a beer together at the King's Head, but if this is how we're doing it, then this is how we're doing it.'

Frank rubs his eyes. No. That is absolutely it. Enough is enough. Everything that's happening here is all his fault, but he's not hanging around. No more voices, no more seeing things. *Peggy, I am coming home.* Frank scurries up the garden path in the cold morning. Trainers covered in dirt. A feather poking out from his sleeve.

29

That same evening

begins for Peggy at Oxenbridge House with the ready-made brilliance of a Marks & Spencer Thai green curry. Peggy loves it, Molly pokes at her food. Peggy waits until they've finished – Molly thirty seconds, Peggy a little longer – and the dishwasher has been loaded and the table wiped. Peggy has said no to wine, she wants to keep a clear head. She hasn't told Frank what she's doing. She doesn't want to hear him say, *Wait*, or *Are you sure about this, Peggy?* If Frank can keep secrets, then so can Peggy. With an inevitable sinking feeling in her stomach, Peggy takes a small rectangular parcel from her bag and slides it across the table to Molly. It looks lovely, wrapped in linen with a ribbon tied round it. Molly turns her nose ring round and round.

'Before you open it I need to tell you that this belonged to your mother, and Uncle Frank found it with your dad when he died, and I thought now would be a good time for you to have it.'

Molly is sitting with her arms folded, looking at the parcel. She has a distinct feeling she's not going to like it.

'What is it?'

'Open it and find out.'

She undoes the ribbon and the material opens, revealing a black notebook with the name *Sally Smallgood* scrawled across the front in thick white letters. Molly recoils and pushes it away.

'It's been over a year since Dad died. One whole year, so why are you giving this to me now?'

Peggy's speaking with a bagful of marbles in her mouth, the words rolling round and coming out all wrong. She's thinking, *We kept it until we thought you were ready, and you're ready now.* Also, *We're protective, Molly, the time had to be right. For you.* She says, 'Molly, please don't take this the wrong way. Your mother would have wanted you to have this.'

'Well, it really doesn't matter what she wants now, does it? Because she's not here and never has been, and I don't need reminding of her, thank you very much.'

She shouts that last bit and slaps the palm of her hand on the table.

Peggy winces. 'Molly, listen, please. There are things you need to know.'

'No, Peggy, you listen. Whatever this is, it's way too little and way too late, and it isn't going to fix *anything* because nothing can be fixed, and I'm not interested in it and I don't want it.'

Molly scrapes her chair away from the table and leaves the room, slamming the door behind her.

Wonderful, thinks Peggy. *So glad I've done that.* She leaves the notebook on the table and picks up her bag. It's past eleven o'clock, too late to call Frank.

Driving home through quiet night-time streets makes everything feel sad and empty, and Peggy only has herself to blame. She goes to bed all shaky-armed and thin-legged, not at all herself. The lights are still on in the shed and Peggy, now upset with Frank as well, takes ages to fall into a fretful sleep.

She has no idea that Molly has tiptoed down the stairs and taken the notebook back to bed with her.

30

Before battle with your beloved,
fortify the body with toast and Marmite. Frank is annoyed with himself for not checking on the bird before he came in last night but, honestly, and Peggy will most likely agree, if a bird is calling you Tiger, what exactly are your moral obligations to that bird? Still, at the least he could have checked to see if it was still hopping down there or injured.

It's the crow that sits on the garden fence, Peggy, that one.

Is it, my sweet good man? Well, whatever you did, it was the right thing.

What he rehearses in his head scarcely matters. There are thousands of birds in England, and they probably see everything. The real question is how to tell his wife about the underground storage solution.

His wife has not slept at all well and joins him in the kitchen, her battle helmet tightly fitted, visor up to see the enemy clearly, a loose covering of chain mail over her clothes. Her sword is still sheathed in a nice soft leather scabbard, but that could change depending on the conversation.

Frank wipes the toast crumbs from his mouth. *Peggy.*

'Where the hell were you, Frank? You were gone all bloody night. I nearly called the police.' She doesn't say how late it was when she went to bed or where she had been. 'Why didn't you call me? Or at least text.'

'Peggy, it's not what you think. I have to tell you something.'

'Whatever it is, I don't want to hear it.' She puts her hands over her ears, swallowing a mouthful of regret. She should never have given Molly the notebook. It was too much for her and now everything's too much for Peggy.

'Please, Peggy, listen.'

'Why didn't you call me?' She clanks around in her armour. 'And what the hell do you do in that stupid bloody shed?'

Peggy has been out at sea all night

in a small boat bobbing on the waves. Lonely and fearful that the love she trusts more than she trusts anything in the world is drifting away. She tries to haul herself back to shore but her heart won't let her. It thumps in an extraordinary way. Molly and Frank, Frank and Molly, what is the world without them? It is nothing.

'We'll talk later,' she says. 'I can't do this now.'

Ten minutes later she slams the front door behind her and drives to work with a low-pressure system coming out of her ears. She's too early for customers, and she's too early for herself. Her emotions have ridden out in front of her and she's struggling to rein them back. Frank can stay in the shed with his beloved king or whoever or whatever it is keeping him so distracted; however she turns it in her mind, and she turns it many ways, the inescapable fact grows that Frank's absences and inattention are signs he doesn't love her anymore, and without that nothing really matters. *You're too hasty, Peggy, always jumping to the wrong conclusions.*

Frank has admonished her a thousand times for the same offence committed over the course of a life well married, and everything is worsened by her not having said anything to him about Molly and the notebook debacle. And that makes her just as bad as him and she can't stand living like this.

'Sort your life out, Peggy Tremble, sort it.'

Today the shop is her hideaway. She locks the door, turns the sign to *Closed*. No one can see into the back of the shop from the road. In the tea cupboard, bottom shelf, sitting below the Earl Grey and the sugar and long-life milk, is a neatly folded green plastic Harrods bag, which is exactly what she's looking for. She'd deliberately put it on the bottom shelf as if it was the least important thing in the world.

A dress falls

through her fingers. Pale pink like the dawn, it's still the most beautiful thing. She remembers how Frank gasped when she wore it all those years ago, but the first time she wasn't wearing it for him.

She's had three missed calls from Frank. What to do? She holds up the dress, watches the light fall through it. Despite its loveliness, it's a reminder of the past. Maybe this is how Molly feels about the notebook, although that's from her mother, and this is just a silly dress and you're always doing silly things when you're young.

She could fling it into the river, but knowing her luck it would end up on the front page of the *Oxenbridge Bugle*: Dress Found, Where's the Body? What on earth was she thinking all those years ago?

She remembers that warm August night. Everyone was asleep in bed and she, Peggy Smallgood, was the only human alive in the world, and how exciting that was. She walked over the rickety bridge, the stream burbling in the night. Up to the house, creeping past everything with the back door key in her pocket.

She let herself in. Sally and baby Molly and Marcus were upstairs sleeping. She walked through the kitchen, undid the lock at the top of the cellar door, climbed down the steps into the room where the man was said to be. Sally had told her, *Peggy, he is an angel, he has come to visit us. I have seen him in my dreams.* Sally had been down to the cellar by herself to see if she could find him. Marcus had grown frantic and said Molly needed her mother in the house with her, not creeping around after an imaginary angel. Sally had gripped her arm with such intensity that Peggy was scared. *Peggy, he's here. I can hear him,* she said. *He's whispering in my head and he's coming for my soul.*

Frank and Marcus had told them both that the man in the cellar had gone, disappeared — 'We will never see him again' — but Peggy wanted to find out for herself. What if Sally was right and he was special? What if her sister could see something no one else could see?

She was wearing her camelhair coat and the dress underneath, with a pair of wellies over her tights. She told herself all kinds of stories on the way there. Just going to check the cellar, that's all, make sure it was empty, and she was doing this for her sister, Sally, because she was very shaken, she was not at all well. Peggy needed to make sure that whoever or whatever it was that had startled them from their dreams was no longer there.

She wanted to say, *Come out whoever you are so you can see the truth of me. Margaret Smallgood in my pink silk dress. Show yourself so I can see the truth of you.* The week before, she'd spent the day in London. Her wedding dress had to be different. Not the usual creams or whites. She was Peggy Smallgood, soon to be Tremble, and she did not want to wear a full-length gown. Frank said he didn't care what she wore, she would always be beautiful. In London she had trawled through market stalls and shops in search of the ultimate fabric and was just about to give up and go home when, finally, she saw it.

'Can't go past this,' said the woman in the Berwick Street shop, showing Peggy something beautiful under the ruin of sky that was England. Pink silk ran through her hands like water.

'When all the little silkworms die,' said the woman, 'they leave us this little gift. Pure mulberry silk, protein from a silkworm's bum. Make sure you cut it right, won't you?'

'I will,' said Peggy, delighted with her purchase. There was nothing she liked more than the folds of some new, beautiful material waiting for her clever hands to turn it into something special. She could picture this dress so easily, draping the silk round her before her scissors sliced into it. She loved bringing the dress into existence with small perfect stitches. When it was done, she twirled round the house, excited that the promise of the material was kept and made. She couldn't wait to show it to Frank on their special day, with Frank's ring on her finger. The dress hugged her body and warmed her skin. It made her feel special, taller, stronger, more powerful, and for some reason, when she wore it, she thought of the man under the house. If he was a man. If he was still there. She could lure him out with this amazing dress and take him to Sally. *Here he is, plain and ordinary Cellar Man.* It was all going to be better, especially for Sally, who was struggling with everything now she had a baby to care for.

Peggy gave her a hand with Molly as often as she could, but this time was different. Peggy was going to find that strange being, and help him, and help her sister, however she did it. It was as if his arrival had struck into all of them an unreasoning of the spirit, a desire, each one different, each one springing from that moment when the doors opened and, in the maelstrom of night, a creature from nowhere burst into their lives.

How things have changed. The dress probably doesn't fit her anymore and she thinks it's a blessing Cellar Man wasn't there because what would she really have done? Dragged him out with a rope, looking all fancy in her dress? Thank God she never found him. Let him fester in the dark.

Oh Peggy, what fools we were. If only we had done things differently, the dress tells her now, winding itself round her wrist, remembering the emotions sewn in with the thread. It wants to be worn. She'll give it to Molly and if Molly doesn't want it, it's hers to do whatever she likes with. Decision made. Peggy stuffs it back in the bag, calls Frank, no answer, pops out for coffee – *Where's Edward? That's his job.* The Khans' newsagency is open but then it always is. After twenty minutes and a double-shot latte, she's back in the shop. She doesn't feel well. The shop's spinning round. She drags the pavement sign for the shop down the steps – again usually Edward's job, she'd forgotten how heavy it was – and makes sure it's not obstructing Abbey Lane, while she imagines a cheering multitude willing her on. Everyone wearing white cotton T-shirts and high-waisted linen trousers, the colour-coordinated citizens of Oxenbridge all dressed in breathable easy-to-wear fabrics. *Calm down, Peggy, it's going to be all right.*

The day speeds past, she barely notices the hours. Every time the shop bell jangles she hopes it's Frank, coming to claim her. She pictures him in the shed with a glass of shiraz, his glasses steaming up as he dreams of riding with the king through the countryside, and hopes desperately this is all he's getting up to. Does he miss her? Does he want her by his side? She thought she always knew the answer, but now she's not so sure.

31

The library is a good way

to spend a chilly afternoon, and on Saturdays it's open till four. Warm and comforting; DVDs, newspapers, magazines, and books. Edward settles into the bean bag by the window with piles of books at his feet. Special subjects: kings, princes, quick meals, and whisked sponges. Cooking with Mr Oliver and Mr Ottolenghi helps balance the weight of history. Did his mother know her son and Young Prince Edward shared the same birthday? Prince Edward was twelve in the summer of 1483, thirteen if he had lived until November. Now he's five hundred and forty-three years old. Edward thinks it's funny how you can be quite fond of someone even though you've never met them. Prince Edward and his brother, Richard, forever known as the Princes in the Tower, were just boys, playing on the grass like all boys do. He imagines them with their bows and arrows playing at the Tower of London in those febrile final days of summer. Perhaps kindly Uncle Richard sharing a bowl of strawberries with them. The boys couldn't see into the future. They didn't know their lives would be written about like this.

Perhaps one day someone will write about the Not So Royal Edward Farraday, after the untimely death of his mother, emotionally off balance but still managing to make the perfect muffins. Every time he reaches for another book the bean bag rustles in an annoying way. It's one of those persistent sounds that teenagers make. Other library users give him disapproving glances for breaking the sacred peace and quiet of the library where they have escaped for five minutes on a weekend.

Books by his mum's favourite author, Katie Fforde, sit on the shelf looking bright and cheerful. No wonder she liked them. All his books are regal and solemn, weighed down by the past and two lost boys and a worried-looking king. Fancy thinking you were going to be king at twelve years old. That was when he, Edward Farraday, was in his first year at high school, struggling with algebra and girls and spotty cheeks. Not much has really changed: cheeks less spotty, still can't drive. His mum was going to teach him, but then she sat him down one day after school and told him the results of her mammogram. 'It'll be okay,' she said as she squeezed his hand, 'we'll be all right.'

No wonder she liked escaping with Katie Fforde.

The librarian gives him a quizzical look when he presents his mother's library card. Everyone knew Nancy Farraday. She whispers to Edward, 'You really will have to get your own card next time.'

Once he's home, he makes himself a big bowl of pasta with cheese and soy sauce. Sits on the carpet surrounded by books and no bean bag so he can't annoy himself.

Edward, please eat at the table.

'I'm not going to spill anything.'

Just do as I ask without arguing. I'm the one who cleans the carpet.

'I do it now, Mum.'

Those princes wouldn't have had any shit like that to deal with, being royal, especially not the older one, Prince Edward. He would have had valets and servants, and men to tuck him in, and men to tuck him out. He had his own beloved uncles until Uncle Richard arrested them for no reason other than they belonged to his mother's side of the family and Poor Young Edward never saw them again. After that he might have had an idea which way the wind was blowing. Still, he had everything done for him. Edward studies the painting by Sir John Everett Millais, *The Two Princes Edward and Richard in the Tower*, a centrepiece in one of the books. How could the artist know what the boys looked like? They didn't have photos back then. He reads more: the painter paid a couple of boys to model for him. Two skinny kids, caught forever in posterity, lending their faces to a story, and ending up in velvet breeches and pointy little boots on a staircase in the Tower of London, with only each other for comfort.

Edward wants to lead them into the light. He wants to make them safe and happy, look after them. They can be brothers together, and he's the wise strong one, making spaghetti for lunch and standing up for them at school. Keeping out the injustices of the world. His heart beats in an odd thin way. He wipes soy sauce from his mouth. Thinks of the man in the cellar as a message from the world. Telling him to *stop fucking around, Edward, because you never know what you're going to find.*

I've already found him. 'Who is that man in Molly's house, Mum? What's he doing there?' He's going to have to ask Molly. He takes his bowl to the kitchen sink and stuffs the last digestive biscuit in his mouth. In his mind he's Jenson Button going out for dinner, but here's the tricky bit: he needs to wash his biscuit down with milk, but there is no milk. Jenson Button would never need milk.

A train rumbles in the distance. Everyone's going somewhere. His mum's not there to tell him he's lonely and his father never was. He rarely sees his friends, with their cars and girlfriends and confidence. If he told his friends about the tunnel, they'd either laugh at him or want to join him, and maybe that wouldn't be so bad, sharing things with mates, but he hasn't talked to any of them for ages.

You still working in that girly shop?

Yes, I am.

He watches *Countryfile* so he can tell his mum about the hedgehogs. An old prickly fellow often wandered by the back door, and she'd leave a saucer of water for the thirsty beastie. She loved his snuffling nose and small spiky body. *I'm not a prince*, he thinks, *I'm a hedgehog, always out at night.* He waits until the downstairs lights are out in the Trembles' house and then he gets into his warm gear.

The night is cold, stars are stretched across the sky. Edward creeps through the garden, kicking overgrown plants and shrubs on his way, ones his mother grew and nurtured. *Sorry, Ma.* With a bit of luck no one will see him, unless someone is having a night-time conniption and looking out the window at three am. Then they would see young Edward Farraday making his way to his neighbour's shed *because he left his watch there and his mum gave it to him, he can't sleep without it, you understand, it's a talisman for him, and yes, he is a bit peculiar these days, but aren't we all? Grief turns you inside out, you know what it's like. Oh, you don't, well, let me tell you how lucky you are.*

Frank keeps the spare key for the shed under the cracked flowerpot by the shed door. *Most unoriginal, Frank*, but one thing Edward knows now is that you can't have everything. Can't be a good cook and think of unusual places to put your keys. He's going mad, half of him wants to be doing this, the other half wants to go to the cinema with Molly Stern. *She's super cool and we could eat m&m's and laugh, and I could just be normal around her, whatever the fuck that means.* Anyway, he's a hedgehog and the rest doesn't matter.

Quietly does it. Can't have Mr Tremble knowing what he's up to, but Mr Tremble is in bed snoring next to his wife. Everything is exactly as it was. The table pushed back against one side of the shed, just enough to roll up the rug. *Storage, Edward, it's storage.*

That little brass handle was the giveaway, Frank. Trapdoor opens, ladder unfolds, it's one easy move compared to the beam in the toilet. As he climbs down he wonders how Frank ever manages to do this. Then, instead of finding a pile of cardboard boxes, he's in Frank's underground disco, lit with fairy lights. *God bless you, Mr Tremble. That's really going the extra mile.*

'Ricardo? Where is you?'

Raven's back in the cave after his kerfuffle with Frank.

'Here,' says a voice in a corner.

'Come out, old mate, where I can see you.'

Ricardo shuffles out from his corner, looking the worse for wear. Legs not doing so well, feathers bedraggled and the hair, well, better not to say.

'The thing is, Ricardo, I'm a taxpayer,' says Raven, as Ricardo finds another part of the wall to slump against. 'I pay my taxes, yes I do, and I have a licence for Being Bird, and All Kinds of Soul Collecting, Straightforward, Difficult or Otherwise, which might or might not be you, my Kingly King. So, considering the affront to my personal person, I do believe it's only right that Mr Tremblay should procure his own licence for Not Panicking in Tight Situations at Your Own Actions type of thing. Yes or no, my Liegeless Liege?'

Ricardo says in a quiet voice, 'I just need the angel to take my soul to Heaven, only I am very tired now.'

Raven cocks his head to one side. 'The investigation, Ricardo, is ongoing. All lines of inquiry are open.' He flies up to a ledge, making the ascent look easy, and eyes the roof of the cave, preparing to launch himself once more, but then he stops. He has heard something in the world of men.

'Ricardo?' Voice calling down.

'What?' Voice calling up.

'Visitors incoming. Perhaps, my Liege of Nothing, we can offer them some ice cream.'

Ricardo sighs, remembering his icy fingers. He will never understand that bird.

Time flows

from one dimension into another, downhill, uphill. Edward swigs some water. There's a powerful quietness in the dark, away from a world where he has to work things out for himself. The lost boy. Like the lost prince, except nobody wants to kill him, although Frank might if he knows he's broken into his shed. His mother didn't mean for it to be like this, never once thought she would not be there for him. His father's nowhere to be seen, and even if by some miracle he did contact Edward, what would he say? *You're nearly twenty years too late, mate, so don't even think about starting now.* More than anything he wants a hug. A goodnight kiss. He wants the sound of his mum's voice in the morning and to come home to at night, but that can never happen now, so he just keeps walking.

It's cosy down here. The more he walks, the more he forgets the world above, until he hears footsteps behind him, and someone's big gaspy breath, and, without thinking, he breaks into a run. *Don't let it be that man again, please don't let it be him*, and before he knows what's what and who's who, his legs buckle beneath him and a tubby man in an anorak tackles him to the ground.

In his ear, the voice of Mr Frank Tremble telling him to quieten down. 'I'm not trying to kill you, Edward, it's okay, quiet now, there's a good lad,' and whatever else a man like Frank tells a boy like Edward yelling his head off in the middle of a dark tunnel.

After a while his sobs subside and once he's calm Frank lets go of him and rearranges his anorak. 'I saw you, Edward, in my garden, late at night, and thought I'd better come and check, and here we are.'

Edward blows his nose and blurts into the tissue, 'I miss my mum.'

'Course you do.'

Frank offers him a piece of gum, and they sit with their backs against the wall chewing in companionable silence, just to steady themselves.

'All right then,' says Frank, getting to his feet. 'Now you're here, there's something to show you, but one thing first.' He can sense Edward's disquiet. 'How did you know about this?'

Edward tucks his hair under his beanie. 'I watched you from the bathroom window. You were gone for hours, so I figured something was keeping you.'

'Right, I see,' says Frank. 'Well, next time, don't break into the shed. That's not okay. But you're more than welcome to ask if there's anything you need.'

Edward stuffs his hands in his pockets. *Caught, caught, caught.*

'What I'm saying is there's another way to do things, all right? Come on. Let's get going, I don't want to be gone all night.'

Frank thinks this might be a good time for a soothing chat on aspects of England's underground creations.

'All this, Edward, happens very slowly.'

Edward barely sees him as he gestures in the dark.

'Way before England had bears and wolves, and then way before that — we're talking millennia, really — water comes trickling through the ground, making gaps and spaces in huge unmovable objects. Then crystals form, and tunnels like these develop …'

Edward's grateful to be thinking about boring things like erosion. Stuff he learnt at school but never paid much attention to. 'Could there be other tunnels?' he says.

'There might be — you asked me that the other day.' Frank turns abruptly under a stone archway and Edward follows him into a jaw-dropping shining cave. The sheer size and height of it is breathtaking. Frank runs his hands over the walls.

'Look at this,' he says, 'it's magic, all these tiny crystals clumping together. They look like diamonds, don't they?'

Edward cranes his neck in every direction. 'It's like a great big chamber of stars.'

'That's a nice name for it,' says Frank.

'Peggy must love this.'

'Peggy hasn't seen it yet.' Frank clears his throat.

Should I tell him about the other tunnel and the man? wonders Edward.

The walls glitter.

Should I tell him about the bird? thinks Frank. *One thing at a time.*

'How high d'you reckon it is?'

'Dunno. Fifty feet, maybe more.' They stare upwards at the roof, the walls, the rippled stone ledges.

'What do you think made these?'

'Not sure. Maybe a flood, water flowing over time. Just guessing, I don't really know,' says Frank. 'I'm not a spelunker, although I am now, and so are you.'

'A what?'

'Cave explorer.'

Edward runs his hands up and down the walls, poking fingers into corners, squeezing himself into one of the hollowed-out steps.

'Fancy a climb?'

Up he goes, Frank clambering after him, emboldened by youth. Going for the same handholds and footholds as the lad, Frank inches higher. After a lot of panting, and a few big breaths, they reach the top of their shining kingdom. Two strange birds on a stony ledge, ruffled and bright-eyed in a world where everything feels possible. If Francis Tremble can climb a wall, then Molly will start eating again, the council will agree to fund the plaque, Peggy will relax about parking, and they will return to their best loving selves once more. Life will go back to whatever it used to be before the bones of the king.

Frank wishes Peggy was with him now, but Peggy is sleeping lightly on her side of the bed, worrying about Molly and Frank with every exhalation of breath.

'Frank,' calls Edward, 'something's up here.'

Frank wobbles on the ledge – *Careful, you're not Tom Cruise.* A jump to the ground will break his legs. His heart sinks. Not that bird again. Yep, it's the same bloody bird, and what a bird it is. It seems to grow larger the closer it gets. Its beak opens and words come out. The bird hops from ridge to ridge without a care in the world.

'Hello, Mr Tremblay. We meet again. And who might your friend be?'

Raven takes a good look at Edward Farraday in his puffer jacket and beanie. Edward answers as if this were the most normal thing in the world.

'I'm Edward Farraday.'

'Don't,' says Frank, 'start a conversation with that bird.'

'Hello, mate,' says Raven to Edward.

'Hello,' says Edward.

'No,' says Frank.

'Relax,' says Raven. 'Chill. Do you know,' he continues, waddling along the ridge nearest to them in as grand a manner as possible, 'what this place is?'

'A cave,' says Edward.

'We don't know what we're dealing with,' says Frank.

'It's a bird,' says Edward.

'My young mate is right,' says Raven. 'Can't get anything past him. Anyway, Gentleberries, here we are.'

Raven turns to Frank. 'Mr Tremblay, it has taken a very long time to ask you a simple question. Are you ready?'

'For what?'

'If you would be so good as to please tell me where the Angel of Oxenbridge might be, so my special guest, the one and only Ricardo, may finally leave.'

'What is it saying?' asks Edward.

'Something about an angel,' mutters Frank, feeling hot and cold at the same time. He knew in his bones. Everything always went back to the same night so many years ago. And now it's here again. Like this. He's not ready, he will never be ready. He was showing Edward round the cave and now his heart is spiralling downwards quicker than a deflating balloon.

'I think we'd better go,' says Frank.

'Frank, I have to tell you …'

'Not now, Edward,' says Frank, clambering down as quickly as he can.

'Frank, there is another tunnel, and it goes to the cellar of Molly's house and there was a man in there.'

Frank stops momentarily. 'That is absurd. There are no men in any tunnels,' he says, forgetting that he's one.

The bird is waiting. Edward is waiting. Frank is climbing down, all that exhilaration trickling into his socks.

'Mr Trembelle,' says Raven, hopping down effortlessly beside him, 'do not be afraid of me. How about an invite for tea, and then we can have a real man-to-bird chat. Nod if you agree.'

Frank realises he must have nodded, as there is a flapping of feathers and then nothing. The cave has fallen silent, apart from the grunting of breath and the sliding of trainers and feet.

'Ricardo,' calls Raven, 'you getting all this?'

Ricardo watches from the shadows against his comfy wall.

'There you go,' says Raven, 'Messieurs Trembelle et Farraday. Your everyday grocers, no bargains for the soul considered too small.'

Ricardo watches an older man bustle out of the cave followed by a younger one.' 'Do we accompany them to the angel?'

'Ricardo. They're human, they'll always come back. Did you not learn anything from being a kingly king? All you have to do is put your feet up.' He indicates the ledge. 'Have a kip. Get used to your new home.'

Lesson number five hundred and thirty

for the ageing: staying up all night is for young people, not old men. *The angel.* Hearing that name has set something off inside Frank, some sense of inescapable wrongness, and he doesn't like it. That's his punishment for keeping things from Peggy. He wriggles through the trapdoor, his head emerging like a giant mole, with Edward not far behind, bidding Frank goodnight and thanks for the adventure. The boy jumps the garden fence and is back in the safety of his home in less than two minutes, leaving Frank brushing dirt from his face and watching Peggy making tea at the kitchen window. Peggy in her dressing gown and morning face. Peggy who has messed things up with Molly. Peggy who doesn't want to hear what her husband will say. Peggy who leaves the tea bag in the cup for far too long, ruining it all.

32

Molly hasn't spoken to Peggy

for weeks since she gave her the notebook. She misses her, but not this personal relationship nonsense. Look where that gets you. Absolutely flipping nowhere. She asks Suzi what she would do about the notebook.

'I'd get a big bottle of Prosecco, and a joint, and then I'd read the fuck out of it,' she says. 'I mean, Mol, why wouldn't you? You've only got one mother. It's a gift, so enjoy it.'

Lenny saunters in, wearing his cool but expensive stripey cotton shirt. Molly waits for a quiet moment and asks him, in an odd unlike-Molly voice, what her mother was like.

'You really want to know?' he says.

'That's why I'm asking.'

He thinks for a minute. 'When I knew her, she was the loveliest, most talented girl I had ever met. A tiny bit' – he holds up his thumb and forefinger – 'like you.'

Then Lenny gets on his phone about the upcoming exhibition and the gallery hums with its usual life of sales, prints, photos, people, and Molly's barely listening to anyone. Apart from Lenny half an hour later showing her a picture of the model Celia Hammond in the 1960s. 'A bit before Sally's time, but back in the day, she looked like that. Bloody gorgeous.'

A wild energy sweeps over Molly. She talks to visitors about the choices the artist has made; for example, the way an artist has translated the moon in all its stages – waxing, waning, quarter half comet Jupiter Earth meteor shower right there in the corner of the tile, the woodcut, the lazy afternoon. 'There is so much light in this gallery, ladies and gentlemen, it is coming out of my ears.'

People look bewildered and then amused by Molly's enthusiasm.

'Is the colour palette of Anish Kapoor a choice, or a compulsion?' she muses. 'I don't know, but my guess would be red is for power. Red is for love.'

When people tell her they would like to wander round by themselves, she floats to the top of the ceiling, watching the people below watching her.

She can just hear Lenny. 'Molly, are you all right?'

She checks in with her father every day, same time, ten to eleven, the time Marcus always liked his coffee.

'Hello, Dad,' she says.

Hello, Mol. Tone it down. They'll think you're mad.

'Maybe I am.'

She tries not to think about anything, but the notebook from her mother has opened something inside her and thinking is mostly what she does, apart from Gabe. The problem with Gabe is his wife, Valerie, has a permanent residency in his head. He never talks about her, but Molly can feel her sitting alongside him, marking him with her absence. Anyway, it's Friday night, and she's the one having dinner with Gabe. They often end up at Molly's place with a Thai takeaway, but this time they're going to eat at a restaurant. Her treat: she's sold three small, very expensive prints of the moon by a German printmaker whose name she can almost remember. She's pleased with herself. Looking forward to the date with Gabe. Both finished with work for the week, so it's normally a happy time.

Frank loves cooking curry,

she tells Gabe, who has never met the fabled aunt and uncle of Oxenbridge. She's about to invite him to the house for the weekend, and is working up to it, but can't quite utter the words yet. She wants to wait for a special moment and take his hand and say something like *Seeing as we're getting along so well, shall we go to mine, my other home, my large and empty house so you can help me fill it*. She's still not speaking to Peggy, and Frank hasn't phoned her to see what's up and he always, always, phones her. *How's my Molly Chops*, he says, which is always silly, but she loves it.

She's halfway through a mouthful of rice paper roll, light and digestible. Gabe, usually a quick eater, pushes his food around the plate. Instead of smiling, he's concentrating on rolling his serviette into a tiny scroll.

'Molly,' he says.

She knows what's coming. 'No.' She wipes her mouth, not wanting to hear his pathetic whiny voice.

'We've decided to give it another go, we thought we owed it to each other. You understand, don't you, Molly? I never said this was serious. Molly, wait'.

She grabs her bag and struggles out from behind the table, trying not to drag the plates and bowls along with her, as they would smash to pieces on the floor and that would not do at all. Out she goes, heart pounding, trying not to be as upset as she bloody well is. *It's all okay, take it easy, Molly Chops*, and she tries, she really tries to take it as easily as she can. She walks calmly from the restaurant, even though her blood is thumping in her ears. Well, there's another place off the list, because, honestly, the food used to be fantastic, but now it's just terrible.

She sprints across the Baker Street lights, dodging busy Friday night traffic. She races down the street, trying to put as much distance as she can between them, bumping into people in her urge to get away. She doesn't want to hear Gabe's voice or see his tall lean body, but he's fast too and, when he finally catches up with her, he grabs her by the arm and she swings round, eyes blazing.

'Let me go, let me the hell go. Why didn't you tell me sooner?'

'Mol, I'm so sorry, I didn't want to hurt you.'

'Yeah, well, I am nowhere near hurt. Nowhere bloody near.'

She wants to shove him in the chest. Stab him through the heart with her favourite fruit knife, just to see if physical pain is easier to bear than emotional pain. Then she could ask him, writhing on the ground like the worm that he is, *Which, Gabe, do you prefer?* She leaves him standing on the street corner as she heads to the station. Who is she kidding? It's all her own fault anyway, *Silly Molly Stern, you should never have called him in the first place, should you?* She takes a few deep breaths. *What can you do with a fruit knife, Molly?*

Slice an apple.

Peel an orange.

Exactly.

She turns and watches him for a long time, until he becomes a speck of a man weaving through the streets. 'Have a wonderful life with your wife,' she yells into the night. He can't possibly hear her, but that felt good. At Marylebone Station she tops up her Oyster card and buys a double-shot extra-chocolate cappuccino, even though it's far too late for coffee and she won't be able to sleep. She wonders if the policeman next to her in the queue can sense her murderous thoughts. Who cares anyway? She hops on the train with two minutes to spare and, just as they're pulling out of the station, right at the very end of the platform, there is a nun standing by herself surrounded by an eerie nimbus of light, her white robes blowing in the wind with a strange fragile beauty. What a shot that would make. Molly presses her face against the window, and the nun points directly at her as the train goes into the tunnel. *She was telling me she loves me*, thinks Molly, wanting to call Peggy right now but not knowing what to say. Suzi is spending the weekend in the gallery with Lenny. Gabe's going back to his wife, and it will be late by the time Molly returns to Oxenbridge alone.

She sips her coffee and thinks of her father.

Mol, life is hard, life is suffering, life is duty, then you grow rich.

That poor old nun, she thinks, *only gets the first three, and what do you get, Molly?*

The house is cold and dark

by the time she arrives and in her heart she would like to be curled up at number 10, but that's just not possible right now. After she's greeted the lions and hung up her coat, an extraordinary listlessness comes over her, as if the whole house is covered in a thick mist, preventing her from doing anything except sinking further into the chair. She feeds Max, who is always happy to see her and follows her up the stairs to bed.

'You still love me, don't you?' She checks his blue eye, wondering if she can see through it into the past, where shadows wait for her to find them. She sleeps, then wakes at eight o'clock, and her phone tells her it's Sunday, so she sleeps again. *Don't want to get up, don't want the day to begin, don't care if it has, and it clearly has*, as someone is knocking at the front door. 'Stop it,' she says, but they don't. Finally, she throws off the bedclothes, pulls on her moth-eaten jumper and goes downstairs, grumbling all the way, only to find Edward Farraday with his scruffy stupid hair standing on her front doorstep. In his hands, a green Harrods bag.

'Yes?' she says as if they were already in the middle of a conversation.

'Hello, Molly.' He hands her the bag. 'Peggy asked me to bring you this. She says if you don't want it, give it to Oxfam.'

She peers inside the bag. A scarf or something.

'Peggy said also to ask if there's anything you need?'

'Thank you, no. I am fine. Really. *Fine.*'

She cannot stand his teenage boy-band messy hair, and she can hear someone horrible telling him exactly that.

'I'm sorry but seeing as you are standing on my doorstep I have to tell you that long hair is for men who have nothing better to do. You might think that not cutting your hair adds to your charisma, and the girls will love you, but all it does is make you look positively medieval, and you must ask yourself, is that who you are, Edward, someone from the Middle Ages?'

Edward looks surprised. He wants to tell Molly he and Frank met a talking bird and the bird asked about an angel, but he doesn't know how she'll take that. Not very well, probably.

'And I bet, Edward, that even men from those tedious long-ago days soon realised that messy hair just gets caught in the helmet and doesn't help *anyone* with *anything.*'

She might have shouted that last bit, she's not sure, and she's never going to tell Edward that the real reason she hates men with long hair is because Stefan – beautiful, funny, selfish bastard

Stefan – had hair she wound through her fingers and adored as it fell gently, lightly, sweetly, over his face when he was sleeping and how she can't bear to be reminded of that anymore.

Edward doesn't appear to be listening. He seems fascinated by his feet on the doorstep and sniffs loudly.

What is wrong with him? What is he doing? She wants to roll him down the path and push him in the river – *kerplunk, splosh.*

Oi, Molly, what did you do that for?

Just looking at you annoys me, Edward. So, thank you, good morning, and off you fuck.

She's tired, he thinks,

walking back down the driveway, wondering what's wrong with his hair. Maybe he should wash it. Instead of leaving through the gates he lopes along under the trees, following the wall around the garden where he's fairly sure Molly can't see him. Perhaps he'll ask Frank for driving lessons and save up for a car. Spoke wheels, rear spoiler, so he can drive out of Oxenbridge and into the rest of his life. Ask Molly if she wants to come. She'll probably say no.

He finds the path to the abbey ruins through the adjoining gate and watches clouds scud over ancient walls and what's left of the latrine block. He can't imagine taking a shit with someone sitting beside him, but at least they had someone to talk to. He skirts round the graveyard and circles back to the house, past crumbling stones, round by the old stables, and peers through the kitchen windows of Oxenbridge House. No sign of Molly. He tries the back door, locked. What a mess, he thinks, unwashed bowls and plates, mugs half full of tea. *We're the same, Molly, you and me, and I can save you.*

Molly goes back to bed,

and does not emerge until late afternoon. That's what
Sunday is good for. Sleeping. Resting. Eating an apple. Gabe
and wife. Wife and Gabe. She empties the bag Edward gave
her onto her bed. It's not a scarf, but a very pretty dress. Silk,
no label. *I bet she made this herself.* She sits on the bed, stroking
the material, then calls Peggy. It's a relief to hear that familiar
voice again.

'Hello.'

'Hello. How are you?'

'Is it one of yours? I mean, did you make it?' Molly lies on
the pillow. She just wants to cry, but Peggy is talking to her in a
low calm voice about the dress.

'I married your uncle in it, but I won't wear it again and I
thought you would like it. I'm far too old for it now.'

Peggy making it about her, making it easier. She loves her,
she really does.

'Why didn't you bring it round?'

'I've got a lot on,' says Peggy, 'you know, and I wasn't sure
you wanted to see me.'

'Well, maybe I do.'

'I do too,' says Peggy.

'Peg?'

'Yes?'

'It was a shock. Seeing her name like that.'

'Oh, darling, I'm sorry, I should have asked you first.'

'I'm glad you didn't, I would have said no, but I love it and
I'm keeping it.'

'The notebook?' says Peggy. 'That's so good.'

'The dress,' says Molly.

She slips it on, takes a selfie, and sends it to Peggy with a heart underneath.

She needs love, thinks Peggy, *we all need so much love.*

The stony magic

of an afternoon walk round the abbey ruins for the millionth time in her life has a soothing effect on Molly. Perhaps people back then weren't as cold and miserable as she has always thought they were. The lives they lived were the only ones they knew. Like her. Maybe the nun on the station platform was pointing that out to her. She thinks of Suzi saying, *You've only got one mother*, and her father looking at the notebook before he died. That evening Molly takes out her father's neatly folded shirt from her top drawer and by dinnertime she's unlocked the cellar door and chosen an expensive bottle of wine as her evening's companion. She carefully unwraps the notebook from the shirt.

'Forgive me, Dad.'

Nothing to forgive, Mol. It's there to be drunk. Go ahead.

'No, Dad. I mean this, Mum's notebook.'

I know what you mean, Mol.

The cellar has a calm peacefulness, tucked away from the rest of the world, enhanced by a candle and a packet of herb-flavoured crisps. The armchair is deep and welcoming but has a spring that pokes her bum as a way of saying don't get too comfy here. Max pads down the cellar steps after her, and jumps on the camp bed, purring loudly, and she absent-mindedly strokes his ears, enjoying his warmth and company. She has her phone, the lamp, the dangly light bulb, the candle, and a cat, and she could not ask for more. *Do not be afraid, Molly Stern, you have chosen to be here.* She begins to understand why her father liked spending time down here and briefly catches his scent.

Still here, Mol.

She drinks a toast to him, 'Dad, I will always love you.' Then her grandfather, the patrician Jacob Stern. Marcus always told her his father believed stability and family rooted a man in the earth, no matter how badly behaved he had been before. Marriage required a man to sober up and confirmed in him all aspects of duty. That had been his experience and, like all deluded men, he thought his was the only one that counted. He was wrong, said Marcus, because duty doesn't count when you marry for love.

'Where is she, Dad? Why isn't she here?'

Sweetheart, you've got me, and you've got Aunty Peggy and Uncle Frank.

Her father was always evasive when she tried to talk about her mother, and if she asked Peggy and Frank, then she would be the one betraying her father and that never felt right to her. She half wishes Peggy had never given her this book, but her father's not here. She tops up her glass, drinking in the peace and quiet. What did Marcus call her when she was little? *My fearless girl. Well here I am and who the hell are you? You think you can walk out of my life and then just walk back in with your little black book, Sally Smallgood.* Even saying that name in her head makes her heart thump now she's finally alone with her mother.

She turns the first page.

From the beginning

she is spellbound. Page after page of clever intricate drawings. It's like being in an art gallery that she's dreamt about but never visited. The palms of her hands ache like they do sometimes when she gets excited. Each pencil drawing is contained in itself and beautiful, bold strokes of feathers and wings, and petals and leaves all drawn with wonderful precision, which makes Molly's heart yearn for the wonder. Across some of the pages her mother has written over and over, *Winged creatures shall cover the earth, and you will tame them.* Then the name changes – *Sally Stern, Sally Stern, Sally Stern* – in those same thick letters. Towards the end of the book, there are half-finished sketches of a painting Molly knows well. *The Abduction of Psyche*, by William-Adolphe Bouguereau. She liked it when she was a romantic teenager, but now she feels sorry for Psyche. *Why so impressed by a man with wings? Ditch him, Psyche, before it ends in disappointment.*

The final drawing is similar to the others but the man has a giant pair of wings and is standing by himself, with a gaunt hollow face looking up to Heaven. Molly can't stop staring. Underneath it her mother has written, *The Angel, Sally Stern, December 1989.* There's nothing after that, just a couple of empty pages at the end.

If there really was an angel, what the hell has he been doing all these years? She would like to tell her mother that her drawings are beautiful, but how can she? She's reading her missing mother's notebook and talking to the cat. Bugger that. She doesn't know how she's going to change it, but change it she will. Life happens, we're all caught and tugged by desires we claim not to know anything about. Gabe flickers in and out of her consciousness. She half thinks of telling him she absolutely does not love him, but the other half of her can't be bothered.

I value myself, I value myself, I value myself.

She's read enough Philippa Gregory books (one) to see how ancient kings and queens could serve up death to loved ones who betrayed them, like a retaliation for the hurt. Betrayal is a punch

in the guts, a cramp in the belly, an ache in the softest parts
of yourself. A few weeks ago, she bumped into The Betrayers
coming out of Baker Street Tube. They were holding hands,
of course they were. Stefan always liked doing that. She should
have pushed them into the traffic and yelled as the cars squashed
their bones, *I've done very well for myself, thank you.*

The stinky old sleeping bag slides from the bed as Max jumps
down. Mice or rats are scrabbling in the walls. *Time to go, enough
of this maudlin nonsense.* She blows out the candle, checks her
phone is in her pocket, trudges up the steps, turns off the light,
shuts the door, makes a cup of tea, her body light and floaty. *Too
much wine, Molly Chops.* Max scratches at the door. 'Hello, Max,'
she addresses the cat flap. The cat grunts back at her but since
when did Max do that? She's nicely drunk, swaying from table
to chair to counter, so the shock of what happens next is muted
by disbelief. A hand with hideous wormy fingers comes crawling
through the cat flap, attached to a hideous wormy arm. Without
missing a beat, she stamps as hard as she can on that hand.

The grunting turns to moaning, the fingers close like a sea
anemone and the hand withdraws. *Who the hell is that?* If she
hadn't been drinking wine all evening she might have been
tempted to call the police, but instead she rams a kitchen chair
against the cellar door, then goes upstairs with the notebook,
rewraps it in the shirt – *Thanks, Dad* – puts it back in the drawer,
then grabs her hockey stick from the corner of her room where
she has kept it for years for exactly this purpose. *You're coming
with me.*

She bangs the hockey stick on the kitchen floor to show she
is not mucking around.

'Come on then,' she yells, 'show yourself. Whoever you are,
we're waiting for you.'

The cat flap moves again, but this time it's only Max coming through, cool as a furry cucumber.

Oh, bloody hell, Max. She moves the chair out of the way and gets down on her hands and knees then peers through the flap but can't see anything. Max sits there yawning.

'Right,' she says, 'that's it. I'm coming in.'

The whole evening has been very challenging. Back down the cellar steps she goes, fuelled by wine and a hockey stick and a dangly light that lights the way down but not much more. Checks her phone is in her pocket. She's not sure what she's going to find. Someone with a sore hand. She shouts into the darkness to make herself feel better, 'I am coming to find you, and I'm not leaving until I do.' Her voice skips around the walls, bounces from the wine rack into the bricks, and into Dedalus, hiding in shadows out of sight, clutching his arm, sucking in the pain.

It's the angel coming into the house for the very first time.

'You would have made him a nice cup of tea, wouldn't you, Daddy?'

That's right, I think he would have liked that.

As if it's a bloody angel. She imagines her father keeping company with some mad old hermit, his long beard matted with wisdom, just the two of them talking nonsense and sharing a glass of wine by candlelight. She calls out again and is met with more silence, so she bangs the hockey stick against the wall. Tough, fierce Molly Stern, forgetting how low the ceiling is and hitting her head. *Bloody hell, that hurts.* She doesn't want to die here — *Not like you, Dad, with Uncle Frank finding me like a skeleton, like that bloody king.* Dry throat, throbbing head. *Get out of here, Molly. Leave and never look back.* It was the wine making her hallucinate. There is no sign of anyone and nothing she hasn't seen a hundred times before. She's at the foot of the steps when someone clears their throat.

She turns around.

'Who's there?'

Her heart is the loudest thing in the room.

'Don't even think about it or I will hurt you if you come near me,' she says, so they know she's not messing about. She steadies herself, and at first she doesn't understand what she's seeing.

He's so completely still, his eyes drinking in what's left of the darkness. He's gripping the back of the chair, and this looks so perfectly normal that at first she almost disbelieves what she's seeing. *Molly, he's not really there, is he?* But he really is, and somehow she's not frightened, although her arms tingle and her heart threatens to jump from her chest. She rests the hockey stick against the wall and carefully pulls out her phone to put the torch on.

'Who are you?' she says, without moving an inch. She has the advantage and can still grab the stick and whack him if she needs to. 'What are you doing here?'

Thin face, big hollow eyes, hair falling everywhere. *It's Jesus, come to save me from my sins.*

'Who the hell are you?' she's shouting, but shouting won't do any good. He's not deaf, he just doesn't understand. He raises a painful hand to shield his face. The light is clearly blinding him, but she cannot look away.

33

It's only when

she's calmer and guides him up the cellar stairs to the kitchen, and offers him a cup of tea, that she realises there's something wrong with him. Hermit or not, he needs some help, so she, Molly Stern, will help him. After all, he might have been a friend of her father's, although what her father saw in him, she's not sure. His breathing is laboured. He holds on to a kitchen chair and watches, transfixed, as water runs from the tap.

'Can you tell me your name?'

The kettle shrieks in the corner. He's riveted by everything.

Dad, what am I going to do with him? Who is he? Dad, seriously, is he the reason you made up the story? Everything she thought is wrong. He's just an odd man living an odd life and the least she can do is feed him before she works out what to do next.

'Fried egg?'

She gets the eggs out of the fridge, and he reaches out a hand to touch them. He's giving her the jitters and she talks to fill the space. 'They're free range, obviously, although why I'm telling you that I really don't know.'

Five minutes later, she plonks a mug of steaming tea in front of him, then watches him rub his nose on his ragged robes. She pushes a plate of food over to him. 'Eat,' she says, so he eats with his fingers. The egg glistens, twirling in the light. Her nerves stretch tight across the room.

'There must be someone I can call. A friend? Your family?'

If he gets too comfortable, he may never want to leave. She should call Peggy and Frank, they'll know what to do, where to take him, they might even know him. He sits with his head on his arm, digesting the food. She watches him. *Call them,* she thinks, but something inside her does not want to. She's searching for an answer, but maybe there isn't one. *What's wrong with you, Molly, he's just another messed-up man,* and she's letting him sit and eat at her table. She's not running a rehab clinic. She doesn't want the dirtiest man in the world wobbling about in her kitchen. Perhaps she should drag him back down the cellar steps and listen to the thud as he falls. *There, problem sorted. That's where you like it, that's where you stay.*

He slides to the floor and looks more comfortable there.

'I'm sorry, but now you've eaten, you have to go.'

Look at him. He's clutching the table leg like it's his only friend, and when she tries to pry away his fingers and help him to his feet, his strength belies his feeble appearance. He gets up slowly, unfolding himself. Stretching his arms, flexing his legs, moving his head from side to side, and taking in big deep breaths, filling his lungs with new air. He straightens his back and seems to grow an inch or three as he takes a long slow look at everything in the room, including the worried face of Molly Stern. She steps away from him, unsure of everything. Not wanting to listen to her own thoughts. Ten minutes ago, he was a tramp living in the cellar; now he's different, changed, not an odd old man after all, but someone younger, as if a thick swirling fog has lifted from him. The longer she stands there watching him, the more familiar his face becomes, but she can't place it in her lexicon of being.

'Who are you?' she asks again. 'And why the fuck are you here? I'm Molly. Molly Stern. Do you understand?'

After a pause that seems to last for hours, he says her name. Repeating it back to her in a way no one has ever done before.

34

She wonders what to do.

'Dad, he's all yours.'

Maybe he'll set fire to the place. Maybe he won't. Maybe this is all too much for her to handle and she needs space and work and routine and a sense of normal, normal, normal Molly Stern.

'Dad, I asked him his name, and do you know what he said?' *Dedalus.*

'I mean for goodness sake, Dad. Did you really spend years in the cellar with *a hermit named Dedalus*?'

What if he isn't a hermit? There is always a gap between how you imagine someone to be and how they really are when you meet them. And if she can't trust a face she knows, why not start with the unknown?

Dedalus. Of course it is; it could never be anything simple because nothing in her life is simple. She laughs, doesn't mean to, and says, 'Well, you're a legend then. Father of Icarus, maker of wings and mazes.'

Dedalus. She's giving him plenty of chances to disappear back into the past or wherever this being in rags sitting so calmly in front of her has come from. All these years she's thought of the angel as a strong benign presence, but if this is him, then she is truly done. There will be no avoiding someone like him.

She knows that without knowing how she does. She gives him a bottle of water, a sandwich. Leaves the cellar door unlocked. 'Make yourself at home. I'm not staying. I'm going to bed.'

Dedalus. The sanity of her life in London seems like a good idea. Leave it all behind, especially him, because, really, what can she say to Peggy? She wants to tell her everything, but more than that, she wants joy and sex and love, and she's not going to find that here.

She rehearses all the things

she wants to tell Peggy. 'Peggy, you're never going to believe this but I came down this morning and found him watching a tea bag spin round and round in a bowl of milk. Milk everywhere. He doesn't understand how we do things. Watching the kettle boil is better than the telly and he hasn't even seen that yet. The gas stove is more powerful than God.

'Peggy, I've met someone. The cellar is his home. He's been here for a long time, but you know that don't you? Remember the story Dad told about the angel? Well, I bequeath him to you. All of it, house, Dad, grounds, ruins, tourists, parking, driveway, lions, all of it. Peggy, Frank, have it all. Have him. I give you … Dedalus.

'Peggy, my mum left me, so I'll leave him. It's easier that way.'

Energy flows through her as if something has changed, but it hasn't. She's seen him, that's all. She'll go back to her life as if nothing has happened. Which it hasn't.

Peggy, this is my new plan for living.

There's no point locking the cellar door anymore, he could always come through the cat flap again, except she knows he won't. Wherever she is in the house she is aware of his presence.

She doesn't sleep well. Early the next day, which isn't early at all, after a spoonful of yoghurt and half an apple for breakfast, pretending no one is there, she heads down the cellar steps to say goodbye.

There he is. Waiting for her with his big curious eyes. He gets up when he sees her, as if he's going with her.

'If you can't handle a kitchen in Oxenbridge, a train to London will probably kill you. Anyway, you're too sad to go anywhere.'

She can see it etched on his face, at least sadness is what she thinks it is – sadness is what she knows – some dislocation of self, a misalignment with who he thinks he is, and where he finds himself now. It's like looking at herself. And he looks so cold, and she can't help it, she moves closer and strokes his hand. He closes his eyes as if a memory has woken inside him, his breathing slow and settled, which quietens her anxious thoughts.

'All right,' she says. She really will go now because she's touched him and he's real, and she isn't afraid of him, and maybe the light is playing tricks as he always looks taller when he stands. She hears herself say, 'Come on then.'

She hasn't planned anything, just finds herself doing it. Leading him out of the cellar with an odd feeling that he is miles ahead of her, even though she's way ahead of him.

A mountain of lime and coconut

bubbles before him in the bath like a foaming miracle. He wriggles his toes. She adds the cold, doesn't want to scald him, doesn't trust that he knows how to do it himself. Doesn't know if he hears her. Doesn't want to touch his filthy old rags, they're disintegrating anyway. Doesn't know what's inside his head. What he understands or doesn't. Maybe more than she thinks.

'I have a train to catch,' she tells him. 'But it's okay, I'll get the next one, or the one after that.'

'Thank you,' he says, because that's what he's good at saying.

She closes the door and leaves him to it. His feet absorbing the shock of the water before he sinks into the foam. Molly listens outside the door to check he's not gurgling or drowning, then enters that timeless zone when you think you need to see what someone is doing, but also want to give them the benefit of the doubt for just a little bit longer. She pulls the notebook out of the drawer, sits on the bed and studies the last few pages. Mr Lime and Coconut has the same face that her mother had seen. Her heart beats loudly in her thin little chest. She puts her head round the door, as anything might be possible with this man. Drowned, flown, or fled, never to be seen again, but bits of him are still here poking through the foam. When he sees her, he covers his privates.

These are mine, he is saying.

You can keep them.

After several years, when he's finally hauled himself out of the water, and when he's dry and glowing pink, she notices a scar on his face she hadn't seen under the grime. The shoulder-length hair is a problem, but she can deal with that.

She's given him an odd assortment of clothes, some from her father, including an old pair of track pants she'd tossed in the bottom of the wardrobe. They're too short, but what the hell. At least he's clean. His robes are so old they're like worm castings; they'll never survive the wash. He looks like he wants them back, so she offers him the bag, *You're welcome*. His hands brush against her skin, and again he closes his eyes at such softness, breathing her in.

The bath is filthy, the towel goes straight into the wash. *How did he get that scar on his face?* She hasn't asked yet. He looks at himself in her bedroom mirror, as if his reflection will provide him with clues in this new reality. She watches him, thinking of her mother. *She saw you just the same as me.*

The outside world

doesn't seem so exciting anymore. The next day, or the one after that, she must return to life and work. Part of her wants to stay. She likes the company of this strange recalcitrant being, but Suzi is having a dinner party, and she was looking forward to it, and if she doesn't go Suzi will want to know what she has been up to because there is nothing to do in Oxenbridge. She won't tell her she thinks she has an angel living in the house. Although she hasn't seen any evidence of that. No wings, no clean unworldly skin.

Next day she packs while he sits in the kitchen looking at a thousand things.

'I have to go now,' she says.

What was her father thinking? He's nothing like she thought an angel would be. She texts Peggy, *See you soon, thanks for the dress* ♥♥✿. She had to fight the urge to take photos of him before and after his bath. She stopped herself, knowing it was wrong to intrude on his inmost being, but she wanted to. She told herself to let him be because he's different. His eyes have a grace about them, a light that's coming from inside him, whichever way she looks. But it's time to go, it really is. The everyday world carries on around her as she walks to the station, puzzling over everything before the train takes her thirty miles back to the present.

35

It's November already

and Edward Farraday is nearly twenty years old. Birth sign
Scorpio, his mum was Pisces. He doesn't care about star signs,
but she was always telling him what they meant. Edward would
like his mum to make him that special birthday chocolate
cake, but he has to do it now. Birthdays should come with
rules. The person undergoing the birthday must never make
their own cake. Penalties apply. For his birthday he would
like Molly Stern to love him. She did say *Hello, Edward*, so
that's a start. He rolls up his sleeves; he'll feel better once
he begins. Separate the eggs. Melt the chocolate, stir in the
ground almonds.

Let it cool properly before you make the ganache.

'I know, Mum.'

Half the ganache for now, half to finish the cake. He blows a
kiss to his mum. She loved the way melted chocolate looked so
beautiful. He sings 'Happy Birthday, dear Edward' to himself and
to each of the princes in the tower. Don't need candles. Would
prefer a hug from Mum and his hair ruffled in that endless loving
way she had of reminding him what a little bugger he was as a
boy, all those sleepless nights and wet mattresses, but that's what
being a mother is all about, and she still loves him.

He takes a couple of slices round to Peggy and Frank, lite sour cream for Peggy, otherwise she'll die from a surge of cholesterol before midnight.

'Should have told us it was your birthday,' says Frank, eyes swimming in his head. 'This is bloody delicious!' Frank points his spoon at Edward in appreciation of his skill. Peggy is annoyed with herself for not remembering, and annoyed with Edward for not reminding her, and upset with Frank and feeling slightly better about Molly, but she still should have known about his birthday and made the cake herself, or asked Frank.

'Ever thought about your coat of arms?' asks Frank, out of the blue.

Peggy rolls her eyes.

Edward eats his third slice of the day, licking the ganache off his fingers. 'I think the Farraday coat of arms would be a spoon, and a whisk,' he replies, 'and a head torch.'

Peggy and Frank both look at him.

'They're useful,' he says. 'What would yours be?'

'A shed, a saucepan, and a sewing machine,' says Peggy.

'We could get one done,' says Frank, warming to the idea, 'and hang it from the shop, you know, like the Royal Coat of Arms, if you're a tailor to the Royals.'

'I'm not though, am I? And I don't think it would attract anyone, would it, a garden shed?'

'A sewing machine might,' says Frank.

She shouldn't have said anything. Now he'll want to do that as well as the plaque. His mind leaping from one idea to the next, while Peggy Tremble can't remember her Young Man's birthday. Head like a sieve. She wipes her face with a tissue.

Anna Wintour never became a world-famous fashion doyenne with chocolate round her mouth, but Peggy does not want to become like Anna Wintour. She wants to be more like herself, if only she could remember who that used to be.

36

When he's not selling

wool-and-elastane-blend tartan socks to match the trousers,
Detective Farraday keeps himself occupied on the case of the
man in the cellar and the talking bird. Since his birthday, he
has temporarily suspended his baking days. The cupboards are
empty apart from half a packet of rice and a tin of tomatoes, and
there's not much in the fridge. He's polished off the barbecued
chicken, which was a day past its use-by date, and a slice of toast.
He cut the mould off the crusts, threw them outside for the birds
and toasted what was left, accompanied by a wrinkled tomato,
which was the lonely vegetable left in the fridge.

Edward slurps his discontent down with his tea.

A tomato is a fruit.

'Mum, I don't care what it is. Something's going on in
Oxenbridge and I'm going to find out what it is. There are
strange men and strange birds, and I think it's something to do
with Molly Stern. I'm going to see her tonight, so I'll ask her.'

Are you going on a date, Edward?

'Just at hers.'

Edward, I think you should find someone your own age.

'I'm twenty years old now, Mum, that's old enough for
anything. Besides, Molly needs someone, why can't it be me?'

Beanie on, hair flicking round the edges.

Time for a cut, Edward.

Edward bounces along to 'Happy' with Pharrell Williams, all the way to the abbey ruins. He's not tunnelling tonight, he needs air, the deep familiar of the night, landmarks he knows. Thousands of stars join him from the galaxies. As he sings he exhales puffy little clouds of breath, his voice winding through empty streets. He's already determined he'll be the only night-time visitor to the abbey. The boy on a date with a girl who doesn't know he's there. The lad with nothing better to do than hang around ancient walls and old houses. When he ducks into Abbey Lane he's almost tempted to dive back into the toilet tunnel but fights the urge. He's a cold, hardy investigator. Fresh air is doing him good.

Twenty minutes later, after a few stumbles on the overgrown path, with his head torch mostly off – can't draw attention to himself – the abbey walls belong to him. He takes a few deep breaths behind the women's block, unaware of all the prayers and devotion to the Lord contained in those small rooms. Oxenbridge House is covered in darkness. *Please do not climb or sit on these walls. Thank you.* There's always a sign that needs disobeying. He edges past the old church, half a building open to the sky, over the bumpy courtyard, and tries the kitchen door. Locked, of course, why would it be open? He's wearing gloves, so no fingerprints for Detective Farraday, and he was hoping Molly would be here, cooking and laughing and inviting him to share a bowl of mussels and sweet chilli sauce, but life doesn't work like that.

All year he's hoped Molly would take a little notice of him, but she's busy, distracted, and he knows what that's like, but he's here now, keeping an eye on things. He trudges round the house, trying every door. At the front door he pats one of the stone lions, which ignores him completely. Front door also locked; the place is a fortress. The living room windows are secure; they overlook the front garden where he now stands churning up the winter flower beds. The curtains are drawn so he can't see in, apart from one small gap where they don't meet. He takes his head torch off and puts it in his pocket. That's better. He peers in, remembering the house from childhood. The times he played with Molly, not often, and not for years. He had forgotten how large the rooms seemed to him. He can just glimpse the hallway through the living room door, one sofa, and half the fireplace by the window. No welcoming fire. He longs to sink into that sofa, put his arm around his girlfriend and for Molly Stern to kiss him on the cheek.

Hello, my darling, what can I get you? How was your glorious, wonderful day? I've made so much food just for you, and dessert is a lemon polenta and poppyseed cake.

Those little bits of Molly's life look so plush, so soft. A shadow walks down the stairs, moving fast, too tall for Molly, heading Edward's way towards the living room windows. A man; long hair, tall, skinny. *I don't want him to see me*, thinks Edward. *Molly, you didn't tell me you had a visitor. Who is he? Doctor? Painter? Electrician? Boyfriend?* Edward can't see too clearly, but he's walking around as if he owns the place. Maybe he does. Edward loses sight of him and ducks away from the windows, and in doing so he blunders straight into the unmistakable form of Muffin Man. He's a fast mover if that was him in the house, and he looks different from last time, but he's out here now. No time for questions. Edward wants to get away.

Muffin Man is in his bare feet, a worn striped shirt, way-too-short track pants and Marcus's old Christmas jumper. His eyes are glowing like Christmas lights and the more Edward moves away, the closer Muffin Man comes. Edward tries to kick him, but he dodges everything. Edward has no idea Muffin Man can see five times better than he can in the dark.

'I will hurt you if you come closer,' says Edward, knowing he won't.

Muffin Man bows to him. 'Please,' he says, 'you are most welcome.'

'I'll call Molly.' Edward panicking.

'As you wish, it makes no difference to me.'

'I'm going to call her.'

I don't know her number and she won't listen to me anyway. There's nothing else he can do, so Edward makes a dash for it, pelting down the driveway, but he doesn't get far before this badly dressed freak catches up with him. Edward is yelling his head off, but there's no one to hear him and the man picks him up and throws him over his shoulder as if he were made of nothing. Muffin Man walks to the end of the driveway, taking absolutely no notice of the young man on his shoulder, barely breaking a sweat. Edward might as well be a feather, a banner, a bunch of dried lavender.

'Let go of me, you maniac.'

Maniac won't release him. Maniac is walking back in time with him. Over the cobbled courtyard. Fieldmice twitch in their nests, worms burrow through the rich soil, and voices travel through the air. Maniac puts him down at the gates.

'Now,' he says to Edward, 'what is it you wish to say?'

Edward straightens himself out and picks his beanie up from the ground where it has fallen. Maniac stands very still, watching, breathing in winter.

'I'm going to sue you for assault,' but by the time Edward has said this, Maniac has effortlessly climbed the front steps and is closing the door behind him. Edward doesn't know how he reached the house so quickly. His knees shake and his stomach hurts. If he goes home, perhaps the man will follow him, and, if he does and Edward invites him in, he might share a bowl of pasta with him and some cake, and if that happens Edward's enemy might turn out to be his friend.

By the time he's reached Crown Street, his mind is full of little jolts of thought, like lightning in a distant storm, and he stops, trying to gather the parts of himself knocked out of place by this encounter. He considers turning back. His tummy's still doing somersaults and the pavement looks all wobbly. A weight is pressing on his shoulders, and it came through the man's hands. *Who is he? What will become of him? Whatever shall he do?* He covers his face with his hands. *Go home, Edward Farraday, go home.*

Jessica Khan, the newsagent's daughter,

up late studying for her GCSEs, opens her bedroom window for some fresh air and sees a young man standing on Crown Street. She recognises him. It's Edward Farraday from Off the Peg. He passes the shop most mornings to buy coffee and she served him once when he bought some stickers.

'Hello!' she calls to him, and he looks up.

He gives her a little wave. 'Hello.'

'What are you doing?' she asks.

'Nothing.'

'That's better than studying.'

Passing traffic makes it hard for them to hear each other, so after another quick wave goodbye he sets off for home.

Jessica watches him making his way down the high street. *He's funny*, she thinks, closing the window, suddenly way too tired to study anymore.

37

Days and nights lengthen into darkness

as the earth sleeps under its quilt of winter. Some parts of the world remain the same: bare branches, brown fields, muddy paths, scarlet berries draped through hedgerows. Dedalus sleeps for hours, with little sense of passing time. The abbey ruins are closed for the season, and Molly Stern, the woman with the nose ring, is nowhere to be seen, which is better for him. Less distraction for his endless tasks of discovery. His strength is returning. The more he eats, the faster he moves. He saw the boy walking past the old church, his church, the place his journey started, and he hasn't forgotten. The past rises inside him. That boy reminds him of Silas creeping around with his broom, peering through the dark. That nothingness waiting to be ignited into something. When he slung him over his shoulder, his bones dug into his body and he could feel the sorrow in his heart. Seeing him for the second time must mean something is shared between them, but what to do? Pray with him? Walk with him? Carry him?

He is slow and careful with everything he touches. Metal, plastic, tin, paper. How have these things been made? He does not recognise his face in reflections, but no one else is there. Every day he walks round the ruins of the abbey. Parts of the northern wall of the church are still intact, faring better than most, but there's still not much of it left. In low winter sun he runs his hands over the walls of his life. The women's block is now a jagged wall. He turns his face to whatever warmth he finds, trying to feel the memory of her breathing through the stones.

He is like a man waking from a deep troubled sleep, only to discover some of his family have died while he was sleeping, and the world has changed now he is so much older. The life he once lived remains unreachable. Time has slipped past him, and he doesn't know how. If he is here, where are the rest of them? Some of the graves in the churchyard have no markings, they're too old. Is one of them hers, and if it is, what would he find? Nothing but bones. Not her sweet face, or the shock of her hair sliding from her veil. His pulse still quickens at the thought of her. He remembers how she called him to save those souls. He has not done what she asked him to do. He can feel a faint drumming coming through the earth. A beat of otherness calling like a misplaced star spinning on its lonely path.

Everyday life is puzzling and ordinary. People laugh and cry and eat and sleep and walk over the same cobbled stones. All the bowls and pails, pots and ink, ledgers and rolls, knives and quills, flour and corn, linen and latrines, the altar, the altar cross, the candles, the miller's dog, the shriek of Jessop's breath. Gone.

The Holy Mother. Gone.

Silas. Gone.

Sister Alice.

Gone.

He's become so used to the dark

he hardly sees it anymore. It's just what he goes through to reach the light. When Dedalus walks into town, history walks with him, marvelling at itself in shop windows. *Is this me? Is this really who I am? You have raised me, Lord, from darkness to walk upon this earth again. If I am not Dedalus the monk, then who am I?* He heads towards the giant moving things. There are many different lights, on the roofs, in people's hands, in shops; the world is full of startling lights flashing in so many forms he does not understand, and he longs to ask someone, anyone, what do they *mean*? Buttons and shining levers, steam, and food. No one ever told him it was going to be like this, but no one ever really told him anything, except what he must not do. He longs for the certainty of Jessop. He dreams of cabbages and goats, and the warm hands of Sister Alice. He asks himself what has the abbey become now but holes in the sky?

The shaking of the earth announces a shining metal beast. Behold, the arrival, and he cannot help but tremble with excitement as the thundering beast passes by. A hurtling mass of sound and doors and wheels. Where are the cherubim and seraphim? The beating of drums, the radiance bursting forth from the heavens? It is all jumbled up in his head. A voice speaks from the clouds as the stink from the beast lingers in the air: 'For your own safety, please stand behind the yellow line.' If that is God at his most instructional, then he obeys, but standing behind the line does not make him feel any safer. The noise of the world drills into his bones.

The station manager has seen worse than Dedalus, staring at everything and nothing as the train pulls out of the station.

Dedalus memorises the way home, otherwise he will turn and turn again and end up crying in the hawthorn. There are so many streets, so many houses, so many objects falling into his eyeballs. Shops full of faces, glasses, hats, bags, books, bottles, pictures of food he's never seen before. He does not know what they are or why they are there. His body takes him onto Crown

Street, past the shop with staring lifeless people. He leaves a patch of breath on the window. Walks on and the way becomes familiar again. The parish church, St Stephen's, is at the far end of Crown Street.

The church pulls him like a magnet to its gate. Will the Lord offer comfort to his soul? The doors open and beckon him in. He's half expecting to see the Holy Mother on her knees at the altar, and Jessop whispering in her ear. This church is full of benches, numbers, plaques, books, bowls, hassocks, the font he recognises. The smell of wooden pews and flowers almost overpowers him. He sits at the back looking up at the rafters of the ceiling and the stained-glass window. It seems to be dedicated to men who fought in a great war. As he slowly reads about them, he tries to imagine such a thing, a battle bigger than the one which killed the king.

We didn't pray hard enough, says Jessop.

Be quiet, he says, *be quiet*.

He kneels at the altar, praying to the Lord.

Too late, Dedalus, too late.

He cannot tear his eyes from the wooden statue of Christ, head bowed, suffering on the cross. The candles aren't lit. A huge bunch of flowers stands to one side. The pulpit, large and wooden, is like nothing he has seen, but the church he knows and understands. Humans are sinful scheming creatures and need forgiveness. He tries the vestry door. Locked. The side door does not lead to the crypts but out to the graveyard, which he'll wander through when he's had enough of the church. The hymn numbers are still on the board, and he recites them to himself, not knowing what they mean.

This world is full of numbers, but goodness is beyond measure. Goodness is virtue and virtue is prayer, and prayer and salvation are the only way to stop sin. Every day you have to start again and define yourself with virtue, but how easy is it in the world he has just walked through? This world he is in. On his way out he sees the church notice board welcoming everyone to the Sunday services. Through the glass he can see only one day a week devoted to God. There are other pieces of such thin paper with so many names that mean nothing to him.

Feb 14th: Dr Wesley Blackwood on Poisoning in Victorian Times. Come and enjoy an unusual talk for St Valentine's Day.

March 30th: Alison Swindlehurst on Wildflowers of Oxenbridge.

April 12th: Mrs Khan's Cookery Club Classes recommence. Places limited, book now!

Inquiries to Mr Francis Tremble regarding the Oxenbridge Commemorative Plaque celebrating King Richard III at the Abbey of Stern. 1483–1485: The most interesting dates in English history! +44 1865 188 126

He reads the name again: *King Richard III*. Rain edges into his boots; he found them in the cellar. They don't fit him, they belonged to the man. Cold feet are his punishment. One life swirls into another. The king's visit to the abbey. His perfect teeth. His fingers glittering with rings. His hands running through the lavender. *I remember you*. There's a persistent echo in his head. One thought collides into another. *The king has followed him here*. He needs the peace and quiet of the cellar, the chant of

Morning Redemption, the cobbled stones, the whistle of the red kite. *How can the king be here?*

He breaks into a run, feet slipping in his boots. Time has strengthened him, he is stronger now, lighter, faster, the road becomes his in this borrowed world. His arms outstretched like wings, like a bird. Only memories belong to him here, and the king, at the heart of them. And her. His boots beat out the rhythm: *God's Grace, God's love, God's forgiveness for our sins, for my sins.*

We didn't pray hard enough for the king.

38

Peggy's morning drive to work

isn't quite early enough to avoid the commuters. Headlights blazing, she joins the never-ending line of cars on the old London Road crawling through the rainy darkness. She usually enjoys the simple peace of driving alone in her car with nothing but the radio between her ears. It's a buffer between home and work, a way of soothing an anxious heart, but today she's finding the heavy traffic annoying. One bright thought is that the bones of King Richard the Third will finally be reinterred in Leicester. Put him back in the ground, get him out of the way. All the worry. All those arguments she had with Frank.

'Doesn't matter where he's buried, does it, he's dead? He won't know and he won't care. He'll get a nice service, and a tomb, and a headstone, which is a lot more than some people get.'

'Son of York, Peggy, that's his spiritual home.'

'Why do you even care, Frank? A man like him. He killed his nephews. Children need protecting, no matter who they are.'

'You are absolutely right, Peggy, they do, and it might seem daft to you, but maybe one day we'll discover the great villain of history isn't so bad after all.'

'Well, I bet wherever he is, he's loving the fuss. After all this is done we could go on holiday. Maybe Florence? Check out the Renaissance.'

'Florence?' says Frank, surprised. 'What's wrong with Leicester?'

'Leicester is Leicester, Frank, it's nothing to do with us, is it?'

Peggy thinks of Edward, eating pasta for dinner on his own. She wants to rewind the days. She doesn't want to worry about Frank in the shed anymore. She wants walks in the woods, and laughs, and cuddles in the evening watching some snow-laden Scandi drama. Goodbye tartan trousers. This year the colour palette is ochre, lemon yellow, and cream. She has bamboo socks and merino wool thermals, thick creamy knitted scarves, and gloves. The oncoming traffic has slowed, car horns are beeping, she hopes it's not an accident, a mass of broken lights and twisted metal reminding her of the strange fragility of life.

For God's sake. She swerves so hard her bag falls off the back seat. He just flew out of the dark, she didn't see him until she almost hit him, the man running in the middle of the road. *Get off the road, you bloody idiot!* She nearly swipes a car coming in the opposite direction. *Fuck, fuck, fuck, get off the bloody road!* She mounts the pavement, engine running, hands shaking, no one hurt, nothing damaged, just a shock, a shock. She sits behind the wheel, shaking. That's what she gets for being angry with her husband. Everyone beeps as they wait to drive round her. The man causing such chaos is standing in the middle of the road as if he has every right to be there. Tall, bedraggled, long wet hair, face briefly lit in the headlights.

Rain spatters her head as she yells out the window. 'What the hell do you think you're doing? I could have killed you.'

Her voice sounds thin and small. He turns in her direction, so she gets another look, and then a sickening in her guts shatters her quiet morning. She eases back into the traffic. *Slowly, Peggy, slowly, turn the wheel, run him over, knock him down now you have the chance.* She indicates right into Crown Street, turns round at the bottom of the road where she usually parks in the spaces reserved for the church, chugs back the way she came, turns left out of Crown Street and heads back down the old London Road.

Light is coming

in the gloomy sky. Unaware of the mayhem he has left in his wake, Dedalus, now back in Oxenbridge House, kicks off his boots and leaves the outside world behind. He dreams his way back to horseshit and dust in his nostrils, his brain brimming like an overfilled pail. Is the king here too, a spirit in this world like him, rearranged in some God-given form? His hacked and beaten body. He cannot unsee it. The pail spills his thoughts into confusion. Spared by God, His Most Sinful Servant, look at him now, flushed with guilt over so many things. He begins to understand that once your soul is pampered and fed, that's how the Devil tempts you. A loyal monk, devoted to God, but who is he when there is no abbey to hold him? As a loyal subject you pray for your king, but he only knows the one he prayed for and look what happened to him. The abbey is in ruins, his old life has gone. He barely recognises the world God is making him live in, where people have more possessions than he can understand and yet there are always more to be had. Perhaps this is one last chance to assuage his soul as he didn't pray hard enough for the king.

Back in the cellar he breathes more easily. The woman in the car said he was an idiot, yet where should he walk if it is not this path? He asks God to take him back to the river, to the courtyard, to the stables, to what he knows. The life he lived, the skeleton walls, the bones.

The windscreen wipers comfort Peggy

with their quiet regularity and she just sits listening to them as the car engine idles in the rain outside the gates to Oxenbridge House. Gone are the days when she and Marcus would have coffee together after taking Molly to school. If Molly was late, and she frequently was, Peggy would end up driving her anyway after Marcus told her to walk and take the consequences. Where have those days gone? There is no sign of the idiot on the road; hopefully he's been dragged away for making a nuisance of himself or washed away in the rain. She knows what she saw, but who to tell? Molly is in London, Marcus has gone, Frank is distracted all the time. Rain pounds on the car roof. *It is not him*, but every fibre of her being tells her that it is. She never forgets a face, and it was impossible to tell how old he was with all that hair. If that is who she thinks it is, then he has been around for a long time, but he didn't look or move like an old man.

Perhaps most men, when they reach a certain age, want to run down the road wearing a long coat. She thinks about Frank, and her father, and wonders if men over fifty should be fitted with a warning, like flammable material. *Keep away, keep away, keep away*, because wherever that fire burns, everything around it burns too. Even her father. The seemingly Respectable Mr Smallgood could not stop the desperation of middle age. It started with him taking guitar lessons at the age of fifty-four. He'd paid for each of his daughters to learn the piano and now it was his turn. *At least it's not flying lessons, Peggy*, her mother had said. Now they just bring home a euphonium they bought on eBay. They've always fancied it, didn't you know, didn't you listen carefully enough over the years? Everything is your fault and so is the affair they'll inevitably have with someone younger at work. That too, will be all to do with you and what you didn't offer him.

She can hardly bear to remember the arguments between her parents and the sorrows of the Smallgood family. Something deep and precious ruined so easily. She learnt from her father that men do shitty unpredictable things to those who love them the most. One last rush of testosterone before those ageing bodies end up on the pavement with wobbling knees and hairy ears at four in the afternoon, crying for a good lie-down. Reliving those days and how she supported Sally and her mother turns Peggy inside out. She believed life with Young Francis Tremble would be kind and loving and fun, and it was, so she cannot bear to think of Old Francis Tremble now finding happiness with someone else. It happened to her mother, surely the same thing won't be happening to her.

Peggy, the truth is the truth.

The car has fogged up. She's surprised she hasn't seen Frank flapping his arms and flying out of Oxenbridge.

Look, Peggy, I'm a bird, I'm free.

Yeah, whatever.

Peggy's anger turns to the idiot. She'll have him arrested on suspicious behaviour, although apart from the fact he was in the middle of the road, he's no more suspicious than anyone else. *The past never goes away, does it, Peggy. He's here, he's bloody well here.* She takes some big deep breaths and tells herself it will be all right. Then she reverses out of the driveway and drives slowly to the shop. The morning disappears somewhere. She calls Frank after lunch.

'I've made a quiche,' he says.

'I don't care if you've made a replica of the Tower of London out of jelly,' she yells and then hangs up. That's not what she intended, and nowhere near as exciting as it used to be on a good old-fashioned telephone. Then you could really bang the receiver down. Now it's just a button on a screen. A long slow scream is building inside her. When she's home she watches *MasterChef*, which she usually hates, and longs for the days when Frank was happy making butter chicken.

Talk to him, Peggy, tell him who you saw today, then let him tell you he doesn't love you anymore.

Frank spends the evening

picking at the sleeve of his cardigan. It's the unravelling; once they start to go, they go. Sewing is Peggy's thing. He cooks, she sews, that's how they've always worked. He's never questioned it. They've kept their promises and they've always trusted each other, and now she's watching cookery programs in the living room and he's thinking about sewing in the kitchen. They're normally chatting away about the day they've each had, with queries and jokes, but tonight they're both overly concentrating on the Pad Thai noodles and king prawn stir-fry that Frank threw together with just a little too much chilli.

'What do you think?' he asks.

'Bit hot.' She finishes her glass of water. She can never say hard things straightaway; she has to unfold them in her mind, otherwise she'll blurt out any old thing and ruin something that wasn't meant to be ruined.

I gave Sally's notebook to Molly, Frank, without telling you, so if you can just tell me who you're sleeping with, everything will be fine.

'So, is this worth mending, Peggy?' He holds up his sleeve. 'Or shall I splash out and buy a new one?' He has a dob of sauce on his sleeve and a large hole.

Peggy can't stand it anymore. She finishes her water, should have had the wine.

'I need to tell you something, Frank. I can't bear you not knowing anymore. I've given Molly the notebook.'

Frank looks stunned for a minute. 'Sally's notebook? You gave that to her without talking to me about it first? I bet that went down well.'

'I thought it would help, but she was really upset.'

'I should have been there,' says Frank. He pauses and gives her a Stern Frank look. 'Did you tell her the rest?'

'She didn't want to know.'

'I'm not bloody surprised. I wish you'd told me, Peggy. I can't believe you just went and did that.'

'For God's sake, Frank, I'm not the only one keeping secrets, am I? Why don't you tell me what the hell is going on with *you*?'

Frank twists the thread from his sleeve into a tight little ball and snaps the end. He wipes his mouth with his silly serviette and peers at his wife over the top of his glasses.

'How is she?'

'Working hard. She texted me. I think she's all right.'

Frank lets out a big after-dinner sigh. 'Next time she's home, we'll go and talk to her, agreed?'

Peggy nods.

'Now get your coat. We're going to the shed.'

She groans. 'It's half-past eight, Frank, it's cold and I'm tired.'

'You want to know what I get up to, so I'm going to show you.'

Peggy has never felt more doubtful in her life.

She follows Frank

over the quagmire that used to be the garden, hoping against hope that her new waterproof Eco-Tuff boots won't get too muddy as Frank ushers her into the safety of the shed.

'Now Peggy, don't say anything yet. Please, just wait.'

Rain drips from the end of his nose and his glasses steam up. He looks like a mad hobgoblin kneeling on the floor, rolling back the rug. She watches intently as the trapdoor springs into life and the ladder unfolds.

'Oh my God, Frank!'

A series of terrible thoughts flood her brain: he's been having affairs *and* murdering people, or smuggling cocaine, or running an underground sex den for the over-sixties. Secret scenarios in the life of the man she thought she knew. All ending in disaster and dismay. He gets to his feet, smooths his anorak, and takes hold of her hands. 'Trust me, Peggy.'

She peers into the waiting hole, hardly able to believe what she's seeing.

'How long has this been here?'

'When we had the shed converted, the tunnel was underneath it.'

'What tunnel? Answer me, Frank, what bloody tunnel?'

'This one.'

Wind throws itself against the shed. Fairy lights sparkle below her.

'What are *they* for? Did you put them there?'

'Of course I did. I'm not completely incompetent, Peggy.'

'You can't sew a button on a cardigan.'

'And you couldn't cook nice fluffy rice even if I paid you.

What does it matter? Just follow me. I'll go first, then I'll help you down.'

'I don't need help, I'm not decrepit.'

'The ladder's wobbly, watch your footing.'

Down they go. Frank flicks the switch, and the tunnel is bathed in twinkling lights. Peggy reaches for his fingers, but he's hurrying on and there's not enough room to walk side by side, so she follows close on his heels.

'Wait for me,' she hisses, fighting an impending sense of doom – if only it wasn't so bloody dark. 'Where have all the lights gone? Frank, please tell me where we are going. I don't like it.' She's sweating like a beast. She's never liked small dark spaces and isn't going to start now.

'Not long to go, you'll see, I promise,' says Frank. He can't shake the feeling that with every step he takes, something is moving beyond his control. He's never had that before. It's Peggy, she's making him nervous.

'Francis Tremble, are you bringing me here to knock me on the head and get rid of me?' Peggy stops in her tracks.

'Yes, Peggy, the fairy lights are to make sure I can see what I'm doing.' He stops and fumbles for her in the darkness. 'Come here, you silly thing.'

He holds her face in his chilly hands. 'Don't you know I would never do anything to hurt you? And I'm sorry I didn't tell you about this before, but I didn't know how to, and I didn't want you to be cross with me. I love you, Peggy Tremble, I bloody love you.'

When he says that, all the tension explodes out of Peggy and she bursts out crying and Frank wraps his arms around her, as she sobs noisily into his jacket. He strokes her hair. 'It's okay, sshh, sshh, Pegaluna, it's all okay. I'm sorry, I'm *sorry*. You were so preoccupied with Molly, and I should have been there, and I'm sorry, I'm really, *really sorry.*'

'I'm sorry too, Frank, we should have talked to her about everything a long time ago. Maybe it's time to end all the grief and the secrets,' says Peggy, her sobs subsiding, mouth still half buried in his jacket.

'There's something else I have to tell you, Frank.'

Frank keeps stroking her hair.

'I saw him today.'

'Who?'

'You know. Him. *From the cellar.*' Peggy takes a deep shuddering breath and wipes her face. 'He was running on the bloody road. I nearly ran him over.'

Frank peers closely at her. 'Are you sure? Only it was a long time ago. What was he doing there?'

'I could never forget that face, it was definitely him,' says Peggy.

'Goodness,' says Frank, his legs suddenly shaky, 'where has he been all this time? Surely not still in the house? We have to tell Molly.'

'I followed him there, Frank. Maybe she already knows.'

'She would have called us if she'd seen him.'

'She hasn't been the same since I gave her the notebook, Frank.'

'Oh, bloody hell, Peggy. It's all kicking off.'

A beat of silence hangs between them.

'Well, we're here now, let's just see this before we face the rest.'

The hairs on the back of Frank's neck tingle as he flashes his torch light over the walls. He prays for the bird not to be there; he hasn't told Peggy about the bird, but he can't handle any more revelations. He takes her by the arm and they continue on until they reach a gap in the rocks under an archway that's easy to miss.

'There we are.'

Frank goes first and Peggy follows him into the splendour of the cave with those magnificent walls lighting up the dark like magic. It's a glistening private show shining above them with all the ceaseless wonder of the natural world.

'Look at this, Peggy,' says Frank, relieved there is no bird, and trying to forget everything that Peggy's just told him.

'Oh, my goodness,' says Peggy, looking everywhere at once, 'this is truly wonderful.'

The cave has such a quiet luminosity they barely need torch light.

'Told you, didn't I?' The crystals glitter back at them, and they whisper to each other like visitors in a cathedral. The grandeur of the place bestowing a mixture of awe and humility in their hearts, both of them caught in such beauty, and both thinking the same thing.

'Peggy, if you really did see him … maybe all this is connected,' says Frank, taking Peggy's hand. 'And maybe, after all this time, we'll get a chance to find out who he really is.'

Frank has hardly finished speaking

when the cave fills with a whirring of feathers and a voice comes through the glittering dark. '*Mesdames et messieurs*, have I told you that I love you? So worry not, *mes amis*, the Bird of Your Dreams is here,' says Raven.

'Oh shit,' says Frank, taking Peggy's hand and hurrying to the other side of the cave, searching desperately for somewhere to hide. There's a ridge of stone with just enough room for them both to wriggle under and Peggy crawls in as far as she possibly can so Frank can squeeze in after her. They sit there trying not to make a sound as an animal smell drifts towards them, accompanied by the sound of loose raspy breathing. It's all Peggy can do to stop herself screaming, *I knew we shouldn't have come*. The sound of someone scuffling along the floor of the cave draws nearer.

'Peggy,' Frank whispers, 'I have to see.'

He bobs up like a giant meerkat, then bobs back down.

'It's a man and a bird,' he says to Peggy. 'I've seen the bird before.'

'What bird?' says Peggy, who can't see anything. Frank's blocking the way.

Neither of them knows that Raven can see them both. Two Tremblays for the price of one. Raven could pick them off like wriggling worms, if only he were ten times bigger.

'My dear Tremblays, I am so glad you have come to us here in this palace of stone,' says Raven, as the cavernous cave looms round them, 'made by the tears of the dead.'

'Oh no,' says Peggy.

'Well that's one name for it, I suppose,' says Frank.

'Speaking of which and whom …' Raven turns his beady eye back to the king.

Ricardo isn't at all well, he has a terrible cough, he's shivering and shaking and not enjoying the final stages of redemption as he once thought he might.

'Here is one of them. Please let me introduce my most Kingly King.'

'I'll have another look,' Frank whispers to Peggy.

'Frank, no!' Peggy grabs his jacket, but Frank won't be stopped. *Frank, what are you doing? For God's sake*, but Frank is crawling out from under the ledge and taking another good look. Peggy follows after him on her painful knees, emerging on all fours in the cave only to find her husband staring like a madman at the man in front of him. If 'man' is the right word to describe him. He is the oddest creature she has ever seen.

She gets to her feet. There is no outside world to hang on to. Shadows play on the walls, everything is mutable, changing around her. Created over thousands of years, eroded through time, reshaped by floods, by crashing rain. Peggy Tremble is standing in eternity. The man in the cloak has very dark eyes and very pale skin. For a few seconds she can see him clearly, but then everything blurs and drifts in and out of focus. She rubs her eyes and desperately wishes she was at home watching telly, so she could turn it off if she didn't like it, and now would be the time to do that.

'Frank?' Heat courses through her body; if she stays here a moment longer she'll explode and become part of the walls.

'Frank, we need to go.'

'Peggy,' he says in a low steady voice, 'I'm not sure what's happening, but I think it's all right.' He turns to the man in the cloak. There is an odd familiarity about him, and Frank tries to remember where he's seen him before, but he can hardly think.

'My name is Francis Tremble, but everyone calls me Frank.'

The man blinks.

Frank's face is glowing with excitement.

'And this is my wife, Peggy.'

The man inclines his head to Peggy. The dark shape of Raven swoops across their heads. 'Transitions,' says the bird, 'are not the easiest things for Ricardo. Formerly King Richard the Third of England, now a disembodied feathered soul, halfway to redemption.'

'Goodness me,' says Frank, not knowing where to look. His legs turn to jelly, his lower lip trembles, he groans to Peggy, 'I don't think my heart can take any more. How can that man be King Richard the Third?'

'I don't believe what that bird just said,' says Peggy, as Raven, much to her great alarm, flies onto her shoulder. For a bird, he's surprisingly heavy.

'Get your claws off my jacket,' says Peggy.

'Happiness as a concept is highly overrated, think you not, dear Peggle?' says Raven. 'But Him and Me, we're waiting for an angel to take this poor old soul to Heaven, and that would make at least one of us ecstatic, so do tell us where one might be?'

Peggy shakes her head. 'I have absolutely no idea what you are talking about, now scram.'

She is gripped by an intense disbelief, a sinking in her guts: *What is happening to us?* Is she, Peggy Tremble, the mad one? Wonderful practical Peggy with her little black torch. When she shines it on the man in front of her he almost disappears. Frank has taken off his glasses and is peering at what is and isn't there.

'Peggy, did you hear, we've just met the soul of a king. Can you believe it?' Frank sounds excited, lowers his voice, 'And the time before, I saw my mum over there.' He points to the corner of the cave. 'She was waving at me.'

Peggy's bad dream keeps getting worse.

'I think this whole place is like a breach in the universe, and he's stepped through. Like Mum, they must be connected.'

'They're both dead, Frank,' Peggy hisses. 'That's the bloody connection.'

Frank blurts out, 'Peggy, what if it's him? You know, the man in the road. You said you followed him to Oxenbridge House.

Maybe that was the angel all those years ago. You remember? Of
course you do.'

Gripped by a heady mixture of belief and excitement, Frank
wants to tell everything all at once.

'Be quiet, Frank,' says Peggy.

'Hear that, Ricardo? The angel is in the House. Monsieur
Tremblay has saved the soul!'

Frank is promising both the bird and the man that he will
come again, as if he was attending a band rehearsal, and not
some surreal event in a cave, while Peggy, with a headache that's
getting worse every minute, has had enough. She is leaving and
taking her husband with her. There is clearly nothing else for
her to do but set fire to the shed and burn all of Oxenbridge to
the ground.

39

Over the centuries

Raven has found that the more he looks for something, the less he finds it. He has developed his Great Distraction Technique as he freewheels through the heavens and that is the consideration that he might write his autobiography. It would run to thousands of pages and be called either *The Unsung Story of Mr Ubiquitous* or, with a greater focus on his work, *An Illustrated Guide to Soul Collecting*, but, as he will freely admit to anyone who asks, and no one does, he's not much good with a pencil.

Leave the thing, find the thing.

Through darkness and light and all states of being in between, the place in Oxenbridge visited by the king now becomes visible to Raven's glittering eye.

Namely, the Abbey of Stern.

Raven can see the path of belief made by the monks from the abbey on their journey to the king. All the doubt and self-deception floating like atoms through the air. Dedalus dragging his feet. Jessop pissing in the hedgerow. Through Fylche, Lesser Dytchewicke and Shroude, all the piety and bubbling stink, while the king is in his splendour, paying for his soul. *Oh Ricardo, if only you knew*, but he could not know what was to come and now is all he knows.

'Time is always time,' squawks Raven as the world flashes past with all its grief and glory. Once again, his eye follows the line between the living and dead, from the abbey ruins to the cellar in Oxenbridge House, where Raven can see much more than a candle burning. There's a hollering incandescence filling up the dark, and something about this tells Raven his autobiography will just have to wait.

Lying on his stony ledge

deep beneath them all, Ricardo dreams of lavender. Swaying in the summer breeze, scenting the land where he once lived. He dreams of the sun burning his face, the shimmering fields where he once stood.

40

Peggy's heart races with anxiety

at the thought of starting a fire in the tunnel with a scented candle. What a mess it would make and then flames would leap through the town and she would not be in control. The tunnel would burn, and blurry man and bird might burn, but so might Frank and then where would she be? Frank has only just managed to drift off and now he's twitching and snoring beside her. Why does everything happen at the same time? The idiot is real. Frank said he was the angel. She nearly killed him, and now this bird and this man, whatever the hell they are, have entered their world, and it's just something else to deal with. She longs to call Molly and tell her everything that's happened, but it's three in the morning.

A little while later Peggy is gliding above the abbey ruins, calling the cat in a high-pitched voice, as you do in your dreams, and there is the man running in the road with his long hair flapping in front of him like a strange wet bird. *Who are you? What do you want?* Now she has Molly, the baby, safe in her arms, and she's flying higher and higher above the house while the house beneath them gets smaller and smaller, until Frank nudges her, '*Peggy*, stop moaning.'

She rolls over and tries to go back to her dream, but she just can't sleep. In the morning she makes a call to Worthing. Charming place, Worthing. She's always liked it.

'How is she?'

She had a walk today. She's resting. Very sleepy. No real change. She bit the night nurse. She messed the bed three nights in a row. She tried to hang herself from the ceiling. She drew an angel and flew away with him. Every morning she used to say, 'I wish I was dead.' Now she says nothing. She's sitting up today so that's an improvement.

Peggy gives the usual thanks, prepares the usual card to send.

41

It's Christmas again

and Molly should have stayed in London. The walk from the station takes longer in the cold and she's tired after the train and the long hours in the gallery in the madness of the festive season. The lions barely bother to greet her when she turns the key in the door and she knows how they feel. The house is very dark. And quiet.

Honey I'm home, but you're not, and we all thank the Lord for that.

Half of her hopes Dedalus will be gone. The problem will be solved, but at least if there's a power cut and they need candles for another two hundred years, he won't care. She bought him a pair of hiking socks for Christmas, she doesn't know why. They're not going to do a tour of Hadrian's Wall in the spring. For Frank, a non-stick wok with a glass lid, from Cook Now You Have the Pan. For Peggy, *The History of Silk*, with beautiful illustrations that Peggy will love. Molly chucks her bags in the hallway, thinking there's a chance he might be feet up watching telly — *Just be normal, eh* — but that's the last thing he'll ever be. She's jittery and nervous and wants everything the way it was, but that's never going to happen.

As she walks back down the old London Road she wonders if he can hear her coming, sense the imprint of her emotions vibrating through the earth. She's wearing her favourite Dior perfume but she kids herself it's just for her, not for him. Once she's in the house she pours a large glass of wine before making her way down the cellar steps. She's greeted by a table full of flickering candles, as he waits, sensitive to every detail of her presence, knowing she would come. 'Wow, you've really transformed the place.'

She thinks of her father in the armchair now occupied by him.

'You'll strain your eyes reading like that.'

He can see better in the dark than Max, but he doesn't tell her that. He puts the newspaper down; he found it in the street, blowing about in the wind. His face has filled out, his eyes seem brighter, and she wants to take a little time looking at them. The cellar is too small for him. 'Come on,' she says, feeling hungry for the first time in months. 'There's a whole house waiting for us, why stay here?' He moves past her on the stairs, leaving a slipstream of energy in his wake. She didn't say he could do that. He's sure of himself now, stronger, confident in his being. She wants to say to him, *Somehow we're the same, we are both so hungry*, and she doesn't mean food, although she is ravenous and hasn't eaten properly for days. She watches him watching everything, like a meditation. Breaking down the facts of the world before he puts them back together in his head. She piles food on their plates and they eat together, mostly in silence.

She hates talking when she has a mouthful of food. When she was with Gabe, she was always wondering how she compared with Valerie, who probably ate with birdlike daintiness and never spilled anything. Some people eat confidently wherever they are and whoever they're with. She's not one of those people, but eating with him, she doesn't care.

She twirls spaghetti round her fork, sucks it in, dribbles it on her chin. He takes a strand and dangles it over his mouth like a worm. He doesn't seem to care either. Why should he, why should she, and they're both covered in sauce by the time they're finished. Her stomach groans. She wipes her mouth on the back of her hand.

'Where are you from? Really, tell me, I want to know.'

His world is so far away that when he speaks, the memory both shocks and delights him, sliding to the outside deep and easy, after being dormant inside him all these years.

Who am I?

A boy in front of a door.

He has flashes of memories, clear and present.

He was a boy once, he tells her. His name was Tom, after the man he called his father. His aunt became his mother, scolding and cajoling while the fire burned. Swallows nesting in the roof, the grunt of the sow, her belly heavy with piglets.

He can see another boy, Cousin Will, his favourite, closest in years. As a boy he made friends with the ache in his chest, he rubbed it at night with his fingers. Sometimes he cried before he could sleep, knowing something was coming his way, but he was a boy, and he could not know, and his cousins learnt to ignore him. At night his feet were always cold while Will's slabs of tough skin and dirty nails were always warm. Most days his nose streamed with snot, and like his cousins, he thought a bowl of stew and a mouthful of bread was happiness.

Molly listens, transfixed as he speaks about this long-ago world, trying to fit this into the complexity of the new.

The Holy Mother renamed him Dedalus; God had instructed her to name him like that, so she did. Like the rest of his life, she is a fragment, real and unreal, and as he doesn't know where he begins or ends, so he leaves Molly and walks into the night to breathe the darkness. Faster and faster over the ruins, trying to find what is here, waiting for him if he can just touch it: a tree, a wall, a woman. His body brimming with energy and strength and light.

Will has disappeared, one world has gone, another has taken its place. He spreads his arms wide and feels the wind rushing under him, a fierce guttural cry burning inside him: *Why am I here?* He can feel a power gathering round him, but what to do with it, where to go?

Molly strokes Max's ears, pulling at them in the way he loves. *Look at him, Maxie, he's bloody bonkers*, but she doesn't mind. It's better than telly, she could watch him all night. Eventually, he returns to the cellar, when she's upstairs in bed, his absence filling the air beside her.

Her stomach complains all night. Next morning, Christmas Eve, she piles on leggings, trainers, sweatshirt, and, despite the endless drizzle, she runs. Past the old stables, the church, the abbey walls – the tangle of undergrowth almost hides the gate – then the stile and the sign back to town, partially obscured by ivy. The grass underfoot is slippery, and by the time she reaches Abbey Lane, her lungs are bursting, and she's slowed to a walk.

She wants to talk to Peggy about everything, just so she knows, but she's left her phone at home, which is just as well, because where would she start? The drawings in the notebook? Perhaps like her mother, Dedalus has opened a door in her mind, and everything is flooding through. She wants to swim in it, like a river of clear water, unclouded by the past.

42

At number 10 Castle Road

Frank is serving his Christmas lunch special, roast turkey with stuffing and cranberry sauce, and all the usual accompaniments, washed down with fizzy apple juice. Molly tucks into a turkey drumstick. Frank looks very pleased and offers her some more gravy. Peggy hardly has an appetite. She eats a bit of turkey, takes a sip of juice.

'There's Nigella's lemongrass and raspberry trifle if you still have room for pudding,' he says proudly. 'Never made this one before. You might like it, Molly Chops.'

Molly's never liked Christmas pudding, though Edward, the permanent Christmas guest, will eat anything. It's early afternoon and not quite time for the Queen's Christmas address. Half of Molly wants to sleep in front of the fire forever, and not deal with anything, especially as Edward is here. She's not spilling secrets in front of him with his silly hair, look at him, sprawled in front of the telly.

'Enjoying Christmas, Edward?' asks Frank.

Peggy pulls a face at Molly to say, *Come with me*, and Frank bustles in after them, wiping gravy from his chin. They gather in the kitchen round the kettle like a holy triumvirate.

'Molly, now we don't want you to get upset.'

'I won't,' she says.

Frank continues, 'But Peggy thinks she saw someone heading to the house, and for some reason' – Frank beseeches the heavens with his hands – 'Peggy thinks it might be the angel.'

Peggy glares at Frank. Why does he do that? Make it out to be all her twitches and imaginings when he's the one who's said the same thing to a talking bird and a blurry man. *Peggy, it's all right, we are simply confused by life*, she tells herself.

Molly's heart leaps around.

'It was early and raining,' says Peggy, 'so, you know, maybe it wasn't him.'

I had dinner with him the night before last and cooked spaghetti. Why doesn't she just tell them? She can't, he's her secret, she's not ready. She'll never be ready. Edward mutes the telly, stands in the living room doorway, ears flapping. He wants to join in, tell Molly he's seen him, and not only seen him, but thrown muffins at him, and is still recovering from his latest encounter with whoever Muffin Man is. He wants to tell Molly how Muffin Man picked him up and carried him as if he was nothing, and after that Edward's brain was on fire and he wanted to do things differently.

'Thank you, Frank.' Molly kisses her uncle. 'Thank you, Peggy.' She hugs her aunt. Not a really strong *I love you, Peggy* hug but a *That's all you're getting for now* kind of hug. 'Lunch was wonderful, and I think I would have told you if there was a bloody angel in the house, and now I really must be going.' Molly grabs her coat. For a sleepy lad, Edward moves fast, leaping up before Peggy can protest.

'Molly, I'll walk you home, shall I?'

'Absolutely no need, Edward, I am fine.'

Undeterred, Edward nods graciously to his hosts, thanking them for a lovely lunch, before the front door opens and closes with the whirlwind of young people heading to the rest of their lives. Peggy and Frank are left surveying the aftermath of Christmas dinner in a rush of cold air.

'Now look what you've done,' says Peggy.

Edward rustles alongside Molly,

arms swinging in his jacket. 'Molly, I'm on your side. I've seen him. If you need me to do anything—'

'How about you just leave me alone, Edward. That will help.'

She walks on ahead, while he stands in the rain, staring after her. He would like very much to go back to Peggy and Frank's but instead he just goes home.

Rain throws itself

against the window, making Edward wonder why, out of all the people in the world, the Farraday family has turned out to be just him.

'Only me left now Mum.'

He's perched on the side of the bath. One frayed toothbrush in the cup where there should be two. Mum bought the new ones. Mum made appointments for the dentist. Mum made the bathroom smell nice, not like him, boy's socks and stink. If he's very quiet he might hear her breathing beside him. Frank's shed appears to be glowing, lit up by the rain.

'Molly doesn't like me, Mum.'

It hurts, doesn't it, but you'll get through it.

'Everything hurts,' he says to the sink, to the bath, to the toothbrush, to the soap, his words drifting through the air as he switches off the bathroom light because no one is there.

Why does Edward

irritate the hell out of Molly like that? He's lost and needy. *Help yourself, Edward. Stop it with the hangdog face and doggy eyes.* But whatever Molly thinks about him she's saying to herself. *Just please stop being lost.* What is happening? Even Frank's not the same as he used to be. *Oh look, there's a Christmas message from Gabe, who is he again? A Very Valerie Christmas to you too, Gabe.*

She thinks briefly about getting her things together and heading back to town. The Christmas season is permanent party mode for Suzi, and if Molly goes back she'll be drinking too much and waking with a hangover and an urge to vomit, and when she's kneeling over the toilet she'll remember how she blabbed to Suzi, who'll insist on coming down and seeing Dedalus for herself and everything will change. The world within the world will break wide open. For now, it still belongs to her.

When she's with him it's like there's something wild and free waiting for her to find it. A meadow with mile-high grass and a thousand trees. She can do anything, be anyone, things become possible, even when he's not there. But so far, he's there and she can be in the house with him and feel everything coming loose inside her, despite the length of his hair.

Dedalus is in the living room

wearing her old pink candlewick dressing gown, arms poking out of the sleeves, legs sticking out at the bottom. He's so thin, as if time has stretched him from one place to another. Pink is for roses, and cheeks, lips, and fingers, sunrise and sunset, and he likes it, and the gown keeps him warm. On the coffee table there's an empty bowl and a spoon, and a battered magazine,

History Today. Fished out of a rubbish bin. It has a special feature on King Richard the Third of England and the discovery of his bones.

'Oh God,' she groans under her breath. 'Not you as well. What is it about this bloody king?'

This bloody king has been inches from his face. He will tell her that this king, the one he recognised in the papers, the name he's seen on the church, this king was once his king. The only king. He wants to ask her why they have dug him from his rest. Images rush into his mind of the monk from Grey Friars conferring with Jessop. He wants to tell her about the heat and the stench in the square as they brought in the king, how, at first, he didn't know it was the king. He wants to tell her how it was when he saw him after the battle, but how can he tell her that? A part of him is still puking onto the stones. He wants to tell her that before Bosworth this king was clothed in flesh and walked upon this world and round the ruins of the abbey, there, he can point to the spot – *That's where we stood, this king and I* – but the words don't match his thoughts. They are too big, too real, and from a place that no longer exists in a time that has disappeared. She knows nothing of the life he once lived. In her world, the private self under the private flesh is flattened onto paper and revealed.

His life is made of moments that do not make sense. *Who am I? What have I become?*

'We have a woman on the throne now, Queen Elizabeth the Second of England, and when she dies, her son, who is a prince, he will be king.'

Molly has never known any other monarch except the Queen and cannot imagine a day when she won't be there.

'Was there a battle to take the throne?'

'The queen didn't fight in any battle but there was a war, a bloody awful world war, if that's what you mean. Her father was the king, and when he died she became queen.'

'He died in this war?'

'No, I think he was sick, but I don't know, and it doesn't really matter now, does it? The question is, what are we going to do with you?'

A woman has the throne of England, but all things change, and the longer he's here, the less he knows.

When the shops reopen

after Christmas, Molly gives him twenty quid and walks him to Oxfam. Silver objects fly past like birds through space. Speed astounds him. Red kites whistle him back to the old, the drumming of hooves, candles sputtering, everything soft and low beneath the senses. His heart beats faster dealing with so many different things as everything inside him grows stronger. He doesn't know the names for all these things; she tells him, and he forgets. Sugar, tea, coffee, taps, planes, trains, detergents, chemicals, perfumes, bath wash, toilet paper, soft, pink, everything pink.

He's so odd to start with, let him be odd. His choice, a lady's jumper, bright green and covered in pink flowers.

'Men's clothes are over there,' says the lady at the till, but he doesn't want men's clothes. They remind him of his robes, very brown, very dull. He wants colour now, and life. He is mesmerised by the flowers on the jumper. The lady behind the counter looks at his hair, his eyes, his skinny legs in Molly's jeans.

'It's five pounds,' she says, 'there, on the label, see. After Christmas, everything's reduced.'

Molly pops over the road to see Peggy, but the shop is still closed over the Christmas break, which is unlike Peggy. Molly hurries back to Oxfam. He looks so totally out of place in a shop. He should be on a mountain top with his robes flowing and a staff in one hand and a mighty orb in the other. Other customers enter the shop chatting. To Dedalus, their voices sound like the murmur of bees round a berry bush. They do not bless each other. They do not thank God for the day or ask where they are from or what they have seen. People talk all the time but fail to say the things that matter.

'Will?'

'What?'

'Can I come home?'

The scruffy boy in the tunic shakes his head. 'You've got to pray for us all, it's your duty. You can't stay with us. There's not enough food. They'll feed you there.'

'Dedalus?'

'What?'

'Buy the jumper.'

He thinks women might be made of light but he's not sure. *There is a queen on the throne, after a war. When she dies, there will be a king.* His ears pick up a sound. Could be the wind. Here it is again, through walls, over cold floors, crooked stairs, glittering spider webs and piles of crumbling dust, through the door, down the path, until it finds him with the lavender and the rain spitting on his head. The voice always finds him.

Dedalus, you dawdling piece of piss. Do your duty, Dedalus, pray for us all. You are the one who will save us.

He buys the jumper. Wears it through the streets of this strange new town.

The next day

Molly has managed to start her father's old hatchback that's been kept alive by the occasional ministrations of Frank and Peggy. Once the engine wheezed into life Molly knew it would be a difficult ride. She tries to imagine a world without cars, and how hard it might be for him, never having been inside one before. She finds him walking down the driveway, feet firmly on the earth.

'Come on,' she says, pulling the car up alongside him. 'Hop in and we'll go for a spin.'

She studies his face studying the car.

'It's me,' she says, 'Molly Stern in my father's old car, opening a door for you and inviting you in.'

At first he refuses, but then curiosity gets the better of him and he squeezes himself into the front seat. He wasn't expecting Molly to tie him to the seat. She gives him a reassuring smile but any moment he's going to change his mind and escape out of there. She pats his leg to comfort him as the beast growls and vibrates and begins to move. He hangs on to anything he can find, the door, the window, the edge of a seat, his face turning green, his heart thumping in his chest. Once they're out of the gates, they are going faster than he has ever gone in his entire life. He thinks he will die if they go any faster, and soon he is longing for death and for this all to be over. He grabs hold of Molly, who tries to shake him off.

'For God's sake, I can't steer like this.'

Houses flash past so quickly he cannot bear to look. A field, another field, a fence, a street, all the people in the cars not looking at all the other people. This is the world where God has sent him. Giddy with fear, the colours, the grass, the streets, the beast rumbling along with him inside it, until he can bear it no longer. He asks Molly to stop. He has to get out. After a long time retching on the side of the road, he stands up slowly and takes a good long hard look at the car with Molly inside it. He runs his hands all over it, feeling the warmth of the engine, trying to find the heartbeat, the spirit of God that makes it what it is. He refuses to get back in. He watches Molly driving slowly back down the old London Road and jogs after her, steadily gaining on the car until he's almost caught up. It's better outside the beast than in it and if this is God teaching him what humans have made, then Dedalus is at a loss to know what any of it means.

Things to contend with:

people – what they look like, their clothes, hair, glasses. Some men have beards, moustaches, others nothing, but their clothes are the same. He hasn't yet encountered anyone in robes. Some people have drawings on their skin. Others do not. There are no rules for him to follow. A woman passes him with a small butterfly on the back of her neck. It is drawn on her skin. It doesn't fly away. Who drew it? How did it get there? Men wear jewellery, earrings, dangling things. He's getting the hang of nose rings, Molly Stern has one, but what does it mean? Molly Stern names things for him; she says, 'Dedalus these are coats, jackets, hats, macs, scarves, trousers, boots, shoes, trainers, sneakers,' until he clasps his hands over his ears and looks away.

The aisle of the supermarket lengthens and curves into nothing. 'Would you like that sliced? Your bread?' Machines chop through the freshly baked dough. Molly Stern points out more things to him: crackers and cheese, yoghurt and milk, sliced meat and chocolate biscuits.

'Why,' he asks, 'does the car beast growl and not the cart they push in the shops?'

'This cart is called a supermarket trolley,' says Molly, 'It doesn't have an engine.'

Dedalus is entranced by the trolley's small wheels; he tries to imagine Squirrel pulling one along; she would not be impressed. If he wanted to, he could pick up that trolley and hurl it into the air, but he doesn't want to, not yet. Once in the shop, the abundance of so much food disturbs him. Shelf after shelf there is always another piece of cheese, meat, fish, bread, always more cake, more pastries. The milk is kept in cold air which shocks him – a moment ago the air was warm.

The first time Molly took him to Tesco's he lay in the car park, staring at the sky, absorbing the warmth from the cars, the metal, the tarmac. People asked Molly if he was all right, before giving him a wide berth.

'He's fine, he's always like this,' she said, tempted to lie with him and look at the clouds before being run over by a Vauxhall Estate, or a Volvo.

'Only a car park isn't the best place for a lie-down, is it?'

'Some people spend five hundred years in one.'

'He'd better move, otherwise he'll be flattened.'

Up he jumps. His soul loose at the edges, flooded with useless things. He wants the world the way it used to be. Fires that spit and hiss and boil the water and bubble the stew. Scent of dill and mint. Leaves floating in his cup of water. The curl of his sandal, incense, greasy tallow candles, the green flash of a pheasant flying over a hedge to escape its bitter end. He misses the horses, their hooves and tails, the heft of their bodies, dung, the snickering and whinnying when home draws near. The instinctive rhythms they bring to life, without the screech and roar of metal.

When he's back in the cellar

in the quietness of night, without all the movement and noise, it makes him feel all right again. He's so deep in thought that at first he doesn't hear Molly knocking on the cellar door. He forgets he is only wearing trousers and is naked from the waist up.

'I'm sorry to bother you so late.'

She's not at all sorry. She wants to bother him. Bothering him is the best thing for Molly to do. Whether she likes it or not, she is drawn to this man and, besides, it's her door, her house, so she can bother as much as she wants. She hands him a jumper.

'There are lots of spare ones,' she says, but then remembers she's given the rest away. He pulls it over his chest in his own languid way and, as she watches him, the sky inside her head threatens to fold her up inside it. Besides and besides and besides, Molly tucks him inside her like a secret. *Will you look at that face, Molly Stern, go on, take a good look. He looks like a feel-good veggie socialist, and we can't have that around us without asking lots of questions.*

He's a bloody angel. She wants to say this out loud to the world, but she doesn't know for sure. It's just an excuse for keeping him here. He's slow to speak if he speaks at all; he's somewhere else in his head, waiting for something other than her with that restless disconnection she knows so well.

Sometimes at night she glimpses her father, wandering amongst the stars, fragments of Marcus Stern filling the sky like the tail of a comet, circling the cosmos.

'Can you see me down here, Dad? I'm bothering him.'

That's good, Mol. Have you made him a nice cup of tea?

She needs to stay centred, but where is that? Anger brings her back to life, warms her bones. She'll tell him the whole thing is madness, whoever he is, and she doesn't know what's true or what she believes. Find someone else to beguile. The story's done, finished, over. She'll haul him out of the cellar. Put him on the next train to nowhere. The sound of her father's voice echoes in Molly's head. She wants to tell him about Dedalus now, how the story is here, in the house, as her father had told her, how the only questions that matter now are the ones that become real.

She still hasn't told Peggy or Frank about Dedalus, and her usual weekends have turned into three-day events, sometimes even four. *Suzi, please Suze, please, but don't make me tell you how I'm spending all my time in the cellar with him.*

Accept him or leave him.

He does not belong to Molly any more than she belongs to him. She can feel him coming closer, but a part of him is elsewhere, pulling away. *Do not go there*, she says to herself. A wave of that old anger washing over her, she doesn't know why, and anyway, she can't sleep. She's spent days and nights thinking about him. She knows Oxenbridge House has been his home for years, more than she ever realises. He's been waiting forever, for her to find him, but how can he live like this? What is he here for?

There's nothing normal about him. He can't just say, *Hi gorgeous, here's some soup I made for you. How was your week?*

I sold three prints, none of my own work, and bought Thai beef salad from M&S. How was yours? Oh, silly me, you don't know what M&S is — it's a shop. Can't call yourself British and not know M&S, but then you're not even properly human, are you?

Night-time swallows her

at the top of the cellar stairs, driving her further, like an engine she can't switch off. Her chest feels tight, brittle like glass, and if she stops and takes a few deep breaths she'll probably be all right, but she's Molly Stern and she won't stop and she knows there are moments in her life when she should turn back but this isn't one of them. He's there, watching her, breathing in her scent; even in the darkness she can see that light burning through his eyes, and he has this way of opening his eyes wide so that what's left of the darkness falls into them. He straightens his back, and his bones click into place, reminding her how she hates that noise, she hates him. 'Right,' she says, 'you're coming with me.' He follows her determined odyssey up from the cellar and through the kitchen as she grabs the scissors and marches him upstairs.

'Relax,' she says as he sits on her bed like he's made of wire, tall, tight, expectant, doesn't know what's coming his way.

What has made you like this?

She peels off his jumper, puts a towel round his shoulders. Holds up a piece of his hair and snips it with the scissors. His hand shoots up and grabs her wrist. *What are you doing?* She shows him his strand of hair, and he stares at it as if he's never seen it before. Then he reconsiders. Nods at Molly: *Whatever this is, yes, you can do it to me.* She's not the best barber in the world, but he doesn't seem to mind. Half a lifetime to grow, half a minute to cut. It's a bit hit and miss, and you wouldn't pay to look like that and there are a few straggly bits still, but my goodness, Molly Stern, look at him now. Almost beautiful. His face looks back at her.

What have you done to me?

He runs his hands over his head, coming to terms with loss, and gain, and renewal. And her. He showers using a tiny piece of soap Molly's left in the soap holder. Dries himself on a towel that's going bald, and stares at his reflection in the steamed-

up mirror. Wearing nothing but the towel he sits back on her
bed and she sits beside him, thinking, *Look at those eyes.* She
must find out for herself what is real. 'Sorry,' she says, 'sorry',
but doesn't really know what she's apologising for, except
everything, except nothing. So it's her and him, and he reaches
out from the past to the present to touch her face with his long
cool hands.

A memory rises in him as he inhales the truth of her, the
shape of her, the feel of her. They sit together hardly touching,
the air cracking and jumping between them, and he looks at her,
so full of doubt and uncertainty, and that's when she sees it. All
this time she has had it right. They're not driven by differences,
him and her, they're the same. Molly and the angel. Two lost
creatures, compelled by forces they barely understand, but here
they are, with the same need to love, to know, to understand
what lies in them and beyond them at the same time. The hunger
for what is good, what is right, the mystery at the end of things,
and the need for each other, even though neither of them knows
where any of this will lead.

'It's all right,' she says over and over, because by telling him,
she's telling herself, inch by inch, flesh on flesh, just how it is.
This is me, and this is you, and all the rest is in between. And she
kisses him, and he kisses her so tenderly, so gently, that she
cannot help but fall into the heat and light pulsating through his
body. She kisses him again and shows him what to do and how
to do it, and then she fucks him with all the grace and kindness
she can give him, all the grace and kindness he doesn't know he
has. He had no idea desire could be like this, and the first time is
over before it's begun, and there is so much he doesn't know, so
she has to teach him and show him again. She is the one to take
him from the darkness, and when he enters her, she knows this

is a slow learning, a dream never to wake from, and every time they start again, their days of madness begin.

They do it once more, just to make sure they can, so they won't forget each other when the world comes calling with all its needs and obligations.

She takes her pill, at the right time every morning so there's no angel baby, and nothing to disrupt whatever this is between them.

She turns her phone to silent so that when *No one* calls, she can't answer.

And she knows she's wrong, and she knows she can help it, but she doesn't want to. All day and all night her skin is burning, feverish. She thinks one of her eyes has changed colour, like Max, and she doesn't even care.

And when the night comes, his eyes burn like stars, and she follows him anywhere he wants to go, until she hardly knows herself anymore. And all she does know is that when she's with him, the world feels like it's exploding into light.

43

Time goes faster

the older you get. It fizzes and pops along with your cells. Shedding, changing, sagging, and drooping as the months progress. Wear lighter colours, eat less meat, more white cheese. Smile. Walk every day. Dance. Take up yodelling. Peggy's innards grumble, her heart thumps for no reason, the uncertainty of life shifts beneath her bouncy shoes. Peggy's policy is to cope with one thing at a time. Her plan was to go to the house and make a citizen's arrest, but she's been shaken by events and twice she's had to clean the toilets herself, which induced a slight fever and a desire to sack her Young Man. She hasn't returned to the cave since the night with Frank, and if Frank is late to bed, and full of talk, she blocks her ears and pretends to be asleep. More and more these days she thinks of her sister, Sally, and every time she calls Molly, Molly declines her call. *I thought things were all right between us, but maybe they're not. Madness is creeping up on me*, thinks Peggy, and it's wearing an ill-fitting coat with none of the buttons done up straight.

Frank is in heaven

after a phone call and a congratulatory email. Mr Frank Tremble, triumphant in the abbey ruins. A full-page spread in the *Oxenbridge Bugle*. One leg up on a pile of stones, arms folded, surveying the world. He gets so caught up sometimes it's a shock for him to realise other things exist.

'Peggy, I'm famous, look!

> Retired deputy mayor of Oxenbridge Council, Mr Frank Tremble, Chair of the Plaque for the King Committee, agrees it will be a huge boost for Oxenbridge now the council has agreed to fund the plaque. The plaque will commemorate King Richard the Third's visit to the Abbey of Stern. Please see council website for more information. Council envisions the plaque will become 'part of the cultural capital of the community'.

'Peggy, what d'you think: a perfect spot at the entrance to Abbey Lane?'

'The toilets are there, Frank, and the sign for the shop goes there.'

'Well, the sign's a movable feast and it's a plaque, Peggy, most likely fixed on the wall.'

Frank kisses the top of her head. She frowns at him. Frank doesn't know how to get her to share his enthusiasm. He imagines a continuous line of hikers and tourists, with cameras and sandwiches, filling the ruins with wonder and Oxenbridge cafés and shops with prosperity. Peggy sees every parking space filled, her daily life radiating with frustration. She sees grubby fingers on the shop window and smears of ice cream on the linen shirts, despite the sign saying *No Food Please.* Hiking boots leaving clods of earth on the pavement. Molly's privacy in the house disturbed by the stragglers, the lost, the thoughtless nosy parkers, the endless trail of people gawking and knocking and being where they should not be. Never mind the brambles and nettles and columbine and cow parsley. Never mind the ancient walls.

Peggy writes her own headlines.

Claw Marks in Jacket Proof of Talking Bird
Woman Grieves for Old Husband Who Loved Cooking

Peggy foolishly bought him a membership of Your Heritage for Christmas, and since then he's barely looked up for a slice of cake, a cup of tea, a bowl of rice.

Frank Tremble. Cook, husband, uncle, not in that order.

Frank Tremble. Took his wife to see the soul of a king, a mile underground and five hundred years into the past.

Some want the plaque, some don't.

Can't give a child-killer acknowledgement.

We don't know if he killed the boys one way or the other. King Richard came to Oxenbridge, so what's not to celebrate?

What do you think about the plaque for the king, then? They're putting it at the abbey.

Why are they putting it there?

Well, he didn't come to the bakery, did he?

Peggy's not sure what to say to anyone anymore. Frank's never been a quarreller, or a man of confrontation. He has always been a man of rice, and green vegetables, and peace, of balance and stability and knowing where things are and who is coming for dinner. That's how he likes it. That's how it works for him. She's been down to the shed once since that night. The trapdoor was open, the table pushed back against the wall. Frank looked at her and she looked hard at him.

'Imagine if people knew about him.' He pointed to the floorboards. 'The soul of the king in a cave in Oxenbridge, waiting for redemption. I need to see what's happening down there, Peggy.'

'No one will ever believe you, Frank. They'll think you've been cooking the wrong sort of mushrooms and then where will we be?'

He sighed. Closed the trapdoor. Put the rug back into place.

44

Ricardo rolls to the other side

of the ledge and groans as Raven calls to him. 'Righto, my Kingly King. Up you get. Smarten up! Time to change, my Right Honourable Lord Mutable, Lord Doubtable, Sir Unreliable. It's time to ebb and flow, to dissipate and transformate. It won't be long now; I've found the Big Lug and just have to get him here.'

'Please stop talking,' Ricardo says to Raven, watching handfuls of his feathers falling to the ground.

'Anyone would think you were tired of the afterlife, old mate. Cheery yourself up, it's all gonna change.'

Ricardo is saving what's left of his energy for the arms of the angel. Whatever he needs to confess, he'll confess and then he'll re-emerge blinking in daylight, gasping at the beauty of the world. Threadbare survivor. Medium height, matted hair, naked body under feathery cloak, a shifting energy, a cloud shaped like a king. Beneath him will be air and ground, a dirty brown puddle, the shine of the sun, the gape of sky, the song of a field, the bark of a tree, the brilliance of all life thundering back into him.

45

Edward sits on the bed

having a heart-to-heart with his mum.

'Mum, what shall I do?'

Put a load of washing on and clean the kitchen.

'Mum, what do I do?'

Iron your shirts and wash your hair.

'But Mum, what shall I do?'

He gathers his supplies: two dry scones – he hasn't made a new batch yet; a packet of cheese and onion crisps; a banana, on the turn but just about edible, try not to squash it; and half a packet of chewing gum.

Water, Edward, don't forget the water.

'Got it. Keys, torch, phone, food, ready. Bye, Mum.'

He locks the back door, takes one last look at the house, then off he goes, Mr Midnight, also known as Detective Farraday. He is so good at being quiet in the dark. When he reaches the high street, he crosses the road so he can see the newsagency; the shop is shut, lights are out. He waits for a minute, expecting everyone to be doing the same things in the same way, like him, but since his meeting with Muffin Man he is trying to see that things can be different. Jessica Khan is not there. The window is closed. He's almost disappointed. He was going to say, *Hey, I'm a spelunker taking a stroll*, if she had asked what he was doing.

He unlocks the toilet door and when he's ready, he swings through the beam. The more he does it, the easier it gets. Into the cavernous dark, walking underground from one side of Oxenbridge to the other. It might catch on. He could take tour groups down here, but then that might spoil things. Waiting for him, further in, beyond the cellar, beyond anywhere Edward Farraday has walked, lie the deep recesses of the subterranean world. The slow geological carve of rainwater trickling through stone. The deep unlit water waiting for no one. Edward Farraday will become the first man to fully discover this hidden world, a renowned explorer, travelling the globe with Molly Stern, award-winning photographer and partner in life. The two of them crawling into unknown spaces, each telling the other how much they love them.

A soft slow silence permeates the dark. Something bigger than himself exists between these walls. He doesn't think he believes in God, because why would God let his mum die like that, but this is the closest he gets to being comforted by darkness. It's like going into the deepest parts of yourself and finding things that guide you, like courage, and happiness, and feeling okay.

'This is the toilet tunnel' – he pads along, recording on his phone – 'and this was the first place I discovered, and today I'm going to see if this part connects with a massive cave over there.'

He flaps his hand. No one can see him.

'It's called the "chamber of stars". A friend of mine showed it to me and it is truly amazing.' He stops for a bit. Doesn't know what else to say. Small lumps of stone crumble from the walls, landing with a loose *pitter-patter* on the ground behind him, and he nearly jumps out of his skin, his bravado melting faster than an ice cream on a sunny day.

'Is that you, Muffin Man?' Silence. 'Muffin Man,' he whispers into the phone, 'is someone who actually lives down here, and I'm going to see if I can find him.'

He is sure he arrived at the cellar sooner than this the first time; any minute now the cellar archway should appear. But this time he's missed it and, without realising, he's headed west, under the old London Road.

After more walking, and an uneasy sinking feeling in his stomach, he comes to a massive rockfall. Lit up by his head torch, it's huge, floor to ceiling, and effectively a dead end.

The boulders are massive great slabs, wedged and nestled against one another, and impossible to move. There's nowhere else to go. Molly would never accept defeat like this, she would find a way through. One of the boulders has a series of small smooth craters on its surface, and there's just enough grip for Edward to manoeuvre himself up a little, and then a little more, using the wall behind him as a back stop.

The stone is slippery but his big Farraday feet grip well in his trainers and nothing comes loose. It's hard sweaty work and he stops when he's almost at the top and can just make out a gap that might lead somewhere. On he goes. The boulder levels out a little more and he thinks he can still climb down the way he came up. So far, so good. There's a couple of feet between his head and the roof and, beyond that, a wider ledge opens out. He crawls along the top of the boulder for quite some way, until he reaches a stony ledge.

The air sits on his head, dense and warm. He wriggles forward on his stomach like a giant worm until he reaches the edge and peers over. There it is. In the distance. His reward.

The chamber of stars looks further away than he thought. Shining with crystalline light. Backpack by his side, phone in his pocket — this is how Molly will remember him, the bravest man she knows, quietly absorbing the beauty and wonder of the subterranean world.

He lies there for a few minutes, resting. Climbing is exhausting work. His head torch isn't powerful enough to shine more than a few feet beneath him, but he can just make out a series of ridges and tries to remember whether this was where he and Frank climbed. He doesn't think it is, and from where he lies, everything looks different. Every place has its secrets. Over the years he imagines the water flowing down the rocks, weathering, transforming. There's no way down that he can see: the ridges below him are narrow and too far away to reach. The only thing to do is to return the way he came. He gets to his feet carefully, grabs his backpack, and inches his way along, using the wall to steady himself. *Ready? Yep. One last look then.* Step by step he makes his way to the edge. *See, Molly? How brave I am.* He peers into the cavernous dark. Some loose stones crumble on the ledge, startling him, and, before he knows what's happening, he's flying through the darkness, screaming as he goes.

46

Under a rare blue sky,

the street quickly fills with press, officials, and dignitaries trying to find the best spot. Peggy and Frank are in the thick of the action, at the start of Abbey Lane, where the path to the abbey ruins begins. There's the Mayor of Oxenbridge Council – Peggy can never remember her name – in her long puffer jacket that looks like a giant quilt. Peggy prefers a well-cut nicely lined woollen coat. Frank is in his best grey worsted, leather gloves, lambswool scarf.

He takes a deep breath and rubs his hands together. 'What do you think, the air's not too bitey.'

'Bitey?' *Be kind to yourself. Practise compassion. Ask what you need from the universe today.* Four hours ago, Peggy was warm in bed, dreaming of a crown tumbling through her hands, and woke with a start, thinking she'd dropped something, only to find Frank bringing her a cup of tea.

'Today's the day, Pegaluna.'

Peggy, in her cashmere scarf and woollen blend coat, is not feeling the cold, and not for a moment considering the freshness of the air. Her hair is tucked into her scarf, she's growing it until she can't stand it anymore. The rule that says women over fifty must have short hair is done. Bugger that. No more Anna Wintour haircuts. Who will be her role model now? Cher? That's a wig. Meryl Streep, shortish? Helen Mirren, always fabulous?

She's staring at the assembled crowd, unable to believe that the plaque is finally happening.

There's a stir of excitement when the mayor, after a short speech from Frank about persistence and celebrating history, pulls the covering sheet from the plaque. *Huzzah!* Mr Francis Tremble clapping behind her. *It's on the wall*. Peggy breathes a sigh of relief. A brief historical interlude for the good people of Oxenbridge, going about their daily tasks with a mixture of love and dissatisfaction, as most people do.

In the following days, small crowds gather for a look at the new addition to the town. It's on the local six o'clock news. Oxenbridge, Buckinghamshire, the World, Universe, Place of Great Importance. A shiny red plaque about the king. Clouds rumble on the horizon, crackling with energy. In a few weeks the bones of King Richard are to be reinterred at Leicester Cathedral. For most Oxonians, this has little significance in their lives; he came here once, but so did lots of people; some stayed, some didn't. Mostly it's nothing to do with them. Now, whether they like it or not, the king is officially part of the town, merged into daylight on the wall.

Raven watches the proceedings.

> This commemorates the visit by King Richard the Third
> to the Abbey of Stern before his death at the Battle of
> Bosworth in August 1485.

His morose medieval king. His fearless feathery king. His lost and lonely king. His Kingly King, now a passing interest. The king with a crown that didn't belong to him, but all kings had blood on their hands. That's how they stayed king.

47

The shed has become

a little refuge for Peggy. Sometimes she spends a few minutes in there quietly by herself, the trapdoor firmly shut. She hasn't been able to get hold of Edward, and it's most unlike him not to reply to a text, even if it takes him a while. She's checked his house, cupboards, closets, and stairs, the usual mess in the kitchen, but of the occupant, no sign. He's a young man and Peggy can't go chasing him all over the place and she doesn't have any other numbers to call. The shed is small and comforting and holds her in place as she contemplates where Young Edward Farraday might be.

The king is dead,

but staying dead is one thing this king resolutely refuses to do. Frank pores over the details for the reinterment of the bones. Mass will be said, dedications made. There will be celebrations and services with poets and actors and bishops and King Richard the Third devotees, which looks to Frank like it's half of England. Frank longs to return to the cave and see whether the soul of the king is still there, but the more he thinks about it the more fanciful it seems, and anyway Frank must stay above ground and prepare for his talk. He can't be so absorbed in his own adventures when he has become the public face of the king. Even Molly said she would come to Frank's talk, which is such good news, and afterwards, in the warm glow that public occasions can bring, Frank and Peggy think this will be the perfect time to talk to Molly about Worthing. About everything.

The next day, after Peggy

closes the shop, she pops over to see Mrs Khan at the newsagency, and an hour later she has her new Saturday assistant, Jessica Khan. Nearly eighteen and studying hard for her A levels. A few hours on a Saturday would suit her perfectly and if her parents stand outside the newsagency, they can see Peggy's shop, and their wonderful daughter. They'll know exactly where she is. They tell Peggy that Jessica Khan is the brightest girl in the world. She will make a great doctor, but she's slightly less great at selling socks. *Still, can't have everything*, thinks Peggy, missing Edward even more, and wondering where on earth he is. How will it go when he finally appears and meets his replacement? Frank soothes her, tells her Edward has finally taken himself off for a big adventure.

'Young men do that, he'll come back when he's ready.'

'But where has he gone? And why didn't he tell us?'

'We're not his parents, Peggy.'

Who are you trying to fool with all that rational nonsense, Frank Tremble? It's all your fault with your tunnel and your stupid little lights.

A wave of guilt washes

over Frank. Edward's met a girl, or he's staying with friends, no need to panic yet. It's late and Frank's gone all scented candles, and that's down to Edward. Frank didn't think he was a candle man, but Edward gave him a pink one that smelt of roses, and now he's hooked. A candle hunter, pursuing the best scents, the most durable wicks. Tonight he is burning fig and cassis, slightly fruity, slightly sweet, with a wick made of wood, or so the candle lady said. He bought three on impulse and they do make the shed smell divine.

He loves being here but now he has a little nervous cough, and the top of his head wants to join the bottom of his body. For the first time that he can remember life is worrying him rather than exciting him. He feels a little bit sunk but doesn't know what he's sinking into. Tomorrow is his talk and Edward said he would help him with the section on the princes, but he's not here. The shed is warm and fuggy, the candles are sending him to sleep.

He looks around the walls and table. The king is present in the shed, watching him amongst all the articles and photos, the pictures and books and facts and dates.

'Here's what I think,' says Frank, 'if you do exist down there. I think you're stuck, and you're waiting for something, absolution maybe, but I can't give you that. I'm nothing to do with God, I'm just a man in a cardigan.'

He thinks of all the distress his behaviour has caused Peggy. 'And not a very good one at that.'

He wonders why they have waited so long to talk to Molly. You can hide from facts, but you cannot change them. They change you, just as truth can change according to who's telling it. Frank loves the unearthing, the discovery of the king. He was real, and he existed, and here are his bones, but he will always be the man responsible for the princes in the tower. His nephews who were never seen again. It doesn't matter how bravely the

king fought in his last battle; just as Molly and Marcus and
Sally belong to Frank and Peggy, the boys always belong to the
king. You cannot untie the threads to your family. They're the
strongest ones of all.

The only thing Frank can change is his perspective. History
is alive and ruthless. For kind, curious Frank, history is one way
of discovering the truth, and if he's learnt anything at all, it's
that he and Peggy owe the truth to their big beautiful fierce tiny
scared impatient wonderful girl, and they need to tell her before
much longer. Frank is sure that Peggy's sighting of the angel is a
sign that things must be told. Secrets fester and multiply. They
cost you in the end. They coat your life with inauthenticity.
Frank doesn't want to believe the king was dark and murky. He
has invested so much time in him, he wants him to be good. He
wants to tell him that sometimes even a decent person can do
terrible things. He wants him to shine, like a beacon of light from
the abbey walls, fully human, good and bad and in between.

48

Fuck, oh fuck,

oh fuck, it all happened so quickly, one minute upright, the next Edward's flat on his back on the floor of the cave unable to breathe, his mind trying to register the terrible shock of the fall. He's been winded by the impact, and the slightest movement brings waves of jagged stabbing pain. His eyes widen; at least the pain is telling him he's alive and gasping for air. His backpack is digging into his side; he must have been clutching it when he fell but he doesn't remember. His left arm is caught in the strap, and he tries to wriggle free, but a fresh wave of pain hits him all over again. He wonders how long it will take to die, forty-five minutes probably, that number just popped into his head. *Shit.* Everything hurts. He runs his tongue over his teeth, nothing appears to be missing, *Thank the fuck for that*, but even doing that hurts, all of it, everywhere, hurts.

He tries to call for help, but every breath wracks his chest with agony, and no one is going to hear that small voice except a mouse. 'Help me, please help me.' Every time he moves the tiniest bit, wave after wave of awfulness pulses through him. He vaguely understands his life is ending, and that this is how he, Edward Farraday, will leave this world. He drifts in and out of consciousness. *Mum, I'm really sorry, I'm really very sorry.* He cries hot little tears that trickle down his face.

49

In his new life with flowery jumper

Dedalus is out walking on a wintry afternoon, deep in thought about Molly. He notices small things: cracks in a wall, clumps of moss growing in those cracks, the clouds changing shape as the wind remakes them. All these things tether him to the earth and help him find the place between despair and discovery and the part Molly has played in all of this. Her acceptance of him. The solace and comfort in his dark spaces meeting the same places in her. He wonders if this is love. Walking helps him think.

People stare. Lady jumper, man face, and what a face, imprinted in their minds like the outline of a flare. *Who is he?* They take notice of him without knowing why. His body at peace with all the contradictions it inhabits. Confidence does that. Confidence in purpose, in the corridor of knowing between the outside and inside. Never mind his trousers are too short, or his eyes wide open, cramming everything in. He's impossible to miss as he strides along, taller than most, still a mass of dark hair, and if you look closely, and some people do, trees dip their branches as if they already know him.

He stops for a moment on the old London Road, listening to the many competing sounds. The ceaseless cacophony of the new world. His senses sharper than they've ever been. There it is. A reverberation. A tremulous cry. Something making its way towards him.

Save them, Dedalus, we must save them.

A small sound echoes between the spaces, and he lies on the ground, which is the old London Road, so he can hear it better. Time slips for a moment and he's back with Sister Alice. The flash of her robes beside him. The memory startles him. *Can you hear them, Dedalus, the lost souls?*

Foxes, badgers, humans.

We must save them.

He listens as hard as he can, despite the rumbling of cars and growling of engines, and when there's a break in the traffic, there it is again, a faint noise vibrating like a tremor in the darkness. The power of loving Molly has given him more energy, made him stronger than he was three weeks ago. Five hundred years of love storied in his bones. Cars screech to a halt before him. He gets to his feet and holds up his hands so they cannot proceed. *Forgive me*, he says to the puzzled faces. *I was here first. This is where I listen. Trust me. Then you will see the road you travel on is nothing more than history.* It was a lane, a path, a churned field, a flock of sheep, a wood full of birds. People switch off their engines and open their car doors. The man on the damp chilly road is surrounded by a halo of light, while through the clouds above him comes the unmistakable sound of beating wings.

A large black bird alights on his shoulders.

'Finally, kindally, my Dear Big Lug, it had to be you,' says Raven, squawking with delight, 'My Well-Lit Traffic Stop Angelus.'

Dedalus lets Raven perch on his arm. The bird's eyes swimming into his soul, letting Dedalus drink that unlimited energy in, fuelling himself for the next part of his inevitable journey.

'Now please scurry up.' Raven points with his beak. 'Old mate and I, we've been waiting and debating, and it's this a-way, sunshine. You walk, son, I'll fly.'

Raven expects Dedalus to follow him, but Dedalus hasn't lived in darkness for this long without knowing his way around. He's on the road one minute, then disappearing round corners the next, racing back to Oxenbridge House.

No sign of Molly, he heads down into the cellar, trusting the bird to go its own way, then he's through the low cellar archway and into a tunnel, leaning against the walls to listen for the slightest sounds. Every time he hears the weak hollowed cries, he tells her, *I will save them*, through the damp spent air.

50

Beat the Winter Blues

with Frank Tremble in the Middle Ages! Frank is standing in the church hall of St Stephen's, about to give a short talk on King Richard the Third, before the reinterment of the king's bones later in the month. It's also to celebrate the installation of the plaque, but Frank has started not to care. Frank misses Molly. He misses the three of them. They haven't seen her since Christmas. Peggy went to the house a couple of times to check on her, but the place was dark and locked. She's left messages for Molly and received a few back, sometimes just a flower or a heart. They've never gone this long without giving their girl a hug. His throat tightens, though he hasn't really cried since Marcus. He'd almost forgotten that prickling in his eyes and the awful crumpling of his face. Something's building in him, but *Not now, Frank, this is a public talk. Molly Chops, where are you?*

With difficulty, he turns his mind to the king.

Over the next few weeks, the eyes of the world will be on Leicester for the reburial of King Richard the Third of England. A lottery of five hundred lucky people will be in attendance for the services and processions and dedications to honour the king. His bones will be laid in a coffin of English oak, made by his Canadian relative, a cabinet-maker. *Good man* thinks Frank, although a basket woven from reeds on the banks of the River Ox would do for Francis Tremble. Peggy would dress him in something nice, that's for sure. Molly would have his favourite photo, the one she took, glasses perched on the end of his nose, in the church or beside his basket. Then he would float away to the other side of life, serene in his reedy weavings.

Francis Tremble, concentrate please.

The coffin will be drawn in solemn ceremony through the streets of Leicester to the king's final resting place, Leicester Cathedral. The actor Benedict Cumberbatch will read a poem by the Poet Laureate, Carol Ann Duffy, written especially for the occasion. The tombstone, built from Swaledale Fossil, a lovely lightly marbled stone, has a strikingly simple carved cross running through the length and breadth of it.

The plinth is made from Kilkenny limestone from Ireland and features the king's coat of arms with his name, Richard III, his dates, 1452–1485, and his motto, in Latin, *Loyaulte me lie* – Loyalty binds me – engraved round the base.

That's what Frank feels in his heart. Nothing but loyalty and love for Molly and Peggy. *Molly Chops, we've always been on your side.* He gulps and swallows. *Come on, Tremble, you've got this far.* A huge gust of wind rattles the doors, the weather lady told him an Atlantic low was on the way, but he thinks it's reached him already.

'Biscuits?' Peggy asks, appearing out of nowhere.

'What?'

'Crunchy sugary things?'

'I forgot.'

Peggy shakes her head. It's so unlike Frank not to have food prepared.

'I'll nip out now and get some. Make sure the urn's switched on so it can heat up. Frank? Are you all right?'

He takes his glasses off and cleans them. 'Sugar rots your brain. Have you heard from Molly?'

'Yes, I told you, she said she'd be here.'

'Edward?'

'No sign. I've tried everywhere I can think of.'

For some reason Frank wants to sit in a corner and cry like a baby. Edward should be here. He said he was going to come. *I wouldn't miss this, Frank.* He was excited about it. Frank cannot shake his inner gloom. He's trying to keep focussed on the king, but he would prefer to see Molly and Edward, young people who are alive, and, failing that, he'd like to go back to the cave and talk to the man he saw, not talk *about* him.

The hall is filling up with people. Smile. Shake hands. The new vicar – *Please call me Jerome* – is so enthusiastic. He's not so tall but solid, large black-framed glasses, brown eyes, not the type of thin pale English vicar Oxonians are used to. It's his first community event and he wants to make sure he's shaking as many hands as possible. He has a good strong handshake. Peggy wonders if he goes to the gym.

'Frank, Peggy, this is such an excellent idea. Do you both belong to the Richard the Third Society?'

Peggy wants to laugh. *No, it's just us, very informal. We met his soul in the cave that nobody knows about; he has a talking Raven as well, didn't I say?*

Frank can hear his own voice echoing inside his head. Peggy has a pulsing at her temples. In a minute she'll slip away and take some paracetamol before the headache takes hold. Can't be sick now. She digs her fingernails into the back of her hand. Apparently, the vicar is still speaking. He really is a very handsome man.

'Where did you say you were from before here?'

'Walthamstow.'

'Lovely,' says Peggy, not listening.

'But originally my family is from Kenya.'

'Well, that's lovely too,' she says.

'Burying an ancient king, it's quite exciting, isn't it?' The Reverend Jerome carries on making his way through the hall. It's all too much for Peggy, and she ducks out. She's the white rabbit in the wrong story, but she doesn't know the right story. She loosens her scarf and hurries to the high street for biscuits. By the time she's back, Frank's set up his laptop for the presentation. Peggy lays out the paper plates and takeaway cups for the tea. Long-life milk cartons, sugar, spoons, urn is heating up. She's good with details, tiny little things, a stain on the bottom of a shirt, a loose button, a thread unwinding, but when the big things of life threaten to blow up in her face, what does she do? Counts milk portions, two each, that's all. She makes her way to the front of the hall and scans the faces, but there's only one she wants to see.

Everyone's talking about the same thing, that's why they're here.

'We didn't get tickets for Leicester, they sold out in minutes, but we'll watch it on the telly.'

Molly. When she sees her entering the hall, Peggy's heart leaps. There's her girl and she's the best story of all. Shining like a star amongst the sea of grey, even with her nose ring. Because of her nose ring. Peggy squeezes past people to reach her. Her hair's getting long again, her cheeks have filled out, her eyes sparkle, goodness she's looking so well, she's positively glowing. *Molly, Molly, I love you.*

'What's going on, you all right?' Molly hugs her.

'Yes, yes, we're fine.' Peggy fights to recover her composure.

'Look,' says Molly, lifting up her jumper, and underneath there is the pink silk dress. 'It's gorgeous, I love it, thank you.' She kisses Peggy on the cheek.

Reverend Jerome is still shaking hands and making his way up and down the rows of unbuttoned coats. Finally he stops at Molly and Peggy.

'Molly, this is the new vicar, Reverend Jerome.'

'Hello, Molly, so lovely to meet you.'

'Hello, Vicar,' she says, 'no last name?'

'It's a long one,' he says. 'Trust me, it's easier this way.' As they shake hands, a crackle of static energy flies between them. The Reverend gives her an odd look and she rubs her hand. *It's his energy running through me.* She's bursting to tell Peggy and Frank about Dedalus, but she knows once she does, everything will change. *Change is good, Molly. Change is very bloody good.* Days ago, she mentioned this talk about the king and Dedalus fixed his eyes on the other side of the room. He asked where it was going to be, and she thought that meant he would come, but why would he? Molly's finding it hard to concentrate. Like her head is on backwards and everyone is talking in slow motion. She knows in her bones a public talk is not his thing. Being normal is never going to work for him. He's not going to sit down for a scone and a cuppa or work out discount points on his club card at Tesco's. He is not of this world now. *He was once, Molly, but no longer.* He's always distracted by things she takes no notice of, and he's had a look in his eyes for days, seeing something she can't touch. At night he comes back smelling of cold air and earth. She never asks him where he's been. Why would she? He's a bloody angel. She finds a seat near the doors in case she turns out to be wrong, but she won't be.

A man sitting near them nudges his wife. 'That's Molly Stern,' he says. 'Her father died in the cellar, remember?'

His wife turns round for a quick look. Molly takes no notice — people are always staring at her here — and finds a seat at the back close to the doors. Peggy returns to the front of the hall in case Frank needs her. She's hoping the familiar face of Edward Farraday will turn up out of the blue.

Frank clears his throat to begin. Peggy smiles at him encouragingly. He's just noticed Molly sitting at the back of the hall. His glorious girl. He's about to start his talk but all he wants to do is race over and hug her, because, like Peggy, she's the face he wants to see. He tries to relax.

'Goodness,' says Frank, 'this is nice. I hadn't expected so many people. Thank you all for turning out today.'

Smatter of applause. Another quick smile from Peggy.

The lights go out. The first slide shines on the wall. There he is, Richard the Third, in his hat and brooch and cloak, looking pensive. *He doesn't look like that anymore*, thinks Frank, but he can't say that out loud, not here. More words come tumbling out. He's lived with this for so long. There's a picture of his brother, King Edward the Fourth. They look so similar, the two brothers, Richard and Edward.

Edward.

'You can definitely see the family resemblance: Edward's a bit fleshier than Richard.'

Frank can hear himself saying Edward was charming, whereas Richard was less so. 'He's shorter, and nowhere near as nice looking as his brother.'

I've seen him, Frank wants to yell, *I have seen the soul of the king.*

The heads of the audience recede in front of Frank, then zoom back into view. A small bell starts ringing in his head. His heart thumps and for a second his mum waves to him from the back of the hall. *Hello, Mum, I haven't forgotten you.* He rubs his eyes.

'And here's Elizabeth Woodville, who became his queen. A marriage no one knew anything about, except it was loyal and lasting, which is all anyone needs to know about a relationship, unless you're the king.'

Loyal and lasting. He can see Molly scratching her head. *Goodness, her hair's grown long again.*

The next slide is the painting *The Two Princes Edward and Richard in the Tower*, by Sir John Everett Millais.

Those lost boys.

Edward, Edward, Edward. Don't you disappear like them. Where are you? You should be doing this bit.

Frank wants to stop talking and sit down. The room swims in and out of focus. He hears his voice amongst the endless parade of facts and supposition.

Why does any of it matter now? Are you a good man? Yes or no? Once and for all, why are we making such a fuss about you? What happened, what did you do? Why have I been so excited by a king? What do you want from me?

'Anne Neville, Richard's wife, Queen of England, and their son, also named Edward.'

Time for a joke, Frank, tell it, go on. 'Was there anyone not named Edward or Richard?'

Titter from the audience.

'William, Lord Hastings,' someone yells.

'Henry Stafford, Duke of Buckingham,' says the same person, the man in the audience who thinks he knows far more than Frank and is making Frank work hard for his low-sugar biscuits. Frank undoes his top button. Licks his lips.

Bit hot in here. Sip of water. *Keep going*. So many heads turned towards him. *Right then*.

'King Edward the Fourth, Richard's older brother, well, he died unexpectedly in April 1483 from a cold, a sniffle, a chill, a chest infection, a fever, pneumonia, tuberculosis, anything, could have been anything. Anything was very common then. We just don't know what it might have been.'

'How old was he?'

'Forty.'

'That's not even old.'

Frank's thoughts slip and tumble. A huge dam of unstoppable emotion is building in him, any minute he's going to burst out of his cardigan. History never stops, it just keeps going. Peggy looks concerned, something's happening, but she doesn't know what it is. She imagines the soul of the king in his fine feathery cloak, padding along with his naked feet, with Raven on his shoulder, making straight for Frank. Outside, the wind howls around the hall, rattling the doors. Frank breaks out in a sweat, wipes his forehead with his sleeve.

'This king, who utterly believed in redemption, the saving of his soul through prayer, he came to the abbey at Oxenbridge, and no one's going to believe the next bit. Even my wife thought – well I don't know what exactly she thinks, no one ever does. I mean how do you ever really know anything? I don't know how it's possible, if it is, as I do like scented candles, but you know, I have seen him. And just then, well, I thought he was here, and he might have been. I think he's real you know, I really do.' He looks at Peggy.

'And some of you lot know Edward, he works in the shop, and if you don't, you bloody well should, so there we are, so thank you, thank you.' He searches through his notes.

What on earth is Frank going on about? Peggy waves frantically at him, mouthing things, but he's had enough.

'Bugger this,' he says.

He's going to see Molly. His darling girl. He walks past the rows of astonished faces, to the most wonderful face in the world, *Molly Chops*, gives her a huge hug, and she returns it, which makes him start to cry. Francis Tremble, Uncle Frank. Retired fanatic, keeper of secrets.

'Come on,' says Molly, 'let's get out of here.' She takes his arm and Peggy's not far behind. The three of them tumble through the doors onto the street and into the cold. Peggy is tight faced and serious, fighting a rising sense of panic.

'Are you all right? Frank? *Frank?* Do you have a pain in your chest?'

He leans his head against the wall. The sky's turned a greenish grey, big fat raindrops start to fall, and Molly's in charge.

'Get him in the car, Peggy.'

51

The Reverend Jerome

oversees the emptying of the hall as people hurry to find their cars and get home before it starts pouring. A few brave souls stay and help pack away, wondering where the Trembles have gone, as they didn't get a chance to thank them. The vicar is concerned about Frank's abrupt departure: he left without his laptop, and he wants to check he's all right.

'Has anyone seen Frank Tremble?'

'I think he's gone home.'

Outside, the spirits are dancing in Oxenbridge. Covering the town with rain bouncing through darkness.

The shed is full

of Molly, Peggy, and Frank and a handful of unlit scented candles.

'Right then, will one of you please tell me what the bloody hell is going on? And *Frank*, are you actually dying or are we just here for a drink? And who's been buying all these candles?'

Frank squeezes Molly's fingers. 'I think it was a panic attack, horrible.'

'He was doing so well. Wasn't he, Molly?'

'Never better.'

Molly is used to dealing with the highs and lows of her own emotions, that turbulence pumping through her veins, but she's not used to it with Peggy and Frank. The deal is they stay the same and always love her. That's how it's worked until now.

'I'm sorry, but are we pretending to have a normal conversation?'

'Molly, love, listen. Edward is missing. And we have to find him,' says Frank. 'And I think I know where he's gone.'

'Frank's right,' says Peggy, 'we should have come down here sooner.'

'Why would Edward Farraday be in the bloody shed?'

Frank clears his throat. 'We've got something to show you, haven't we, Peggy?'

Molly groans. 'I don't like this at all.'

Peggy helps Frank move the table, roll back the rug, and open the trapdoor while Molly watches with a serious dose of disbelief.

'We'll explain as we go,' says Frank. 'Watch your footing on the way down, come on.' He switches on the fairy lights, his voice echoing back down the tunnel.

'Excuse me, but what are these?'

'Fairy lights, Molly.'

'Look, you two, if this is your remake of *The Blair Witch Project*, it's not funny. I can't believe I'm doing this. Hey, wait for me, it's bloody dark.'

52

The Oxenbridge storm

has gathered itself around the town, gaining intensity, blowing half the steady world off its feet. The average monthly rainfall for Oxenbridge will pour down in just one night. Rain will drizzle down these walls. The underworld's ancient maw will open its darkling mouth and take this water in. Dedalus doesn't pay attention to the weather in the same way he doesn't count time, it keeps its own wisdom, but with every step the sound he is following grows fainter. *Help me.* He could let time run its course, and the sound fade away, but what's the point of him if he does not attend to the cries of a soul? He once lay in the dirt calling for help and no one came. For all the pleasure he has taken with Molly, he will surely suffer more, if this is suffering for him, which it clearly isn't. Not yet.

Max has followed him from the cellar and trots along beside him, remembering his glory days of ratting in the dark. Dedalus likes the company of this cat. They understand each other's solitary ways. The ground is spongy beneath them, as if it will give way and drag Dedalus into the fire pits he still believes are waiting, despite the damp earth hiding in the walls.

His eyes translate the darkness. Stop, listen, there it is: *Help, help.* Max remains at his side, tail upright, whiskers twitching in the dark, happy until they reach the tunnel's end where a massive rockfall waits. The boulders are huge, as if the devil himself has rolled them into place. *Take that, you puny humans, move them if you can.* Dedalus can just make out a narrow gap snaking between the larger rocks, right at the top and barely visible.

He picks Max up and strokes him, holding the noisy purring animal close. *Go back*, he says, before he climbs, and Max listens to Dedalus in all ways, sending his small catty cries up and down the walls as he returns to the cellar. Dedalus clambers as high as he can, pushing forward through stone and rock until he's at the top. He stops, breathes, and listens. Silence. The only way through the gap is to crawl under the wedged boulder that has been there for a hundred years. It's a tight squeeze, even for him, hauling himself along. Once he's through and out on the narrow ledge he finds there's hardly any room to stand, but not for nothing has he been given his determined feet. From the edge of the ledge he can see far below him, to the body of a crumpled man lying on the ground.

The young man who has fallen

is shivering with pain and passing in and out of consciousness, unaware he is moaning. He is in the kitchen with his mum. The kettle is boiling, bubbling, 'Turn it off, Mum, turn it off. Mum?'

You're in a bit of a pickle, aren't you?

Now she's there with him, cradling him in her arms, her hands brushing against his face. *You're so warm, so soft.* He is so very grateful for her warmth. He tries to touch his mum – *Stay with me, Mum, stay* – but his arm is so heavy, it just won't move. His lips are dry. He can barely turn his head.

In the tumult of his years,

Dedalus remembers flying down the stairs with the body that once was his. He remembers how no one came for him. How he stumbled, lost and hurt, from the past to the future. He remembers Jessop scurrying from the church. He remembers that fragment of hair fallen from his hands. Lost. He must have dropped it when he fell. If Silas had opened the door where would he be now? Somewhere in God's Heaven radiant with prayer. Departed from this noisy world that asks so much from him. He can barely see where he puts his feet, but he trusts the truth of himself now, he was made for this. He leans back against the rock and lets the rock guide him. *Take me down*, he tells the stone, *take me down*. Foothold to hollow, from one small purchase to the next, he's both thrilled and terrified, gathering speed down a vertical rock face, until he reaches the bottom and digs his feet into sandy soil. He looks back up to see the vastness of it, his heart beating louder than ever. Then he sees the boy. Twisted on the ground. Dedalus kneels beside him and places his hand on the young man's chest. His soul is intact, Dedalus is certain.

Edward's eyes flicker open as he croaks, 'Am I going to die?' With every movement pain drags him down to the difficult depths. Who is hurting his eyes with that light? He must be hallucinating, because the face leaning over him and swimming in and out of focus is Muffin Man. That hand on his chest again, an easing of fear, a kindness, a voice.

'You keep breathing,' says Dedalus. 'Come. I will help you.'

Very carefully and gently, he scoops him up, and as he does so, Edward cannot help but let out a terrible moan, and that is how they go, Dedalus carrying him as best he can, trying not to cause him any more pain. The boy is light, a feather in his arms. *Save them. We must save them.* He studies the cave walls. Coming down was easy. He did not know how hard it would be going back up. He steps onto the first foothold. Balancing carefully, he has no free hands and cannot hold the rock, so he uses his shoulders to navigate one step at a time as the ascent begins. He begins to understand salvation is not a word, it is a task. Salvation is the hardest thing he's ever done.

Raven could be in the rain

conducting the rhythms of the storm, but, like all good guides, he waits in the interlude between action and thought, where nothing and everything happens. He knows the angel's on his way, so where is he?

Ricardo is hiding on the ledge. Bedraggled. Feathers moulting. It's an effort to do anything. He shrinks into the wall at an approaching light. He wants to see the angel before the angel sees him.

53

'So long as there are no human sacrifices
at the end of this we'll be all right,' says Molly, trying to keep the
mood light in the darkness, but the mood is tense.

'Is this what's been going on between you two?'

'Sort of,' says Frank.

'I hope we find him,' says Peggy.

Frank wishes he'd had a cup of tea when they'd come
home. 'Here we are,' he says, swinging his torch all over the
walls.

'Oh my goodness,' says Molly, walking into the chamber of
stars. The cave never fails to impress, with its space and height
working wonders on the human spirit. Peggy calls out fiercely,
'EDWARD! EDWARD FARRADAY!'

No answer. Peggy and Frank exchange glances. 'Edward
followed me here,' says Frank.

'Why didn't you tell me about this sooner?' Molly turns to
Peggy.

Peggy shrugs. 'I thought your uncle was having an affair
with someone. I didn't want to say.'

'He's in love with a cave, Peggy,' says Molly, 'Look at him!'

'It's been really, really, stressful, Molly, you have no idea, and
there's something else.'

'Oh no,' Molly groans. She thought she was the only one keeping secrets. It's on the tip of her tongue to tell Peggy everything, but now is not the right time and she holds back. Something's near the roof, and she tries to get a better look.

'*Mesdames et messieurs*, welcome to Our Humble Abode. May I ask why you would keep a king waiting thus? Archaic word, I grant you, but we're all getting on a bit, are we not, my Kingly King?'

'Well that is definitely not Edward Farraday,' says Molly.

By the strained look on their faces, Molly guesses Frank and Peggy have seen this before, but she hasn't. The sight of Ricardo descending from his humble ledge and floating down those narrow steps and drawing ever closer in his cloak of feathers, takes Molly by surprise. Really, she wasn't expecting this.

'And what the hell do we have here?'

'Ah, Molly,' says Frank, his heart thumping, 'now just bear with everything, won't you?'

'Looks like I have no choice, but please tell me I'm dreaming,' she says.

'Molly-Millicent, my deary dear, you are always dreaming,' says Raven, 'but then again, you are not.'

Molly believes and disbelieves at the same time. She's been sharing her days with an angel, after all.

'Molly.' Peggy drops her voice. 'This is, you know, the soul of Richard the Third, the Oxenbridge King.'

'Of course it is,' says Molly, thinking if that's what a soul looks like then she never wants to die.

Ricardo, now halfway down and balancing on a ledge of crumbling stone, fixes his dark eyes on this audience of mortals. A hushed expectancy hovers between them. Raven perches beside the king, dipping his indigo head this way and that.

'What's coming next, Monsieur Frankincense and Mirth?'

Frank clears his throat.

'Ask him if he's seen Edward,' says Peggy.

'He might misunderstand the question,' says Frank.

'Monsieur Farraday has not been seen since he was with your good self, Monsieur Tremblay,' says Raven.

Frank is starting to look a lot less like the happy man Molly has always known him to be. 'Does that mean he's … gone?' asks Frank, swallowing hard.

'We are not waiting for Monsieur Farraday to assail us with his wit,' says Raven. 'We are waiting for an angel. The very same angel you have spoken about, is it not Monsieur Tremblay?'

Peggy nudges Molly. *An angel.*

'Peggy, I'll tell you everything, but not now,' Molly whispers.

'Everything about what?' asks Peggy.

'Later,' says Molly, 'not here.'

This is the most peculiar meeting of Frank's life, and he's had a few. He turns to Peggy and Molly. 'I just want to acknowledge that he is here, isn't he?'

'Yes,' says Peggy, 'we can all see him.'

Raven yawns. Ricardo totters forward.

Molly wonders what the soul of the king will sound like. If an angel can speak, why not a soul? 'Mr Crow?'

'Raven is always bigger than Crow, Sir. The name is Raven, much obliged.'

'So tell me, Raven,' says Molly, perfectly at ease being called 'Sir', she quite likes it, and talking to a bird, 'who is this angel you are waiting for?' She knows but she still asks.

'By the Beak of Exasperation, I saw him, and I showed him. Angel of Nothing and Nowhere, that's who he is.'

Peggy and Frank exchange glances.

'So, this is how it's going to go,' says Raven, 'There's Part A, public confession, and we might as well crack on. Part B, the Big Bread Stick Himself arrives and takes Ricardo off to glory. It's been long enough, eh, my Kingly King?'

'Wait a minute,' says Frank, 'Here and now? With us? The actual confession of Richard the Third?'

'Frank, you are genius level,' says Raven.

'Can I just say,' says Frank, in his guest role as moral arbiter, 'that not everything can be explained and sometimes the greatest mysteries creep up on you before you've had a chance to ask a single question. And this is one of the greatest things that's ever happened to me in my life.'

'Thank you, Monsieur Tremblay. Let us proceed, my Kingly King, for this is the moment, Ricardo. The coming together of all things.'

Everyone is quiet, waiting to hear him speak. He shuffles a little further forward, this feathery thing, this defeated enduring soul of the king. He surveys the holy trinity of Frank, Molly, and Peggy, shining like mad little diamonds in the middle of the cave. His voice is soft and quiet, like breath on a cold winter's day.

'When my esteemed brother died, I made promises before the Lord' – he looks down, picturing a stone staircase at his feet – 'that I would be a good and faithful Protector. Loyal to the Crown, as I have always been.' The king cocks his head to one side like a bird. The great stone walls of York heard his promise of Protection to a slender boy. The name Edward ricochets inside him. Brother. Son. Nephew. All climbing the endless stairs like him. Above them in the faraway world, thunder reverberates through the walls.

Frank can't help himself, he bursts out, 'That's your motto,' says Frank, '"Loyalty binds me."'

'Ssh, Frank!'

Peggy thinks of Edward and hopes desperately that he's all right. She's irritated, tired, and hungry and wants to go home. 'It's all well and good, being a protector, but why don't you just tell us what you did to the boys. That's all anyone wants to know. I mean, you didn't protect them, did you? And we can't stay long, as we need to find Edward.'

Frank thinks maybe Peggy is right. All anyone wants to know is what happened to the boys. Frank's glasses are misting up. Perhaps the king is an apparition, a self-induced hallucination, after all. The temperature drops. No one remembers the lousy weather forecast. None of them can see the rain funnelling down, or the trees being blown over roads and driveways. Peggy can't see the soaking Oxenbridge roofs or the leaks through Oxenbridge ceilings, or the birds taking shelter from a storm where only the brave or foolish venture out.

Frank is never one to break up a meeting, but the king is losing his feathers and whichever way this goes, it's sad. Sad for the boys. Sad for the soul in front of Frank and sad for Frank, for what is his journey with the king if not personal?

'For goodness sake, will someone please tell me what is so special about this king?' says Molly.

Raven flaps his wings. 'I thought you'd never ask, my deary dear. Out of all the souls on the battlefield, this one truly believed he was good. So I shows him, in his great and stumbling afterlife, he's both good king and bad king. It's a balancing thing. And he can ask the Almighty for forgiveness. And we all need that, don't we, Molly Polly?'

'Forgiveness? Doesn't that depend on what you've done?'

Molly takes a deep breath. She hasn't quite finished. 'Whether he's the king or not I really don't care. You have to earn forgiveness. It doesn't just get brought to you on a plate. As far as I'm concerned, he's the same as every other man, with an opportunity for power, always wanting things. And when he gets what he wants he thinks he can just say sorry and all the hurt goes away. Like it's nothing and everything's all right. But it's not and never will be and I've had enough of all this for one evening, and I'm going home, but before I do, let me ask him this. What if he doesn't go to Heaven, what if he's stuck here forever, consumed by eternity, gasping for the light. What if there is no light?'

She shouts that last bit, then says, 'Come on, Trembles, we're leaving.'

'We have to find Edward first,' says Peggy.

'Molly, that's a bit harsh,' says Frank.

'They were young boys, and they were vulnerable and he didn't protect them.'

She looks at Ricardo. 'Did you? Well, answer me. Did you?'

The king struggles to remain on his feet.

'So, the question becomes,' says Frank, drawing himself up to a height of blazing glory, 'are you a good soul? Here's what I think. You were responsible for those boys. You took them into the tower, and you didn't do a very good job of looking after them, did you?'

The king studies the cave walls. It's one thing to be shown the body of a sleeping boy who cannot answer back, it's quite another to have an accusation flung by the living. Frank wants to clasp his feathery arm. 'Look, mate, I respect you, I really do. When you're inside your own life you don't always know the consequences of your actions and by the time you do, it's too late to change them. But in the end you have to account for yourself, don't you?'

Frank has lost track of the hours and is just a little peckish. Some crackers, cheese, and an apple would do. Still, he's said his piece, let life takes its course. He bows to the king. 'Thank you for letting me see you,' he says. 'I hope you find absolution, but it's not mine to give.'

Feathers tumble through the air. Molly glances over at Peggy. She loves her uncle, her good, kind, brave uncle. Peggy looks quite proud of him too. The king walks unsteadily to the edge of the ledge, looking like he's about to hurl himself to the floor. No one is expecting what happens next. He takes a deep feathery breath and flings his arms open, his cloak fluttering like a pair of scabrous wings.

'Forgive me most Merciful Lord for the sins I committed when I sought to be king. May the Lord have mercy on my soul, for I repent all my sins.'

He stops speaking and his head falls to his chest. A moment later he looks up. When he speaks again, his voice quivers with the unearthing of words dug from his bones. From his life and from his death. Words that say true and lonely things.

'I did not protect my nephew, the Prince of Wales. I left him and his brother in the Tower, and, by my gross neglect, it was I who killed them, and I am sorry for it.'

A stunned silence sweeps the cave. Ricardo stares into the darkness before adding, 'And I humbly beg the Heavenly Father to bestow His Divine Mercy on what is left of my soul.'

Raven lets out a piercing cry. 'Bless you, my son, my Kingly King.'

Ricardo sways before him. More stones crumble beneath his feet.

Raven cries again, 'Now the alignment of Heaven and earth can begin.'

Frank rubs his face. 'Oh goodness me.'

Peggy whispers, 'Gosh, I wasn't expecting to hear that. So what happens now? I thought he'd be ascending.'

'Let's stay calm,' says Frank.

'I am calm,' says Peggy, surprising herself, 'but we still haven't found Edward, have we?'

The walls twinkle like it's a big happy occasion.

54

On the far side of the cave

Dedalus stops, listening. A voice is asking for mercy. That's what
he's trying to give this poor creature in his arms whose groans
are filling the air. Dedalus searches the cave for the speaker of
those words, and sees three figures, almost lost in shadows, and
one of them looks a lot like Molly Stern. He looks again. A bird
is fluttering high on the narrow ledge, and, as he looks closely,
he can see a face he recognises. After all this undiluted time. *His
king*, wrapped in the feathers of eternity. And now his king can
see Dedalus. And for a moment both are lost in that shock of
recognition.

Your face has not changed. You are still the king.

*And you are still the monk with the horses. I remember you. I waited
for you.*

Time hurtles past them. *What have you now become?* Dedalus
is back in the Abbey of Stern in his tiny prayer-filled room.
This is what she wanted him to do. *Save them, Dedalus, save
them.* From five hundred years of lonely. From his itchy
mattress. From the church. From the relic box. From his knees.
From his dreams. From the lavender. From the horse. From
his beseeching prayers. God has given him a chance to redeem
himself. His inner light brightens and pulses. Raven flies over

everyone's heads in great dizzying loops, from one side of the cave to the other.

'Ricardus Repentus. A soul can be transformed.'

'What the hell,' exclaims Molly, looking from the shadows of the king to the light of Dedalus. Rain trickles down the cold stone walls and a stream of water starts running round her feet. In the faraway muffled world, huge gusts of wind swirl around the hollow tree.

The burden of carrying this pain-struck young man is almost too much for Dedalus, who wants to put him down and be in attendance on his king. He wills himself on, for what is salvation after all, if it is not the taming of desire first. His feet find the smallest fissures in the rock, for purchase, to take this young man to safety, to bring his soul in, to save him, save him, save him. Then he will return for the king.

Floodwater pours steadily

into the cave from the storage tunnel entrance. Returning that way now looks impossible, so Frank and Peggy hurriedly follow Molly to the other side of the cave. Only an hour ago they were walking on the dry dirt floor.

Molly desperately searches for the shadowy figure halfway up a wall, 'Dedalus! Deeedaaaluuss!'

'Who?' says Frank.

Peggy's heart is knocking in her chest, 'Frank, we should never have come down here.'

At the sound of Molly's voice, and with great effort, Dedalus turns around.

'Oh my God,' says Peggy, flashing her torch at the figure against the wall, 'it's the idiot from the road.'

'He is not an idiot,' says Molly.

'Well what the bloody hell is he doing down here? And Frank, look, isn't that Edward Farraday he's carrying? Frank, look.'

'Well it looks awfully like him, Peggy, and at least he's alive because his head's moving.'

Rain funnels down through the roots of the hollow tree, the entrance to the cave where Raven once perched. The rain slides over stony ridges, bringing mud and debris and turning the cave floor into a pool of dirty water. Above them, Dedalus ploughs on ahead, the young man in his arms.

'We can't stay here,' says Molly, 'it's flooding, we'll have to follow him.'

Peggy shakes her head, 'I can't do that.'

'Peggy, look where we are.' Frank holds her hands. 'We can't go back through the tunnel. We either climb or drown, and we're not drowning, are we Peggy?'

Molly searches for all the fissures and footholds that Dedalus has used. 'Just put your feet where I put mine, you can do this,' she says to her quaking aunt, before beginning her climb. Peggy can hardly bear to watch her in case she slips, but she's following close behind, so she has to, her legs shaking and her boots scraping against the wall. Progress is slow but steady. In the dark, up the impossible wall.

Peggy is close to tears. Frank's behind her, his body aching with every step. He's not sure how much longer he can keep going, his knuckles grazing the rock wall, his body feeling heavy like a sack of potatoes and every step getting harder and harder. The higher they climb the more desperate Peggy becomes, trying not to lose her balance on the slippery stone. This is one of the worst things she has ever done in her entire life, her face inches from the wall. Molly, younger and fitter, has nearly reached the overhang where Dedalus is now laying the young man gently down.

In his semi-conscious state, Edward cannot possibly know his life has already been saved by Muffin Man, whose warmth has flowed into his veins and kept the trembling shock at bay. Dedalus takes a moment to regather his strength. Molly is nearly at the top, so he reaches over the ledge with his wiry arm and pulls her up the last few feet. *Molly. Molly Stern.* She's trembling like a beast as he holds her in his arms, letting his radiant heat flow through her, warming her up, filling the places she so often cannot see. She buries her head in his chest, but he lifts her face to his. *Not now Molly, not now, we must save them.* There are things each of them must do.

'This strength is yours,' he says, 'and always has been.' He kisses her on the mouth where all his secrets lie before he gently pulls away.

'No,' she says, 'don't leave me. This is when I really need your help.' She clings on to him. 'I can't do this by myself, don't make me.'

He runs a finger down the side of her face. 'You have to let me go. You have to save them.'

He cannot mean that, not here, but before she can say anything else, Edward groans and opens his eyes, not sure if he really is seeing Molly Stern above him. He closes his eyes. Molly kneels beside him, feeling for his pulse and pushing the hair from his face. 'Edward, blink if you can hear me.'

He blinks.

'Right, hang on, we're going to get you out of here.'

She looks around for Dedalus, but he is getting ready for the next stage of salvation, which is setting the boulder free.

Molly's heart is beating

like a big old drum, and everything's dark and everything's difficult. Her arms are working like pistons as, with grim determination, she hauls Peggy up the last few feet and over the ledge to safety. Frank's not far behind. Below them the floodwater's rising. The light from Dedalus has gone with him between the rocks and now there's a thumping noise pounding through the walls, which is Dedalus trying to move the immovable boulder. Hearing this, Frank looks up, wondering if the cave is collapsing, and misses the next step. He scrabbles for the wall, but the wall isn't there and he falls backwards, arms flailing as he hits the water.

'He's gone!' Peggy screams.

'Peggy, stay there,' Molly yells, 'I'll find him.'

How the hell will I do that? thinks Molly, frantically peering from the ledge. He's somewhere down there in the water, but it's impossible to see.

Nothing else for it, she takes off her coat and jumper. Stands shivering in her pink silk dress.

'Molly, what are you doing?' cries Peggy.

Molly edges forward. *I am afraid.*

You can do it. Trust yourself.

The moon slips between clouds. The storm renews itself.

Peggy can't look and sits next to Edward to stop herself screaming. Molly is more scared than she's ever been in her life, but she's not letting Frank drown in front of her without doing something. *It's yours, it always has been.* She can hear him pounding the rocks, like a heartbeat drumming inside her.

Now Molly, now.

It all happens so fast she has no time to think. She slithers back down, grabbing at every hard slippery foothold as she goes, bumping and sliding most of the way before she tumbles into the water. The shock of it takes her breath away. It's fast and freezing bloody cold. It's a struggle keeping her head above the water, and she paddles furiously, searching desperately for Frank. She dives under but it's too murky and full of debris to see anything. Twigs and branches hurtle by and she grabs what looks like half a bloody tree to help her keep afloat. She's screaming for Frank at the top of her voice, trying not to swallow filthy water. Twenty yards ahead of her there's an arm grabbing the air.

'Frank, Frank, I'm coming, I'm coming,' she's yelling to her uncle as loudly as she can. Molly can barely keep hold of the branch as the current swirls round her. She swims and kicks frantically trying to steer the branch through the water. Everything feels like it's happening in slow motion. Again and again she lunges towards Frank, while the water tries to drag her away. After what seems like an eternity, she finally manages to reach him. His head is rolling and bobbing in the water, he's heavy and hard to hold, and her hands are going numb with cold and keep slipping.

She's shouting in his ear. 'Frank, hold the bloody branch.'

Breathe, Molly, breathe.

Dad?

You can do it, Mol. You are my fearless girl.

She can't do it. She's going under herself, the branch dipping with their combined weight. Her fingers have lost their grip, her hands aren't working properly. Her legs flail in the water as she tries to hold him, and just when she thinks she cannot go on, her feet touch something hard. It's the cave floor, of course it is; she's fighting to stay upright and hold on to Frank and keep her head above the water. *There it is again. Stand, Molly, stand.* She can't, *shit*, she's losing him. Then she finds the floor again.

*It will hold you long enough, Mol, that's the way. Come on, Mol,
you're my girl.*

'Frank, please wake up. I need you, Uncle Frank, I need you.'

Somewhere in Frank's brain he can hear Molly. He opens his
eyes, spluttering and coughing. Molly needs him. *Molly.* He's so
cold and so tired, but Molly's helping him and a voice in his head
tells him to forget about dying in the flood. Anything for Molly.

'Keep hold of this, you have to help me, Frank, ready? Kick,
Frank, kick.'

Frank is not letting go of the branch. Together Molly and
Frank thrash their way through the water, surging into the
current, trying to get back across the pool of water that used
to be a cave, still is a cave. Molly pushes Frank in front of her
like a giant float, and Frank swimming as best he can. The
cave floor disappears, then reappears under their feet. They
stop, rest, go again, rest, go, until they crab their way over
to the wall. The branch is still in one piece and Frank lunges
forward on it using the momentum of his body, with Molly
close behind, shoving him onto the narrow ridge. Molly
doesn't want to let go of the branch, but Frank grabs hold of
her long enough for her to swing her sodden body up beside
him, gasping for breath. They watch the branch swirl away in
the water.

'We're all right, we're okay.' Frank's panting from exhaustion,
his voice barely a whisper as he hugs Molly tightly, but they have
to keep going. They have to begin the perilous climb again. Step
after step, a bedraggled Frank going first, with cold wet Molly
following behind, one hand on the wall, the other on Frank,
and she's not letting go. Peggy is yelling until she can yell no
more. Another thunderous roar fills the cave. Peggy can't watch
anymore, not until they're over the top. Edward opens his eyes

as Frank's head finally comes into view. Peggy helps him up the last few feet with her quivering arms; he's followed by her wonderful girl, dragging herself onto the ledge again, soaked to the bone in a pink silk dress.

Peggy dries her as best she can with her jumper and coat. Frank sits exhausted on the ledge.

'Where's Edward?' he says.

It's only now they see

what Dedalus has done. He has shattered the boulder. What's left of the rockfall has fallen and crumbled into a mass of smaller rocks, creating a space just big enough to walk through, which is where Dedalus is now. Carrying Edward over the chaos of the world, leaving a tumbled stony path for them to follow. He has done this for Molly, and he has done this for Edward, and he has done this for himself, so he can return and save the king. Back down the tunnel he goes, through the flooding water. Past the cellar entrance where he first saw the young man. Past the cellar where he first met Molly. He sees now that both of them were showing him the way.

Calm Peggy

still has her black-handled torch in her pocket and, like a miracle, it still works. She gives it to Molly, who holds it above her head like an Olympic flame as they clamber down the crumbled boulders. It's hard going, but at least it's down rather than up, and once they're at the bottom they find themselves in another tunnel with water swirling through it. They have no choice other than to wade through it, but so far it's not too deep.

'This isn't the storage tunnel,' says Frank. 'I don't know where this leads.'

'We can't go back, though,' says Molly, 'so follow me.' She has no idea where this tunnel will end up either, but every act of strength makes her stronger. They keep a firm hold of one another, wading through the water like an odd little conga line of people, Molly at the front, and heading straight past the cellar entrance, which is half hidden by the rising flood.

Dedalus comes the opposite way towards them, the force of his body making a bow wave before him. Molly knows he is not coming for them or for her. He studies Peggy and Frank, as now he is inches away. There they are, he remembers them.

Peggy blurts out the first thing in her exhausted head. 'What have you done with Edward?'

'Keep going, then you will find him.' His voice is smooth like silk, clear like water. Drops roll down his face; he brushes them away and takes Molly's face in his hands.

'Don't go back there,' she says.

Molly.

'Come with me,' she says.

She means leave the dark and the soul of the king. *Come with me to the shops and the coffee bar. Come with me to the bright fragile nonsense of everyday life, to work and play, and love and washing up.* He won't. She knows deep in her bones her life could never hold him. Water swirls between them, and she is cold, way beyond desire now, but desire is all she has at the end of things. She wants to say, *I'm Molly, your girl, your lovely, your end and your beginning,* but she is not that for him and never has been. This is what they both knew in the love they made. The leaving, the leaving, the leaving. She takes his hands from her face because there's nothing else to say.

Frank pats Dedalus on the arm. What an arm, it's like a piece of wood.

'Good job mate, good job.'

Peggy's desperate to reach Edward and get her feet dry. They have to keep moving, but now Peggy's seen the way Molly is looking at the angel, she's beginning to understand Molly's absence and his presence.

Molly is done, spent, tired beyond reason, and she takes a deep breath, because she knows the effort it has taken to get here, and the way it will always be.

'*Go,*' she says, 'just go.'

She looks back at him once, forging his way through the water.

The pink silk dress is now torn

and sodden but Molly doesn't care. It scarcely seems to matter. Frank is grey with exhaustion. When one tires they all stop, but they never let go of one another, until all of a sudden, the ground gets steeper, and they find themselves walking up a little slope of mercy where a large wooden beam is floating around in the water. In the wall at the end of the tunnel, a hole is waiting for them, made bigger by Dedalus to get the boy through. Water trickles steadily out of it into the tunnel. Above their heads, a little green moon, and stars.

Stepping carefully through the gap, Peggy is astonished to find herself back in her very own public toilet, where Edward Farraday is laid out on the ground waiting for them, alive and very pale and as comfortable as Dedalus could make him. For a second, Peggy wonders about Edward's late lunches, but this isn't the right time to ask him, *is it, Peggy? Absolutely not.* Frank sits on the floor next to Edward, patting him gently, so he knows someone is there. Peggy tries the handle of the toilet block door. 'It's locked.'

Of course it is. The key is in her shop.

'For fuck's sake,' says Molly, with her ragged dress and her heart in turmoil. She walks over to the door and gives it a massive kick that nearly knocks it off its hinges. 'There you are, it's open now.'

Jessica Khan is trying to sleep

when the sky rumbles and a huge thunderclap shakes the windows of the flat above the newsagency. Storms scare her. She creeps out of bed and peeps through the curtains. Peggy and Frank Tremble are walking up the road. Jess looks at her watch. It's very late. Why are the Trembles out during a terrible storm? They both look a bit bedraggled, and when Peggy Tremble sees her at the window she starts waving her arms madly in the air.

'Jessica! Jess! Call an ambulance now, please.'

Jessica clasps her hand to her mouth. 'Mum!' she shouts. 'Come quickly.'

55

Raven watches Dedalus

make his way over to the king. The angel was here, the angel had gone, and now he is back with that inescapable light that Raven can see inside him. Some don't burn so brightly, but so far, so good. Raven loves meeting new angels. He will be kind.

'You took your time getting here, my Big Lug. Did you know I was at the first flood, and I will be at the last?'

Dedalus stands tall in the darkness. 'Do you know my name is Dedalus, given to me by the Holy Mother of Christ?'

'What a woman,' says Raven, bowing his head in deference. 'Never met her but she knew what she was doing. Maker of wings, that's what we need, a bigger pair than mine. Welcome, Wingmaker,' says Raven, pointing with his beak to the curled ball of feathers on the ledge. 'There he is.'

Dedalus draws closer to Ricardo, who hardly dares look now his time has come. 'Will it hurt?' he asks, struggling to sit up, his energy failing.

'It will be like nothing you've ever felt before, my Kingly King,' and for one last time Raven offers him his wing.

Ricardo brushes it with the tips of his fingers and the scent of lavender fills the air. 'Forgive me,' he says to the bird. 'Forgive me.'

'Already have,' says Raven.

Dedalus kneels on the narrow ledge and kisses the small trembling hand of the king. Ricardo closes his eyes. A silvery light bursts through him as Dedalus lifts him into his arms and carries him under a weeping sky.

56

Rain drips on Molly's head

as she flings another bag of rubbish in the garbage bin. All she really wants to do is sleep, but the house needs sorting after the deluge. She needs sorting. She's wearing her old pink dressing gown; it's so warm, and he made it like that. The bin is full. She leans in, squashing everything down. She's clearing out her life so she can begin again. Gone is the jar of feathers, emptied over the abbey walls to drift like tiny wings. She's kept it for such a long time, but now she's letting go of childhood things. She's hardly slept, but what's new? The cellar will take a long time to dry properly and be fit for use again. Wading through, she found an old wooden box in a damp corner. Well made, bound with iron and still in one piece despite the soaking. When the wood dries out, she will line it with velvet and keep her mother's notebook in there, and when she's ready, she'll ask about her. *Things will change and we will rearrange ourselves.*

Max winds himself around her legs. The cat flap's still there; her father made it, so it endures. Frank keeps her well stocked with meals and homemade chicken soup and sits at the table saying, 'If it wasn't for you, Molly Chops, I wouldn't be here.'

'How is Edward?' she asks.

'Quite a lucky lad, really. Being rescued like that. You can visit him in the hospital if you like.'

'No, thanks.'

Frank nods towards the cellar. 'No sign then?'

She shrugs. 'He has better things to do than eat soup.'

'I can't imagine what they might be.' Frank hugs her, ruffling her hair.

When she calls Lenny, he tells her, 'Take as much time as you need, Molly. What a story. Did you manage to take any photos? If you did, Molly, we would be seriously interested in those. Suze sends love, we miss you, and when you've recovered, come on back. Hey, did I tell you we're planning an exhibition ...'

She spends time at her father's grave and clambering over the abbey's walls. She runs from the ruins of the church along the path, letting the damp earth pound through her like a heartbeat. She stops at the overgrown brambles, looking at Oxenbridge below her. Pieces of her life tumble like a kaleidoscope inside her.

'Dad, if you could see me now. Did you ever think I could do something like that?'

Mol. You're my best girl.

'Thanks, Dad.'

Mol?

'What?'

Try and be happy.

A slow drizzle of rain drifts past her, and rain is nothing but cold water, and she's had enough of that. She never wants to see that cave again. She walks back to the house, shakes off the rain, kicks her trainers halfway down the hall and pads into the kitchen for a glass of wine, thinking of all that's happened.

'What is happy, Dad?'

You are, Mol.

Happiness is not a man, is it, Mol?

'No, it is not.'

And happiness is definitely not an angel. She's not going to spend her life wondering where he is, or what he is becoming. *He's an angel, so he's always becoming*, and she's not doing that anymore. No siree, and no and no and no. She raises her glass because someone has to and it might as well be her. 'A toast to Molly Stern.'

57

Concussion has given

Edward an aching head and he cannot remember how he fell, but his bruised mottled body tells him the story. Cracked ribs, left shoulder dislocated, left ankle broken, he'll be recovering for a while. He does remember the pain when they put his shoulder back in.

The doctor says, 'Someone up there's looking out for you. Could have been a lot worse.' She taps the contraption holding his ankle bones in place. 'Swelling has to go down and then we'll operate.'

His leg looks like a purple balloon. His toes like little alien pods of flesh he's never really noticed before, but now they're all he sees. Tablets for the pain make him feel like a zombie, one who can't walk. He has to watch his breathing, his ribs hurt like hell. When Frank and Peggy visit him, their faces zoom in and out of his vision. Sometimes they're on one side of the bed, sometimes the other.

Once he thought he saw the girl from the newsagency with some chocolates.

'This is Jessica,' said Peggy, 'Jessica Khan,' but after that he didn't know what she said. Jessica was nice though, she kept smiling at him.

The world swims towards him like a mist and swims away again.

'Once your plates are in,' the doctor continues, 'you'll wear a boot and you'll need crutches, and physio. It will take time to heal but you'll be fine. Just rest now.'

Edward's eyes roll in his head. Everything hurts. He tells one of the nurses, 'Muffin Man saved me.'

Peggy plonks a packet of digestives and some crisps on his tray beside his water. 'Make sure you text me if there's anything you need.'

'Jenson Button,' he says.

Frank pats his arm. 'You rest and tomorrow I'll bring you something nice for dinner.'

The next evening, Frank keeps him company with a hastily whipped-up chicken noodle stir-fry. When they've finished eating, Edward leans back into his pillow while Frank pretends to be comfortable on the hard plastic chair. Frank visits him the evening before his ankle operation. Nil by mouth for Edward but his head is clearer now and he leans as far forward as he can.

'Frank, please listen.'

Frank tries to turn the chair round in half an inch of space. 'I'm listening.'

'Frank, the thing is, I've had a lot of time to think in here.' He gulps some air; breathing is a bit less painful. 'I don't really want to work in the shop anymore.'

Frank wipes his mouth. No wine allowed. What a pity.

'Okay, okay,' he says.

'Only I think I'd like to become a pastry chef, Frank, if I could.'

Frank thought something terrible was coming, and he rubs his thighs with relief. 'A pastry chef? Edward, bloody hell, I think that is marvellous. Good lad. I'm happy for you, and Peggy will be too. Anything I can do, I'm your man.'

'You don't think Peggy will be cross with me?'

'Peggy? Cross?'

Edward wants to laugh but can't.

'Peggy will be fine, Jessica's working out really well.'

'Jessica? From the newsagency? She's working in the shop?' Edward sighs into his pillow.

'Ah, sorry, mate, I've put my big foot in it.' Frank kicks himself. *I've put him back into a coma now.*

Edward looks at Frank. 'It's all right, I expect Peggy forgot to tell me with all this going on.' He thinks for a bit. 'She's nice, isn't she, Jessica?'

Frank pats his hand. *Good lad.* 'She really is.'

A companionable silence floats between them.

'Right then, I'll see how you are after the op.'

'You really mean what you said?'

'About being a pastry chef? That would be me in another life, Edward. Go for it.'

58

From the outside to the inside,

the Trembles' bathroom has never looked more inviting. Edward is safe. They're safe. Molly saved them, she's safe. The fuss will die down. People will repair their roofs and go back to their lives. And him? They haven't talked about him yet. From the bathroom window Frank can see the damage to the kingdom of his shed. His storage facility in ruins. Half the roof peeled back like a tin of sardines. Books, newspapers, magazines, a box of tea bags, scattered like leaves around the garden. Some are stuck to the fence, some are scattered over Edward's back garden. Frank stands there watching the wind and rain blow bits of his life about.

'Bath's ready,' he calls, before sliding like a baby hippo into the frothy water.

'Room for me?' asks Peggy, not sure if this is a good idea. She can't remember the last time she had a bath with Frank, just after the fall of Baghdad, perhaps, but then again, maybe not. She comes in wearing a towel.

'Goodness,' says Peggy.

Frank sits up in the bath covered in foam and spreads out his arms, water dripping off his fingers. 'I repent all my sins, darling wife, please forgive me.'

Images of the cave flash before her. 'Oh Frank, you silly thing. Do you think he's going to be all right down there?'

'Course he is, Peggy, he's the king,' says Frank, 'and he has some help.'

'I suppose he does. Ooh crikey, it's hot.' As Peggy gets into the bath, water sloshes over the sides, but for once she doesn't care about the floor. It will dry. Their lives will go on, although they nearly didn't. The hot water is so soothing on her skin.

'You know something' — Frank puts a blob of foam on the end of his wife's nose — 'I'm not going to Leicester. We've seen a close-up already. We can watch it together on the telly.'

So much has happened that they don't know where to begin. In bed, exhausted, Peggy rests her head on his chest, a respite from the maelstrom of the last few days, few months, few years. It's been so long since they lay like this, quietly absorbed in each other. All the rest of it can wait. Peggy sighs, Frank musses up her hair. These are the most important things in the world, everyday gestures of love and belonging, because without them, nothing else makes sense. Out of anyone in the world you have chosen this person to stay with, to put up with all their irritating ways. Love is an arm around the shoulder and endless cups of tea. Love is a button sewn back on a cardigan, a meal at the end of a day, a phone call to say hello for no reason. Love is the strongest thread of all, even if you don't recognise it, or become exasperated by it, or a litany of endless desires gets in the way. Without love colouring in your life, that unique occupation of the human heart, you're back in a bedsit, grilling a piece of mouldy cheese on stale bread, wondering what you're going to do with every long lonely unfulfilled evening. Peggy had forgotten how beautiful life could be with the kindest sweetest man in the world. In the quietest moments, when the planets are still and listening and stars creak past the bedroom windows, they turn to each other and remind themselves once more who they are, and who they have been.

59

'Finally,' says Frank,

rubbing his hands together with glee. 'The Great Day has arrived. This is going to be interesting.'

Frank has been in front of the TV for hours making sure he doesn't miss anything. Peggy potters about with cups of tea.

Molly is coming whenever Molly gets here. She had to ask Suzi to cover for her again and she didn't really want to, not this time. Work absorbs her, distracts her, and it's easier than being in the house, in Oxenbridge.

'It's Thursday, Frank, I can't just leave the gallery.'

'Molly, you must. It's the reinterment of the king.'

A simple oak coffin on a horse-drawn cart trundles through the streets of Leicester. The procession profound and full of respect. Everything thoughtfully done. Inside the coffin the bones of the king have been carefully laid, packed in wool and unbleached linen. People who didn't get tickets for the cathedral service are watching outside on giant screens. The city is teeming with knights and horses, flags, and banners of England. The past is alive and breathing. A golden crown is beamed onto one side of the cathedral.

'Don't you think he would love this?' says Frank. 'It's weird, isn't it, Peg, seeing him in his cloak and now his bones are in that coffin.'

'It's all weird,' says Peggy, who isn't really sure, anymore, what she saw down there.

The camera pans amongst the crowd. There are children dressed as knights, people carrying swords and roses. England has become medieval for the day, with sad, respectful faces. The next shot shows a man walking to the cathedral with his eyes fixed on the way ahead. He has bare feet, and a flowery jumper that has seen better days, and he's carrying a bundle in his arms. Frank peers at the screen.

'Oh my God, look,' he says.

Peggy gasps. 'I have to call Molly.'

Frank lays a hand on her arm. 'Leave her be,' he says, 'she'll be here soon. He's quite something, isn't he?'

People seem to agree with Frank. They move out of the strange man's way as he passes them with his quiet solemn air. A large black bird flies overhead, but no one takes much notice of that. Whatever the man is carrying moves a little, then lies still. Rain is gently falling as people pay their final respects to the king. A woman cries in the damp excited air. The last medieval king killed in battle. They are not his subjects, but they mourn him anyway. Somehow he is still their king. Peggy and Frank share that old deep affinity running through the rainy streets.

'We love our royalty, don't we, Peggy?'

'They're just men and women, though, and none of them are perfect.'

'Far from it,' says Frank, 'but that's why we respect them, with all their imperfections.'

*

The energy of the crowd

affects Dedalus, rising through his bones. *I have you now. I will protect you.* He has made this journey before, but never like this, with the weight of a soul in his arms. *Pray for us now and in the everlasting peace.* The sound of quiet applause follows the coffin on the cart to the cathedral where everyone is waiting for the king.

He is so close now he can feel the people's love for him, and from the safety of Dedalus's arms, the soul of the king opens his eyes to the sky above. Wreaths of white roses. The rituals of death he never received.

The service has started

just as Molly knocks at the door then plonks herself down on the sofa. 'Seen anything interesting yet?'

'There's Benedict Cumberbatch,' says Peggy.

'You know what I mean,' says Molly.

Frank has made a plate of sandwiches so they can watch and eat.

'Delicious,' says Molly. 'Salmon and cream cheese, very patriotic, Francis Tremble.'

Frank pats her leg. Thrilled Molly is eating again.

'For goodness sake, Molly,' says Peggy. 'Look who's there.'

The doors of Leicester's great cathedral, which were closed, have now been flung open, and Dedalus is walking through them, carrying the soul of the king.

Molly stops eating.

There he is. A circle of light emanating from him as he walks up the nave of the cathedral. The congregation accepts this with hushed awe; this must all be part of the ceremony. The choristers keep singing and a few heads turn to see Dedalus, absorbing the service in the way he always did. Now he is part of the reinterment of the king.

'Oh my God,' says Molly, 'look at him.' She cannot tear her eyes away, like everyone else. It's all they can do: watch Dedalus. Shafts of sunlight fill the cathedral as Dedalus continues his walk to the coffin of bones. The soldiers have carried the coffin over to the tomb, where they wait for the blessing. As Dedalus approaches them, they become unsure. This is not what they had rehearsed, but the spectacle holds everyone in its thrall. People try to get a better look, puzzled at the dusty motes of sunshine trawling through the air, because it was raining when they came in. No one can see clearly what the man is carrying in his arms; it's a bundle of feathers or a piece of cloth.

Bishops confer. Anglicans or Catholics, it doesn't matter now, the king is dead. The soldiers look worried, but Dedalus pays them little attention. Whatever Dedalus can hear or see is not of this world. It is outside and inside, meaning and purpose. It is the beginning and the end for the soul he holds in his hands. The congregation murmurs with apprehensive glances as light pours everywhere, flooding over drizzling streets.

The soldiers shield their eyes from the intense brightness as Dedalus reaches the coffin. No one moves except him. He won't let them. This is his power. This is his purpose. A bird follows him into the cathedral, calling to the bundle in his hands.

'Now it is here, my Kingly King.' The bird seems to grow bigger as it flies low over so many startled heads. 'Your fallen bones and your penitent soul united.'

The bird lets out a huge echoing cry and an overwhelming brightness streams round Dedalus, flowing through him and covering everyone and everything. Dedalus holds his arms aloft over the coffin as the light continues to pour out of him. Over women and men, over song and prayer, over that bundle of feathers, that whisper of movement, those atoms dancing through dust. Gathering, gathering all that endless bursting radiance into one point, until all the energy in the cathedral can no longer be contained and is drawn up and up and up from stone, from bone, from dust and breath towards that shining light.

For the three of them

in the front room it feels like hours, but only five minutes have gone by. Molly lies on the floor, as close to the TV as she can possibly get. Peggy watches everything silently until there's nothing left to see. Dedalus has disappeared, but the Archbishop of Canterbury continues. Blessing the coffin with incense. Blessing the bones of Richard before the soldiers step up to the coffin, so they can lower him into the tomb. Commentators talk about the extraordinary scenes in the cathedral. 'Totally unprepared for such a thing. But what a marvellous end to the life of the king.'

'Well, blow me down,' says Frank, 'we met him, didn't we? I mean we actually met him.'

'We met them both,' says Molly. 'An angel and a king.'

60

Truth is a solitary thing

inside Peggy's heart at Oxenbridge House. Molly has stayed for
the weekend and Peggy's at the house with her, making endless
cups of tea. Frank had wanted to come, but Peggy insisted he
stay home. This is on her. She'll tell it, shoulder the weight of
it. Ask for forgiveness. *We all need forgiveness*, that's what the bird
said. She pats her hair. It is a tiny bit longer than usual.

'What do you think?'

'Peggy, you look positively feral with your hair like that.'
Molly sniffs into a tissue.

'Sweetheart, come here. He's gone, and he's not coming
back, is he?'

Molly shrugs.

'Let him go, darling, let him go. He will never make you
happy. He will never give you what you need. He will always be
somewhere else doing God knows what.'

'I know, I know.'

'It'll be Gregorian chants and candles and an absence of
knowing for the rest of your life. And what about your career,
your photography, where is that going to take you if you're
always waiting for him? Lurking about in some dark corner,
and what about children, and a home, real things? We all want

319

stability and love and weekends away, and a veggie patch. And dancing. He wouldn't be very good at that.'

Molly laughs, then cries, something she's become good at recently.

'He would be a really shit dancer,' she says, emptying the tissue box, 'but I still miss him.' She rolls the tissue round in her hand.

'Who is he anyway? A creature from the past? He's never going to be there for you. He's not exactly Mr Reliable, is he? And Stefan was dull, so very dull, Molly, and you're better off without them.'

Molly hasn't told Peggy about Gabe, but he was dull too. He was worse than ditchwater. He was *married*.

Peggy strokes Molly's face, seeing so clearly the child still in her. The child Peggy has loved since the day she was born. Her sister, so intensely happy with this new life, said, *Hold her, Peggy, hold her*, and Peggy has never stopped holding her.

'Molly, I know right now your heart is broken, but it will mend and there are good people in this world to help you. You're smart and funny, and he's not yours and never will be.'

'When I was with him, I thought nothing else mattered, but maybe it actually does.'

Peggy studies her wonderful girl, all her fleeting expressions. Sometimes she can see Sally so clearly in her, other times she thinks Molly is such a mixture of them all.

Molly sighs and rests her head on Peggy's shoulder.

'You know he's been here before.'

'I've heard it a thousand times.'

'One last time won't hurt then, will it, because you've never heard it from me.'

Molly wants to lie down.

'Back then, we didn't really talk about emotions. Not really. Your mother had always been very up and down, since she was a teenager. Our father, your grandfather, had terrible mood swings, and then he had an affair.'

Molly clasps her hands over her ears. 'Not interested in this, thank you, no.'

But now she's started, Peggy's not stopping.

'You were eighteen months old, a baby. Your mum was exhausted. In those days we didn't know about post-natal depression, we just thought everything she was going through was the baby blues. And that she'd get better, not worse.'

Hearing Peggy talk about her mother like this is like having the curtains pulled open in a very dark room and Molly has to adjust as the light comes in. It's the last piece of the puzzle that she's lived with for so long, and to make the telling easier Peggy tries to hold Molly's hand, but Molly's not having that.

'We really did not know how sick she was. And we should have told you a long time ago, Molly. She became very withdrawn, talking to herself. Hearing voices. Your father was around as much as he could be. He and Lenny were working in London then, but that's another lifetime ago, and we were here, helping your mum look after you.'

'That was very noble of you.' Two red dots of anger appear on Molly's cheeks.

Peggy bites the inside of her lip. 'Molly, please just listen. That night, Frank was cooking roast beef, his speciality back then. Your dad was home, and your mum was upstairs with you. We'd all heard the odd thumps and bumps in the house, and Marcus said there was nothing there; he said it was an old house, and old houses make their own music, and he was just going to fetch more wine from the cellar. You must have fallen asleep, as your mum came down and we were all in the dining room eating, and then the doors opened, and in he burst. The food went flying. Your poor mum was very upset. Frank and your father were trying to stop him. Then you appeared at the bottom of the stairs, bawling your eyes out. You must have climbed out of your cot. There was such a commotion.'

'Of course she was upset at the sight of him.'

'We all were. We thought he was a lunatic. He had all these disgusting robes hanging off him, and underneath he was naked. None of us knew what was happening. He probably didn't either. Your mum kept saying, "It's him, it's him," like she knew who he was, but how could she? In all the fuss he grabbed her hand and held it, and she just kept looking at him like she'd had a shock. She was saying over and over again that this was an angel, and we had to let him go, but none of us listened. We had no idea.'

'For God's sake, Peggy.' Molly gets to her feet. She can feel a scream building inside her, a scream from the bottom of the stairs where she once stood. 'She was right though, wasn't she? Why didn't he save her then?'

'Back then he couldn't even save himself.' Peggy tucks a strand of hair behind her ears. 'Your mum was very unwell, Molly.'

'What do you mean?' she asks, her voice shaky as her anger builds.

Peggy grips the side of the table, 'It was very hard for her. And for us. We knew so little. Your father was beside himself. He didn't know what to do. It was like we were losing her every day and she needed more help than we could give her. She needed somewhere with proper care, Molly. And we didn't tell you because you were so young. And your father wanted to protect you.'

Tears come rolling down Molly's face and she punches them away.

Peggy's heart is thumping loudly in her chest. 'Everything your father has ever done, and me, and Frank, has been because we wanted you to be all right. We didn't want you to be always sad, or anxious. We wanted you to grow up believing you could do anything, and nothing was going to stop you. And I'm sorry for all of it, Molly. I'm so sorry.'

Molly is gulping back the sobs.

'Dad told me she was gone. So I thought that she had left us. Left me. Left Dad. And I was always so angry about that. But now you're telling me she was … what … depressed?'

'Molly, she was mentally unwell.'

'Why didn't Dad tell me that, Peggy? Why didn't Frank tell me? How could you not tell me?'

Everything Peggy has held inside her for so long now comes crashing through the walls.

'Your mother tried to kill herself, Molly. She couldn't care for you, and she couldn't care for herself. She didn't know what bloody day it was and sometimes she didn't even know she had a daughter. We had to protect you. Me and Uncle Frank were looking after you when your father was working and caring for your mother. And don't forget I lost my sister too.'

Peggy is just about done. Her legs shake, her hands tremble. She can't help crying as Molly yells at her, 'Just stop, Peggy, I've heard enough.'

Molly walks out of the kitchen, slamming the door behind her.

Peggy should have listened to Frank. He would have been better at this, but she had to do it herself to make up for all those years when she said nothing. Now her salty worthless tears are too late to be of use to anyone except her own self-pitying heart. Perhaps she should have stayed quiet, but then how would Molly know how to make sense of everything that's happened?

The distance between the graveyard and the sink draws closer. She's about to go home when Molly comes back into the kitchen, all the hurt and anger burning in her like fire.

'All this time Dad never wanted to talk about it, but you should have told me. I've been so angry with *her* for leaving me, when I should have been angry with *you*.'

Molly's face is crumpled and red from crying. Snot drips from her nose. Peggy thinks now would be a good time to die, as life without Molly's love and acceptance is no life at all, but there's one last thing to say.

'Molly, *Molly, listen*, she didn't exactly leave you.'

Molly stiffens, anything else is almost too much to bear. She's frozen to the spot, she can't move. Can't breathe. Big fat tears keep rolling down her cheeks. She can hear someone shouting the question that has followed her all her life. Her voice filling the kitchen and the walls and the graveyard and hurtling into the darkening trees.

'Where is she then? *Where is my mother?*'

61

From the House of God

to an empty field, it's all the same to Raven. When a soul is taken up, he finds himself flying at odd angles to the earth, but being Raven, he'll always be okay. It's the angel he's concerned about. What he's just done in front of so many is a hell of a thing, but he'll get used to it. The field rolls and pitches like the sea. Dedalus is easy to spot, halfway to nowhere, exhausted, sunk on the ground, doing nothing but watching the bird. The more he looks, the more he sees it's the bird making the fields move, not the other way around. His arms are empty. The king has gone. It's just him and the bird, the bird and him. When Raven lands, clouds of dust fill the air as he spreads his obstreperous wings.

'Magnifico, my Angelus Dedalus. Magnificent indeed.'

'Where has he gone?'

Raven stretches one leg behind him. 'Do you really not know?'

'Never done this before,' says Dedalus. An inescapable warmth spreads in his bones. Perhaps he knew what would happen, yet now he knows nothing at all. His life slips through him. Memory after memory. Perhaps Sister Alice knew how hard salvation would be, and that it would bring him here.

Perhaps she always knew. Dedalus watches the bird while Raven watches him. The bird opens his mouth and the world rolls in.

'You, my Dedalus Angelus, have kept me very busy,' says Raven, extending his dusty claws.

'And I am sorry for it,' says Dedalus, 'but you also have kept me very busy. Where is he?' he asks again.

Before him, the outline of the king appears, exactly as he used to be, but then it disappears. Emotions swirl like fog inside Dedalus. He staggers to his feet. A horse with an empty saddle gallops past. Dedalus tries but he can't catch it. It's moving too fast. Too late, it's done. He will never see the soul of the king again. He has gone. Passed into dust. Leaving Dedalus as one more thing for the energy to flow through, a conduit between the sky and the earth, for as long as he needs to be.

'We're a team, you and I. Together forever.' Raven blows him a kiss. 'Never had a soul like that and never will again. People make all kinds of assumptions about angels, and all of them wrong. Anyway, you were there when it mattered. That's all you can do, my unwilling angel, my Dedalus Reluctant. You might turn out to be the greatest one of all.'

Dedalus thinks he knows at last who this might be.

'How will I find you?'

'Old mate, I will always find you,' says Raven. 'Now you can go to her. We have saved the best soul for last, have we not? Be gentle, won't you?'

'Always.'

'This one is special.'

'When shall it be?'

'Pray,' says Raven.

He might have said stay, but it hardly matters. What he says, he says. The bird fades in and out of vision as Dedalus walks back across the empty field. Each step seems to take forever, horizon after horizon, dipping into cloud, into sky. When he can almost go no further, he takes a huge angel breath, drawing the horizon deep inside him with the thunder and the rain.

62

One month later,

Molly shuts and locks the cellar door. The cat flap moves a little in the breeze. She cuddles Max and kisses his face. One blue eye blinks at her. He miaows loudly. *We're the same Max, you and me.* A couple of cool cats, but she's not cool, she's anxious and nervous. Frank and Peggy have both told her how difficult this is going to be. The car horn beeps again. *All right, I'm coming,* but she stops still, listening. The house is silent. Nothing but her own breath disturbing the quiet. This is it then.

'Goodbye,' she whispers. *Help me, won't you? I have loved you my angel, but you are not my angel now.* She will see him again, but she doesn't know how and she doesn't know when and that's all right. *Who are you, Molly Stern? What can you give to this world? I am dust and rain. I am small and large. I am strong and weak. I am alone. I am never alone. I am loved.* She closes her eyes. Everything rolls into one point hurtling through her heart like a thousand burning stars.

63

Before the journey begins,

Molly tells Frank she's changed her mind and is not coming.

'We'll be there by eleven' – Frank checks his watch – 'depending on traffic.'

Peggy, almost back to her best self, says, 'Molly, you're sitting in the front because I am not cleaning up vomit today.'

'I don't want to go,' she says, doing up her seatbelt.

The gallery is waiting for her. It's Saturday. She can hop on the train and be back at the front desk talking shit about the image and the space and the persona and letting Suzi paint her eyebrows. A bowl of beef pho after a massive day selling millions of her own prints while Lenny stands there grinning like a Cheshire cat in his best striped shirt. She wants work and money and wine and song, and she wants her work to mean something in this world. She wants life running through her veins in all its fecund glory. She wants her photos to be in every gallery in every city and she wants to be loved and wanted and valued. Forget about this seaside stuff. *Stop, Frank, turn the car around*, but she doesn't say that because they're on the M25.

After an hour of lane changes and lorries, Frank needs some opium and a coffee, but failing that, a slice of carrot cake will do. They stop at Horsham and find a café, and all Molly wants is ice cream. The day is chilly, even though it's meant to be spring, but spring is unreliable. Molly spills a blob of chocolate and vanilla on her coat – *Shit, shit, shit* – then tries to rub it off. Doesn't want to turn up looking scruffy and messy and all over the place, which she already is.

Recharged with caffeine and carbs, Frank's about to say, 'I miss him, really,' meaning the king, then thinks better of it, but he really does. What will he do without him? He could join the Richard the Third Society, but Peggy wouldn't like that and whatever comes next he's doing with her. Rollerblading? Pottery? Hiking? Oops, just missed the turn-off. 'Sorry, everyone.'

Molly has turned a pale shade of green.

'Use the plastic bag,' says Peggy, 'if you're going to throw up.'

The sea is cold and grey. Gulls swoop and cry overhead. Molly opens the car window, breathing in the sharp air. She wants to swim in the choppy water. She could be in Calais by late afternoon.

'Nearly there,' says Frank, hoping he can remember the way once they reach the town centre. He has his phone, and he has Peggy. He always has Peggy to direct him. He takes a few wrong turns, drives down a one-way street, does a ten-point turn, sorts himself out, and there it is. On the corner.

A signpost out the front.

Molly says she is definitely going to be sick. Front garden full of lawn, some shrubs. Frank parks. Molly stays in the car. Peggy waits for Molly to slowly get out. Their footsteps crunch on the gravel drive. Through the doors. Smell of air freshener and disinfectant. A large cheerful lady welcomes them. Apparently she's called April. Same as the month, thinks Molly. She signs a register. Her hands are sweating. She should know the date and the time, but she doesn't, she looks at Peggy. 'It's April,' she says. Peggy puts an arm around her. She's just standing there dry mouthed, waiting to see her mother.

'This way then,' says April.

Molly's legs are shaking. Frank walking one side, Peggy the other. April is saying something to her, but Molly can't hear. There are so many elderly people. Molly has never seen so many gathered in one place. *Mum's not old, she's younger than Peggy.* A TV blares nonsense in the corner. On they go, room after room, until they reach the name *Sally Stern*.

April is talking. 'So, Molly, I'm not sure how much you know.' She glances at Peggy. 'Sally does have difficult days, but I am sure she'll be happy to see you.'

Through the open door, Molly can see a chair by the large bay window.

April says, 'Just talk normally to her.'

Molly doesn't know what's normal.

'Shall we come in with you?' asks Frank. Molly shakes her head.

April says, 'You will be fine.'

'Yes, I am fine,' says Molly, following April.

'Sally, my darling, there's someone to see you.' April pats Sally on the arm. 'Leave you to it then, I'll wait outside.'

Someone is sitting in the chair, but this is not her mother. She is tiny, like a bird, her hair short and wispy, her hands curled, her eyes watching something Molly can't see. Molly's hands tremble. She's unsure what to say. *Hello. I am your daughter.*

'Hello,' she says.

Sally Stern keeps staring at the garden.

'Mum,' Molly whispers, 'it's me. It's Molly.'

They are inches apart now, mother and daughter. How long has it been since Molly was a toddler on the stairs, a five-year-old wriggling on the back seat of the car? A six-year-old listening to her father's story. All through those years a life she knows nothing about, apart from a notebook giving her clues.

April sticks her head round the door. 'Everything okay? Tea? Coffee?'

Molly strokes her mother's hands. Sally looks at her fingers. Pats them.

'I'm Molly, Mum, I'm your little girl. Do you remember me?'

Sally looks back at the garden. Molly's legs won't keep her upright anymore, so she kneels by the side of the chair. She wipes her face, doesn't want her mother to see the tears. April brings her a cup of tea. There's an alarm on the wall by the bed and the windows have locks on them.

'You're all right,' says April.

Peggy comes in, kisses the top of Sally's head. Molly holds her mother's hands lightly in her own. Sally pats Molly's hand again. 'Draw me a feather,' she says. 'A feather, draw me a feather.'

Molly looks around for a pen and some paper, but Peggy comes to the rescue. 'She means on her hand, Molly. Use your finger.'

Sally closes her eyes as Molly traces the shape of a feather on her mother's hand. She sighs, pats Molly. 'Draw me a feather,' she says.

The room is very warm and stuffy. At some stage Frank appears, puts his arm round Molly, and says, 'Drink your tea,' but the knot in her throat won't let her, so Frank says, 'Come on,' and walks her outside. As they're waiting for Peggy, April has a word with Molly. 'It's always hard the first time, but it's lovely that you came. She's very special to us all. Thank you for coming. See you next time.'

Molly walks to the car. It's still Saturday.

That evening

Frank makes dinner. It's just heated-up leftovers, but it's food and Molly hardly notices. She's not going back to the house on her own, not tonight. They're sitting digesting the day when there's a knock at the door.

'Oh no,' says Peggy, 'who the hell is that?'

Frank answers and five minutes later two heads pop round the door.

'It's the vicar, just called in to say hello,' says Frank, his eyebrows raised.

'Hello, Vicar,' says Peggy.

'Please, call me Jerome.'

Molly jumps up, glad to have her mind on something else, even though she's exhausted. There are no handshakes this time, just an easy energy running between them.

'I'll make some tea. Jerome, how do you like yours? And now you're here, can I ask you something?'

'Sure,' he says, 'fire away.'

'As a man of God,' says Molly, 'do you believe in angels?'

Frank gives Peggy a worried look.

'I absolutely do,' says Reverend Jerome, with that happy smile. 'Why do you ask?'

Molly likes that smile. 'Just wondered, that's all.'

She's too tired to say much else. She puts the kettle on. It has been a huge day. An image of a chair looking out the window comes into her mind. She regrets not taking a photo of her mother, but she's also glad she didn't. Save it for next time if it feels right. Jerome doesn't stay long, and leaves in a flurry of warmth, but not before inviting everyone to the vicarage for tea.

'That's a yes and a no from me,' says Molly once he's gone, thinking maybe one day, when she's ready, she could talk to Jerome about everything.

Peggy yawns. 'I am so done.'

'Then we're all done together, aren't we?' says Molly, hugging her dear ones. 'Thank you for taking me. Thank you for being here for me.'

'That's our job,' says Frank. 'Good night, Molly Chops.'

The three of them lean into one another, in the old and best alliance of love. Molly says softly, 'I will always love you.'

Peggy's voice has gone all wobbly. 'And we will always love you.'

Where would they be without Molly? An hour later Peggy snuggles down in bed. A lump rising in her throat again, like it's the end of something, and she wants to bawl her eyes out, but she's just tired and overwrought. She's always like that after seeing Sally, as if some big unexpressed thing has been released from deep within her. The past pouring itself into the present, fracturing and refracturing into the nights and days ahead. Frank jumps into bed and Peggy groans as a car hoots loudly in the street.

'That's Jess dropping Edward home,' says Frank.

'Does she have to do that every time? She'll wake the whole street.'

Peggy pulls the duvet over her ears. No more words, not tonight, they have earned their rest. She kisses her husband's prickly ears; Frank twitches, on his way to dream land already. The night sinks low on Castle Road, Oxenbridge. No one wakes, especially not Molly, as she is fast asleep.

*

Time is slippery

in the darkness. It's two or three or four in the morning and it's funny how sound travels at night, especially when a large black bird comes squawking down the street.

Night gathers round Molly. She doesn't hear Raven fly in through the open window.

'Wake up, Molly Chops,' he says, 'Sweet of My Dreams.'

Molly sighs. There's a bird on her bed and she's talking in her sleep. 'I'm never going to get rid of you, am I?'

'Well,' says Raven, 'seeing as I am such magnificent company.'

She turns over and buries her face in the pillow. 'Go away,' she says. 'Don't you know when you're not wanted?'

'I have made her the most beautiful cloak,' says Raven. 'Look, Molly Chops, there's a way through for everyone.'

Now there are feathers falling from the sky. Onto the houses, the roofs, the shops, and the cafés. The whole town is cloaked in a gently swirling cloud of feathers, and there in the middle of them is her mum. Exactly as she had been in the chair, curled and small, but there is no chair. She is being carried by the angel of her dreams. The road is covered in feathers.

When Molly wakes, it's eight o'clock on a Sunday morning. She's slept for hours, something she hasn't done for a long time. She yawns and stretches. The house is quiet, the street quieter. How blissful. There are no cars, no dogs, no children, no delivery vans. What a day this is going to be. A feather falls from her bed. She hasn't seen it before. She picks it up. It's a deep rich indigo blue. She opens the curtains. It's April. Early morning sunlight dazzles the street.

ACKNOWLEDGEMENTS

My dear Gentleberries, as Raven would say, this book would not exist without the love and support of so many of you for this writer with a quill.

Huge thank you to my daughter, Freya, for her many insightful lectures. And all that goes with them. She upholds me every day and I am so grateful for her big loving heart.

So much love and gratitude for all my beautiful family – Isaac, Bridget, Arlo, Freya, Bede, Jazmin, Arwyn Joe, Ali Paice, and Angie and Neil Lemon – over the many hundreds of years it has taken me to write this book. I would be lost without this compass of love and certainty you give me to guide my way. Thank you June P. Griggs, for keeping faith with me and willing me on.

Bill Jansens, your love and support for me in the early drafts of this book always meant the world to me. Our life together was the most precious thing and I thank you for that.

Special shout out to my sisters, Ali and Angie. You gave me the time and space to finish the edit in the garden shed while you cared for Mum, fed me cheesy snacks and hung out the washing with the sporadic use of pegs. Ali, I know you would have liked me to stay in the shed, but that old rope was frayed and I escaped. I love you both dearly for this special time we shared with each other and with Mum. Thank you to my beautiful cousin, Sarah

Vaux, for your bravery and resilience and that lovely talk we had in the walnut tree meadow.

Huge thank you to my agent, the wonderful Caitlan Cooper-Trent, for always believing in me and encouraging me to make a deranged manuscript into something readable. We shall prevail! Catherine Milne, what a journey it has been; I blow you kisses and sing a strange quavery song under the moon. Thank you for seeing what the book could be and challenging me to bring that into existence with kindness and patience and humour.

Scott Forbes, thank you so much for your brilliant editing and word wrangling. If I say any more it will be repetitive and you will have to delete it. Fiona Daniels, thank you for your masterful copy edit and your patience and insight with my many ridiculous mistakes.

Thank you always to my two Catherines: Catherine Newell for being there and loving me through it all, and Kate Tayler, the other Raven on my shoulder, for those long conversations about life and death and the in-between.

To my dear ones, Tim and Nuala Orlik, a huge thank you for the space, love, wine, and food you always share so generously with me. The temperature in the morning room was sub zero, my choice I know, but it was perfect for editing my excessive use of commas and illegally placed dangling modifiers.

Chantal Pilandon, every soy cappuccino helped my brain edge a little closer to the finish line. Thank you for all your love and care over the years, but especially this last one. Maria Wiley, you're always so present and accepting of all my nonsense and I love you for that and the fire and passion you bring to every word. WTF, says Viktor, your favourite Slavic philosopher. Wendy O'Malley, thank you for the love and the clothes and shoes. I'm still wearing them! Sue Barnett, thank you for always believing in me and being there with poetry, cheese scones, and gravy. Sally Ann Bird, you're a legend, and a brilliant friend, and I thank you from the bottom of my heart for always being there for me and us. Big thank you to Sally Brown, wonderful gardener and maker of cakes, soup and everything else you and Miles so graciously plied me with, especially the afternoon Baileys. Miles, thank you for telling me about bats and driving the lawnmower to Chesham.

Thank you to Gary Wheeler for love and support. Liz Scrimgeour for encouragement and love. David Hillman for lunch, love, and support, and Dominick Reyntiens for the long-distance chats. Tracey Martin for keeping me company during dinner and tethering me to the earth. Meg Pomfret, psychologist extraordinaire, for helping me through the dark and encouraging me to see the light; and thank you to the lady in Wendover Post Office, Carol in Wendover Library, and all the volunteers who helped me with the printer.

Last but most and never least, I would like to thank my beautiful brave mother for her eternal patience, and laughter, and chicken soup. She and Dad always believed in me and what I could do, so I hope I've done a little of it here.

If there is anyone I have forgotten, forgive me.